Like home

LOUISA ONOMÉ

Delacorte Press

Text copyright © 2021 by Louisa Atto
Jacket art copyright © 2021 by Bex Glendining

All rights reserved. Published in the United States by Delacorte Press, an imprint of Random House Children's Books, a division of Penguin Random House LLC, New York.

Delacorte Press is a registered trademark and the colophon is a trademark of Penguin Random House LLC.

Visit us on the Web! GetUnderlined.com

Educators and librarians, for a variety of teaching tools, visit us at RHTeachersLibrarians.com

Library of Congress Cataloging-in-Publication Data is available upon request.
ISBN 978-0-593-17259-9 (hc) — ISBN 978-0-593-17261-2 (lib. bdg.) — ISBN 978-0-593-17260-5 (ebook)

The text of this book is set in 11.5-point Bell MT Pro.
Interior design by Cathy Bobak

Printed in Canada
10 9 8 7 6 5 4 3 2 1
First Edition

To Nneka, Uzezi, and Efemona, the mandem

I can't stop looking at the glass. It's *everywhere.*
I've never seen the ground shimmer like this before.
Never heard the sound of the wind whistling
through the storefront like this.
I breathe out, letting my eyes wash over the scene.
I don't have it in me to struggle anymore.
All I can do is watch.

CHAPTER ONE

My shoes scratch against the uneven pavement, and I know right away that they've been scuffed real bad. I immediately think of my mom—I pretty much begged her to buy these shoes for me. "Take it out of my college fund or something," I told her, like an idiot, and she laughed in that stiff way she does whenever we talk about money. If she sees them scuffed up so early, I'll never hear the end of it. I'll never hear the end of the shoes, the same way I'll never hear the end of this— this *bra* thing. I gotta tell Kate.

It is April, and Ginger East is quiet early in the morning, so my light footsteps sound like heavy boots as I run. The sun creeps over the top of the highest building on the main road, casting stale light on dusty storefronts and barely swept roads. A set of duplexes that used to be cash-and-carry outlets stares back at me as I reach the end of my street, Ginger Way. Mom used to buy fish and bedding from there. Two different departments, same store. They moved out a long time ago. Now it's a coffee place open bright and early at seven a.m. Man, the only people up this early in Ginger East are us schoolkids who need to catch a bus, the few homeless people who live in that shed behind the liquor store, and the Trans—Kate and her family—because they run Ginger Store.

My feet slow as I round the corner approaching Ginger Store, and then stop as I pull open the door. It's hard to get in with how the wind seems to be pushing at it. Mrs. Tran is at the register and immediately leans past the counter to see who it is.

She frantically waves at me and says, "Chinelo? Shut the door, please."

I do as I'm told, and the fierce wind tunnel dies. My carefully straightened hair, which I tried so hard to smooth down this morning, is frizzing around my shoulders. "The back door is open," she says, settling onto her stool behind the counter again. "Kate's dad is mopping the storage room, and with all the doors open—*whoosh*," she explains, waving her hands around to symbolize the movement of air.

"Why doesn't he tell Jake to do it?" I ask. Jake is Kate's useless older brother who's gotten away with doing the absolute least because he's a boy. He'll straighten one shelf and complain for hours. He outgrew his cool-older-brother phase ages ago.

Mrs. Tran makes a face like she knows her son is useless and why would she even consider asking him? I laugh, a difficult feat after sprinting all the way here, and ask, "What about Kate?"

The sound of a freezer slamming in the back rings out, and then I notice Kate trudging up the middle aisle, her arms extended in front of her. Her lips are curled into a pout as she approaches, her stark dark hair gathered messily around her neck. "How many things do you want me to do in one morning? Like, damn." She grunts, shaking her hands.

I look at her fingers, because I feel her eyes are urging me to. They just look dry. "What's your problem?"

She ignores me and takes a slow step toward her mom at the counter. "Mom, my hands are *fro-zen*. Can't I organize the ice cream after school? No one's out here buying ice cream before noon."

Her mom frowns all strict. Mrs. Tran is definitely the nicest Tran, so the small tic between her eyebrows really strikes fear into my scuffed-shoed feet. I loop my arm with Kate's instantly, saying, "I'll help you."

"See?" Mrs. Tran cuts in with a wry smile. "Nelo is a good worker."

Kate's mouth drops open. "Worker? But you're not even paying her, though. You're not even paying *me*—"

"Ah, so I should pay you to live in my house?"

I snort. My mom and Mrs. Tran are pretty much the same person at this point. They probably share insults on some group chat called Neighborhood Moms. "Come on," I say to Kate, tugging her down the aisle.

From where we disappear to, I can hear Mr. Tran sloshing a

mop across the linoleum tile in the hallway. Even so, the smell of chocolate is strong back here. Ever since that hot-chocolate-machine explosion incident when we were nine, the store has smelled like chocolate—and old building and cardboard and musty floor wax.

Kate shimmies free of my grasp as soon as we're hidden. She gives me a knowing look and says, "I got you," before dipping into the freezer for a Vita ice cream bar. It's seven a.m., but I don't argue. I snatch it from her, peel off its wrapper, and stuff it into my mouth as if it was made for me. She tries not to cackle. "You're so extra!"

"I love these," I say through a cold mouthful. Vita ice cream is the best ice cream, my absolute favorite. Ginger Store is the only place around here that sells it, and every time I eat it, it reminds me of some of the best times I've ever had.

Usually, in the summer, my friends and I used to meet up here and buy ice cream. Sitting at the curb by the storefront, watching customers come and go amid the humidity and heat. We were all about the stickiness of sunrise-to-sundown adventures and the cool, calming wave brought on by tubs and tubs of ice cream. Nothing really has come close ever since.

Life split us up. I guess that's normal, but it still sucks. Our friends moved to a nicer neighborhood closer to school. It's only Kate and me who live on Ginger Way and who still talk about summers with too much ice cream. A small part of me feels it's a matter of time before she leaves too, but I know the Trans, and they wouldn't leave. Ginger Store is as much the neighborhood's as it is theirs, so they'd never sell. So many businesses have come and gone around here, cash-and-carries turned into hair salons turned into loan offices, but Ginger Store is a staple. Ginger East would be nothing without it, but if I'm being honest, maybe I'd be nothing without it too.

Kate purses her lips, biting back another laugh. Then she points a stern finger at me and says, "Do *not* say anything to my mom. She's doing inventory."

"Uh, why would I?"

"You and my mom are obviously like this," she says, crossing her fingers.

I snort, say "Shut up," and punch her in the arm as lightly as I can. I barely feel her thick sweater on my knuckles, so I punch her again, but this time deeper. She gasps and returns the favor, except she misses my arm by an inch and her knuckles land square on my left tit.

Her face says it all. Her mouth makes a perfect O, and her brows arch so high, they almost meet her hairline. I instinctively bring a hand to shield my chest in case she does it again. And she does, but this time she leans forward, tipping the top of my animal-print sweater so she can see down my shirt. When I try to swat her away, she takes a step back and gapes even wider. She whispers, "Are you, like, padding your bra now?"

My face is burning up under the store lights and her growing shock. Her eyes—she's watching me so hard! "No! Why would I?"

"Then what . . . ?" she asks, letting her eyes drop to my heavily sweatered chest.

I take a second and cast a quick look over my shoulder through the store. Everything is undisturbed. The aisles of food, scissors, telephones—you know, corner-shop stuff. Mrs. Tran's shelf of used books stares back at me from the wall. The lotion that's mad scented when you apply it but then dies after an hour is untouched on the counter. It's quiet and safe enough for me to turn back around and whisper to Kate: "Okay, so this morning my mom comes to me, right, and peeks down my shirt, and was like, 'Chi-chi—'"

"Who's that?"

"Me."

Kate screws up her face with disbelief. "Since when?" *Exactly!* Even she knows that no one has ever called me that.

"I don't know. Mom just started calling me that one day, maybe literally the day Dad left to go to Calgary for work. She'd never call me that if he was here." There's a Chi-chi in every Nigerian Igbo family, and I don't know why my mom is trying to turn me into Chi-chi when I already have a cousin who claimed the name.

"It doesn't suit you."

"That's what I'm saying! And she was like, 'Chi-chi, we

need to think about getting you a bigger bra.' If you *heard* how she enunciated 'bra.' And I was like, I mean, I didn't even say nothing. Just ran. How awkward is that?"

Kate's shock morphs into amusement, and she laughs, despite her previous attempts not to. "You're blossoming," she teases, fanning out her hands to symbolize the growth. "You're changing, *Chi-chi.*"

I cringe. Joke or not, hearing those words from her mouth makes me feel some kind of way. Hearing her refer to me as a thing to *be* blossomed is making me feel mad awkward too, like I'm growing too big for my body. I don't like it. "Don't say 'blossoming.' That's nasty," I groan, and she laughs harder. "And don't call me 'Chi-chi.' Shut up. We gotta catch the bus," I remind her, trying to sound stern and assertive over her ringing chuckle. I can't kick the mental image of my chest growing bigger than my head, though—a girl named Chi-chi Agu whose Nigerian mother cursed her with the strength of a thousand chests. A girl whose chest is so damn big, it swallows her entire face.

Mrs. Tran waves us to the register. Kate is still snickering as her mom gets to her feet and pulls something out from under the counter. It's a plastic container with rice-paper rolls. That seems to be enough for Kate to finally shut up. Man, Mrs. Tran used to make these all the time when we were younger and spent our evenings hanging around at the store. When I think about it, it sort of feels like she was bribing us to stock shelves, but whatever. These rolls are too good. When everyone moved away, she stopped cooking so much and bringing us extra food. This feels like a remnant from some other time. "Leftovers. Both of you share when you get to school," she says, and then frowns. "Speaking of school, won't you be late?"

The bus gets here at seven-thirty every morning. Just like clockwork, we hear its squeaky-ass wheels run down the street into Ginger East, and we race out of the store yelling our goodbyes. Sometimes we're unlucky and the bus gets here at 7:29, the driver decides in a split second that no one is coming, and speeds off. This is one of those days.

The bus barely even does a real stop before it starts back up and speeds through the main street, leaving in its wake nothing but the memory of getting to school on time. "Fuuuuuuuck," Kate groans as we watch it round the corner at the very end of the street. It's headed on to brighter suburbs. Cleaner too.

"What now?" I ask.

"Jake can drive you." Mrs. Tran is standing by the door, smiling stiffly as if she knew we were going to be late all along. I want to ask why she'd have Kate organizing ice cream at the crack of dawn if she knew we'd be late, but I keep my mouth shut. We're like family, me and the Trans, but that's actually none of my business.

Before either Kate or I can protest, Mrs. Tran goes to her phone to call Jake, and we're standing awkwardly outside

Ginger Store, taking turns eating rice-paper wraps, waiting for him to show up. I bet Mrs. Tran had to really convince him. I bet he said no first.

Kate's family lives four houses down from me, but it still takes Jake five whole minutes to make it to the curb. He parks in front of the store, window rolled down, looking like some sort of wild animal that just woke up. He doesn't say much, only waves us over so we can get inside. Kate sits shotgun, and I slip into the back, clutching the container of wraps. "What's that?" he asks.

"Food," I say.

"From my mom?"

"Obviously," Kate grunts.

"For who?"

"For me and Kate," I say, and then I add, "Because *we* helped her clean the store."

I press into that "we" a bit too hard, and it has him rolling his eyes as he pulls onto the road, mumbling something under his breath. Kate turns around in her seat, her lips pressed together like she's fighting another burst of laughter. After a stoplight and a second of silence, Jake says, "I got in late last night and I was tired. Why's everyone so up my ass about cleaning?"

"Because you never clean," Kate says. I nod once in solidarity. "It's *your* parents' store, you know. Poor Nelo has to do everything."

"Everything," I say with an exaggerated sigh.

"And soon her back's going to be hurting her with all that—all that extra weight," Kate continues, motioning to her chest. My snickering is done. We're off the same page.

"What?" Jake says, trying to lock eyes with me in the rear-view mirror. I avoid him and kick the back of Kate's chair instead. "Why? Are you—"

"She's blossoming," Kate cuts in, a giggle still hidden in her voice.

Jake looks mortified, and I don't blame him at all. I don't want to think of myself as a blossom, and I'm almost dead sure he doesn't want to either—especially this early in the morning.

CHAPTER TWO

Kate and I have the same free block for third period, so we sit in the cafeteria, vibing to music on her phone. Actually, it's her music—songs fresh from her mixtape. She's been working on it forever, which is why sometimes we sit and listen to playlists of her old mixes too. The school is pretty familiar with those because she plays them at school events. One time, she did some megahits R&B and country-rap mash-up with the best transitions, and people went wild for it, like this girl really has all that skill in her. Her social has mad followers too. Although, honestly, I think the school is too small for her now. She was asked to do the upcoming football game, but she said no. She's got big dreams. Hence the mixtape, and the new DJ name: DJ Kaytee.

I mean, I don't know why she picked "Kaytee" when her name isn't even "Katie" and her childhood nickname "Kitkat" was right there for the taking. Sometimes I think it's because she doesn't want anyone to call her "Kitkat" anymore, but I still don't get why. The nickname wasn't that bad.

I'm eating my second-to-last rice-paper wrap while I nod to the beat. "This is good," I say slowly.

She smiles, wide. Kate is a sucker for praise. "Man, you think? I was afraid no one would, you know, get what I was trying to do with the Gemstones' bridge. It's *such* an old song."

"Yeah." I laugh even though I don't know what song it is. "This is legit. You could really get famous off this. We'll do a full social media thing and push it out to blogs and stuff."

Her feet are tapping under the table, and she's rocking side to side in excitement. "Okay, okay. How about this for a name?" she asks, and holds up her hands, bracing me for the inevitable glory of the official title. "DJ Kaytee Tran, Volume One."

I'm hit with a jolt of excitement too, and suddenly we're high-fiving over the table and squealing. "That sounds dope!" I tell her. "When are you gonna decide on cover art?"

"Soon," she says, and giggles. "Should I go black-and-white or something else? Hot colors or cool colors? Sepia?"

"This isn't a sepia event, sis." I snort. "Go full color."

"Hot?"

"Cold. Go purple and blue."

"Purple and blue volume one," she sings, dancing around in her seat, and I have to turn away before I die of embarrassment. "I trust your judgment, you know."

I nod and reach out for our handshake. Over the years, it's become less of a handshake and more of bumping our knuckles. I realize you can just do that with anyone, but Kate and

I have been friends for so long that it still feels like it's more special.

The cafeteria gets a bit louder, and I turn my neck stiffly to see what the commotion is. Kate is peering around for the source of the noise, but the scowl on her face tells me all I need to know. I take out my earbud and twist in my seat just in time to catch Maree walking into the caf with her new minions behind her. No way she'd have the same friends from two weeks ago.

Kate groans, and I turn back around. "Never mind. Let's listen to another song," she says, and flips through her phone.

Maree settles with her people onto a bench not far from ours. One of them is laughing even though no one is speaking, and it makes me uncomfortable, because why is she doing that? Maree's golden blond hair is flowing all over the place, and it sort of feels as if she's only moving her head so everyone can see all fifty million highlights she got in after her vacation. They do look nice, though. For a second, it looks like she's staring at me, but I turn away before I can make sure. Maree used to be our friend a long time ago, back when it was me, Kitkat, Bo, Maree, and Rafa. We don't all live on the same street anymore, and we're not all friends, but Kate, Maree, Rafa, and I ended up here at T.L. Collegiate. Bo goes to the decidedly nicer, spring-trip-to-Greece-having Santa Ana Academy. I was shocked when I saw Maree on the first day of high school. She lives in a way nicer neighborhood now, so I figured she'd be at Santa Ana too and not T.L. The rumor is that her mom sent her here so she doesn't catch an attitude about being a pseudo-celebrity, but it's too late for that. Maree walks around like she owns everybody.

In fact, Maree was the first of us to change, even though she cried the most when her parents said they were going to move. Man, she was *always* crying. The day she moved, she stood on her front porch, large tears dropping down her pale face while she moaned her goodbyes. We all got up one by one to wish her well and give her a hug. Me, with my multi-colored braids (it was such a grade-seven thing); Bo with his messy cornrows and thick-ass magnifying glass–like glasses; Rafa with his uneven tan and long, sun-kissed hair; and Kate, with her checkered wristbands and obscure band T-shirts. Maree even had the audacity to say she'd miss us *so, so, so much*, and we believed her too! It only took two weeks for her to get brand-new friends and have new pictures up online.

In the caf, Maree says something loud enough for us to hear but not clear enough for us to make it out, and her friends laugh. She smiles and preens like a cat in the sun. I'm getting tired of her, so I nudge Kate, who already has a song queued up for me. "What's this called?" I ask.

She runs her tongue along her teeth, nervously. "It's mad rough, but you're going to love it. It's a Midtown Project mash-up with, uh, bass."

"What?" Midtown Project was our favorite boy band in

middle school, but it's embarrassing to say now. They had really good R&B harmonies, but once Sol Cousins entered the game and merged smooth harmonies with rap, it was over. Sol is local, but internationally famous. He grew up literally fifteen blocks from T.L., and we liked that he always gave our city a shout-out no matter what. We're collectively over him, though. He dropped a really wack collaboration project that tanked on the charts, and almost every kid I know pretends that they don't know him anymore. He still gets some radio play, but honestly, it's hard to tell if anyone here even likes him or if he's just become part of the fibers of the city.

"It's so good, though," Kate says.

I feign enthusiasm when I put the earbud in, but when the sound erupts, I'm genuinely surprised. I'm furrowing my brows and scowling and nodding my head—all the things you do when you're really into the beat of a song. "This is *good*," I say again.

While I'm listening, a notification pops up on my phone from T.L. Chats. I look around. Almost everyone joined the private online forum, and whenever we want to talk about teachers or school or anything, we put it in the group. The admin is some twelfth grader named Carlos who's done a victory lap twice. We joke that he's only hanging around to retain his group admin privileges, but the more classes he purposefully fails, the more it's like we're not lying.

The message comes from a girl whose name and face I

don't recognize, but I know it must be one of Maree's new friends. It's a link to Maree's latest YouTube video, and she never posts those herself. The picture is a shot of her, with perfect makeup, sitting in her brightly lit room and making a weird face as if someone told her something stupid. The freeze frames always have obnoxious titles splashed across that say things like "OMG" and "LOL" in crooked font. This video is aptly called "The WTF Challenge."

I show Kate my phone, and she groans so deeply, I can feel the table vibrate with her anger. "Of-fucking-course," she says. "Why wouldn't she post a new video? It's been a whole-ass week."

As I stare at the video and study Maree's contorted face in the picture, I can't help but notice the views. It was posted ten minutes ago, and they're at three thousand and counting. I keep forgetting she's YouTube famous now. Honestly, she can keep it. I never want anyone knowing who I am, what I ate, or where I buy my clothes.

"Don't click on it," Kate hisses at me.

"I'm not," I tell her.

My thumb is hovering dangerously close to the video, but I divert quickly. I hate that I'm so curious. Maree hasn't said two words to either of us since she peaced out of Ginger East. She hasn't even said anything to us since we all started going to T.L., and we're in the same grade! If that isn't high-quality snake behavior, then what is?

Kate watches me carefully as I stash my phone away. She has less patience for Maree than I do. "I hope you're not going to go home later and watch the rest."

"Ugh, no," I say with a grimace. "These challenges are dumb anyway—just people recording themselves watching the weirdest videos. There's a wolf pack video and I saw it— it's not even that good. A bunch of dogs go running through some mall somewhere, and this lady starts shrieking and saying, 'Whose dogs? Whose dogs are these?' and then the person filming laughs, and that's all. It's stupid."

Kate snorts and sits up straighter. "I kind of want to see her reaction, though."

"She's not going to fail the challenge, fam."

"Yeah, she's probably already seen the video beforehand and is faking like she hasn't."

"True," I say, smiling. "She has a reputation to uphold."

CHAPTER THREE

Vicky Sanchez compliments my sweater in the hall after
school and asks where I got it. I'm on my way to the buses,
and her question comes out of nowhere. She practically hurls
it at me. I tell her I made it myself, and she sneers, smacking
her lips as she leaves. I wasn't even lying, though. I did make
it. It was just a plain black sweater until I cut out the tiger
from another shirt and stitched it on. She's probably going to
spread rumors about how I'm a fake bitch tomorrow, which
means I should consider wearing something that won't draw
attention to myself. I have a black shirt with giraffes on it that
I was looking forward to wearing, but I might have to forgo
that. I'll probably have to dig for it later, and I'm not about
that right now.

At the head of the bus line is where the only bus that stops
in Ginger East sits. It leaves first because it has to make the
longest trip. And it isn't that Ginger East is far; it's that the
bus makes a lot of small stops along the way and does a huge
detour around another neighborhood before it slinks into
ours. Ginger East is the last stop. The end of the road. The
other side of the tracks.

It's five minutes after the last bell, and the bus is already sort of packed. I waited too long for Kate, but she's stuck talking to the principal. He's really trying it with this football game thing. I'm not about to miss the bus home, so I left. Most of the seats I like to sit in, up front with a clear view of the road ahead, are taken by first and second years. They get nervous about sitting at the back of the bus since that's where the cooler and older kids, or other third years like me, tend to sit. I go down the row looking for the first available spot. I'm secretly praying that I won't have to sit near the soccer team. They're all loud and suspect, and sometimes they yell ugly things at the bus driver. It's not a good vibe.

I'm treading into their territory now and wishing I waited for Kate. One guy on the team, Marcus, always likes to creep on girls the second they get into his peripheral, especially if they're solo. He sees me and we lock eyes, and I'm suddenly so conscious of how my jeans are clinging to my legs and how fitted this sweater actually is and how I probably went up a bra size. I need to disappear.

I slide my backpack off quick and duck into the first open seat nearby. I don't even look at who I'm sitting with, but suddenly I hear a voice: "Nelo?" It's Rafa.

I'm always so shocked to see him these days because our group quietly disbanded, and he's so different. He's tan, tall, and lean; he's halfway between being a boy and a man, and it still throws me. All the girls say he's hot, but I have to stare at him a bit longer to see it. It's not my fault, though. Every time I look at him, all I can see is that annoying kid with really long hair who used to follow me around and come to my house every day asking me to play soccer. He was obsessed with the Brazilian men's team and almost always wore their uniform to school, to the store, to go to the park, anywhere. He still plays for the school, and he's friends with all the obnoxious guys on the team. They're assholes and he's become asshole-by-association.

"Hey, Rafa," I say.

He frowns. "It's Raf." Raf. Rafa. Rafael.

I shrug and settle into my seat. He eyes me for a second, and I pretend not to notice, bringing out my phone and opening up my email. Why's he watching me so hard? Then he says, "Switch seats with me. I wanna sit at the end."

"Why?"

"Because you get off last."

It makes sense but I don't want to move because I don't want Marcus to look over here. "Can you just crawl over me?" I ask.

His lips pull into a tight line because I know he wants to laugh. "Are you serious?"

"I hate getting up after I sit down."

"It's not that deep."

"Oh my God," I groan. I'm making a huge show of it, but Rafa doesn't care about my feelings anymore, not the way he used to. Now he's tough for no damn reason. He moved out of Ginger East when we were eleven—as far as I'm concerned, there's no reason for him to be so hard anymore. Ginger East is rough; everyone knows that. It's not the safest for a kid to go out after a certain time, and there are places you should stay away from, even in the daytime. Now he lives in Cooksville, where all the houses are two or three stories high and there's a condom-less community park. The Ginger East park always has used condoms around the trees and goalposts. It's nasty as hell, but it's kind of what it's known for. He doesn't know anything about that used-condom park life anymore.

Reluctantly I pick up my bag and stand in the aisle as he slides over to my vacated seat. I can hear Marcus start to whistle, and I want to shrink into my own body and die.

Rafa is mean and doesn't get up so I can slide into the window seat. Instead he gestures over his lap, assuming that I'm going to crawl over him.

"Actually?" I grumble. He shrugs. He's the worst. "Hold my bag," I say, and shove it square into his face. I'm mad that he catches it, because that was as close as I was going to get to punching him in the face for real. I crawl over him and settle in by the window.

"What's going on over there?" Marcus calls out in the ugliest voice, and Rafa twists around to look at him. They're either talking or sharing hand signals or chuckling, but I don't care. I snatch my bag from Rafa and slide downward so I can press my knees against the back of the seat in front of me. If I can't completely disappear, this will have to be good enough.

The bus starts to move, and Rafa turns around again. We don't talk.

I shift a bit and open my bag while I grab the container of rice-paper wraps. There's one left. I should eat it and drop the container off with Kate's mom before I get home.

"Did you learn to make those?" Rafa asks suddenly.

"No," I say, taking a bite. "Kate's mom gave them to me."

"Kitkat's mom?"

I have to smile because he still uses it too, Kate's nickname. I let myself get all nostalgic for maybe two and a half seconds before I remember he made me crawl over him just now. "No one calls her that anymore," I say, looking up and over at him.

He nearly pouts. I wasn't aware he still could. The lines of his face are so rigid, like he's performing masculinity or something, and someone told him "Boys don't cry." It's only funny because he used to cry a lot, most notably that one summer when I wouldn't stop pulling his hair. It was getting so long, though, and I'm pretty sure my mom thought it was a sew-in. "I still call her that," he says eventually.

I snort, my mouth still somewhat full. "You don't talk to Kate."

"Yeah, I do."

"Kate's my best friend. I talk to her all the time, and she never talks about you."

"Well, I talk to Kate all the time and she doesn't talk about you either," he says with a scoff, like he's won.

I take the entire wrap and stuff it into my mouth. He silently watches me, eyebrow twitching, and I know it's because he thought I would share it with him. But I don't know him like that anymore, and besides, food is sacred out here. You can't just share with anyone.

His phone buzzes, and my eyes shoot over to his screen as if it were mine. It's a message from Marcus. I bet I can guess what it says.

Before he opens up the text, I see a glimpse of what is on his screen already: Maree's latest video. I guess no one is immune. "You watch those?" I ask, barely stopping the judgment from bleeding into my voice.

He hides his screen, annoyed. "Why're you looking at my phone?"

"It was a mistake." It wasn't, and the look on his face tells me he knows I'm lying. "How many views is she at now?"

He locks his phone and pretends like he's not going to check, but then he swipes his screen back on and loads up the video. He scrolls under the image and flips it around to show me. She has almost thirty thousand views after four hours. "Who's even watching this?" I say.

"I don't know," he says. "There are only, what, three

thousand kids at our school? And I doubt all of them care about her."

"Must be the endorsement deals and 'huge' fanbase from where she lives," I say. "The bougie part of the city."

He cracks a smile, and it makes me feel like it's old times. It doesn't last long because soon he's clearing his throat and pushing his hand through his dark brown hair and looking away. Trying to be cool. "Yeah," he says, glancing over his shoulder.

"Yeah."

He brings out his phone again and starts tinkering with it. I guess we're done talking, but when he thinks I'm not looking, he texts Marcus back. I want to know what they're saying and if it's about me. Marcus is so greasy, and even thinking of him makes me cringe. I don't know what Rafa sees in him. I think I'd be a way better friend to him than Marcus. I think I *was* a better friend to him.

"She's always . . ."

"Huh?"

"I don't know," he says quietly. I sit up a bit straighter to listen. "Maree. She's always talking so much shit about the old neighborhood."

"Yeah, she is," I grunt.

"Pretty much in every video, she has some shit to say about how she grew up," he says. "You know?"

"Yeah." I'm happy he noticed it. Not that I watch a lot

of her videos, but she always finds a way to smack talk Ginger East. The last video she posted was about how she was going to spend her vacation. She said she wanted to travel and go somewhere exotic, somewhere different from "that trashy place" where she grew up. What? Ginger East may be a bit scary and sketchy, but it's not trashy. She never called it trashy when she was playing kickball with us on Bo's birthday and we let her win twice. She never called it trashy when my mom let her come over for dinner after she lost her house key and her parents were out of town. And she most definitely never called it trashy when Jake and his friends took us to the park and showed us where only the older kids went. But *now* it's trashy?

"She's fucking fake," he says, and I laugh louder than I intend to. "Ginger East ain't that ghetto anymore."

"You mean it ain't that ghetto *at all*," I say, and nudge him. He doesn't look at me like I'm crossing a line. It's nice. "We used to have the best time, and she's acting like she had to suffer or something."

"Exactly. Fake."

"Remember when we went with Jake's friends to that bike path? We saw a snake there that one time, and we screamed so loud that we had sore throats for a week or something."

He scrunches up his face like he's trying to remember. He obviously does. That snake was so damn big—is he kidding! But he's not going to let me win. "What I remember," he tells me, "is that you used to have the biggest crush on Jake."

I'm choking. "Ew, no? No fucking way. Why would I? That's Kate's brother."

"Yeah, but he's *older.*"

He says "older" as if it's an incentive. I'm way more sophisticated than to like a guy only because he's older than I am, and if Rafa knew anything about me, he'd at least know that. "You're so waste," I grumble. "I'm not even surprised you'd say that."

"Why?" he says with a snicker. "Because it's true?"

I can't even say anything. It's definitely not true. I definitely do not like Jake, and I don't need to defend myself to Rafa.

I slip down farther in my seat and bring out my phone. I'm going to ignore him until he gets off. Then maybe I'll say bye if he looks at me, but I won't say it first. He and I really aren't friends anymore, so I shouldn't need to try so hard.

I never used to try. We got along as well as me and Kate do these days. She's always been my best friend, but Rafa and I were, I don't know, inseparable.

I was really into astrology the year we all turned ten. Rafa turned ten first—April 9—so the day before his birthday I told him, "Did you know you're an Aries?" He was biting down on a lollipop, his long hair tangling in the wind as we headed to Bates' Arcade. Man, the Ginger East arcade was *it.* All the kids would hang out there after school. Once you got past Derek and his boys at the doors—tough ex-military types who tried to get kids hooked on whatever they were selling—it was fine. People used to line up when there was a new game, and sometimes we'd stay real late until the kitchen started throwing away the old fries.

"What's an Aries?" Rafa asked me after he'd finally chewed the lollipop to a pulp.

"It's the—wait." I read from the browser tab on my dad's old phone. "It's a ram. It's a fire sign, so that means you're hotheaded and childish."

He laughed. "No way. I'm not childish."

"Listen, it's science. I don't make the rules."

"Science is stupid. I don't even believe in that stuff."

"Bro, you don't believe in *science?*"

"What are you doing tomorrow?" Rafa always had this weird habit where he'd ask me things out of nowhere as if he wasn't paying attention to me. Most of the time, it made me want to pull his hair. So when I reached for a loose strand, he ducked away because he knew what was coming. "I'm serious. It's Saturday."

"Yeah, and it's your birthday."

After a moment contemplating, he said, "Let's hang out tomorrow at the arcade. We can come when they open."

I grimaced. "Who's trying to be at the arcade for nine a.m.?"

"No way they open at nine."

"Yes way they open at nine."

"Hey!" Maree's voice was shrill and peppy, which was how we always described Maree. She was sweating from her multiple rounds on Dance Dance Revolution with Kate, back when it was cool to be good at DDR. "Why're you guys always late? School was out forever ago. Kate and me did maybe ten rounds just now."

I scoffed, tossing my bag onto the floor by the growing pile. Maree's pink backpack, Kate's black-and-white checkered backpack, and Bo's anime messenger bag were huddled by the wall. "You did not do ten rounds," I said.

"They did maybe four," Bo piped up. He was sitting in the racing simulation chair beside Kate's DDR station. Man, he still hadn't fixed those damn cornrows. If he needed help, I wished he'd just ask me. I had done half my braids myself, and they were pretty good.

"How's that even possible?" Rafa asked, tying his hair up and getting into the car beside Bo's. "Mountain Hill Road on hard?"

Bo frowned. "Mountain Hill Road on normal, bro. The uphill climb is mad rough on hard and my calves can't take all that."

"Shut up, Bo. Jeez," we groaned, and snickered as Bo grinned, stunned into silence by his own cheesiness. He shrugged before selecting normal on the racing game.

Kate had skipped back to her position on the dance mat, and spun around to hang off the balance bar. When we locked eyes, she laughed. "Do a round with me?" She stomped her foot on the up arrow to select the song. It started up fast and angry, like how all the music Kate liked back then sounded.

Maree jogged over to where Bo and Rafa were focused on racing through the desert. She crouched down between the two cars, focusing on the screens. Eventually her eyes were only following Rafa's. "What are you doing for your birthday tomorrow?" she asked.

Rafa didn't break concentration once as he uttered, "Uh, nothing."

"Nothing?" I missed a step by accident and watched a trail of arrows zoom by on my screen. My coordination was completely shot. "We're going to the arcade tomorrow. How's that nothing?"

Rafa crashed, and I only remember it because Bo cheered so loud. Maree gasped, popping up to her feet. "What?" Her mouth hung open in shock and offense. "You guys are going to the arcade without us?"

Rafa and I said "Uh, no" simultaneously, but my face was hot with nervousness.

Maree was almost on the brink of tears. God, she always was. "But we can come too, right? Rafa, you have to say yes. I'm gonna ask your mom, and then you have to say yes."

Rafa groaned, leaning back into the car seat. "Yeah, whatever. If you want."

Bo glanced over his shoulder at us. "I might be busy tomorrow. I have to go somewhere with my grandma."

"Well, that's cool, because I didn't even invite you," Rafa said. Bo buttoned up right away, pursing his lips and looking at the ground. Rafa snickered, knocking him in the arm. "Bro, I'm kidding."

"He's kidding, Bo. He's kidding," Kate echoed with a frown. When she looked at Rafa, she scowled, though. "You're so mean. Are you just mad because Yvonne said you were pretty at recess today? There's nothing wrong with calling a boy pretty."

"I like boys who are pretty," Maree piped up.

Suddenly Kate grabbed my elbow and tugged me aside to the farthest dance mat. She leaned in and whispered. "Okay. Don't tell anyone, but I asked Rafa, if he could spend his birthday with anyone, who would he pick? And he picked you, so then I was like, 'Ask her to go to the arcade, then.' And so maybe that's why he asked you."

"What? How come? Why would he pick me?"

"Because I think he likes you," she said.

"Why would he like *me*?"

"Man, I don't know. You're cool, though, so it's not hard to understand." She sighed, her shoulders rising and falling dramatically.

"Why would you even ask him?" I frowned, crossing my arms. "What if he meant as friends? I don't understand why you would say something to him."

She shrugged, and for a moment, that was it. I want to believe her mind was racing, trying to come up with the perfect answer, something that couldn't be conveyed with a shrug. But she shrugged again, and said, "Because it kinda looked like you liked him too."

Kate is a Sagittarius, but at that exact second, I was like, *Damn, this is Aries behavior.*

CHAPTER FOUR

Last year, Dad went to Calgary for work. Better job, he said, and Mom's hours as a personal support worker were getting cut, so we needed the money. I've never been out of the province—barely even out of Ginger East—but I searched for pictures on the internet, and parts of the city he's in look really fake. The sky is so blue and the snowcapped mountains are so white that it looks as if they've been Photoshopped. I still can't believe Dad lives in a place like that. I don't really know what he does over there, but my mom says he works with some sort of machinery. She doesn't ever outright say it, and I feel weird not knowing when people ask what my dad does. It bothers me sometimes. Other times, it's not so bad. Like when he sends money, and Mom is finally able to fix her car. She buys fresh fruit, tomatoes, and bags of rice. She stocks up the pantry with all the necessities, lining each shelf so that I almost forget how empty it was a second ago. Those are the times when it's not so bad.

He sends cards too, and he likes to text me all the time. The cards sometimes have money in them, maybe five or ten dollars, and the messages have prayers. The last time we spoke, he said he would come to visit for the summer. Mom says not to get my hopes up; if work is busy, he might not be able to come. "So we should go visit him," I offer. She just laughs. Mom's laugh is easygoing without an ounce of bitterness, so it doesn't bother me. I know too that we can't really afford to travel.

I'm sitting at the table, and it's Saturday. My rice is getting cold, but Mom won't let me leave until I finish it.

"You're so skinny, girl," she says, pinching my arm as she walks by. She's making food for the week, and suddenly the kitchen smells like Nigeria. I assume this is what Nigeria smells like, even though I've never been. The air is nothing but pepper, crayfish, and melon seeds. "Eat all of it. I don't want your dad to say I'm not feeding you."

I sit up straighter. "So is he coming to visit?"

She gives me a look that screams *What kind of question is that?* "No," she says. "When did I say that?"

"But then how will he say I'm skinny if he never sees me?"

"He'll know. You don't think he knows?" she tells me. Mom wasn't born in Nigeria like Dad was. She was born here and lacks the harshness that comes with a village upbringing—the harshness my dad has. She doesn't speak Igbo like grandma used to, but still, her speech is different and foreign sometimes. I can't explain it well, but Rafa used to get it. His parents didn't grow up in Colombia either, but they still clung to an accent and speech pattern that wasn't really theirs. I wonder what that's like—being firmly in between two places. I get it, but only a little.

"Hrmmm," I grunt, shoving a forkful of rice into my mouth. Mom smiles but turns her back to me while she strains various meats from pot to pot.

The kitchen is always extra cluttered on weekends, but it feels even stuffier in here because of all this unopened mail. Mom is usually pretty organized, but she has letters and papers piled high on the table across from me. I stare at them and chew obnoxiously until Mom hisses at me to stop.

The TV is on. It's hanging on our otherwise empty wall directly across from the kitchen table where I'm now groaning into my plate. That news channel that has ten marquees going at the same time is on. A commercial begins playing for Spice of Life. A blond woman is on the screen talking about how they're excited to be expanding. "We offer the best selection of herbs and spices in the greater Toronto area," she says. I chew through another forkful of rice.

"We have three new stores opening this year. Get all the spices you need at Humber River, Georgetown, and Ginger East."

I scowl. "Which Ginger East?"

Mom looks over her shoulder at me and then at the TV. "They're opening one here?"

"I guess."

She is silent for a while, and then all she says is, "Oh." It's not a confrontational "oh" or an angry one. It's very calm, almost a whisper.

I swallow another scoop of rice. Mom gets all her spices from Ginger Store, and she has for years. They carry spices that the neighborhood cares about. We're their market, after all. Why would we go anywhere else?

"It's like what you used to say when we were watching those debates on the news," I tell her, remembering the many times when Mom forced me to watch election results or live debates. She gets way into these things because she has a sociology degree, and as a result, I have to suffer. Those debates were literally just old people yelling at each other and breathing heavily when they tried not to swear on TV, but they were always yelling about the same thing: economics and displacing people and stuff like that.

Mom raises an eyebrow, impressed, but she stays quiet.

"It's true, right?"

"Yes," she says. "Unfortunately."

Dad and Mom are both into politics in a weird way. When I was younger, Dad used to let me flip through a bunch of his and Mom's old textbooks for fun. I pretended I was smarter than my age, but really, I wanted to look at the cool diagrams. Dad made me practice reading the words. "Displacing People" was high on the list of bolded headings that I remember, which included "Property Tax" and "Gentrification," a word I couldn't spell till I was twelve.

"I'm surprised they're bringing one here," Mom pipes up, her back facing me. "This place isn't what it used to be."

I frown. "It's the same to me."

Now she turns to face me, a pitiful smile pressed into her lips. "You're a kid. How much do you think you even noticed growing up?"

"Uh, a lot."

"Where's that arcade you used to play at?" she asks, and I sigh into my chest because I know what she's going to say. It closed how many years ago—"It closed how many years ago?" she goes on. "And now what's there for you kids to do around here? Drugs, or drinking, or getting pregnant—"

"No one is getting pregnant, Mom," I grunt, even though I definitely saw Janine from the next street a few days ago, and she's finally starting to show. Janine and I were in the same second-grade class back in the day. "Besides, just because the arcade closed doesn't mean we need Spice of Life to open. They're not even related. Plus, where would they even open here?"

Mom hums. "I don't know," she says. "They tore down a bunch of houses at the end of the, uh, the main road. Maybe there."

"Which houses? Where the old couple died?"

Mom looks over her shoulder at me. "What?"

"We used to play there as kids. The lady would give us rum cake and candy at Halloween," I tell her. She looks suspicious of my story, but I'm actually telling the truth. There really was an old couple and they really did die in there.

"Who asked you to be playing around there?"

I roll my eyes back into my food. "Well, I don't go there *anymore*, now that they're dead," I mumble. "Plus, that was back when Bo used to live there."

"Who?"

"Oh my God, Mom," I groan. "Bo? He had crazy cool cornrow patterns and really bad teeth. Remember?"

She doesn't, but she still nods like she does. How can she not remember Bo? I know it's been so long since I hung out with anyone but Kate in the neighborhood, but he was one of my closest friends back then. How could she have forgotten him?

I suddenly don't have an appetite anymore. Instead I want to find where Spice of Life is opening. It's already April, so if they're planning on opening this year—and especially if they're running ads on TV—they must have a building already. They must be opening real soon. I can't imagine it being here. Ginger East has always been mainly residential, with the odd small business here and there. The main road is made up of money loan places, fast-food restaurants with no seating, and small rotating shops that really only sell flags around World Cup time. People like to hang out on the street corners, and everyone here knows each other, even if you're up to no good. Like, *Yeah, I know Sunny sells dope, but he has the best firework hookups for holidays, so I can't even hate.* It's like that. Not really a big box Spice of Life kind of place, to be honest. What made them think we'd need one here? It's probably the high concentration of people who cook with spices.

I push another forkful of rice into my mouth as I get to my feet. Mom still has her back turned to me, but she senses me trying to escape. "Finish all your food. You owe me after ruining those shoes I got for you," she says, glancing over her shoulder until she catches my eye. Guilt is plastered all over my face. I take another bite before she eventually turns back around.

I scrape my fork across the plate so it sounds as if I'm eating, but I'm already slipping away from the kitchen table. My eye catches a glimpse of the stack of letters there, and suddenly I'm reading the bold, black text from where I'm standing. I couldn't see it clearly before, but it's so obvious now: "RENT INCREASE NOTICE." All caps. Staring me right in the face.

I lean forward and flip it upside down as if that actually makes a difference. Mr. Tran got a similar letter from his landlord too. Maybe something's going around. The words "rent increase" are swirling around in my head, and it's giving me a hollow feeling in my stomach, but it's probably fine this time. Nothing to worry about.

Mom isn't happy when I finally run from the kitchen table. She's calling after me—"Chi-chi, come finish your food!"— and I'm still running because I hate that nickname so much.

If this were back in the day, I would get on my bike and ride down to the old house where that couple used to live, but now I press my feet into my shoes and start jogging. It's more difficult to jog all the way there now, past the rows of houses and around the main street. There used to be a cool ice cream place over here and a different burger place over there, but they're all gone now. Even that cash-and-carry-turned-salon-turned-I-don't-know place looks as if it'll be vacant soon. There are a lot of the shops that are boarded up and others with FOR SALE signs on the front door. Some of the signs are new, and I hate that I slow my jog a little to try to read them. Reesor and McKenzie and Hillcrest—all these real estate companies swooping in at the last second to buy up our stores. I can't even be mad because we let them do it.

The group of houses with the dead old couple's house is gone. Bo's house too. I joke about it, but to see its absence puts a new kind of emptiness in my chest. It's so messed up because I can remember the long, uneven stone walkway we used to trip over during Halloween, and I remember the way the front step used to creak with the wind. I'm squinting at the place in front of me, trying to—I don't know—get it to come back or something.

Things close here and there on the main road and people move away, but this was a whole house, a whole block, that isn't here anymore. Instead it's been replaced with a sprawling building that has huge glass doors, the kind that probably open when you get close to them. The property is surrounded by a thick, metal fence. I've stopped jogging and I'm breathing heavily, letting my eyes fall on the huge sign in front of the fence. COMING SOON, it says. It has the Spice of Life logo on it. This is the newest store, and soon it'll be filled with people shopping through their million aisles of exotic spices. Man, I don't know about that. People around here don't care about this. We already have Ginger Store.

A branch snaps somewhere beside me as Mr. Brown hobbles up to the fence a few steps away. Mr. Brown owns the longest-running cash advance place on the main road. Tons of other stores start up, the owners thinking they can handle owning a loan place in Ginger East, and soon they crumble under pressure and scare tactics, but Mr. Brown is a hard-ass. An OG. He's been here since he moved from Trinidad in the eighties, and he'll probably never leave. I get it, though. Sometimes I look at him, his tall, sturdy stature and thick glasses, and think I'd want to be someone like him. He really believes in something. I can see it in his eyes as he scans the fence, taking a tired step toward it. I can sense it when he gives the fence a swift kick.

"Damn," I breathe, and he looks at me. We stare at each other like we didn't know the other was here the whole time. I'm trying to play it cool, but Mr. Brown can be scary. When he cusses you, all you want is for the earth to swallow you up. He made Maree cry once like that.

He walks over to me quickly, hands firmly at his side.

"What are you doing here?" he asks. His accent makes it sound as if no time has passed since he last lived in Trinidad.

I shrug, feeling my voice shrink a little because of his gaze. "I don't know. Just looking."

"Uh-huh," he grunts, turning back to the fence. "Me too. I'm just looking."

The distant sound of cars and life takes over while we look at the fence and the unfinished building. I step a bit closer to read the COMING SOON sign. There's an email address and phone number there. WE'RE HIRING! it says. CALL OR EMAIL FOR JOB OPPORTUNITIES.

Mr. Brown cuts in front of me, fixing both his hands on the sides of the sign. In one swift motion, he yanks the sign down and toward him, pulling it from the fence. It slips from his fingers and clangs onto the pavement before it finally settles, overturned and scuffed. I may be imagining it, but it seems as though Mr. Brown kisses his teeth before he turns on his heel and slumps off back down the road. It's a power move. It's exactly what I expect from an OG.

CHAPTER FIVE

Kate doesn't text me in the morning on Monday. Usually she does. She sends something like *I'm up*, with an upside-down smiley face. She does that because she knows that if she doesn't, I'll call her, and she absolutely hates picking up the phone in the morning. Kate isn't a morning person.

I'm throwing the rest of my outfit together for school: black shirt, black leggings, denim jacket. My shirt says ALL BLACK in the center in black lettering, and the letters pop more than usual today. I know that if my mom sees, she's going to mention the bra, so I gotta dip before she gets out of the shower.

Mom didn't turn the bathroom fan on, so the steam is seeping into the cramped hallway. It's making me sweat, and it's way too early to start sweating. After snatching my phone off the table, I head down the hall and stuff my feet into my shoes. "Bye, Mom!" I call, even though I know she can't hear me.

I'm dialing Kate's number, and her phone is ringing off the hook. The call goes straight to voice mail. "Ugh," I grumble, and text her instead. *Where the h e l l are you????* I doubt she'll reply before I walk up to the store. She's probably there, helping out her mom before the bus shows up again. Maybe she'll slip me another Vita ice cream.

The normal quiet hum of the street is gone. Instead the air is tense and thick with something foreign. It's weird. Usually the undesirables, the ugliness of the neighborhood, hide while the kids come out to play. The second we're at school, the busyness, the good and the bad, starts back up again. But today there's this creepy rustling in the distance and it's loud, like crunching papers, broken glass—and then there's the voices, lots of them, speaking quietly but forcefully. It's a hum. "Step back, step back" and "Stay behind the line," they say. "Oh my God!" cries another.

My feet quicken along the sidewalk. They're scraping now in these damn new shoes. New shoes are always like that, so loud and awkward. I have to press my feet into them harder and wiggle my toes more so they feel like home. I can see people now, a small crowd with phones out gathering at the intersection at the end of the street. That's where Ginger Store is.

I'm running. My feet come to a stop at the sight of police cars—two of them blocking traffic one way—and yellow caution tape sloped lazily from signpost to signpost. And the police are blocking the shop; they're blocking Ginger Store. They're trying to make sure no one gets in.

I rush past the crowd and nearly smash into a police officer.

"Kate?" I call over his shoulder. He has his hands gripped tightly around my wrists, and I can't fight him off.

"Miss, we're going to need you to step back," he says. He's being calm, but I can't hear anything, can't really see much over his tall, lanky figure.

He twists a little to the right, and that's when I finally see it. I hold my breath, gazing, gaping at this large, uneven hole in the window.

CHAPTER SIX

Jagged pieces of glass litter the ground in front and on the inside of the shop. I can't stop looking at the glass. It's *everywhere*. I've never seen the ground shimmer like this before. Never heard the sound of the wind whistling through the storefront like this. "Shit . . ." I breathe out, letting my eyes wash over the scene. I don't have it in me to struggle anymore. All I can do is watch.

"Kate?" I call again. My voice doesn't carry. I whip out my phone and dial her number. She's really not answering at a time like this? Where is she? I get on my tiptoes and try to peer around the officers, but they're steadily watching me. One has his eyes so focused on my every move that I feel crippled under his gaze, tripping over my feet and stumbling until I give up. It's not worth it. I'll never be able to get around him.

I try Kate's phone again. It's ringing and ringing before it goes to voice mail. My heart is beating quickly, and a whimper escapes my lips. Is Kate okay? Why's the window like that? Who would do such a thing? Everyone in the neighborhood knows the Trans. We're all cool with each other. Ginger East isn't this kind of place anymore.

Another officer emerges from the storefront talking quickly with Mr. Tran. My heart pounds in my chest as I take another step forward—only to be nudged back by the officer in front of me. "I know him," I plead, pointing to their retreating figures, but the officer isn't budging. "Mr. Tran!" I call, pushing away from the officer. "Mr. Tran, is everyone okay? Where—where is everyone?"

Mr. Tran looks as somber as I've ever seen him. His lips don't even turn up at the sound of my voice. He just looks at me, spent and tired, and shakes his head like *Not now, not now.* It hurts to see, and I don't know what to do. I call his name again, but he's walking away, his head low, nodding, timid, at the officer's words. I've never seen Mr. Tran act like that in my life. He's never had to. He is much bigger than I am, but he seems so small now.

Someone bumps me from behind, and I turn around as Paco Velez utters an apology. He's four years older than me, but I remember him because he used to run these makeshift summer camps for neighborhood kids when we were eight. Really, it was just a glorified hangout. He once taught us how to tie a figure-eight knot, and I'll never forget when Kate cried out "This is *useless!*" in the middle of the lesson. God, where is she?

When Paco and I lock eyes, all he can do is frown and

sigh, nodding toward the wreckage. The *wreckage.* He opens his mouth as if he has something to say, but his resigned sigh takes the place of stilted words. I still understand.

"It's . . ." His eyes are boring into the building as though he's searching it for answers.

"I don't know," I utter. I feel like I have to say something, but the words aren't there.

"It's getting worse," he blurts out. "You know what I mean?"

I didn't.

Ginger East isn't supposed to be getting worse; it's supposed to be getting better. It *is* getting better.

"Something like this could happen to Ginger Store, of all places, you know?" he goes on, glancing around the crowd. "Nothing is sacred. Not even the store is as safe as it used to be."

"It's just as safe as it used to be," I tell him, my voice sounding firmer than I want it to.

Paco frowns. "No disrespect, Nelo. Ginger East is my hood too, but even you have to admit that things are unsafe around here."

"But this c-could've been an accident," I stutter out, my eyes darting back to the building. The more I look at it, the less I'm sure I even believe it.

Paco sighs. His resignation makes me itch with anger. "Come on. You really think that? Nelo—"

I can't even listen to him anymore. My heart is beating faster as I duck away, swerving through the crowd until I am safe from his—his lies. Or whatever that was. I can't take it today. Him too? My mom first, and now him? Paco always believed in this place; he cared so much about making sure us kids had something to do during the summer, even though he was just a kid himself. And *now* he thinks it's not safe? Now suddenly it's different?

"Holy shit . . ."

I stop walking when I come across a group of neighborhood kids, crowding around, phones up and filming, snapping pictures, everything. I recognize one of them immediately, a seventh grader named Mikey whose mom used to own a Caribbean Chinese restaurant on the main road. He gasps again, letting his phone's camera take in the scene. "What the fuuuuuu—"

"Yo, don't swear," one of his friends hisses at him. "Can't you see the Feds are everywhere?"

"They're just local cops," I utter, my voice tired. The officer near me glares, but I shrug because I didn't stutter.

Mikey and his friends turn to me and nod a quick hello. They take pictures of everything as if someone's about to ask them for evidence. Another of his friends who steadies his phone as if he's filming turns to me. "What happened to the store?"

"I don't . . . I was waiting for Kate, and . . ." My eyes are drifting back to the shattered window. Mr. Tran nodding at the police officer. Everyone speaking in hushed tones. Crowds growing, trying to see what happened here. And what did happen here?

"Was it a gang?" he asks.

I frown and sniff, trying to hold back tears. No way—*no way* could it have been a gang. Ginger East isn't known for that anymore. "Don't even ask that out loud. Someone will get the wrong idea," I say. My voice is shaking even though I really don't want it to. I'm so scared that I might be wrong.

"Yeah," Mikey says. "But someone from here couldn't do this."

"Exactly," I go on. My words come out jumbled and disorganized, but there's a fire behind them that burns as I talk. "Everyone knows everyone, and I swear, shit like this only happens in places where . . . I mean, no offense, but rent has been going up because of all those new stores. Who else would it be if not someone who isn't from here? I swear—I *swear* people who don't know anything about what it's like to live here will come in, do whatever they want, and then leave, pretending they did us any favors—pretending we *need* them."

Mikey's friend groans behind his phone. "Yeah, eh? It's messed up."

"Yeah, it is," I grunt, crossing my arms. "You know, honestly, and don't tell anyone I said this, but this is *exactly* the kind of thing that the Feds would do."

Mikey cackles, staggering back as if his body can't contain his laughter. It's such a crass sound in the hollow sadness of the sidewalk, and I wish he would stop. "That's what I'm saying!" he says.

"I see people talk about it online all the time. Feds show up, vandalize property, send in local cops like it's a local problem," I say. "These people won't ever leave places like this alone because they *hate* seeing when . . . uh . . ." Wait. It takes me longer than normal to realize Mikey's friend's phone is still focused on me, still stuck in my face like he's a reporter and I'm giving an interview. I swallow my words and let my eyes lock on to his. In a second, he knows he screwed up. He drops the phone, stuffs it back into his pocket. "What are you doing?"

He stutters, "I w-was just filming the window . . ."

I am standing between him and the storefront, so he could be telling the whole truth. Still, that phone was way too focused on me to even get a decent shot of the building.

Before I can say anything, Jake appears through the crowd. He purposefully gets in the way of one of Mikey's friends who's trying to take a picture of the store, and glares at us. "What are you doing here? Don't you have school?" he growls.

Mikey and his friends disperse in all different directions, cutting through the crowd to get to their bus stop. Jake turns his attention on me. He's hunched over, his jacket zipped up to his chin. He looks as tired as Mr. Tran. "You're going to be late too," he grunts.

"Are you okay?" I ask, trying to catch his gaze. "A-and your mom? And Kate? Where is she?"

He sighs this time, his shoulders stiff as they rise and fall. "You should go to school, okay? She's probably not coming today."

There's something about his voice when he says it, but it reminds me of when we were younger, when he would try to calm me down after I lost my house key or forgot my dad's work number. It reminds me of home, and it makes me want to cry. He doesn't look at me, and I want to believe it's because he might start crying too, even though I know that probably won't happen.

The police officer who was blocking my view before shifts away when a man in a long coat comes parading through. The man says all of two words to the officer, and then he's climbing under the tape toward the shattered glass. The crime scene. The officer with Mr. Tran cuts their conversation short and sweeps over to the long-coat man. He brings out a see-through bag, practically shoves it into the man's hands. The officer was holding it this entire time, and I didn't even notice, this see-through bag with a brick inside.

A brick.

Another "holy shit" falls past my lips. Someone bricked the store? Someone bricked the store.

Jake's voice cuts through the fog in my head. "You're going to miss the bus," he says, and nods toward the bus stop. It's seven-twenty-eight, and the bus is making its way down the road, mad slow. The driver must be watching all the commotion. I don't want to go—I don't want to tear myself away from the scene—but I have to because I can't look anymore. I cross the road impatiently and wait for the driver to stop.

"What happened here?" he asks aloud. He might be talking to me, but I don't have the energy, so I skip up the stairs and make my way to a seat in the middle. There's no one on the bus. I'm the only one, aside from the driver, who can hear my whimpers and almost-sobs. I'm mad that I'm sitting here on a bus crying before school.

The bus lurches forward, stops, and starts again as the driver cranes his neck, trying to get a good look at the scene in front of Ginger Store. I know what he must be thinking: *Stuff like this always happens here.* Well, it doesn't.

I can see the store better from my seat, but I try not to look. If I see any more of it—if I see Kate, or Mr. Tran, or Jake—I might cry even harder. I have five minutes before we hit the next stop and more kids get on. I need to get it together.

It takes one stop for the tears to dry and two stops to fully compose myself. I still feel hollow and drained. Can't stop thinking about the store and that huge hole.

We drive up to Rafa's stop. I hate that I even remember

that this is where he gets on. It isn't as if I'm making a mental note of it. In fact, once I realize that it's his stop, I direct my attention away from the aisle. If he looks at me or anything, I don't know. I'm too busy thinking about the store, Kate, and all that broken glass. I'm too busy thinking about my home.

CHAPTER SEVEN

I don't have anything for lunch. I don't know if I was hoping Mrs. Tran would have leftovers for me or what, but the more I hear my stomach grumble during lunch hour, the more I begin to regret not throwing some rice into a container this morning. I cross my arms tightly against my stomach, trying to press it in and stop the gurgling sounds, while I head into the cafeteria. Kate didn't show up and she's still not answering her phone. Mr. Tran didn't say anything to me when I looked at him. Jake wouldn't even tell me anything. And the store—the store is ruined.

The cafeteria is dreary. It feels extra horrible because Kate isn't here. The benches are filling fast with kids who have this period for lunch. They're snacking on fries and rubbing the residual oil onto their pants, scrubbing it from their fingertips. So many boys, tall and lanky and pimply, hang by the kitchen doors. They ask for extra money, one dollar or two, so they can buy a bag of chips or something. Girls sit in small groups, sharing small fries like they aren't about to be hungry in an hour. The boys never ask them for money. They only ask other boys.

I want to talk to someone about Ginger Store, but I can't because no one knows. No one knows about where I'm from, so they don't get it. They'll say things like *That must happen there all the time, right?* I must always be so scared, right, growing up there, living in a place like that? But no, this time is *different*. Someone wouldn't just do this, not to the store. And the only other person who knows or cares is Kate, and she isn't here.

I text her again: *where are you sis???* Suddenly I'm at the entrance to the cafeteria, barely on the inside, avoiding eyes and keeping my head low. She has to text back at some point. She *has* to.

I even text Jake: *are your parents okay? have you heard from Kate?* He definitely won't reply.

Eventually I shift into one of the empty benches by the canteen. A group of boys, varying heights, descends on me at once. "D'you have a dollar?" one asks me. The code is broken, I guess.

I shake my head, leaning forward on the table in front of me. "No." My voice is so much smaller, so much hoarser, than I remember it.

One nudges my back. I sit up straight and whip around to stare right at this blue-eyed demon kid. "Don't touch me," I say.

He's nervous now and takes a cautious step back while his friends snort and laugh. "It wasn't even that deep," he crows back, his eyes shifting nervously from me to his boys. "I didn't even *touch* you—"

"Yeah, you did. Don't lie—"

"I'm not *lying.*"

"Let's just go," one of his friends says. He has an ugly, throaty chuckle. It matches his ugly, throaty face. All neck, no forehead.

"Wait . . ." One of the boys lingers, slipping around the table to get a better look at my face. I don't have the energy to play nice, so I stare back at him, watching him watch me. Then, as if he couldn't get any weirder, he pulls out his phone, and as he scrolls, he says, "You're that girl . . . 'It's the Feds,' right?"

"What?" I croak. "What are you talking about?"

He doesn't speak, just turns his phone around to show me.

And it's my face.

My face is on his phone screen.

Somehow he's streaming a video of me—that's me! What the hell!—from this morning when I was going on and on about Ginger East and the store. For most of the clip, I'm talking around the camera, not even aware it's there. But then I suddenly cross my arms, and the camera catches me as I say: "Honestly, and don't tell anyone I said this, but this is *exactly* the kind of thing that the Feds would do." I'm glaring as I say it. It's almost funny how serious I am—but then it's not funny at all because my face is on the internet, damn!

"How did you get— What is this?" I swipe for his phone,

but he moves it away from me, snickering. "Where'd you find that?"

He is still chuckling as he says, "I hear some guy from that middle school posted it. You know Calderstone? Yeah, like, one of my boys sent it to me an hour ago, and it's blowing *up* online."

I spit out "Take it down," like I don't know how the internet works. The boy laughs again as the video starts up. "How many people saw it? Only you guys?"

He shakes his head right away and scrolls down a little so I can see the video info. The title is a pretty basic "THE FEDS SOON COME FOR THIS GIRL LOL" and the total view count? Two thousand people and counting.

"Shit," I say under my breath.

The boys disperse and descend on their new victim, a mousy boy who honestly played himself by sitting alone. My mind is buzzing with that video being out there for everyone to see. Damn, I knew Mikey's friend must have been filming me! No way could he have been focusing on the storefront that long. And I really ran my mouth about the Feds? This is different from all those crime shows I watch. Could I go to jail for this?

It's then that I notice the TVs. They're all tuned to the same news station, that same one my mom makes me watch at home. There's a reporter with thin lips speaking into her microphone, gripping it tightly, as though she's clutching pearls. And maybe she is. I take a closer look at where she is, and I think, *Yeah, maybe she is clutching pearls.* She's terrified. She's in Ginger East, at Ginger Store. She's on the other side of the tracks now.

I push myself away from the bench and gravitate closer and closer to the nearest TV. My neck hurts with how I have to crane my head to get a good look at it. It's hard to make out the words because it's so damn loud in the cafeteria, but as I take another step, I hear a sharp, "Shush! Shut up!" erupt from my left.

The voice, Rafa's voice, pierces through the thickness of the room. I feel like only I can hear him. He is standing too, staring up at the TV closest to him. His eyes are narrow and his chest is rising and falling, rising and falling, so fast. He's mad. I can tell just by looking at him, because I know him—I still know him so well.

Text appears on the screen underneath the reporter's face. "Break-in at Ginger East Convenience Store," it says. Break-in? No way that was a break-in. The glass—didn't they see the glass? That's not. It just isn't.

I walk as close as I can to the TV, straining and squinting and praying I can hear the reporter better. ". . . live from Ginger East," she says. I can pick out pieces and read her lips a little. The wind is in her face, so she keeps pushing her thin hair away from her eyes. "I'm standing in front of a neighborhood shop known as Ginger Store, a staple here in this area. Late last night, the store was damaged after a brick was thrown through the front glass." She turns her back and takes a shaky step toward the storefront, carefully tiptoeing her way around the sidewalk. "The brick has completely damaged the entire front window, leaving this neighborhood hot spot in a very sticky situation.

"Violence isn't new to this area," she continues. "It was the site of a tragic homicide just six years ago. Luckily, today's incident has resulted in no injuries, and nothing has been reported stolen . . ."

"*What?*" I snap almost at once. A few of those tall boys near me jump at my outburst. "What the *fuck*? Nothing stolen? Then it's not a break-in!" The news is so ugly, calling it a break-in when it's not. They're always reporting things however they want, just to make us look bad and reinforce what everyone thinks about us. Why else bring up that homicide? People are thinking it anyway.

The cafeteria doesn't quiet down. It's still as loud and boisterous as ever, but I am seething inside. My brown eyes can only see red. My teeth are chattering and my eyes sting with the onset of tears. A break-in, a break-in, a break-in. Nothing was stolen. No one was hurt either.

Then why would this happen?

Rafa and I lock eyes across the room. I don't mean to look at him, but when I turn and he sees me, we're stuck in a moment of panic. I'm rooted where I am, and he wouldn't dare come over either, because as far as anyone is concerned, we don't know each other. The only thing running through my mind is the neighborhood.

It must be running through Maree's mind too. She's standing near a TV, biting her bottom lip to keep it from trembling. Her eyes search for me or Rafa. It's like a lightbulb goes off in her mind and suddenly she remembers who we are.

CHAPTER EIGHT

Vicky Sanchez eyes me as I dart out of the school's main doors on my way to the bus. I can tell she wants to say something, based on how she shifts her body weight back and forth in her squeaky new high-tops, but she doesn't approach. Instead she gives me a nod, kind of like *I saw the news and I hope everything's good.* Vicky isn't from my neighborhood, but she's from the kind of place where the news would bring up long-passed homicides too. She probably saw me in the cafeteria. I think everyone in the cafeteria who saw how Rafa and I froze to watch the news report knows about it now. Maree too. I haven't seen her that shaken up in a long time.

I'm two steps from the bus when I feel a tug on my arm, sending me backward and away from the curb. Damn, I just want to get on the bus and stare out the window in peace. I want to go home.

"Nelo?"

Maree keeps her eyes low, avoiding my face and the air behind me like she's about to say something shady. Her hands are trembling, but she clasps them together to stop them from shaking. She's nervous as hell. Probably doesn't want anyone to see me talking to her either.

"Maree."

"Yo . . . ," she begins, her voice as low as her eyes. "Seen your video."

"What?" I ask, but before she has a chance to respond, I remember my rant video from earlier. "Ugh. The Feds?" I grumble.

She nods right away. "It's racking up a lot of views. You should track those."

Maybe that sort of thing would get Maree excited, but to hear people are watching that video just makes me antsy. Who knows who's watching it now.

"So," she goes on. "I don't know . . . Was there really an attack or something? On the store?"

She's speaking different. Her drawl and accented speech make it sound as if she never left Ginger East, like she's always been one of us. It makes me mad because she has nothing good to say about the neighborhood, but now she's trying to pretend we're friends? Man, her accent is as fake as she is.

I shrug, casting a careful eye at the bus behind me. It better not leave with me standing right here. "I mean, you saw what it said," I tell her. I want to sound confident, but my voice is still shaking. I want to be hard and resilient, but I'm not even close.

She offers a weak smile. "I'm sorry, girl. Like, that's so shitty. Where's Kate? Is she okay?"

"I—I don't know."

"You don't *know?*"

"No. I tried—"

"I thought you talk to her pretty much every day?"

"I do! I just didn't see her today."

"What are they going to do?"

"What?"

"What are they going to do?" she presses again. "Kate's fam. Are they going to sue?"

A nervous chuckle escapes my mouth. "Sue who?"

Maree is frowning now like I said something to personally offend her. "Nelo," she goes on in a hushed tone. "The assholes who did this can't get away with it."

"No, really? You think I don't know that?" I say, trying to bite back the sarcasm in my voice. I'm not sure she remembers what justice looks like in Ginger East.

She rolls her eyes and crosses her arms. She's getting defensive with me? What did I do to this girl? "Okay, whatever," she scoffs. "You can't be that good a friend to Kate anyway if you're actually about to tell her that suing isn't a good idea."

"Oh?" I cough out in shock. "I didn't even know you remembered who she was, though, so."

She opens her mouth to say something else—probably something useless, as per—but Rafa walks up before she can get another annoying, bougie-ass word in. I'm just as shocked as she is to see him, but this time I know why he wants to talk to me, why his eyes are urging me to get on the bus and get away from this wannabe celebrity.

"Rafa!" Maree's shock subsides once she realizes Rafa is hot now. Honestly, it's an adjustment for all of us. "Oh my God. I didn't realize you guys still talk to each other."

She's really trying it.

"Nelo, hey. We're going to miss the bus," he says to me, pointedly ignoring Maree. He nods toward the steps, and I follow, leaving Maree at the curb.

He's following me closely as I walk down the aisle. I settle into the nearest empty seat, and he scoots me over so he can sit down beside me. "What? What are you doing?" I'm hissing. "Go sit somewhere else. Don't you have friends or something?"

He snorts. "That's really bold coming from you, whose *one friend* was absent today."

"Shut up."

His chuckle is strained and he slouches down farther in what was supposed to be my seat. "Have you talked to Kate? How is she?"

I swallow the lump growing in my throat, but no matter how many times I do, it doesn't help. I can't speak.

A few other people get on the bus, and he averts his eyes from them as they walk past. He doesn't want anyone to see him sitting up here—and definitely not one of his soccer friends. They'd have something to say, for sure.

I get into my usual position: hunched down with my shins pressed up against the seat in front of me. It's more comfortable for me to sit this way. It helps me hide too.

More people get on the bus, cackling and stomping their feet as they walk past. He shifts a bit closer to me. I bring out my phone. "What—what are you doing?" Rafa says.

I make a face at him like *What's your problem?* "What do you mean what am I doing?" I say, waving my phone in front of his face. "I'm minding my business. You should try it."

He eyes the small plastic device, watching it sway back and forth, before he finally looks at me. "Oh, did you know you're on Hive Man?"

I nearly drop my phone. "Damn, actually?" Hive Man Clips is this blog that posts nothing but viral videos, usually of people talking smack or getting their ass beat. I immediately know which category I fall into. "That explains my phone."

"What happened to your phone?"

I tap on the screen to show him the growing number of notifications. I can't believe my social is blowing up with randoms. Messages upon messages with nothing but *lol girl the FEDS* and *you're right tho honestly* and *man your face when you saw you were being filmed!!* fill my inbox like no one's business, and it gets worse every minute. Rafa scrolls till he gets to the bottom. "Sucks," he says, hiding a smile. I hate him. "But, you know, Hive Man."

"I'm aware. Thanks."

"Uh-huh."

"But, I mean, four hours? That kid posted this, like, four hours ago. It doesn't even make sense how fast this is happening. . . ."

Rafa isn't listening to me anymore; he's digging up the video on his phone. I'm about to say "Don't you dare!" before the video loads up and starts playing again. ". . . Like, no offense, but rent has been going up because of all those new stores. Who else would it be if not someone who isn't from here?"

"You're so serious," Rafa says, pausing the video. "All this stuff about the store—"

"Well, it's true," I tell him. "My dad used to say it all the time, that there are people out there who don't like to see communities like ours be okay. You think shit like this would still happen to the same Ginger East we grew up in? No way."

"Yes way." He snorts. "Did we grow up in the same place or what? You remember what happened to the arcade, right?"

The news didn't mention it by name, but all of us in Ginger East know that the neighborhood's most tragic homicide happened at the arcade. It was that year we were all turning ten, the end of summer right before the days started to get shorter. This guy came out of nowhere with a gun and started shooting. He was from another neighborhood, and to this day, my mom thinks it was a gang thing. A lot of people do. Around that time, there was a lot of weird gang stuff happening in the shadows, so maybe it's more probable than I want to think it is.

The worst thing is that the shooter didn't even live here. He wasn't one of us, but he thought whatever vendetta he had with some local gang was enough to open fire in an arcade. An *arcade*. Two people got caught in the crossfire, including this girl we knew growing up. Cassie. She never had the chance to turn ten.

It feels like yesterday, but my memory has so many gaps. I hate that I can't really remember. I hate that the arcade shut down right away, and one by one, everyone started to move. Maree, then Bo, then Rafa . . . almost everyone.

I shift a bit so my knees press harder into the seat in front of me. "Whatever," I grumble. "That's not what I meant. It's— everything is so . . . so . . . ." Different. Everything is so different, but I don't want to say it out loud.

Another boy gets on the bus and reaches out to Rafa for a handshake. They bump knuckles as the boy lumbers past. I flip over my phone, but there's only the same messages. Nothing from Kate, at least.

Rafa turns to me as soon as the boy is safely from view. "Honestly," he says. "It's not like I thought, you know, that shit didn't happen down there anymore. It's just that I never thought it'd happen to Ginger Store."

"Same," I grunt. "That place has been there for years.

Mr. Tran and them never had issues with anyone. Who would do something like this, anyway?"

He rolls his head against the back of the seat to face me. "You think it was someone they knew?"

"No way."

"You think it was a gang?"

"No one runs Ginger East anymore," I whisper. Mikey's friends thought it was a gang, Rafa thinks it's a gang, but we both know there are no gangs that have a foothold in Ginger East these days. Community initiatives started to block them after the arcade incident. There was a church group from some neighboring borough that wanted more police in the area. They really thought that would fix things too. Ginger East community groups refused to have any extra police walking the streets. Kids wouldn't go outside, they said. The neighborhood wouldn't be the same. No one wanted these pretentious officers from the other side of the river trying to police our streets and our kids when they didn't know the first thing about us. In the end, the community won, and that's the most important thing.

Another boy stops by the seat and reaches out for a fist bump from Rafa, but Rafa doesn't see because he's looking at me, pondering. I wish I could read his mind. He's probably thinking about Ginger Store, or how the Trans are doing, or where Kate is. I nudge his leg and say, "Your friend," before he finally notices the boy in the aisle.

The tall, bright-eyed boy is snickering, spluttering, and

tripping over his words. He's so restless, bouncing back and forth on the heels of his feet, just waiting to speak. "Raf, bro," he chortles. "You're not going to come sit with us?"

I turn away, because suddenly this random boy is looking at me as though he wants something. Rafa says, "Later," and the boy chortles his way to the back.

"Why don't you go sit with them?" I ask.

Rafa shrugs. "I don't know. You still haven't answered my question."

"What question?"

"Have you talked to Kate?" he asks again, and my mind is racing back to this morning, my shoes scraping down the sidewalk, the caution tape, the glass on the sidewalk, the brick. I curl into myself further.

"No," I murmur. "No, I haven't."

Now there are tears running down my face and I can't stop them. I feel bad for Rafa because seeing me cry is probably the last thing he's emotionally capable of dealing with, but I can't stop sniffling. Rafa doesn't say anything. He barely even moves beside me.

Suddenly, in one swift motion, his hand is on my knee, and I almost choke from shock. He's staring at the seat in front of us, stoically, his brown eyes blinking quickly while he concentrates hard on the seat's navy pleather. And he says: "Yo, stop crying."

This is truly the bare minimum.

CHAPTER NINE

Rafa doesn't switch seats. He sits with me the entire time, though his hand flies off my knee so fast, the moment another of his friends comes bumbling down the aisle. It's nice of him, but he doesn't need to keep me company or anything. I don't know him like that anymore, and he doesn't owe me.

When the bus pulls up to his stop, he gets to his feet and reaches out for a fist bump. I snort and almost refuse, but my hand is extending, my knuckles touching his, before I can really protest. "See you tomorrow, eh?" he says.

"Yeah," I reply. "Tomorrow."

I am the only one who gets off at Ginger East. The street beside the large park and across from Ginger Store is so empty. It's echoing out here. My head is buzzing with all this nothing.

The caution tape is still up and the gaping hole in front of the shop where there once was a window strikes fear into me. I'm not prepared to see it, now that the cameras have gone, now that the intersection has cleared. There's nothing between me and the tape, nothing between the tape and the open hole.

My eyes get misty again, but Rafa's stark "Yo, stop crying" is burned into my ears, and recalling his voice dries my tears so fast. In a backward way, I guess his consoling really did help.

I trudge across the street to the sidewalk in front of Ginger Store and stare inside. There's no life in there. I always used to be able to hear my voice echoing back to me, but now it's just nothing. A lot of nothing.

An older woman I know by face but not by name comes toward me pushing a few heavy shopping bags in a cart. I step back to get out of her way and offer a tight smile as she passes. That's an invitation, enough for her to backtrack a little to stand beside me. "You're that girl," she says, which means she knows me too.

"Chinelo," I tell her.

"Janet's daughter?"

"Uh-huh."

"You say 'yes,'" she says, pressing into her thick Jamaican accent. "It's a shame what happened to this place, you know. It's the last of the old stores. The last of the old neighborhood."

Her words root me in place. They're trying to get to me, to burrow into my head, but I won't let them. I don't want to hear any of that. Ginger Store is important to everyone, to me, but it's not the last of anything. Ginger East has been okay before this, and it'll be okay once this is over.

Luckily, she presses on. "Those neighborhood kids are always up to no good."

What is she talking about? *I'm* a neighborhood kid. "You think it was a kid from around here who did this?" I ask.

"Should be," she tells me. "Who else? Mr. Tran and them are so nice to everyone here, and one of them really went and broke up his store like this. Now where am I going to get my Chinese movies with the good subtitles?"

I shrug. The internet, maybe? "I don't think it was a kid from around here. I mean, we would never do something like this."

"Well, then who, my dear?" she asks pointedly, as if I should know the answer. A part of me feels as if I honestly should. I really should know who did this.

There's a shuffle in the store, like someone is moving a large cabinet, and it echoes in the emptiness outside. The woman jumps a little and mumbles under her breath as she huffs her way back down the sidewalk.

The shuffle happens again, coming from deep inside the store, and then it's quiet. "Hey? Hello?" I call as quietly as I can. Residual glass crunches under my feet, and I wince at the mental image of the glass coming from the storefront. "Hello?"

There's another crunch and fast footsteps coming from

inside the store. I must have scared Kate, because I've never seen her look so shaken. Her face is pale and her eyes are wide as she rounds the corner inside the shop holding a duffel bag. She lets out a sigh of relief when she sees me through the broken window, and not even Rafa's voice in my head can stop me from crying. "Nelo," she whispers, making her way toward the door. She opens and then shuts it gently behind her. Irritation flashes on her face. The irony of closing the door while the glass window is smashed in doesn't escape her at all. "What are you doing here?"

I bite my lip to stop my crying. "What do you mean, what am I doing here?" I say.

She laughs, though it's dry and missing her usual spark. "Yeah," she sighs, and pushes me playfully in the arm. I stumble back a bit and regain my footing along the glass-peppered sidewalk. Glass everywhere. "I'm sorry."

"Why are you sorry? I'm the one who should be—"

"Why would you be sorry? I'm the one who didn't reply to your texts," she says timidly. "I wanted to reply, but I—I don't know. It's been so busy here today, and I didn't get a moment alone. . . ."

I wipe my face quickly. All I've been doing today is wiping my face. "No way, don't apologize. I get it." My eyes are drifting to the gaping hole in the window again. Now that I'm this close, I can see how specks of glass have spread across the counter, dusting the stool where Mrs. Tran sometimes likes to sit. Where Mr. Tran finishes his shift with a beer.

"No one's hurt, right? They didn't take anything?" I ask, still mesmerized by the storefront.

Kate gives a weary glance over her shoulder. "Nothing," she mumbles, and hitches the bag higher on her shoulder. I don't realize until right then how it seems to be weighing her down. She's shifting her weight from one leg to the other, trying to support its contents.

"What's in there?" I ask with a nod to the bag.

She wrinkles her nose while she looks down at it. "Documents and stuff. Things from the back office that Mom and Dad didn't want to leave here overnight, you know, just in case."

I nod again. "Oh."

Kate hitches the bag up her shoulder again, trying to steady herself under it. "Let's go. We should get out of here before nightfall, anyway."

"But wh-what about the hole?" I ask, and again, my eyes are tracing its jagged outline.

Kate guides me by the arm away from the store and back toward Ginger Way. As we duck under the caution tape, I take one or two glances over my shoulder at the building's terra-cotta brick side. The building looks so empty standing there like that. It's as though it lost its spark too.

Kate doesn't say a word while she's pulling me past my

house down the street to hers. I don't protest because I want to see her parents, her family. I want to tell them I'm sorry and ask if they need help. We're family, me and the Trans. We've been like this since day one, and nothing can change that.

People are gathered on her front lawn. I'm not surprised because people at Ginger East really show up for one another. They're talking, sharing drinks. A few are sitting on the grass, praying or something like it.

As we come up to Kate's open front door, a tall black boy with thick-rimmed glasses walks out of the house, scratching his brow and squinting at the sky. I freeze, watching him step aside for a disheveled Jake, who immediately heads down the three steps to the garage and driveway. The boy follows, eyes moving lazily around the street until they fall on me. He squints, tilting his head when we lock eyes, looking at me as if he knows me. And maybe he does. Maybe I know him too.

A jolt of shock rushes through me, and I gasp, "Yo, is that Bo?" It's louder than I want it to be, and everyone turns at my sudden outburst.

Bo winces and tiptoes toward me. He adjusts his glasses and smiles. Wow, his teeth are so straight now. And his glasses are mad stylish and hipster chic. In fact, the more that I look at him, his entire vibe *is* hipster chic. He sticks out like a sore thumb in Ginger East, like a cranberry kale salad at a fast-food place. He's got that "nicer neighborhood" glow. He's evolved.

"Beethoven Junior," I say with a snicker.

"Don't call me by my government name," he tells me, nearly hissing.

Beethoven Junior Kingston Williams. He hates his full name more than anything else. When we were younger, he'd joke about changing it. He skipped church one Sunday, faking the least-believable cough ever, and invited the rest of us over to help him Google how to change his name. A bunch of eight-year-olds who could barely spell spent three hours navigating the government website. We were two seconds away from calling the first number we found online when his parents walked in and screamed. They never let him skip church again.

"Damn, what . . ." I'm so shocked, I can barely form words. I turn to Kate as if she should have an answer for me. Realistically, she'd better; this is her house, after all. Instead she nods toward the front door like we have better things to do. Forget that—does she not realize Bo is in Ginger East? At her *house*?

Bo turns away sheepishly, looking eagerly toward Jake, who is punching buttons on the garage side panel. "Bro, what are you doing here?" I ask him.

He chuckles nervously. What's there to be nervous about? "Uh, I wanted to help out, after hearing the news."

"How long have you been here?"

"He's kind of been here all day," Kate jumps in, chewing the inside of her cheek.

"What?"

"Well, everyone has," she adds, gesturing loosely to the people in the front yard and glimpses of the gathering through the doorway.

"Okay, but how has he been here all *day*?" I say, eyes drifting back to Bo. "Don't you have school?"

"Bo! You coming?" Jake's voice rings across the lawn, and Bo, apparently looking for a reason to disappear, dips so fast to where Jake has successfully opened the garage door.

I cross my arms, eyeing the two of them. "What? Is Santa Ana on vacation or something?"

Either Kate doesn't hear me or she pretends not to. She waves him off, but something about this whole thing seems fishy to me. He's been here all day and she didn't mention it? Is this the first time he's been back since he moved? By the way he helps Jake pull out plywood from their garage, so at ease in a place he supposedly hasn't seen in years, I'm gonna say no. Jake isn't acting as if this is someone he hasn't seen in years. He hands him wood and maneuvers around him like it's been mere weeks.

Maybe it's not that deep, but the more I stare at Bo, the more irritated I become. He's been coming back to visit Kate, but he hasn't been back to visit me? We used to all be best friends. What's the point now in picking favorites? And why wouldn't Kate say anything to me? I'm not that petty, but this hurts. It hurts more than Rafa telling me to stop crying in the worst monotone voice ever.

And now I'm chuckling because I hear it in my head again.

Kate is frowning. "What's so funny?"

"What?" Jake calls from inside the garage. He emerges with two panels of plywood, and rests them against the wall. Bo grabs one under each of his arms, holds them unevenly, and tries not to struggle so much in front of us. Jake appears with more plywood held under his arm effortlessly. He blows his hair from his eyes. "What's so funny?" he asks in the exact same tone as Kate. They're way too related.

"You guys are going now?" Kate asks.

I frown. "Going where?"

"Board up the storefront," Bo answers. He tilts his head back and scrunches his nose, trying to adjust his glasses without his hands. "We figure it's better to do it before it gets dark," he adds as the two of them take off toward the sidewalk.

"D'you guys need help?" I call after them.

Jake turns, chuckling. His laugh is strained. He's still so tired, but he tries to keep things light anyway. "You can't lift for shit," he says to me. A hint of a smile crosses Bo's lips as he scurries along. "Some of my friends are meeting us at the shop to help. Don't worry. You guys stay here."

"I got everything in the back," Kate says to Jake, patting

the duffel bag at her side. "So just board up the window and come home."

"Yeah, okay," Jake calls back before he and Bo make their way farther down the road.

As they turn the corner, a sleek, silver sedan pulls onto the street, speeding and then slowing every so often as if it's trying to find the right address. Some people shift away from the curb as the car pulls up and parks. The driver doesn't move. I crouch a little, craning my neck to get a good look at this guy who's rolled up to the Trans' place. All I can see is gray hair and a gray suit before Kate tugs on my arm. "Let's go, let's go," she says, suddenly impatient. We dart into the open doorway before the gray-haired man gets out of his car.

Kate ushers me inside first as though I haven't been here a million times. She's so eager to get me into the house that I have to kick off my shoes fast just to keep up with her.

There are almost as many people inside as there were outside. I spot the woman who owns the sandwich shop on the main road, huddled with some of the nail salon girls drinking tea on the sofa. Mrs. Tran comes in with a bag of chips for a small boy seated on his father's leg—I think that's Mr. Stewart from seven houses down. His kid is getting so big now. Mr. Nowak from down the road is serving fruits to people like he lives here. He offers me a small bowl of grapes, but I say no and he hands it to a woman in the corner instead. I even see Mr. Brown in the corner, looking exhausted as he breathes slowly in and out.

We can hear Mr. Tran in the adjacent room, his voice loud, his inflections distorted. He must be angry, angrier than I've ever heard him. As I peek into the room, I see him on the phone, pacing, yelling. Mrs. Tran comes in with a heavy manila folder and hands it to him. He's rough when he snatches it from her, and they have a short, harsh exchange of words in Vietnamese. They're so taken by their argument that they don't even notice me or Kate amid the growing group of people—or the paper that slipped from the folder when Mr. Tran grabbed it. It has that same logo, the same red letters, as the letter he was looking at from the store.

When Mrs. Tran finally notices us, she forces a smile. She's doing that same thing Jake was. Faking it. "Ooh, is that Nelo?" she asks, exaggerating a gasp as she approaches. "I haven't seen you all day—"

"Mom," Kate interrupts with a swift shake of her head. There's a long pause where I'm not sure what's going on— Mrs. Tran is staring at Kate with sad, sad eyes and Kate is chewing her lip, pensive and slow. "Mom, he's outside," Kate finally says.

Mrs. Tran's smile falters a little, but she doesn't respond. Instead she rubs my shoulder and moves past me. "Are you two hungry? We have real food. The neighbors have been bringing things all day," she calls on her way to the kitchen.

I'm so hungry, but I don't say it. I feel so foreign and out of place here among Mr. Tran's harping on the phone, Kate's nervous shifting, and Mrs. Tran's broad, stiff smile.

I must be taking too long to answer, because Mrs. Tran pipes up, "Yes, yes, stay for dinner. Someone has to help us eat it all." I can't see her anymore, but I can hear her voice and her footsteps in the other room. She's opening drawers and stuff. It's so noisy.

Mr. Tran's voice rises in the corner of the other room. I'm hesitant to peek in, but I do anyway. He holds a hand to his eyes, pressing them and massaging them while he says, "I already *told* you about the policy number! Isn't there anyone else I can speak to?"

"Insurance people," Kate puts in, as if she knows I'm thinking about it. "He's been on the phone all day trying to figure out what we're covered for. Can you believe those bastards are coming down to do *another* inspection this weekend? They've already sent two different people since the morning. What did they miss the first time? It's so annoying."

"Yeah . . ."

"They need to hurry up," she grunts. "Give us a quote and be done with it, you know?"

Finally Mr. Tran snaps a loud and angry, "Yes, thank you!" before slamming the phone down onto the table. Mrs. Tran yells something from the kitchen, but he stays silent, breathing heavily.

The doorbell rings. The sound is absorbed into the room, drowned out by voices and community. Someone even yells, "Why would you ring? Just come in!" and a few other people chuckle. I immediately crane my neck to the doorway where that gray-haired man lingers, uncertain, on the porch.

Kate nudges me in the arm. "Come on, let's go upstairs," she says.

"Kate! Kate?" Mr. Tran calls, emerging from the adjacent room. He doesn't even look at me or acknowledge that I'm standing there. "When those insurance people come here next time, huh, you go show them everything. Show them the window, show them the front counter space. I'm tired of them. I'm so tired."

"I know. Okay, Dad."

"You took everything from the back already? You got everything?"

"Yes," she says, and turns so he can see the duffel bag better.

"Good." His final word is stern. Kate grabs ahold of my arm and steers me to the staircase before Mr. Tran puts on his fakest smile for the man at the door.

Kate's room looks the same: neat, with her oak bookshelf and organized desk taking up most of the space. She had a pile of old *Rolling Stone* magazines on her desk that she must have hidden somewhere because I don't see them there anymore.

I was supposed to borrow one, but this probably isn't a good time to ask.

I settle into my spot on her bed, with my back against the wall and my knees pulled into my chest. She drops the duffel bag by the edge of her desk and goes as far as opening it before she gives up, collapsing into her chair.

We are quiet for the first time in maybe forever. I'm not talking about some show I watched, and Kate isn't play-bashing Sol Cousins. I want to break the silence, but I can't seem to piece my words together fast enough. My feet burrow into the cotton covers beneath them, and I rest my head atop my knees, waiting.

"Who is that?" I ask. "That guy at the door."

"My mom calls him 'vulture' in Vietnamese," Kate says. "But his name is Mr. Horst. He works for a land development company."

I snort. *"Horst?"*

"Man, it's his name."

"What's he want with your dad?"

Kate sighs and gives an exaggerated shrug. "Vultures circle. That's what Mom says," she goes on. "His company— Reesor or Hillcrest or whatever—they want the store, or they want the land. I don't know. But . . ." She chews on her lower lip as she leans in closer to me. "They want Dad to sell."

I push away from the wall and sit bolt upright. *"Sell?* As in, sell Ginger Store?" She nods, and I cringe so hard, my back cracks. "No way. Papa Tran would never. He knows how important . . . H-he just knows how important the store is to everyone. He wouldn't. You guys—you guys can't leave." Kate has been my best friend forever, and I can't imagine a Ginger East without her or the store. In fact, even thinking about it feels like betrayal. Everyone else left, but in my mind, I never imagined her leaving too.

Kate bites her lower lip as she looks away, and it makes me feel more uncomfortable than I think she realizes.

"The store's been here forever," I press on. "We pretty much grew up in it. No, once the inspectors come by this weekend and they see it was an accident, they'll fix it, and everything will go back to the way it's supposed to be."

Kate is still nodding, and it's making me antsy as hell.

"Is that why this Horst guy is here?" I scoff, settling back against the wall. I remember his silver sedan, how boxy and old it looks. It looks exactly like the kind of thing a vulture would drive. "He doesn't even care about what happened. He doesn't care about the neighborhood. He's just taking advantage of your dad."

Kate's nod finally slows to a normal pace, but now it's her silence that's freaking me out. She agrees with me, right? She has to.

But then she says, "Dad has been seriously considering it," and my heart sinks. She must think I didn't hear her, because she repeats, "Like, seriously considering selling the store, I mean," as if she already knew the reaction I'd have. I am paralyzed with a fear that I didn't know I could feel. In one day, I find out someone bricked the store *and* Mr. Tran has been thinking of moving? Kate could be leaving?

I move to get to my feet to run, pace, something, but Kate pipes up, "Girl, sit down." She knows me so well.

"Are you serious?" I gasp, my throat tightening against my disbelief. It gets harder and harder to swallow. "There's no way."

She purses her lips, and I can't tell if she wants to smile or cry. Maybe a bit of both. "Yeah," she utters.

"If you leave, what am I supposed to do?" The words flub out of my mouth, and in my ears, I can hear how horrible I must sound. But I can't help it. Everyone else left, but Kate has always been here. No way I can picture a Ginger East without her. "Your dad . . . I bet he's only considering it because he doesn't know . . . H-he's like me."

"How is my dad like you?"

"If he could find out who bricked the store," I go on, "he wouldn't even consider leaving. Legit. I bet he'd stay."

A tired sigh escapes her lips when she looks at me. She pushes her hands through her hair, sighing out again, trying to get out all her frustrations. I can already hear her disagreeing with me. I can already feel the weight of the "no" hanging in the air, and I hate it.

She brushes her hair off her shoulder and leans toward me. "How do you figure?"

"Because then he'd know it wasn't one of us," I say, and she rolls her eyes. "It's true! People out here really already think someone from the neighborhood did it, but you know as well as I do that it can't be true. No one around here would ever do this."

Kate groans, rubbing her hands down her face. "That's not all this is about, Nelo."

"But that's part of it, right?"

"I mean, I guess, but—"

"So then what's the problem?" I ask with a defiant shrug. "He'd feel safer. He wouldn't want to leave Ginger East if he knew that the people who bricked his store are a bunch of outsiders. That'll just prove that outsiders are the problem and it's safer here—"

"Safer? Nelo—"

"Honestly, though, the police might care too," I press on. "If they found out it was someone who wasn't from here."

She scoffs, waving away my comment. "Man, nothing will make the police care about this place. You saw what happened after the arcade. How they twist words," she says, and she's right, because I did. I know why they say things the way they do about Ginger East. It's easier to make it seem as though everyone out here is waiting to do something horrible—rob from each other, burn things up—even though that's not the case. We're a community.

Suddenly she gets to her feet and crosses the room to peer outside. I get up on my knees too and set my eyes on the silver car by the curb. The more I look at it, the more annoyed I become. It's the ugliest symbol of everything wrong with the world, and it's sitting on my street.

"Does your dad have any idea who might've trashed the store? Probably not, right?"

Kate's eyes don't move from the window. "He thinks it's those new kids down the road. The ones who look like mini pre- and post-*Believe* Justin Biebers. The Avery brothers, I think. Says he saw one or two of them hanging around the store, trying to take something, and he chased them off."

"You think they would?"

"*Tch,* yeah," she scoffs. "If we're going by your theory, they're not really from around here, you know? They don't come to the store a lot, so Dad was kind of like, 'Why would you guys be here?' Their mom doesn't even shop there. He sees her sometimes walking past, turning her nose up as if she's got somewhere important to be."

"Yeah, she's mad shady."

"Definitely."

"Did the security camera catch anything?"

Kate winces like I cut her. "No. . . . You know how Dad likes to turn it off and drink before the night is up, right? Well, that's kind of what happened last night. Popped a beer, shut off the camera, you know."

I groan, tossing my head back. "Old man Tran, why?"

She chuckles. It's the first real chuckle I've gotten out of her. "Cops are saying it's kind of his fault he turned the camera off. They're just pissed they gotta do real work now. You know how it is."

"Yeah."

"Those same cops took some pictures and took statements. That's probably the last we'll hear of them," she says.

"Yeah . . . ," I say again. This time, I'm thinking more of that woman I talked to outside the store and more of the hole in the front window. I'm thinking more of my words this morning, everything I said in that video. The police don't take crime seriously around here, but that doesn't mean we don't either. Ginger East isn't a community of delinquents, and if the police can't see that this isn't just an ordinary crime, then I don't want them here anyway. I could probably do a better job figuring out who did this.

So I say, "*We* should find out who threw the brick." I mean it from the second it comes out of my mouth, and as I hear the words flood the room, my chest swells with a kind of pride I didn't know I had.

Kate shakes her head immediately. "No."

"What? Why not? So you want to move?"

"Oh my God, Nelo, this isn't like those TV shows you watch. This is real life, *my* life."

"I *know* that, obviously," I say. "But I mean, if we already know the police won't do shit, then we should figure it out. Why not? We know everything about this place. We *live* here, and everyone knows everyone. If someone from outside the neighborhood did it, we'd figure it out in maybe two days, and we could get whoever did it to pay for a new window."

"The insurance will pay for a new window."

I frown. "Okay, so? Are you above getting extra money now?"

"You're naive."

"And so?"

"I don't know . . . ," she utters, and for the first time since we left the store, I can see the vulnerability and sadness etched across her face. She's hurting, maybe more than I realize. "I get what you mean, I get how you think it'll help my dad want to stay, b-but y-you know . . ." She clears her throat. "My parents told me to grab the important stuff from the store office, but they don't want me anywhere near that place while things are still up in the air. Said they'd take away my mixing equipment. Can you believe that? I'm so close to finishing this mixtape too."

She averts her eyes, and even in that fleeting glance, I can see it's too soon for her. "That'd be a second tragedy," I utter. I don't want to push it, but I can't sit at home and pretend I'm okay with all this, with the idea that Kate might be moving, with the idea that some outsider is coming in to ruin the place I live in. If she can't help, then fine. I can do it myself.

It's like she can hear me plotting, because she shakes her head again, this time more sternly. "Don't think about it too much," she tells me. "Give it some time. It'll all work out—for the *better*, you know?"

The way she says "better" rings in my head. It's crisp and light on her tongue, but it bores into my ears like a drill. It gives me hope that somehow, once I figure out who did this, everything will be fixed and go back to the way it was.

CHAPTER TEN

All I have is the store. Boarded up and broken, it's the one place I hope will give me answers. I try not to look at it too closely when I approach, because I'm still not used to seeing it this way, but if I want to figure out what happened, I have to pay closer attention.

By Wednesday afternoon, both the front and back doors are locked. Kate won't give me keys, and if I can't get in, how am I supposed to find any clues? Clues and evidence are so important in every crime show I watch. A person would have to practically bleach and burn everything and everyone to bury the evidence. To think someone from outside the neighborhood would go to that extent is just so ugly.

Evidence and clues work on TV, but things are a bit different around here. It's more about who you know and what they know. I stop pressing my ear against the door and instead turn to face the park, where some boys are making their way down the winding path. Mikey is one of them.

He's kinda one of the last people I want to see right now. His friend posting that video is the reason why my social notifications are all on mute. But I can't even lie—most of the people contacting me completely agree about the neighborhood thing, and it makes me feel good that they do. If random internet people out there get what I'm trying to say about Ginger East, then why is it so hard for the media to understand?

"Mikey!" I call, and he and his crew stop in their tracks. He points a finger toward himself, and I nod. *Yeah, you—obviously.* "Mikey, come here."

He jogs toward me, his friends trailing behind. "Yo, I told him to take down the video," he mumbles, glancing sideways. "But Hive Man got it already and—anyway, you know how the internet works."

"Yeah."

"Everyone at school is watching it," he tells me, a small smile creeping onto his lips. "You're famous or whatever. It's crazy. Even the older kids! We haven't been telling anyone that we know you, though. It's been real low-key."

"Low-key?" I snort.

"Yeah," he says. "My friends were dead at the end, the part when you notice you're being filmed. And the part where you talked about the Feds and the store. You looked so serious!"

They chuckle, and I glance over my shoulder at the boarded-up building. "You know anyone who's talking about the store, though?"

"What do you mean?"

"I mean, do you know anything about this," I ask, gesturing to the store beside us, "or no?"

He scrunches up his nose as he stares at the building. He is shorter than I am, so he cranes his neck to see its rooftop. "Nah," he says finally, shaking his head. "But I've been hearing some other stuff, if you're interested."

"Obviously I am."

He crosses his arms, a smug look on his hairless face. "You know how the produce truck comes down the main road here every third night to go to the pizza store, right? Well, it came down at the same time it always did that night, but when it did, a loud crash happened—*tchtchtch!* That was the glass being shattered, fam! It was insane. It was like *zoom!* truck, and then *tchtchtch!* glass. Pretty much at the same time. So, more like *zootchtchtch!*"

I purse my lips at his story. "Okay, and? We see the produce truck all the time. It almost hit Mr. Daniel once."

"Exactly. Anyone *from around here* would see it all the time. But you know that already, right?" he mocks with a snicker.

I bite my lips together harder, trying to make sure my face doesn't betray me. Anger rises slowly in my chest, and it's replaced with this weird mixture of hurt and betrayal and sickness. I think I'm going to be sick. I think I'm going to need to sit down or lie down and be sick at the same time.

I can't lose face to a kid like Mikey, so I say, "Of course I knew that," real confident. But I am not confident; I'm hollow.

Someone around here would definitely know when the pro-duce truck comes. *Only* someone from here would know that.

"Shit," I sigh.

Mikey smirks. "Exactly."

"Why're you so happy about this?" I hiss. "That just means it's either you or one of your dumbass friends."

"I'm not happy about it," he tells me. "It sucks. I was collecting these Sorcery trading cards and I was two away from a full defense set. And now where'm I supposed to get a healer?"

One of his friends pipes up, "That grocery place in front of the Eats might have them. Yo, have you seen? I think it's new," and I watch them debate over which grocery store, what aisle, the window display, all of it. They never talk about how that place literally didn't exist a year ago, a few months ago. They don't say that it's strange to see it pop up so suddenly, strange to see something so shiny and out of place between what already exists.

Quickly I reach out and give Mikey a smack on his fore-head. Light, but swift with meaning. He recoils, grabbing his head, and his friends burst out laughing. I don't budge an inch when he steps to me, puffing out his chest and acting like he's sprouted any facial hair in the past year. Then I say, "How's your mom?"

He softens instantly. "O-oh. She's cool."

"Cool."

"Actually, she's applying for a job at that big spice store," he goes on. The lightness in his voice is endearing when he talks about his mom. It almost makes him appear cute, but then I remember that time when he and his friends borrowed my bike and never gave it back. Makes me want to smack him twice. "Hey, it's wack, right?" Mikey says. "Can you believe there's just one huge store for only spices? What a dumbass idea. They don't even sell food to season. It feels like a waste of space."

CHAPTER ELEVEN

The week went by fast with a whole lot of nothing—leads that went nowhere—and by Saturday, I'm up too early for my own good. This is even worse than waking up at seven a.m. on a school day. Usually I lie in bed and think about how I can fake sick, how I can convince my mom that I'd be better off sipping her pepper soup in the kitchen than going all the way to school and infecting my classmates with my nonexistent disease. But today, on a weekend, I'm awake at the crack of dawn and moisturizing my ends so I can make it to Ginger Store for the final insurance inspection.

Mr. Tran was pissed when he found out they'd be in on Saturday. "This is my store, you know?" he snapped at them over the phone. "It's my livelihood! You're making me wait *so* many days for something that should be *so* simple!"

"Chi-chi!" Mom catches me as I'm headed to the front door. She presses a container filled with rice into my hands. "It's for Kate's mom. Tell her I said sorry again."

"Yes, Mom." I hold the container close to my chest. The rice smells really good. It'll take all the willpower I have to not eat it myself. She reaches forward and adjusts the corner of my shirt, to which I groan, and I try to maneuver my way out of her grasp. "Mom, please."

"I'll buy you a new one soon," she says, and tugs at my bra straps. I nearly shriek. "It's getting way too noticeable now."

"Mom, please, I'm going to die—"

"And you be careful," she warns. "I don't know what's been going on with this break-in. Who knows if the neighborhood is safe?"

"Oh my God," I groan, tossing my head back. "It's probably nothing." My voice breaks awkwardly with the remnants of all the thoughts I have fighting each other in my head. I don't know where to go from here after hearing it might be a local who bricked the store. I put it out of my memory for now. Today is about the inspection.

My phone pings, and I know it's another notification from someone who's watched the rant on Hive Man or whatever. I can't believe people are still messaging me about this. The law of internet viral videos states that after a day, everyone should be over it, so I don't know why I haven't been replaced with a cat meme or something. I've just been clicking on the alerts to get rid of them because I'm past reading them at this point. But when I swipe open my phone, I see that the notification isn't from some wayward slacktivist; it's an email from a news station. And they want to interview me.

"Uhh . . ." I can't stop staring at my screen. They know

my full name—how'd they get my full name? *Miss Chinelo Agu, everyone is talking about your viral video*—who even talks that way?—*and we'd like to interview you to hear more about what prompted the response.* What prompted it? They don't even know? What's the point of interviewing me, then, if they don't even know anything about what happened to the store?

In the end, I do a quick search online for "Ginger East store" and pull the first article I can find about the break-in. I copy-paste the link into the reply and hit send without so much as a hello.

My phone pings again, and for a split second I think it's another random, but it's a message from Dad. He is either three or two hours behind, but I can't remember. I was good at keeping track when he left, but he texts so sporadically anyway that sometimes it seems like we're still in the same place. It's a nice feeling.

Dad: Hello . . .

Chinelo: hi dad

Dad: How are you?

Chinelo: fine. how are you?

Dad: Am good . . . Just at work.

Chinelo: on a saturday??

Dad: Yes . . .

Dad: Just for a while . . .

I'm chuckling because Dad is always texting with all these ellipses. It makes whatever he's saying sound super ominous, even when it isn't.

Chinelo: ok well i'm going to see kate
Dad: Ok . . .
Dad: How is she? Heard about the store. Be careful.
Chinelo: she's good
Dad: Good. . . . and your mom?
Chinelo: she's good too
Dad: Good . . .
Dad: Well am just saying hello
Chinelo: ok!
Chinelo: have fun at work, dad!
Dad: Ok . . . be safe . . .

I barely have a second to exit my texts before, as always, a thousand-paragraph-long prayer comes in. Dad has these saved up, probably gathered from the secret network of Nigerian parents online. They trade prayers all day, several times a day, and I bet no one even questions where this chain mail comes from.

Dad: I just gave one of my friend your number, He says he loves you but I told him that you have someone in your life, but he insisted that there is no one like him. Don't get angry with me for giving out ur number. He was so convincing, he told me how much he loves you and how much he would care for you. So I told him he could call you at any time if that's OK with you. Before I forget, his name is JESUS. Please give him a chance!! Please Don't ignore send to all your good friend.

Oh my God, Dad, please.

I race to the store. It's past sunrise, but clouds fill the sky, almost like they know what's happened here. When I think of it, of everything, of knowing someone in the neighborhood did this, my chest gets heavy.

The feeling doesn't let up the more I run past houses on Ginger Way. For one thing, each house has the same weird black-and-white poster tacked onto it: bold letters with short words splattered across the front. My feet slow for a second as I take in the posters, and I gravitate to the closest one hanging off the back of someone's old car. "Silent protest?" I murmur, brows furrowing at the page. My heart skips and my mind immediately goes to Ginger Store, but the more I read, the more I realize it isn't about Ginger Store at all. It's about Spice of Life, the rent increases, all of it. TAKE BACK THE NEIGHBORHOOD, the poster says in block letters. SILENT PROTEST IN FRONT OF SPICE OF LIFE TO PROMOTE UNITY AND COMMUNITY ACTIVITIES. ALL ARE WELCOME.

"This is dope," I say to myself, eyes scanning the poster

over and over again. Nowhere on the poster does it say who's organizing the protest, but I bet with a bit of digging, I can figure it out. I wonder if Kate knows. Quickly I fold the poster and stuff it into my pocket.

By the time I get to Ginger Store, I almost forget how bad the storefront looks. Almost. I was just here, being held at a distance by the caution tape, afraid to get any closer. Though the hole has been boarded up with planks of plywood, the image of that smashed-in window will never leave my memory. It's burned in there now. I don't want to think of Ginger Store like this—fragile and broken. After this last inspection, the insurance people should give Mr. Tran what he's owed, we'll figure out who did this, Kate will stay, and things can go back to normal, back to the way they were. And honestly? I can't wait.

Kate is standing outside wearing her limited edition Supreme hoodie. It's technically Jake's, but she bought it off him for ten dollars after she wore it out. It suits her more, anyway.

She stiffly grins when she sees me, and I try to return it. Kate is in better spirits now; I can see it on her face. Since the incident, she's been fake smiling at me. In any other situation, as her best and closest friend, I would've called her out, but I can't do it this time. Maybe she cries a lot at home when no one is looking, but in front of me, she never once acts as if anything is seriously wrong. She is always just Kitkat. "Yo," she says with a wider grin. "You got here before the inspector. Nice."

"He's not here yet? Wow." I sigh. "Making people wake up at who-knows-when, and he can't even get here on time."

Kate snickers and rolls onto her heels before rocking forward. "Yeah. But it's the last one. That's what they said, anyway. After this guy, Dad should be able to finalize his claim or something. I don't even know. All this insurance talk is too stuffy for me. Jake knows more about it."

"Oh yeah? Then where is he?"

"Asked him to grab me coffee from Tim's," she says. "It's *early* out here, you know?"

I laugh. "Yeah, yeah, it is." I pull out the folded poster from my pocket, smooth it out, and show it to Kate. "Look. How cool is this? Someone's planning a protest or something."

"A silent protest?" she says, looking down at the paper. Her eyes skim the details fast. "About Spice of Life and stuff?"

"Guess so."

"Who's organizing it?"

"No idea."

Kate glances at me with a cheeky smile and chuckles. "You're going to go to this, right? This is the kind of stuff you're into."

I don't even bother lying. "Yeah, okay," I chuckle. "I mean, I'll go, but I also wish I knew who was running it. I kinda think it'd be cool to help plan and stuff, you know?"

"How do I know you didn't secretly put up all these posters?"

"Because I would've needed your help, genius." I snicker, and she laughs because it's true. And we would've hit Ginger Store first, with posters going all up and down its brick walls.

"Would you join with me?" I ask her. "If I found out who's running it."

Her smile fades a little, but not enough to make everything mad awkward. "Uh . . ." She hums. "I don't know. Social justice seems to be your thing."

"*My* thing?"

"I saw your video on Hive Man too," she goes on. I look away, embarrassed at how easy it was to run my mouth, and annoyed at Hive Man for even being a thing. "I appreciate the energy."

I narrow my eyes at her. "You're trying it."

She laughs. "I'm being serious! I love that you looked so pressed! But honestly, you have more views than Maree's latest video now."

I snort. "Oh my God, please."

"It's true! You better watch out before her PR people come for you in the night."

Jake's car pulls up moments later, and he parks on the side of the road where the bus grabs us from school. He looks tired and cold and miserable as he crosses the street with a steaming hot cup of coffee for Kate. She accepts it before he can even hand it to her. "Did you ask for a French vanilla shot?" she asks, bringing the cup to her mouth. "I know. I'll know when I drink it, anyway." She takes a quick sip and warms at the taste of vanilla. "Yessss. This is legit."

Jake grunts in response, stuffing his hands into his jacket pockets, and stands waiting beside her. He doesn't look too pleased overall, and he gives me this look like *Why are you here?* He's so annoying. "You could be asleep right now," he says.

"Yeah, I know," I reply, and hold out the container clutched to my chest. "Was supposed to give this to your mom. I thought she'd be here, but I guess in the meantime I can keep you guys company."

Jake snatches the container from me. I barely have a second to react before he's ripping it open and the smell of warm, just-cooked fried rice is wafting on the cold April air. He's basking in it as if the steam is clearing his pores or something. "Fried rice? It's mine now," he says, and hands Kate the lid while he awkwardly eats, mouth to container.

I gasp "Wait!" but my shock turns to amusement, and I have to look away to keep from laughing too hard. Jake is always so serious these days. Maybe college does that to you. I didn't know if he knew how to joke around with us anymore, but suddenly, standing out here in the chilly air on a Saturday morning, I'm feeling more like we're friends than I have in years.

"That isn't going to work," Kate tells him. "You gotta tip it, like, into your mouth."

He does as she says, angling the container so the rice can fall into his mouth easier. I frown. "My mom's gonna beat both your asses once she finds out you ate all Mama Tran's rice."

"She's gonna beat *your* ass for not getting it to my mom," Jake says with a mouthful of rice and vegetables. "She won't say anything to me."

"No way. You're not the golden child anymore."

"Like you are?" he teases. Suddenly he nods to the flyer in my hands. "What's that?"

I hold it up to show him. "This is happening in front of Spice of Life at the end of the month—I'm not planning it, but if I could have, I would," I add hastily. He snickers at that.

"Yeah?" he says. "That's cool. Cool to see some people actually care about . . . you know."

I frown. "Know what?"

"Some people are really excited about the new store," he says, his voice losing its edge. "Not that they don't feel a type of way about our store, but they're—I don't know. Spice of Life is new and shiny, and I guess they're into that."

I grimace. "New and shiny? That's all they care about?"

"There's no loyalty," Kate utters, and I nod right away because this snake revelation is almost too much to deal with. I don't even want to believe people around here are looking to abandon Ginger Store like that. After all the Trans have done for us too.

Jake shrugs. "It's not even that deep."

"Who's been saying that stuff?" I ask him.

"Does it matter? Are you gonna shake down a bunch of senior citizens?"

"Ugh, no," I say, even though the mental image of me doing so is pretty funny. "I just want to know."

Jake sighs as he takes a long, good look at me. For a second, I expect him to spill a name I know, like Caddy Smith, this weird boy who failed his way out of high school and now stays home all the time, sweeping his front step. Or even Annie Jenkins, this militant, religious lady who says her church won't let her wear pants. But then, he opens his mouth and says, "People," and I don't know how to take that. "Maybe more people than you realize," he adds.

That can't be true. It's so vague. "That could be anybody," I say.

"Shh, shh," Kate cuts in, waving a hand between us. We fall silent when a dusty old BMW pulls up to the curb. My dad always calls these kinds of cars "dead or alive." It barely functions, it's rusting in places where cars usually never rust, but because it's a BMW, a luxury car, the owner *has* to drive it for the status.

Jake stops chewing while a square-faced, brown-skinned man exits the vehicle. He fixes his shirt and smooths his slicked hair back while he surveys the street. His eyes do a once-over of everything, and I feel as if I can read his mind: the park is big but too ominous and probably has loose drug paraphernalia lying around, which isn't a wrong assumption; the roads look clean, but when's the last time a drunk passed out on them; the buildings look quiet enough, but it's early so maybe the troublemakers aren't awake yet. And so on. And so on. I see it all the time when people who aren't from here roll through. They get that look in their eyes like they don't want to touch anything. This man is too bold. He does know his car is a piece of shit, right?

He stares at us, unsure if it's safe to approach. Jake hands the container to Kate, who fumbles it with the lid and her coffee. Jake approaches the man. "Are you with the agency?" he asks. He's using his polite, customer service voice. The lazy drawl is gone.

The man wrinkles his nose and stares up at the store behind us. "Yes. I'm Dhaval. And you are?"

"Jake Tran," he says, and reaches out for a handshake. The man reluctantly accepts. "I can show you around. I'll take you through the back."

Dhaval doesn't take his eyes off the building as he follows Jake around the side. Kate and I gravitate toward the front door, staring as best we can through the faded stickers and stamps pressed onto the glass door. The NO ID? NO WAY sticker is particularly huge, blocking most of the inside. I can spot the spice aisle, where Mr. Tran started to stock very specific West African spices just because my mom asked; and the snack aisle, where I spent hours going through all the different variations of white cheddar popcorn. In the corner, there's the book rack with its few missing spots. I'm happy no one took those.

CHAPTER TWELVE

Dhaval is really picky. Maybe that's how an insurance inspector is supposed to be, but he's asking so many questions, and it's making my head hurt. "Was this wall always damaged?" "Was there a claim filed on the pipes in this room before?" "What temperature is it in here normally?" Jeez. Jake can take care of the inspector on his own. We're no help, anyway, and Kate is super antsy. It's as if she doesn't even want to be here. I understand why she wouldn't, though. It still feels so new, the "break-in," the vandalism. Being this close to the store—being *inside* the store—makes it too real. Realer than real.

Kate finds her old Bluetooth speaker under the front counter, and she's about to hook up her phone, but Jake catches her before she presses play on her music app. "Does this look like the time for Midtown Project?" he hisses. The look on Kate's face makes me laugh so loud that crusty, stuffy Dhaval does a double take.

Kate frowns. "Who says I was gonna play Midtown Project? What if it was my mixtape?"

"Are you kidding me right now?" Jake goes on in a hushed tone. "Get out if you're not going to be useful."

"Oh my Goood," she groans, throwing her head back.

We leave Jake and Dhaval to comb through the store. Kate is walking quickly across the street. When we were younger and she used to get mad at Jake or her parents, she would always go to the one place out of her house and Ginger Store that she found comforting. And even though I'm convinced that Jake questioning her taste in music isn't that deep, I know that's where she's headed, her shoes scraping with purpose against the ground.

We used to go to this swing set all the time with Bo, Rafa, and Maree. It was the best because it was situated in a large sand pit at the edge of the park. We used to swing as high as we could and jump off right at the top, hoping we could land—on our feet or otherwise—outside of the pit and on the grass. I only made it once, but I sprained my ankle and couldn't go out for a week. Still a victory.

"Wait up!" I call to her, jogging to catch up. My mind flashes back to Mikey, who came down this same path with his friends the other day; Mikey, who's so convinced a local kid had something to do with Ginger Store. I feel my joints freeze, stiffening under uncertainty as I walk. There's no way I can tell Kate that. She'd tell Mr. Tran, and he'd be more convinced that leaving is the right option.

Kate looks at me and snorts when she sees the conflict in my eyes. "Are you good?" she asks.

"Yeah, why not?" I brush it off and even force a smile so she won't get suspicious.

"How's your, uh, thing going? Trying to find out who bricked the store."

My jaw tightens under her gaze. She's not even staring that hard but I still feel so naked. "It's cool. Just—just looking at some stuff. It—it's hard to tell right now, so."

"Right," she chortles, uneasy, before digging around in her pocket for her phone. "Can you listen to this mix for me? Don't laugh, but did you know that Sol's 'I Ain't Never' goes so good with Midtown Project's 'Waterproof'?" She flashes a grin. "And—" My phone beeps before she has the chance to load her music app. She snickers, though it's forced. I know her well enough to know she's pretending not to be annoyed. "Another admirer?"

"Please," I groan, and open the notification. It's that same news company asking for an interview again. I guess they still want to talk to me.

Immediately I show my screen to Kate, and she skim-reads. Her face morphs from fake interested to really interested. She gasps. "Oh, word? This is legit?"

I roll my eyes. "You thought it wouldn't be?"

"Well, damn, I didn't realize people wanted to *interview* interview you," she grunts. "After that video blew up . . . Are you going to do it?"

"Can I, even? I'm sixteen," I say. "It seems like they just want to know about the store incident, right?"

"Yeah, but why from you? You're not the police. I mean, the Feds," she adds with a snort.

"Shut up," I say, and she laughs. "But whatever. I live here, so that's better."

"Bro, you're only sixteen, so don't you think they'd ask your mom for permission? Would she say yes?"

My mom would never say yes. "She might," I mumble. The longer I stare at the screen, the faster my dreams of being interviewed die. Yeah, there's no way. Mom would kill me if I ended up on the news under any circumstance.

Kate chuckles, "Yeah, okay," and returns to her phone. Suddenly a notification comes up on her screen. She hides it, but I see Bo's name before she moves her phone away. My eyes drop to my feet. I don't want to be obvious, but it kinda bothers me that Bo talks to literally my best friend and doesn't have the time to talk to me. Did I used to tease him that much that he doesn't think he can say hi to me or something? Was I really that bad? I mean, I doubt it. We were all cool. And everyone made fun of Bo! Maybe Kate was nicest to him, but that doesn't warrant him messaging her all the time or visiting her. Unless . . .

"Hey," Kate speaks up. "Bo wants to add you on Messenger."

I frown. "What?"

"He's like, 'Should I add her?'" she continues, deepening her voice an octave to sound like a boy. "And I'm like, 'Yeah, bro, why not?' And he's like, 'Are you sure she won't be mad?' And I'm like, 'Why—'"

"Why would I be mad?" I counter.

She snaps her fingers into a thumbs-up. "Exactly. So can he add you?"

"Sure. I mean, whatever, yeah," I say with a casual shrug. I shrug twice because the first one isn't casual enough. She starts typing furiously the second the word "sure" is out of my mouth. Soon my phone beeps with a notification: *Bo Williams has added you as a friend.* A friend, huh? A friend who doesn't think to contact his friend even after he's been visiting her best friend in secret! Sounds like a snake to me.

"Accept it," Kate barks at me.

"I will, damn," I say. She's watching me swipe the notification and press accept.

"Good." She smiles and skips ahead to the swing set in view. It looks almost unchanged from how it did when we used to come here all the time. The jungle gym, the four rusty swings, the two baby swings, and the metal slide that used to shock you on your way down.

Kate plops down onto a swing, and I join her. I kick my feet off from the ground and push myself higher and higher, feeling the wind chill my knuckles and blow past my ears. Kate matches my speed, and soon we're swinging in time with each other. Makes me feel as if I'm ten, looking up at the neighborhood from this high. It used to be more decorated back then. Less FOR SALE signs too.

"We all used to make fun of Bo, right?" I ask. She nods. "So then why'd he take so long to add me? Even Rafa added me, and I don't really talk to him."

"I—I don't know," she says, kicking her feet higher into the air. "You were extra mean, though. Always talking about his forehead."

"His forehead was *colossal*."

She laughs. "See? You and Rafa were so rude to him, more than anyone else."

"Yeah, but we were all kind of mean to each other," I tell her. "That's why we were friends."

"You're right, you're right."

My phone beeps in my pocket, and I have to slow myself a little to reach for it. Bo sent me a message. My feet are on solid ground now while I stare at my screen. I don't look at the message right away. Instead I browse Bo's profile as though I'm some creep and don't know who he is. In every picture, he has his head tilted so you can see more of his angular jaw and less of his forehead. His designer glasses are the focus in almost every picture. He's actually so photogenic. His profile links to a personal forum page where people tag him in gameplay videos or weird memes about sausage. He gets a lot of likes too. This Bo seems to be very popular, so unlike the Bo I knew.

His message says: *your last name is sondra?? since when?? i thought it was agu.*

That's the first thing he says to me? After showing up in my hood randomly like he never left?

"What'd he say?" Kate leans over as best she can, peering at my screen. "What's that say? I can't read it—"

"Because it's not for you," I say, and she pulls the most unimpressed face. I stare back at the message, not knowing how to respond. Should I be funny? Will he take it personally? Does this new Bo with stylish frames and a strong jaw suddenly have a sense of humor? I doubt it.

"Say something like 'What took you so long?'" Kate says.

"No."

"Just do it," she whines, scrubbing her feet in the sand.

I hesitate, my fingers hovering above the keys, but I type exactly what she says anyway: *what took you so long?* And I wait.

He replies quickly: *thought you were gonna add me first.*

I roll my eyes. "This kid . . ."

Chinelo Sondra: you're dumb.
Bo Williams: is that all you gotta say to me?
Chinelo Sondra: sondra's my middle name, beethoven junior. you should know that.
Bo Williams: wow sorry damn.

I'm stuck. I show the conversation to Kate, who only *tsk-tsk*s and shakes her head.

"Ask him what's up," she says.

"Why do I have to do that? Shouldn't he ask me?"

"Just do it."

I groan, but I do as she says.

Chinelo Sondra: what's up?

Bo Williams: nothin. I feel bad i didn't say hi proper when i was at kitkat's

Chinelo Sondra: you been there all day?

Bo Williams: almost yea. when i saw on the news, i ran over. skipped school. missed a chem test.

Chinelo Sondra: nerd. you didn't get in trouble?

Bo Williams: nah, mom understood. she was maaaad though. thinks it was a gang but i tried to tell her it hasn't been like that at g-east for a while.

I choke on a laugh and show the phone to Kate. She's happy to get a real look since she's been trying to read over my shoulder this entire time. "He called it G-East," I say, chortling. "That's not even a cool nickname."

"No one calls it that," she says, and chuckles with a swift roll of her eyes. "Tell him I don't want to see him come around here saying 'G-East,' or else."

I hear what Kate says, but for some reason, I start typing: *LOL G-EAST.*

Bo Williams: what??

Chinelo Sondra: no one calls it that!!! you been at santa ana academy too long

Bo Williams: whatever

Bo Williams: how's the store?

Bo Williams: saw you in some video online btw! wasn't sure it was you at first, but i'd know that side-eye anywhere

Chinelo Sondra: oh my god

Bo Williams: are you trying to be maree now?

Chinelo Sondra: that's offense number two. that video was an accident. really not out here tryna be like her any day.

Bo Williams: true

Bo Williams: how's kate doing?

Chinelo Sondra: ask her yourself?

Bo Williams: i'm talking to you though

Just then, both our phones go off with new notifications. It's from our school group. Kate instantly frowns. "It's probably something dumb from Maree," she groans. "I'm not going to watch it."

I'm already in the app, so it opens up the notification whether I want to see it or not. One of Maree's new friends has posted a video with a caption that just says *OMG* with a sad face. It's titled "Ginger East Catastrophe."

"Shit, shit, look." I nudge Kate in the arm until she finally turns to face me. She looks at my phone screen unimpressed, but I know it's because she can't read from far away. I shove it closer toward her face and watch her expression go from annoyed to confused to pissed to super pissed in two seconds.

"No fucking way," she utters.

CHAPTER THIRTEEN

Maree opts not to have her theme song play, because this is a very somber topic. When we finally see her face on-screen, she's seated at her usual desk, but is looking inconsolable. She's careful to make sure her lips pout perfectly and the undertone from her blond highlights comes out at this angle.

"Hey, guys," she says with a loud sigh. "I just—it's really hard to even start this video. How can I even begin? Hmmm." She's so good at sighing. She's brushing her hair out of her eyes and rubbing her face and doing all the things you should do when you're flustered. I know them so well because I know her. "First of all, I don't know if many of you know this about me, but like, I grew up in a really tough neighborhood."

The word "whaaaaat?" flashes on the screen, and she swats it away, pushing it to the left, before it eventually topples somewhere off-screen. "Yeah, actually. I really did," she says. "I grew up in a place called Ginger East, and it was—every day was survival. One of those places." She's rubbing her face again, rubbing her eyes as if she's going to cry. Oooh, she'd better not. "Over this past week, something horrible happened to a store in the neighborhood, and that store happened to have been owned by, like, one of my close friends." Her voice is getting shakier. Shiiiit, she's gonna cry. "I—I really—"

The scene changes, and Maree is dotting her eyes and sniffling away from the camera. When the scene cuts back, her eyes are reddened with tears and she's seated, patient, staring at the camera again. "I'm sorry. This is just so emotional for me. Like, growing up and stuff, it was always hard to pretend that things weren't bad. I'm not even joking, guys; there were real gangs where I grew up. It's pretty much the hood."

She's traumatized by this, but she still managed to insert gunshot noises into the background of her video.

"Anyway, like I said, this store that my friend's family owns got robbed, and a lot of their stuff was stolen. It's so sad because her family works really hard and it's not fair. I really wanted to talk about it today because that's my hometown and it's where I grew up, and I really wish things weren't that way, but they are." A tear falls down her cheek, and she dots at it, elegantly, while her eyes flicker to the table in front of her. "In times like these, it's easy for us to feel so small, but it's way more important for us to come together. We're stronger in groups. It's so important for us to stay woke and realize there are things happening every day in communities like Ginger East, and they're not isolated. We shouldn't be afraid to speak up. *You* shouldn't be afraid to speak up either. . . ."

CHAPTER FOURTEEN

Kate is already on her feet by the time I shut off the video. She's restless, can't sit still. She looks as though she might scream. "Is. She. *Serious?*" she snaps and grumbles and groans at the same time.

I'm mad too, but for other reasons. Maree's talking a whole lot of shit about stuff she doesn't understand anymore. And she's giving false information! Who said anything about a robbery? Why'd she make that up? And—and Kate's her *close friend* now? She doesn't even have Kate on Topsnap!

"This wasn't supposed to happen! I can't believe she said that; I can't believe she said all that. Shit!" Kate repeats over and over again. Her pacing becomes uneven and her shoulders rise and fall quickly. Her face twists like she's eaten something sour, and then she inhales so sharply that it sounds like her throat's been cut in half. She's going to cry. I know she is.

"Kate . . ." I get to my feet too and try to approach her. She backs up from me. "Listen," I say. "You know what we should do? Drive over to her rich-ass neighborhood and slap her right in the face. That's the only thing that's going to fix this."

I mean it to be a joke, but Kate isn't laughing. She juts a finger at my phone. "Tell her to take it down or something! She can't just—just *say* that!"

"We can get her to take it down, yeah, but I say we slap her first—"

"Nelo!"

"F-fine," I say with a light chuckle. She's not laughing with me at all. In fact, I think for the first time since the incident, she's being honest. I can see the anger all over her face. "Fine," I repeat, firmer.

She turns on her heel and takes off back down the path, running faster than I've ever seen anyone run. I don't go after her, and it's hard to say if she's going back to the store or to her house. My guess is home, where no one can bother her. Where Maree and her useless lies won't get to her.

Why'd I even watch the video? I know Maree never says anything good about the neighborhood, that she likes to act as if she's better than where she used to live so people will watch, but she didn't need to go that far. She didn't need to be so cold about it.

I pocket my phone and head back down the path to the intersection. Ginger Store comes into view once I round the corner, and I see that the inspector's car isn't there anymore. The store looks eerie with the plywood boarding up the left window. It's like a ghost building or something. The board completely blocks up the front counter and the stool where Mrs. Tran usually sits during the day. It blocks out the rows of chocolate and candy, and the freezer stocked with Vita ice cream. It makes it look as if none of that ever existed.

I hope the inspector got all he needed from his visit. I don't like seeing Ginger Store like this, especially knowing someone from the neighborhood caused it, if what Mikey says is true. Kate says Mr. Tran hasn't set foot in there since the police showed up that morning. She says Mrs. Tran doesn't even talk about the store; she cooks and cleans at home as though nothing happened. But something did happen, and everyone's stuck. Everything is on hold now.

I head farther down the main road, hoping to grab some food before I go home, but I stop in my tracks when I hear a familiar cling-clang coming from beside the store. It echoes in the emptiness of the street, each thud in measured time, while a chorus of throaty giggles erupts from their source. My feet scurry around the corner, and I see the Avery brothers. They freeze, hands held high—smooth stones clutched in their grasp as they're midthrow at some protest posters.

"Holy shit . . ." I take a step forward, but they drop the rocks quickly.

A frightened look flashes across the taller brother's face as he stutters, "W-we didn't do nothing, I swear!"

"Y-yeah, it was like that already," the other one says, and

snickers. They nudge and punch each other like it's some sort of inside joke. Like the poster they threw rocks at and ripped was meant to be that mangled.

"Are you serious?" I snap, and they straighten up right away. "What's your problem?"

I take another step forward. They split, one slipping to my left and the other to my right, and they take off at breakneck speed toward Ginger Way. One of them almost runs into Mr. Brown, who barely misses them as they come barreling down the road. He kisses his teeth, a resounding *"Mtchew!"* cutting the air like a knife.

I rush over. He's carrying a rough-looking, bulky briefcase with a paper sticking out of it. Some kind of newsprint. "Are you okay, Mr. Brown?" I ask, reaching out in case he needs a hand.

But he nearly swats it away, a shadow of a glare on his face. "I'm fine," he says, and continues down the road. It only takes a few paces before I fall into line, stepping lightly behind him.

"Those kids are so annoying," I tell him. He gives me a look over his shoulder that tells me he thinks I'm one of those annoying kids too. "I mean, for real. . . . I just saw them throwing stones at Ginger Store."

Mr. Brown huffs in response but says nothing. What's his problem? Doesn't he care?

For a moment I stop following. Mr. Brown crosses the

street, slumping past that old duplex and the liquor store. He ignores a shaky woman who calls out to him, instead quickening his pace like he's got somewhere to be. And for one reason or another, I try to keep up.

I walk slowly on my side of the street, ready to bolt across the road if he takes a turn into an alleyway. I don't think he notices me. For all he knows, I'm just walking casually down the other side of the road, minding my own business. But it's Mr. Brown, so he knows I don't know how to do that.

He stops, and I stop. He walks, and I walk. He's doing this on purpose.

"Chinelo?" he calls across the street. My name gets carried through a passing truck and whips me in the face where I stand. He's facing me now, clutching the briefcase and frowning. "Well, if you're going to follow me around, you might as well come be useful."

"Huh?"

"Don't 'huh' me. Come here."

By the time I get to the other side, Mr. Brown is shoving the newsprint page back into his briefcase. He's still frowning when I approach. "Hold this for one second," he says as he hands me the briefcase. I take it and Mr. Brown tries to press it closed as best he can. "This old thing . . . I feel as if any moment it can just break on me."

The briefcase is bulky, worn, and definitely looks like it's seen better days. He wrestles it closed and takes it back, shakes it gently at his side, testing its weight to make sure the locks will hold.

He's staring down the street like he's looking for something, and in that instant, my eyes catch a glimpse of his loan store. "Who's watching the shop while you're out here?" I ask absently.

"I have staff. Come on," he says simply, and continues on down the road.

"Where are we going?"

"Just around here."

"What's just around here?"

He looks over his shoulder at me, a sneer settling into his face, before he dips, predictably, into an alleyway. It's mad shady, and I'm hesitant to follow, so I stand at the opening, watching him. He looks as though he wants to crouch down while he opens the briefcase, but doesn't. Instead he holds the briefcase to his chest while he opens it and pulls out a stack of pages and an awkwardly shaped jar of paste. I take a careful step forward as he finally sets the briefcase and stack down before picking up one single page—newsprint. A poster.

He positions a silent-protest poster on the wall before he slathers paste over it. Then he does the same with a second and third poster. I take another step into the alleyway, watching him work. "You're organizing the protest?" I ask him.

He nods. "Who else?"

Who else, huh.

I trudge into the alley to join Mr. Brown. He hands me a poster and nudges the paste toward me. I put the poster up right beside the last one. He moves around me to put up another.

"How do you know people will come out to this thing?" I ask.

He lets out a snarky laugh. "They'll come. There are so many people who live here who are maybe too shy to say anything when things get bad, but they'll be there. You may even know someone like that," he says, and gives me a wink like we have an inside secret.

No way he's talking about me. Since when have I ever been too shy to say anything when it matters? He doesn't know me at all. I say, "You must be thinking of someone else," and begrudgingly grab another poster.

He laughs again. "Oh, so your friend Kate is suddenly the adventurous one?"

"What?" I spit out. "Kate?"

"Yes," he goes on. "She may not be thinking about it, but she'll be there, and so will others who live here. Everyone feels things different, you know? The feeling's different."

I don't say anything, just grab another poster and scan the wall for where to put it.

"Where is she today?" Mr. Brown asks as I wander a few paces down the alley. "You two are usually inseparable."

My mind races back to how mad Kate got at Maree's

video. We have to get that video taken down, even though I don't know what good that'll do. It's up already. It won't make it onto Hive Man or anything, but still. "She's, uh, she has family stuff," I tell him.

"And you're not there?"

Damn, he didn't have to say it like that. Mr. Brown is savage. This is what I get for helping him? My hands dust away a good spot on the wall before I position the poster. "How many people are helping to organize?" I ask.

He wrinkles his nose as he thinks. "There are maybe ten of us now. Hmm. A few young kids like you."

The urge to say "I'm not a kid" is pretty strong. "Can I join?" I say instead. He hands me the paste, and I put up another poster. "I can be punctual and organized. And I care." I hate that I make it sound like an afterthought. It isn't. I probably care the most out of anyone I know right now, even though that's not saying much. After all, it may have been one of those kids who threw the brick. It might not have been an accident at all.

He grunts again, nodding. "You can join. We're meeting in a few days to talk about getting more people interested. I think you'll have good ideas." He laughs at that like it's actually funny.

When he steps back, he nods in approval at the new line of posters, smiling at them like he put them all up himself. Actually, if I'm being honest, I've never seen Mr. Brown smile so much. He's usually very serious because he gets some real shady-ass people coming through the loans place. He doesn't have time to smile.

"You know . . . ," he says, his eyes fixed on the wall. "There used to be . . . It was a band that used to come play in here, you know."

"What? A real band?"

"It was . . . Rocky and them," he tells me, like I know who Rocky and them are. "Rocky, Bill, and that one Polish boy— could never speak any English, but he could play drums." He laughs to himself. I watch him, watch all the memories go by in his eyes. He takes off his glasses and rubs his face, letting out a small, tired groan. "It's all passed now. Some of them moved away; some of them are dead."

"Friends?" I ask. "From when you moved here?"

"Oh, yeah," he answers right away. "In the eighties, it was a whole scene here." He waves his hand across the alley, painting the entire picture. "Miss Lee from the corner used to bring tables and chairs, and she'd line them up and make people drinks. But she'd charge because she was a mean, mean lady. I said, 'Why're you charging me to drink outside here when you don't own the space?' And she said—she said, 'It's for my bail fund when the police come.'" He bursts out laughing. It makes me smile a little to see him so into his story. "Said the neighbors should come get her out of jail for serving in public, and serving minors and all that. Can you believe that? Never seen a girl like her since. She—her grandkids moved her somewhere else and I suppose she's dead now. Bill too. Bill had, uh, something with his brain."

"I'm sorry," I utter. "That sucks."

"It does," he says with a sigh. "You know, things around here, they're always changing. I've seen it my whole, whole life. But now, I don't know." The memories fade from his eyes and his laugh dies out. The Mr. Brown who was drinking questionable drinks in an alleyway in the eighties is replaced with this somber one who can barely remember how his friends' music sounded. He fixes his thick glasses back on his face and sighs again. "This time," he says, "I don't know."

CHAPTER FIFTEEN

There's been a thread in T.L. Chats since this morning about Maree's video. Everyone is watching it this time. Usually you can't even find one kid to own up to watching her videos, but now, before first period on Monday, everyone knows and is talking about what happened at Ginger East. They watch her video and they watch my video, and finally people are piecing it together. People are also speculating about this friend Maree cares so much about and are trying to figure out who it is.

There are so many things wrong with this. First of all, Maree has a new best friend every day and no one even knows their names. At one time, there was Rebecca Howland, and then there was Amber Ramsammy, and now who knows? Secondly, half of these kids are pretending they even know where Ginger East is, when they've barely heard of it—or if they have, they know it by its more common name: "the ghetto."

I'm Maree's best friend, but I've never even been to Ginger East, says one. *Isn't that the hood, LOL? When did she live there?* says another. *Are we sure she meant Ginger East and it wasn't a typo?* says someone else. I'm tired of all this. Too many wrong opinions going around. And honestly, Maree is legit on something. Aside from DMs on social platforms that she probably doesn't even check herself, the only way to really contact her is through a PR email address on her YouTube channel. And what did I get after I sent a thoughtful and well-edited email? *Thanks for contacting us. We'll get back to you within 24 hours.* Well, it's been twenty-four hours already, and that video is still up!

On the bus, I toss my phone into my lap and let my mind wander back to the store. I've been scared to ask more people about who bricked it, but Kate, who didn't care maybe two seconds ago, keeps trying to ask me what I found out. There's no way I can tell her it was someone local. Not to mention, there's no way I really even believe that for sure. I mean, that produce truck starts at the top of the hill and makes a million stops outside of the neighborhood too! What if someone followed the truck in? What if the person who drove the truck is the one who threw the brick? There's no guarantee it was a Ginger East resident. Not a real resident, anyway. I swear it's those Avery kids.

Kate talks about how a producer reached out to her online about collaborating. She does not talk about Maree or the video. In fact, she's doing Olympic-level circles trying to pretend it didn't happen. It's wild to see in real life. When I say, "By the way, I emailed Maree's people about the video. Did I tell you? I can't remember if you said you tried the PR email or not too—" she cuts me off.

With a roll of her eyes she says, "Yeah, ugh. But the producer . . ."

Now I'm hearing about how she claims this producer heard a snippet of that Sol Cousins mix she did and asked to work with her. He'd provide a vocalist if she was down to mix the beats. "I guess some people still listen to Sol, huh?" she says real quietly because, like I said, it's embarrassing to be a Sol fan now. His last album was such trash that even local stations stopped playing it.

"Speaking of Sol and all that," she continues. "The principal—you wouldn't believe how he asked me again!"

"Asked what again?"

"The principal," she tells me. "Remember? He keeps trying to get me to DJ the football game, and I had to tell him I legit one thousand percent dead-ass cannot. I said, 'Bro, I have a mixtape to work on. Sorry.' Well, I didn't say 'bro,' but you get it," she tells me as the bus cruises over a pothole. Both she and I bounce out of our seats a bit, and I have to grab my book bag to stop it from slipping off my lap. It's also keeping my legs warm. I wore tights that are a bit too thin, underneath an oversized sweater. There's nothing underneath my sweater but my bra, so I'm trying to pretend I'm not cold. I'm also very conscious of how often I have to readjust it.

I smile and shrug. "Yeah. He tried it."

She nods and turns to gaze out the window, pressing her forehead against the glass as the road rushes by. "He backed up so fast after that. I'm just happy he's not gonna bother me about it anymore," she says. I almost don't hear it because her face is so close to the glass.

Maybe he gave up because he knew about the vandalism thing. The principal's got everyone's record—he *must* know where we're all from. He must know about Ginger East.

She turns from the glass to look at me. "So are you still trying to figure out who bricked the store or what?" she asks with a sly smile. "How's that been going?"

I swallow, nervousness threatening to murder me in my sleep. "Uh, it's—it's whatever. I haven't found anything."

"What?" She frowns. "Are you serious? Someone has to have seen something, right?"

"Yeah, I don't know."

"You don't know?" She chuckles. "What's wrong with you? You told me two days tops, remember?"

"Maybe I was a little optimistic," I tell her, and she nods heavily, like yeah, maybe. I feel a type of way about her agreeing so easily. What's wrong with optimism? "Whatever. I'll figure it out soon. Don't worry."

Her eyes flash with resolve as she forces a tight smile at me. "Okay," she utters. Sometimes I forget that this must be affecting Kate in a different way. Ginger East belongs to both of us. That gnawing feeling of betrayal comes back when I think of how someone could do this to the store. And the thought that Kate could be moving because of it? Even worse.

She shifts a little so she's staring straight ahead, and a blank expression comes over her. We're both hurting in different ways. I need a bit more time, and then I know I can find something else. Honestly, maybe I'm playing myself, but I need to know that I can fix something, anything. This is all I have right now.

This, and the protest.

So I say, "Join the silent protest with me?" and wait for her to agree. She's been so adamant, asking me about the brick, so I don't expect the hesitation. She lifts her eyebrows and blinks once, twice, and I assume that means no. "Come on. It'll be cool. Mr. Brown is running it and we have a meeting tomorrow."

Kate grimaces. "Like I said, social justice is your thing. I think I'm good."

"Wow, rude."

My phone pings. It better not be another random message about that rant video. Those messages have died down a little, thankfully. People I don't know at school still call out "The Feds!" when they see me, and try to act overly familiar. But still, there's no way it can be another producer asking for an interview. Instead, it's a—message from Rafa?

"What the hell?" I croak.

That's Kate's cue to reach for my phone. She does it so

often that I'm prepared and know exactly how to fend her off. When she dives for it, I shift so her hand digs into my bag instead. "Let me see," she whines, as if I have any reason to give her my phone in the first place. "Let me see, let me see. Who is it? Someone else asking for an interview?"

"It's n-no one," I say. Honestly, why's Rafa messaging me? I know he's sitting a few rows behind us with those soccer guys, so maybe he's just trying to get a rise out of me. Maybe Marcus took his phone and is sending stupid things through Rafa's profile because he knows I'll open it. I don't even know why he'd think that, because Rafa and I aren't cool like that.

Kate is growling.

"Stop that, damn," I say, and she backs down. "I'll show you but don't say anything."

She grins. "Yes, oh my God. Who is it, who?"

I wait a moment before spinning my phone around to show her my lock screen, where it says: *Raf Morales sent you a message.*

Kate frowns. "Girl, why don't you have message previews on?"

"Uh, because I don't want to?"

"Can you just turn them on? How's this even supposed to be news?" she says, kicking me lightly in the ankle. "And why's he messaging you, anyway?" She sits a bit taller and glances over her shoulder, over the back of the seat, to where the soccer guys are sitting. All it takes is one long whistle from those guys for her to spin around and sit back down, her face burning a bright pink. I shrink into myself, slipping down further in my seat. No way I'm going to turn around too.

I glance at her and say, "They're so ugly," in solidarity.

"No, they're not," she hisses back. "That's the problem."

We both divert to my screen while I swipe open my phone and read Rafa's message. He added me on Messenger a million years ago but he's never messaged me. Honestly, he probably added me out of obligation. I've never even seen his profile picture before, but it's exactly how I imagined it would be: Rafa on the soccer field, his hair damp with sweat, while he's leaning forward, hands grasping his knees, and he's staring off into the distance. He has—uh—grown

"No offense, but he's kinda hot now," Kate whispers.

I'm too choked up to agree or disagree, so I click on his message and hope my melanin is strong enough to mask the tinge of red rising in my cheeks. The message says: *did you see the video???*

Kate leans closer to my phone. I don't know if she does it because she's pretending to have forgotten about the video or because she's trying to read the message better. I nudge her away and respond as best I can with Kate leering over me: *yeah. fuck maree.*

The corner of Kate's lip twitches, which looks kind of like a smile. She settles back into her side of the seat and doesn't talk, doesn't say anything else until we reach school.

CHAPTER SIXTEEN

Rafa adds me to a Messenger group chat at lunch. When I get the notification, I'm more confused than anything else. First thing he does is sit two tables away from us in the cafeteria. Who does that? He should just come sit with us or whatever. Then he gets out his phone and stares at me, and when I look away, he starts texting me. Kate waves, and he waves back. He waves at me, but I'm too offended by him sitting two tables away—at an *empty table*—when he could come sit with us at our otherwise empty table. And then this new group chat starts blowing up? What?

Kate KK Tran has joined the conversation.

Chinelo Sondra has joined the conversation.

Raf Morales: nelo, your last name is sondra??
Chinelo Sondra: nooo middle name
Raf Morales: its cool it suits you
Chinelo Sondra: okkkk

Kate KK Tran: why are we in a secret chat??

Raf Morales: who says its secret? its regular

Kate KK Tran: what's this abot?

Kate KK Tran: about*

Raf Morales: didnt you see the maree vid?

Kate takes a deep breath while she reads. She had to have known that's what this was about, right? When's the last time Rafa ever said two words to her? And suddenly Maree drops the most shameless video of all time, and he's talking to us? What else did she think?

I rush to reply.

Chinelo Sondra: like i said, fuck maree.

Raf Morales: thats what i said! why's she acting like she knows anything anymore?

Chinelo Sondra: it's what she does. she says what she says for views and that's it.

Raf Morales: has she always been this fucking waste??

Chinelo Sondra: LOL i don't know!! didn't you used to like her? you tell me

Raf Morales: w o w

Chinelo Sondra: pretending like you don't know her when your girl was out here like this from the beginning

Raf Morales: UM whose girl?

Chinelo Sondra: your*

Raf Morales: shut

Raf Morales: up

Kate KK Tran: do we have to talk about this? she's just doing her

Kate KK Tran: it's whatever

Rafa and I lock eyes with each other across the tables. He's squinting, confused, and mouths a "What?" at me. I know— why's Kate acting all distant? I want to tell him to drop it, but Kate is close enough to me that she'll see me switch into another chat. He tips his head to the side and nods toward her. I give a swift shake of my head, fast enough so he knows what's up but that Kate won't notice, and let my eyes fall back to my phone.

A few seconds later, another message from Rafa comes through.

Raf Morales: what you guys normally do after school?

Raf Morales: watch nelo's Hive Man debut?

Chinelo Sondra: please!! i need that scrubbed off the internet

Kate KK Tran: Nelo is getting interview requests, she's a mini-Maree now

Chinelo Sondra: are you trying to insult me???

Kate KK Tran: plus she's doing a neighborhood protest, so she's so busy these days

Chinelo Sondra: pleeeeease shut up lol! my first protest meeting is tomorrow. it's not like i'm busy all the time.

Raf Morales: so from the times nelo wasn't famous, you guys normally just hang out?

Raf Morales: with food from Kate's mom?

Kate KK Tran: !!!

Kate KK Tran: who told you?

Raf Morales: nelo had fifteen wraps last time and wouldn't give me one

Raf Morales: still petty as fuck

Chinelo Sondra: LOL shut your ass up!! i had ONE and it was MINE

Raf Morales: ok there babe

Raf Morales: @*Kate KK Tran* so can i come through or not?

Kate kicks me under the table, and I bite my tongue so I don't yelp out loud. She shifts closer to me while she whispers in a hoarse and ugly voice on purpose, "Why's he calling you 'babe'?"

I snicker at how annoying her pretend inconspicuous voice is. "Uh, I don't know." She narrows her eyes at me as if I'm lying. "I'm serious! I just started talking to him again, like, two days ago almost. And only because of what happened to you."

She gives a nervous laugh and turns away. "It's so weird that he knows about that. About the store."

"Well, everyone knows," I say like it's nothing. "It was on the news, remember?"

"And in your rant video too," she says, and winces. It's so

subtle that I almost feel I'm making it up. Does she not want anyone to know? I get that. Feeling as if everyone is in your business isn't fun, especially when it deals with your family. Maybe that's what's bothering her. She doesn't want anyone to know what happened to her parents' store—and me running my mouth online probably isn't helping, even if it wasn't me who posted the video in the first place.

Well, why can't she just *tell me* that? Why's she pretending to be okay when she really isn't?

Kate KK Tran: yeah come through!!
Kate KK Tran: it'll be like old times. almost.

Kate and I sit next to each other on the bus like normal later, and Rafa is somewhere in the back with his soccer friends. He doesn't text us or anything. After his friends leave, he comes to sit with us near the middle of the bus. "It's so bright up here," he jokes, and Kate flicks him on the forehead.

The bus lets us off where it normally does. Rafa stares around at the empty street in front and at the huge field behind us. It isn't until he sees Ginger Store across the street that his awe turns to concern. A lot must be different for him since he was last here, but seeing the store like this has to be the biggest shock of all. The store and its missing window.

"Let's go," Kate says immediately. She tugs at my arm like

she's in a mad rush, but she's trying to laugh it off. Trying to be cool. "Rafa, you left before the Eats opened, right?" she asks. The Eats is a new old spot nestled between a low-rise that's been out of commission for a while and one of those new, bougie-ass coffee places. The Eats only came into being when we started high school two years ago, but the owner Jimmy is a local, so it feels as if it's been here for a long time.

"Yeah . . . ," Rafa murmurs, but he's not paying attention to us. Instead he crosses the street and heads straight for the boarded-up window.

Kate taps her foot impatiently. She's dying to get out of here. "The insurance is gonna deal with it," she calls to him, though he doesn't turn or stop at the sound of her voice. "It shouldn't look like that for much longer. Things will be better real soon."

I take a step forward, but Kate tugs me backward, her fingers swirling in my sweater. "We gotta cross anyway," I tell her as softly as I can. I hope she knows that I get it; I know why she doesn't want to go there. Hell, I don't want to go there either.

But she lets go of my arm, practically throws it, and scoffs. "Yeah, obviously," she snaps back. "I didn't say we weren't going to cross. I just said we should go because you know the Eats gets really busy after school." She shoves her hands into her pockets and rushes across the street to the main road.

Rafa watches her leave before he turns to me. I'm standing

beside him now, staring at the plywood, noticing how ugly it is up close. It's a mishmash of different wooden strips glued together. Ginger Store deserves better.

"Is she going to be okay?" he asks quietly.

I shrug. "I don't know. She's been choked up ever since the—the thing." I gesture loosely to the ugly plywood. "Everyone's on edge too."

He winces. "Bad time for a visit?"

"No," I say. "It's probably fine."

"Why's she trying to pretend as if nothing happened?" he asks. I didn't realize he could tell how fake she's being. I thought it was obvious to me because Kate's my best friend, but Rafa used to be her best friend too. It must be pretty easy to see.

I don't want to speak for her, so I just nod toward the Eats. Rafa follows silently. "Do you remember Jake?" I say after a few paces. "You haven't seen him in a minute, but he's mad tall."

A grin breaks Rafa's solemn mask, makes his eyes light up. He's always trying to be so tough, when we all know he really isn't. "What? No way he is."

"Yes way he is," I tell him, and hold up a hand beside him as high as I can get it. "He's taller than you now, obviously, because he's older."

"Mmm older, huh?" he teases.

"Shut up. I didn't mean it like that, damn." I never had a crush on Jake! What's Rafa's problem?

The Eats is packed and loud, but it's shaking with life and I love it. The sounds of oil hissing in the deep fryer, burgers sizzling on the grill, and Jimmy yelling orders to his staff fill the smoky air. Kate is right: it always gets really busy after school because almost all the neighborhood kids descend on it like it's giving away free burgers. Jimmy sometimes does. He lives two streets down from me, so he knows who might appreciate a free meal, but he's never shady about it. He'll ring it up like he's supposed to, and then say "Damn, looks like the computer's acting up again. This one's on the house." He thinks he's slick with it, but he's really not.

Kate is sitting at a table for four by the wall. She crosses her arms and legs, staring impatiently at us as we walk in. "Took you long enough," she says, and smirks. I can't tell if she's mad or not, but the second I smell the smoke from the grill in the back, I don't even care anymore. Let her be mad. Maybe Jimmy will give her a free burger.

"This place is insane," Rafa says, looking around. "You guys come here a lot?"

Kate nods. "Yeah. Jimmy's real cool."

"He's the only place around here that really seasons the fries," I add, and Kate nods frantically. "Other places only put the least bit of salt—"

"The least!" Kate choruses. "But Jimmy puts, like, actual seasoning. It's magic."

"I bet they're not as good as your mom's, though," Rafa says.

I have to pause and think of that time Mrs. Tran walked

into the kitchen with frozen fries and came out with what I assume was some witchcraft, because I've actually never again had fries that good. "Wait," I say, and Rafa laughs. "No, no, wait. Let me think."

"I could judge," he tells me. "But someone has to buy me food."

Kate snickers. "Are you serious? Shouldn't you be buying us food?"

"Why should I buy you anything? I don't even live here anymore," he teases. "You can't invite someone all the way to your house and not feed them. That's rude in my culture."

"You're rude."

"Wow."

"*I* kinda want a burger, though," I mumble, turning to scan the menu at the counter. Instead I lock eyes with Paco Velez. He's waiting for his order by the side with a group of his university crew, his eyes moving from the number in his hands, to the screen displaying numbers on the wall, to the TV, to me. He looks as if he's in a hurry.

Kate notices me staring and follows my gaze to Paco. She waves faster than I can. "Is that Paco? The one who used to play camp counselor for us?"

Rafa leans forward and squints. "Yeah, true, I think it is. He got so old."

"Are you dumb? He's only four years older than us," Kate says.

"I saw him that day, you know." The moment I say it, the moment it comes out of my mouth, I regret it. My mind skips back to the morning of the vandalism, the glass on the ground, the crying, the whispering, and Paco with his arms crossed, worried about safety. I was so pissed that I couldn't even listen to him speak. He looks at me again, and I let my eyes wander back to our table. It's way too shameful to say anything now. I feel so bad for blowing him off.

Rafa nods slowly. He knows enough of what I'm talking about, so he doesn't pry.

But then Kate says, "Maybe *he* threw the brick," and my breath catches in my throat. She shrugs when I glare at her. "What? It's possible, right?" And she turns to Rafa, a smug smile on her face. "Nelo is trying to figure out who would vandalize the store. She thinks it's an outsider." This girl is gunning for a smack.

Rafa narrows his eyes. "Actually?"

"Yeah," I say, as confidently as I can. "I mean, no one around here would do something like that. These are the people who live here," I go on, gesturing loosely to the growing lineup behind us, the groups of schoolkids waiting for their orders, and the farthest table from the door taken over by university students studying. "No one in here, no one who lives here, would ever . . . do that." Everyone in this room knows the produce truck schedule, though.

There used to be a different produce truck that came

down the main road. I remember it because its wheels had this ugly yellow tinge as they rolled down the street. One time Kate and I stood by the curb each with a pebble, trying to time our throws with the coarse steel bolts on the wheel. We thought we could hit them. We were eight, and a week before in the middle of the night, we had heard a loud, sharp, piercing sound. Like a pop. Someone said it was a firework, but it wasn't a holiday that day. Someone else said it sounded like a rock hitting a wheel, so every time the produce truck came by, we tried to re-create it.

I was so confident I knew what it was by the next time we met up at the park. That was when Paco was really into his day camps. It was the first of many and Bo was doing the most, as usual. "We're gonna be late," Bo said, huffing past us with his backpack. He'd packed too many things in his bag for one afternoon.

Kate and I rolled up last and joined a group of twenty other kids sitting cross-legged in the middle of the park. The grass was hot and sticky under our legs as we huddled together with our friends. Paco had said he'd teach us how to survive a fire. What did Paco even know about surviving a fire? We didn't care—he was older and wiser than us, so we trusted him. He was teaching us advanced stuff.

"Okay, so," Paco said, clearing his throat. "The first thing you have to know about fires is that they can happen anywhere, all the time. So you need to be ready."

Kate crawled up to where Rafa was sitting and began to pick at the grass with him. I stayed where I was, wondering how the light could change the color of his hair into a million different shades like that.

"It's really important to remember three things." Paco held up three fingers. "Stop. Drop. Roll."

Maree gasped and stage-whispered to us behind her, "We learned this in school already."

Kate snickered. "See? Let's go to the swings. Or I can go get my bike and tell Jake to take us to the bike path for older kids."

It was as though she had summoned him, because the second she mentioned his name, there he was, standing at the foot of the field, waving to us. Jake stood with his bike by the road, waiting for Kate to approach. We followed her, curious as to what had brought Jake here and away from his bike squad, and also why he looked so damn nervous.

He said, "Mom wants you to come home now."

"*All* of us?" Bo gasped, staring around.

"No, you nerd. Just Kate."

But Kate was really defiant even when she didn't need to be. She crossed her arms and pouted. "Why just me?"

"Because only your mom said you had to come back, genius," Jake told her. "Mom says it's not safe to be outside. Remember last week when everyone got woken up by that noise?"

"It was a rock," I piped up, proud of my contribution. "Me and Kate figured it out. Someone hit the produce truck."

Jake frowned, his brows twisting with annoyance. I had never seen Jake so annoyed till then. His hands gripped the bike handles harder as he shook his head. "It wasn't the produce truck. It was a gun."

It took me a while to understand what he meant, why he was so mad, why he carried Kate back home kicking and screaming. That night when Mom and Dad were watching the six o'clock news like always, I felt a shiver run through the room when the newscaster said a woman had been killed a week before in Ginger East. They showed her face on TV—Mrs. Jones, who ran the laundromat. Stores were closing here and there all the time, but seeing that CLOSED sign on the laundromat door was different. It felt eerie. Made me sick a little.

And now, sitting in the Eats and watching the news, the *breaking news,* flare across the TV on the wall, I'm reminded of that gunshot. Not because there's been another homicide, but because the reporter on TV is standing in the exact same spot where I was when I realized that Mrs. Jones, the laundromat, none of it was coming back.

"Turn it up," someone calls, and the volume on the TV rises steadily. And as it does, so does Maree's voice from the screen.

"What the *fuck* is she saying? What's she even doing here?" Kate snaps. Her voice is loud and brash and fiery. It's nothing but pure anger.

That same reporter who came to Ginger East that day is interviewing Maree. This segment must have been filmed earlier today, because we all walked by that place, and I guarantee, if Maree was really out here talking the level of smack I know she's about to, then we would've had words.

Maree's shoulders rise and fall, and her hair settles around them. "Yeah, that's why I thought this would be, you know, really important, for my friend and for the community. I couldn't stay quiet. See something, say something, right?"

The reporter nods as if she understands. "Exactly. Does it surprise you that this break-in happened in this particular neighborhood?"

Rafa groans. "Don't say it."

Maree touches her neck delicately before giving a shrug. "I mean, it was always like that when I was growing up, so I wouldn't say I'm surprised more than I am saddened that it's happened to someone I know."

"Your close friend, no less," the reporter adds, and Maree nods. Her close friend.

"She's really out here on TV . . . ," I mumble.

"We're setting up a FundRace," Maree cuts in before the reporter can wrap up the segment. "Um, if you go to my website MareeAntoinette.com, you can read more about the tragedy at Ginger East and help by donating. Please, we need as many people as we can get. This sort of thing can't happen to anyone else—"

Kate gets to her feet, her chair scratching against the floor tile. People stop and stare sympathetically at Kate because they know. We all do. There's no emotion behind her eyes, and her lips are pulled into a tight, tight line. They tremble, even though she's pursing them hard, trying to get them to stop. Suddenly she grabs for her bag and darts out of the restaurant without a second's notice. The air is full with the door chimes clanging against one another, and then nothing else.

And I am—shocked, I'm just shocked. And regretful.

It could have been me on TV. It should have been. Maybe if I had agreed to do the interview back when I got that email, Maree wouldn't be on TV spouting all these lies about Ginger East. I wouldn't have to sit among people I know, people I grew up with, and see the disappointment in their faces when someone else who willfully refuses to get it has the first chance to speak. Except the first chance was mine, and I let it go. Imagine: people watching the news could've had the real story if I'd just said yes. People out there would know the truth about life in here.

CHAPTER SEVENTEEN

Mr. Brown's house is stuffy. It's neat and organized, and everything has its place, but the air is still thick and clammy. Mr. Brown doesn't smoke or anything like that, but as he guides me through the front hall to his cramped dining room with posters and notepads and stickers all over the place, I can't help but think he should open a window.

There are six of us at his house on Tuesday afternoon, although I'm probably the only one who had to run here after school. Mr. Brown, myself, some people I don't know, and Paco. I can't escape him, and the way he looks at me makes me believe he's got something to say to me too. He watches as Mr. Brown gestures at everyone loosely as if that's an introduction. "This is the team," he tells me bluntly, and then he points to me, "This is Chinelo. You know, Janet's daughter."

I can't believe I'm still being introduced as Janet's daughter. "Hi," I say with a small wave.

"Welcome," Paco speaks up. He returns my awkward wave with an awkward smile. I don't know where to go from there. "I feel like we've been seeing a lot of you these days."

He's either talking about how he's probably been literally stalking me, or he's talking about the video. I didn't come here for that. This is the last place I want to hear about it, so I smile real polite and say, "You know I live a few houses down." He looks thoroughly unimpressed.

Mr. Brown smacks his thick hands together, and we all stand a bit straighter. "Back to business," he says, circling the table. There's a large stack of untouched posters in the corner that he pushes to the center of his rickety wooden table. "We're gaining some momentum. These days, I see most of the posters are staying up rather than being on the ground."

An older woman in the corner chuckles. I've seen her before leaving the nail salon, but I don't know her name. When she touches her neck, her gold-and-red shellacked nails practically blind me. "So we do more postering?" she asks.

"We could also go door-to-door," Paco pipes up. He's got that same authoritative thing going on from when we were kids. "See what people think of where their property tax is going." He snorts at this, sharing knowing looks with some of the other volunteers. I must look confused, because when his eyes land on me, he rushes to explain, "It feeds into neighborhood security. So, if everyone's rent is going up, if people are being priced out, it's essentially to make room for all this new shiny stuff."

"Gentrification," I say, remembering the news, the textbooks filled with diagrams, the conversations—lectures from my parents. Paco nods, smiling at my admission. "Displacing people . . . seems like a common tactic."

"Exactly," he says, his smile growing into a grin. "That's why we need to go door-to-door. I think it'd be better to hear from people directly, you know? Get a good idea on how many people will come out for the protest."

Mr. Brown grunts. "A lot of people will."

"I mean, yeah," a middle-aged man cuts in. "But there might be some people who aren't exactly fond of us. Paco would know."

My voice mixes with Mr. Brown's: "What do you mean?" Mr. Brown's eyes land on Paco with vigor. Paco must not be afraid of Mr. Brown like most people. He doesn't even flinch.

"I was talking to Jimmy, right, from the Eats—"

I gasp. *"Jimmy's* a snake? He doesn't care about the protest?"

"N-no, no," Paco says with a stifled chuckle. "But some guy overheard me. I think it was Clyde or Craig—some guy who lives behind Ginger Way—and he said it's too much hassle to protest. Asked why we're even bothering, Spice of Life isn't that bad, they're even giving out discount coupons for their grand opening. You know, stuff like that. Plus, now that we're getting one, doesn't that mean this is finally a developing neighborhood, and whatever else. But the thing is, I wasn't even talking to the guy. Every time I'd say something to Jimmy, he'd pop off."

Hearing about Clyde or Craig or whoever reminds me of what Jake said that day we were waiting for the inspector— some people are actually *cool* with Spice of Life being here. They're cool with the neighborhood changing; they're cool with the businesses closing? What if there really are more people like Clyde-Craig out there?

"How old was he?" I spit out, as if it makes a difference. Some of the older generation really love this place the way Mr. Brown does, but some kids like me don't really care as much as they should.

"Why does that matter?" Mr. Brown grunts.

"Uh—"

"You think if he's old, that's just an old way of think-ing, but I'll tell you, things don't die out with age. They just evolve," Mr. Brown says.

Wow, why is he chewing me out right now? I asked *one* question. "I agree with Paco," I say. "If you guys haven't been doing door-to-door, then maybe you should."

"But what about reach?" a woman speaks up. "Door-to-door ensures we only speak to one person at a time. That's no good."

"I don't know. I'm with Nelo," Paco says, and then glances at me. "Plus, she'd know a thing or two about how to get people's attention."

Oh my God.

"What?" Mr. Brown asks, and then he glares at me. I

didn't even say anything! And I'm definitely not going to now, damn.

"She was on—you were on Hive Man, right? Hive Man Clips. It's, uh, a website where they post these funny, viral videos," Paco explains. "The day Ginger Store got smashed, she was in this video talking about how it's unfair people paint communities like ours in a bad light because of one incident. It went crazy viral—almost five hundred thousand views on Hive Man alone. Who knows where else it ended up?"

I groan. "Yeah, who knows?"

"It's perfect, though. We can leverage that. Maybe you could do a promo for us on TV."

I am poised to say yes right away because of what happened the last time I said no. Thinking about Maree on that news program talking all that shit about Ginger East and setting up a FundRace for something she probably doesn't even care about makes me mad. So I say, "I think we should do a fundraiser too," with so much conviction that it almost hurts. Mr Brown shakes his head right away. I'm glaring at him before I realize it. "Well, why not?" I ask.

"Don't mistake the two," Mr. Brown chides. "What we need now—what Ginger East needs now is not money. It's community. It's a way to rebuild the community."

"Exactly! Which is why this has less to do with my video," I say, "and more to do with what we can do for others. We should do the fundraiser—"

"No."

"Oh my God, Mr.—"

"No."

"Mr. Brown, you're so old-school—"

"No."

From the corner of the room, I can hear Paco chuckling, and it makes me want to disappear. "Fine," I say, crossing my arms. "No fundraiser."

"Good," Mr. Brown says, crossing his arms too. "We don't need our own version of that little blond girl."

Honestly, though, maybe we do.

CHAPTER EIGHTEEN

Paco was right. The video really did hit over five hundred thousand views. Wow, what even makes a video go viral? I haven't looked at it since that day, but I take my time watching it now to see if I can figure it out. It's pointless. People like what they like, and they chose to like this. I might not care, but it would be dumb of me to ignore it at this point.

Media has been swarming Ginger East ever since Maree's FundRace reached twenty thousand dollars. They probably just want to get a glimpse of the area where her hard-stolen money is going to make a difference—that is, if we ever see it. That's another story altogether. Dad always says it's common for nonprofits and organizations that are supposed to help people to ignore small communities except when it's convenient for them, and honestly, I see it. I'm seeing it more the older I get. There's even a rumor the news might do an interview with Maree here, but I really hope not. I don't want to see her fake-ass highlights on any block. No, if they're going to interview anyone, it should be me. I live here; I know what's been going on.

Mom would never let me do an interview, but honestly, how would she even know? I click into one of my many emails from reporters and skim through the contents. *Hi, this is Dave with Channel 9. We know all about the tragedy at Ginger East and want an insider perspective. Would you be willing to do an interview with us for an evening news segment?* Dave no last name. I email back yes, and say that they should come here since I'm just sixteen, but also my mom says I can do the interview so they shouldn't worry. It takes an hour, but he gets back to me with an address, a time, and a quick: *See you tomorrow.* I grin.

"Chi-chi!"

Mom is obsessed with this new-wave minimalist movement and has been cleaning out our cupboards all day. By the time I make it to the living room, she has a bag of old jewelry for me to take to the pawnshop on the main road. "I'm going to get you something real special after," she says, and I'm praying it has nothing to do with an item that's supposed to go on my chest. Her eyes keep glancing out the window, and I know it's because it's getting darker and she's reconsidering making me walk all the way there.

"Take your bike," she tells me.

"Someone will steal it, easy," I say, and she frowns because, yeah, it's probably true.

She says, "What kind of place is it if someone will steal a child's bike if it's left out for two minutes? This place is

160

honestly becoming something else," and I immediately regret talking.

"No, no," I rush to correct myself. "I mean—okay, *maybe* someone will steal it, but it's not guaranteed someone will. People are unpredictable."

She frowns, tying the bag tightly in my hands. "Not people around here," she says, and steers me to the door. "Don't be on your phone when you walk. Come right back. I'm giving you fifteen minutes, and then I'll call someone."

I shrug her hands off me, annoyed that she's even thinking I might die between here and the intersection. "I'll be fine," I grunt, and make a show of clasping onto my phone, unlocking it, and scrolling. She scowls at it, but behind her anger is a very real fear that I can't really fight with.

My phone pings when I get to the intersection. I don't look at it because I can hear footsteps coming down the road, but it's dark, so it's none of my business. Maree is all "See something, say something," but if she knew anything, she'd remember that it's "See none, won't be none" in the nighttime around here. Unfortunately.

The footsteps belong to a woman walking quickly with her purse slung over her shoulder. We make eye contact and she gives a small, tired smile as she passes me down the street. Only when she has completely wandered off do I feel safe to check my phone. It's a message from Rafa. *is there food at your house?* is all it says. I laugh so hard, my voice echoing in the crisp night air.

Chinelo Sondra: are you coming to visit or??

Raf Morales: noo lol there's nothing but rice at my place and it reminded me of your house.

Chinelo Sondra: rude

Chinelo Sondra: i'm not even home. went to the pawnshop.

Raf Morales: still trying to figure out who bricked the store?

Chinelo Sondra: I mean, yeah. but i'm here for my mom

Raf Morales: cool cool cool

Chinelo Sondra: might ask the pawnshop people if they seen anything

Raf Morales: waste

Chinelo Sondra: w o w, ok

Raf Morales: if i were you, i'd ask someone on the streets. remember kenny and them?? they see everything

Raf Morales: if they're still alive

Raf Morales: RIP

Chinelo Sondra: lol stop!!

The pawnshop is located on a weird corner where one side leads into an alleyway that leads right into the liquor store, and the other side stretches out onto the main road. The tacky neon signs are flashing, lighting up this desolate corner of the street. I can see shadowed figures hunched in the alley, passing things back and forth, shifting under the faulty streetlights. My hand clutches tight around the bag as I approach the figures. Maybe one of them knows Kenny—maybe one of them *is* Kenny. He had a pretty bad drinking problem, so sometimes he was good to talk to, but most of the time he was bad.

The thought crosses my mind that this, coming up to strangers in the dark, is the stupidest thing I've ever done, but the more I get a good look at the figures, the less apprehensive I feel. Because I know one of them. I recognize him.

His name is Calvin, and he is skinny with wide-set eyes and paper-thin lips. I stand two feet away from him, unsure if I should get any closer. The jewelry clangs together in the bag tied to my wrist.

The clanging is enough for him to fully move into the light. He pushes his black hood off his head and sticks his face, sallow and drained of color, out into the light so he can see more of me and I can see more of him. His eyes drag across my face at a pace slower than I ever thought possible, but soon his silent inquisition turns into a welcoming, familiar smile. "Yo . . . ," he drawls. "Nelo? 'Honestly, and don't tell anyone, but this sounds like the Feds' . . . right?"

Is he fucking serious?

"Is that her?" someone down the alley calls, and Calvin chuckles, nodding down the row. "Yo . . ."

"You guys have all seen that?" I mumble, trying hard to hide my irritation.

"Bro, of course." Calvin turns back and smiles toothily at me, the kind I remember from when we were younger. He's

Jake's friend—or used to be, anyway, back when they were church-going bros. Jake quit going to the Vietnamese church after high school, but Calvin quit way earlier. He stopped hanging around with Jake right before high school and fell into the wrong crowd. Calvin used to be so cool too! We used to memorize songs together, each of us rapping lines back and forth. Man, we really used to be close. Now, looking at his slim, almost emaciated figure in the dark, it's so weird to even think this is someone I used to know.

I crack the smallest smile and nod. "MC Calvin," I say, and he laughs, loud and high-pitched as always. "How've you been?"

"It is what it is. Can't complain," he says, and chortles. As I look down the dingy alleyway, I wish he would. "Got change for a twenty?"

I shake my head. "No, sorry, fam. You know how it's been with rent going up around here."

His laugh fades to a bittersweet smile. "Don't worry, I got you. Shouldn't have asked."

"It's all good."

"You still talk to Jake and them?" he asks.

"No" is on the tip of my tongue because I haven't really said much of anything to Kate since we saw that news report about Maree the other day, but I can't lie. "We're still friends," I say. Best friends, even. And she might be leaving.

"Man," he sighs. "That's good, that's good. Jake was my

best bro. I seen what happened to the store, man. I seen your video too. That's crazy—your video—but what happened to the store is fucked. Can't believe someone would do that. That store is life out here."

I smile and nod, overcome with this strange happiness at hearing Calvin say that. Lately I've been feeling as if I can't say anything about the store without thinking about the brick or the produce truck, or if it's someone from around here who trashed the place. I don't want to think those things. Ginger Store is home for me, and I don't want to think of someone from around here vandalizing it. "Exactly," I say. "Police are useless. I want to figure out who smashed the window, but I—I don't know—I can't imagine it being a guy from here. I don't want to."

"That's because it ain't some guy," he corrects. "It's some *boy*. At least, that's what we've been hearing out here."

My heart falls again. No, no, this can't be. "Are you sure?" I ask, timid. "There isn't anything else people have been saying? Anything . . . at all?"

Calvin rolls his shoulders and stands straighter until we're standing eye to eye. He leans against the brick wall for support, and I try not to notice. "So this is what it is: People are saying it's a young guy, you know. Some are saying it's those two kids, those blond boys. I think their last name is Avery? Anyway, their mom buys a lot of coffee, and I think it's because she works nights. I see her sometimes, you know, just out here. Reggie's seen her too. And who's watching those kids if she's out working? Definitely not their dad." He sniffs and glances over his shoulder.

"How do you know all this?"

He shrugs. "Networking."

"*Tch*, okay."

"There's this guy . . . Ah, damn, you know him, you definitely know him," he goes on, scratching his head. "What's his name?"

"I don't know. Who?"

He groans and pauses for a second, as if he's listening to a voice in his head that has the answer. "Uh . . . snap, I forgot his name," he says. "But he's, like, he's tall. He's black. Got an accent. Owns a . . . a shop on the road."

"Fam, you know you just described, like, half of the business owners around here."

He groans again. "Okay, well, you definitely know this guy. They say he went jogging. First of all, I don't know what kind of Ginger East man goes jogging in the dead of night, but it's weird, right? So this guy's jogging, and I hear he saw someone move behind Ginger Store's building just as he was coming around the corner. A shorter figure, *definitely* someone young. He called twice but no one came out. And then he split because he must've realized it's stupid as hell to call someone out in the dark around here. That's like asking to get jumped." He scoffs and fidgets with his hoodie.

We're silent. I'm taking in everything Calvin said, and he is staring expectantly at me, rocking from foot to foot against the wall. I don't know what's worse: thinking it was a guy, someone older and wiser, who did this, or thinking it's a kid, someone younger than me. But this all but proves it was one of those Avery boys, and if that's true, then I'm still right! They haven't lived here long enough. They don't care about the community like the rest of us—of course they'd pull some shit like this.

"Your video on Hive Man spread so fast." Calvin's voice cuts through my thoughts. "I know tons of guys who are on it all the time. Like Reggie back here."

I don't want to think of a bunch of guys watching that video repeatedly, but I nod and force a smile anyway. "Yeah. It's mad. I'm getting so much attention off it."

"Like that blond girl," Calvin says, and my mouth fills with a sour, sick bitterness.

"No, not like that blond girl," I grumble. I'm different from her. No way am I anything like Maree I don't exploit people. She's on a media crusade trying to reinforce her connection to the neighborhood. I think about how wrong she is, how much she's getting wrong—and how that storefront glass felt under my feet as I crept up on Ginger Store that morning. She wasn't there; she doesn't know. But I do. "I'm doing an interview tomorrow morning. I joined the protest group too, you know. I actually—I mean, I really care . . ."

A smile creaks out past his dry lips. "Yeah, I know. Look at me. I know."

"Thanks, Calvin," I say, more genuinely this time.

He grins. "No problem. Change for a ten, then?"

I take the bag tied around my wrist and pry it open before fishing out a small gold necklace amid rings and earrings. His eyes glimmer in the night as he watches it. "Mom wanted me to pawn this, but I can just pretend I lost it somewhere," I say.

He stretches out his hand and swipes it from me the second I present it to him. "You're a good kid, Nelo," he says. "Tell Jake I said hi, okay? And that I'm sorry."

"Yeah," I say. I don't bother asking what he's sorry about.

CHAPTER NINETEEN

There are silent-protest posters on the sides and front of every building, but the one place you'd never find one is in front of Ginger Store. That's how you know it's for the community. Ginger Store is a poster-free zone out of respect. It's only been over a week since the incident. Now the entire neighborhood is covered in new, colorful posters. They're on buildings and are being mailed to houses. I see them everywhere. The logo, the stark black border, the huge red and white words in bold across the page: GRAND OPENING! COME TO SPICE OF LIFE. NEW IN GINGER EAST. That's why it's so shocking when the Spice of Life poster goes up over what's left of the Ginger Store storefront.

The posters cover the entire plywood board where the window used to be, and it's not just one or two either. There are seventeen, eighteen. From corner to corner, edge to edge. I stare at them, hitching my bag further up my back. Something about these posters reminds me of a virus. There's more and more of them every day. I reach out and swipe at one in the middle, and peel it from the plywood. There's another one, slightly faded, underneath from the day before.

"You don't want that as a background?"

Dave from Channel 9 still hasn't told me his last name, but he shows up bright and early in the morning before the school bus comes. I don't tell him that I'm contemplating ditching school today. This was the best time to have the interview, and I left early like normal so Mom wouldn't get suspicious. It's foolproof.

"Let's try a different background, maybe?" I ask.

He shakes his head, eyeing Ginger Store with a twisted look in his eyes. "No, it has to be this one." Of course it does.

His cameraman is setting up the shot a few paces away, checking for the best lighting and the most optimal view while Dave marches over to me. "So . . ." He straightens out his collar. He's taking a long time to start speaking, and it's making me anxious, so I start smoothing out my sweater and adjusting my clothes too. He watches me. For a second, I'm frozen under his beady eyes and I don't know what to do. "You can't say anything accusatory, got it?" he warns, and that's when I realize what that look means. It's a warning. He's reminding me that I'm from here and he's from out there, and out there will always be better.

"I know that," I grumble in response.

"This is airing twice today, noon and six, since it's pretty timely stuff," he goes on, squinting over my head. "I'll prep you before the interview. There will only be two questions. You have to answer like normal. No swearing either."

Fucking obviously. "Yeah, okay."

"Or three. Maybe we'll do three questions. Hold on." He turns and brings out his notes, and flips through the small notepad pages until he finds what he's looking for. "Yeah, let's do three. It's not live or anything, but I don't want to be here all day. I assume you have school as well."

I nod, and that's good enough for him. Honestly, I'll only go to school today if Kate does, but I don't think she is. I haven't seen her in a minute. I texted her and asked what was up, but all she said was "family stuff" and told me she's fine. She's been brushing me off a lot ever since this whole thing happened. I don't really get why she's pushing me away like this. We're best friends. We've always been as close as family, so why would that change now? She should be joining the protest with me. We should be trying to fix our community.

Dave barely goes through the questions with me before he signals the cameraman to start filming. I am nervous, but I don't show it. Dave is smiling, but he really shouldn't be. It doesn't suit him. "We're here in Ginger East, home to the violent break-in that has left a neighborhood staple out of commission," he says. I zone out the moment he says "violent." I'm thinking about what I'm going to say. I think about the protest and people like Paco who care and people like Clyde-Craig who don't. I think about Mikey and about Calvin and my stupid video—but mostly about Kate and how she should be doing an interview like this too. About how she shouldn't have to leave her home because of something like this.

Dave places the microphone in my face just as I hear him

say, "We're here with Chinelo, who you might have seen from a popular viral video making the rounds. . . ." I blank for a second. *Don't look at the camera, don't look at the camera.* I am so focused on Dave's face that I'm sure I'm glaring at him. My forehead hurts.

"How has the break-in affected the community?" he asks me.

I don't break eye contact with him as I give my rehearsed answer: "The community is really different now. Most people feel a bit betrayed because, you know, Ginger Store is everything to us out here. It's kinda unfair that this had to happen in general, but it sucks even more that it happened to the store." My best friend's store.

Dave nods as if he gets it. "Of course. And what do you hope people who don't live here, who maybe don't really understand the gravity of the situation—what do you hope they take away from this tragedy?"

I take a deep breath and let my eyes flutter to the camera lens just once. "Um," I mumble. "Uh, that we're good people." My voice is sincere when I say it. I think about all the people who will listen to me and agree, and all the people who will listen and change the channel. I think about how those people probably all live next door to one another too. "We're good people, and this kind of thing can happen anywhere. It's not just about the store, you know. It's the community—I mean, it's about the community. That's—that's why we're having the silent protest."

Dave's eyebrows rise in mock shock as though we didn't

go over this a second ago. "What are people in the neighborhood protesting?"

"Change," I blurt out. "I grew up here my whole life and, I mean, y-yeah, bad things happen, but isn't that everywhere? People in the neighborhood are mad too. Well, most people. We don't want to be portrayed like this is a place where bad stuff always happens, because it isn't."

Dave nods for a second. Then he asks, "And how would the FundRace help people living in this part of the city? What would it mean to residents here?"

There it is—the big tie-in. How is Maree's work saving the neighborhood? How are charity dollars funding the underprivileged? Fuck that noise. This man does realize I'm the one who called him for an interview, right? He wouldn't have a story without me, and my story is not that Maree is fixing everything. My story is, I've lived here my whole life and I've never felt like a stranger till now. My story is, my family and my friends are being forced to leave a neighborhood they helped build, because they can't afford to live here anymore. My story is, my best friend could be leaving and I really, really don't want that to happen.

I make sure to enunciate every word as I tell him: "It would mean we are now a neighborhood that has had a FundRace set up for us."

CHAPTER TWENTY

I'm still thinking about the interview by the time Dave and the cameraman have packed up their van and left. I wonder which parts he'll use and which parts he'll cut together to make me more digestible. I wonder if the news segment will say anything about "the Feds." Honestly, they'd better not. That video is making me sick of myself.

Kate didn't text me again, so I make the executive decision not to go to school today. Instead I'm going to hang around the neighborhood. Anyone who would snitch on me is either at work (my mom) or holed up in their house (the Trans). I'm going to buy ice cream even though it's cold and nobody even sells the good Vita ice cream, go to the park, and swing as high as I can, and after that I'm going to Spice of Life.

Chinelo Sondra: yooo i'm gonna be on TV soon
Chinelo Sondra: also i'm off school today, but if anyone asks, you saw me around
Raf Morales: why?? on both counts

Chinelo Sondra: one because of the feds, and two just because

Raf Morales: want company??

I break into a warm smile. It feels as if Rafa's been talking to me a lot because of this whole Kate thing, but I think the real reason is because he secretly misses hanging out with me. Honestly, I think I miss hanging out with him too. We were almost like best friends for so long, and it's hard to throw that away. He might have his annoying soccer friends now, including Marcus, who is definitely the worst boy ever, but it's different with us. We have real history.

Chinelo Sondra: yeah come through, bring me some snacks

I text Kate: *don't know if you saw the chat, but i'm around if you need anything.*

She replies almost instantly: *yeah cool. thanks.*

Mad suspicious! So you definitely saw the chat and just decided to ignore me? And when I tell you I'm around, all you say is "yeah cool"? What about a *sure, come through?* Or an *ok, see you soon?*

Can I even be mad at her? I want her to open up to me, but if she doesn't want to, then what can I do? I'm already nervous about her moving away, so I try not to get too in my feelings about her blowing me off. I can't help it, though. I can't call her out for being fake. It's none of my business, but at the same time, I don't think it's wrong of me to want to know what's going on. Her family has never kept secrets from me before. Don't I deserve to know too?

The school bus passes by, and the driver gives me a look like *You're really not getting on?* I shake my head and smile pleasantly. This bus driver isn't the type to park the bus and ask me about my home life. He gives me a look as if he's going to say something, but then quickly carries on. He doesn't care enough to talk to my parents or anything. Besides, it's not like I'm skipping school to do something illegal. I want to be around in case Kate needs anything or in case anything comes up with the protest planning. Just want to be around the neighborhood.

Rafa pings me and says he's nearby. That boy can't drive, and he sure as hell didn't get a ride all the way here, so I'm not sure what to look for. *meet me in front of the park,* I text him. *I wanna go to spice of life.*

Rafa doesn't text back, but I only have to wait ten minutes for him to show up. One of his cousins drops him off by Ginger Store. I recognize that cousin from when we were young. Thick, curly hair has been replaced with a close-shaved head and a five o'clock shadow. He waves at me a little, but even from where I am, it's hard to tell if I'm imagining it or not.

The first thing Rafa says when he steps up to me is: "You're gonna be on TV?"

I forgot that I even mentioned it. "Yeah. Because of that video, though, so it's not what you think," I say.

"The Feds?" he snickers. "They make you repeat it on TV, or what?"

I shake my head. "No way, fam. I talked a bit about the protest. And they asked me about the FundRace too."

"So you're organizing a protest now, huh?" he asks as we set off down the road.

I chuckle. "No way. I'm just helping out. It's been cool so far. People there really care about fixing stuff, you know? It's such a nice change, especially because outside of this place, people only care about Marce and her FundRace."

"Yeah, true," he agrees, but he doesn't sound that convinced. Maybe he doesn't see it like I do because he doesn't live here anymore. "But do you really think a protest will help?"

"Yes," I say right away. "It has to. Once everyone sees that there are people here who actually care, maybe other people will start to speak up too. Other people like those who saw the person who threw that brick, for example."

"You're serious about this."

"So serious."

"You expect whoever threw that brick to just present themselves to you at the protest?" he says, and snickers. "Tell me that's not what you mean."

I laugh. "Why'd you say it like that? Obviously it sounds stupid when you put it that way, damn."

We walk a few paces with nothing but my laughing to tide us over. It's nice how easy things are with Rafa. I'm tempted to reach for my phone and text Kate again, but I doubt she'd reply so soon. I don't know what hurts more: texting and waiting for a reply that may not come, or not texting because I know she won't respond.

"So where's this spice place?" Rafa asks, and I point farther down the road. "What? It's at the crack house?"

I snort. "No, not the crack house. . . . We don't even have a crack house."

"Anymore," he adds. "Remember when the old loans place used to be crazy busy in the nighttime and the police kept coming through to shut it down? They'd come maybe, like, five, six times a week."

"What?" I grimace and shake my head. "When was this? I don't remember the police coming through *that* often, especially for the loans place. It was never a crack house. Look, look." We walk by the house he's talking about, the one that used to be a cash loans place. It's a sandwich shop now, and a young, thin woman pops out wearing too-big heels. She gives Rafa a quick once-over, and I roll my eyes because it's so obvious she's checking him out, and he doesn't even notice. He's too busy staring at the shop sign. Boys, I swear.

"A sandwich shop?" he says plainly. "They turned the crack house into a sandwich shop?"

"It wasn't a crack house—"

"Crack sandwiches. Is that—is that *kale*?" He gravitates toward the window and presses his face against it, trying to peer as closely as he can at the counter without actually having to go in. The attendant inside is shocked but doesn't do anything. Just stares back.

I press my face against the glass too and look inside. Damn, this has to be the cleanest shop in Ginger East. No grime on the tiles, no dust in the corners. It's as though it was transplanted here from some other suburb.

Rafa peels himself from the window and smooths a hand through his hair. He looks over my head at the street, narrowing his eyes at the open stores, the passersby, the road signs. He says, "This place *changed*," and right then and there, I can feel those words in my stomach. I want to protest, but as I take a step back and really look around the street, I know what he means. The street is brighter, the business signs are on straight, and there's a popular coffee chain at the end of the road. Gourmet coffee? We don't need that, but it's still here. And with the shop comes gourmet coffee drinkers who demand cleaner streets, working traffic lights, and safety. They demand sandwiches with kale, even if that shop used to host illegal poker parties upstairs and—maybe—more than illegal dope cookers in the back. They demand security, and that costs money.

Gentrification. Displacing people. Property tax. All those things we talked about at the protest meeting.

"Rent's been going up, I think . . . ," I utter. I don't want to say it, but Rafa's my friend and I feel like I can trust him.

I always was able to. And he's from here, so he understands why my voice gets quiet when I talk about rent or why I can't keep eye contact and my hands get sweaty. He knows. Rent in Ginger East has always been a touchy subject. It brings out the differences, shows the cracks that supposedly divide us. When we were kids, we knew when someone's family was struggling with rent. We wouldn't see them outside and they wouldn't look us in the eye at school. We're all the same until one thing—one heavy, ugly thing—takes away our anonymity. It takes away the shield.

Rafa looks at me, his brows twisted with worry, and I give a measly shrug in response. My eyes are still skirting around him. "I've been seeing notices. Like, Mom's got one. Papa Tran had one about the house. They're going around."

"You guys are screwed, fam."

"Well, damn, tell me how you really feel," I say, frowning. "We'll probably be fine, though. It's gone up before."

"No, but this time, you have *this.*" He juts his lips at the sandwich shop, and I purposefully turn so I don't have to look at it. "Rent is going up because you guys suddenly have to pay for expensive sandwich shops and a—a spice store. And that crosswalk didn't exist before." He points to a striped walkway that crosses the street, with two huge yellow signs hanging above it, signaling for residents to cross there or else. No more watching the older kids play chicken in the summer.

"No way. It did exist before," I say, even though I don't remember if it did or if it didn't. I don't want there to be a new crosswalk that I didn't even notice. That will mean I haven't been paying attention.

"No, it's new," he replies coolly, and I'm a bit annoyed because no way it's new. I swear it's been here all along. "But it's not that deep, I guess. The same thing happens to every suburb. New people move in—new people who want organic everything and hate it when you don't speak English—and then the old people—the real people—can't afford to live here anymore. Everything changes."

I don't want to think of Ginger East as a place where everything changes. It's my home, and it's never gotten so new and shiny that I haven't ever been able to recognize it. That's impossible. I'll always recognize this place.

"Come on," I say, and reach for his hand. Our knuckles graze, and I retract my hand, shocked by the sudden hit of electricity. Rafa and I never used to hold hands, so I don't know why I thought . . . "Let's go. Spice of Life is at the end of the street." I look away completely when we pass the crosswalk.

When Rafa sees Spice of Life, he quickly snaps his fingers and says, "This used to be the block where the old couple died. Right?"

I nod and chuckle a little at how enthusiastic he sounds. "Yeah. What'd I tell you?"

"My mom used to be like, 'Why is this lady always giving you guys rum cake?' And I was like, 'I don't know, Ma. It's her culture. I'm not about to ask.'"

"Remember when Bo said you could get drunk off rum

cake?" I say. "And then my dad would sniff us to make sure we didn't eat too much of it?"

"Your dad used to offer us beer, but he was so self-righteous about us being drunk off cake."

I laugh, remembering how militant my dad got about this whole rum cake thing. How he would literally line us up and sniff the tops of our heads. "True, true!"

"Also, Bo was *always* lying. Why'd that boy lie so much?"

"That's what I'm saying!"

The building is open now, and it looks so different from the last time I saw it. There's a huge parking lot, which is just weird. Ginger East is mainly corner stores, and corner stores don't have huge parking lots like this. This one is expansive and has room for more than ten, twenty cars. The sliding doors work, and every now and then, they push and pull open to let more people in and out. And, man, are there ever people going in and out of this place. It's a steady stream.

I see the Avery brothers' mom, and I sneer at her, even though she doesn't know who I am. I almost want to smack her on account of her snotty-ass kids, especially after I saw them throwing stones at the store. They seem capable. If someone told me it was true right now, that they were the ones who bricked Ginger Store, I'd believe it.

The inside of Spice of Life is surreal. I've never been in a store this big around here, and I can't stop my jaw from dropping when we walk inside. Rafa snickers and touches my chin, sending my jaw right back up to where it belongs. He doesn't seem fazed by the size of it all, the rows of spices and fresh herbs. There's a small appliance section with blenders and grinders that have hefty price tags. TVs at every corner are flashing sales and advertisements too. I'm in awe a little, and I hate that I am.

Rafa clearly isn't. He stuffs his hands into his pockets and waltzes in, bypassing the greeter creeping by the doorway.

"H-hello!" the greeter spits out, nervously clutching a stack of flyers. She hands one to both of us before taking a deep breath. "Welcome to Spice of Life. Is this your first time shopping here?"

Rafa shrugs and defaults to me. I shrug too. I don't want to talk to this lady either.

"Well, g-good," she continues. She probably rehearsed this. "We have a sale on all spices in the South American section— thirty percent off until noon. We also have specials on Indian spices. Really good stuff. Indian spices are so flavorful. Have a look."

Rafa is strangely quiet, so I pipe up with a, "Cool. Thanks," and steer myself away from her. I take the flyer and fold it in half, and am getting ready to stash it on a shelf somewhere, when Rafa hands me his. "What do you want me to do with this?" I ask.

He shrugs again. "I don't know. Keep it for when I become famous or something. I'll sign it for you."

"What?" I snort. "You? Who's going to make you famous?"

He touches his hair so effortlessly, so cool. He's so annoying. "I'm going to get signed, obviously."

"Uh, and who's actually going to sign you?" I say. "I've seen you play, and ugh. Marcus even dribbles the ball better than you."

He laughs, all teeth. "Whatever. You know I'm good."

"No way."

"You're only saying that because you probably like Marcus—"

"Why d'you think I like *every* guy?" I ask, crossing my arms and leering at him. "You said the same thing about Jake too."

"Because I *know* you liked Jake," he says as though it's so obvious and I'm the one being stupid. "You always wanted to sit on his shoulders and get him to carry you everywhere."

"Because he was taller than I was!"

"Mmm, taller," he teases, and a jolt of frustration rushes through my chest.

I throw my arms up and groan. "Shut up, whatever, shut up! Let's just go," I say, and gesture down the aisle to the next. "Let's go check out Spanish spices or something. Get you reacquainted with the food of your people."

He snickers. "What? I'm not Spanish. I'm from Colombia."

"No, your *grandparents* are from Colombia. You were born in Rexdale."

He rolls his eyes and walks ahead of me like I'm not right.

Rexdale isn't even that bad! I've heard it's a nicer spot than Ginger East now, if "nicer" means cleaner and more accessible or whatever. They've had a Spice of Life for about a year.

I slip away in the opposite direction and wander through the aisles until I get to an intersection. A roundabout of spices. There's a rotating table that has flash sales. Rosemary and paprika are on sale for the next half hour.

Spice of Life has an African aisle, which makes me more excited than I'm willing to admit in public. It feels like betrayal almost, coming into this store and then daring to be excited about it. I'm betraying Ginger Store and the Trans. But it's not like they've really gone out of their way to tell me what's going on. What's Kate doing at home all the time? Why doesn't she ever call me? When's the store going to open back up? Will it ever?

The African aisle is aisle seventeen. It's strange because I didn't smell it coming. I know exactly what that aisle should smell like, and yet when I walk into it, it's so sterile and smells a lot more like curry than anything else. Lots of curry. Where's the burnt smell of dried crayfish or the spiciness of ground melon seeds? Where's the sickeningly sweet smell of Maggi? They've grouped the entire continent into one aisle, and it smells like nothing. I'm uneasy walking through, like someone's playing a sick joke on me and I'm waiting for the reveal. *Surprise—this isn't anything like Africa. It's just what we think you'd think it's like, based on, I don't know, half a documentary.*

I start thinking about my mom and her kitchen. And now

I'm thinking about Ginger Store again. At the store, I can turn the corner into the spice aisle, and my nose will tell me what I'm looking for. I can find bay leaves beside thyme, because they go together. Everything is in a couple. I don't have to think—I just know. But here, I let my finger trace the shelf, where every spice is in alphabetical order. It's so organized. It's so ugly.

A woman's low voice cuts through the quiet. She's toward the end of the aisle, and she eyes me momentarily before leaning in to whisper to her friend, another woman beside her. They're being shady as fuck near the ground pepper. Whenever I hear people trying to have a normal, private conversation, I hold my breath because I think it will help me listen better. So I do that and I wait, pretending I'm so interested in whatever spice is in front of me. Guinea pepper.

". . . great that it's here now," says the first one, the shadier of the two. Her slicked-back ponytail makes the edges of her face look hard and rough. She's shifting her weight back and forth to each leg nervously.

"I know, I know," the second woman says. "I know this is technically on the border, but it's closer than the other location. You just gotta . . ." And she clutches her bag under her arm super tight. They share a knowing look with one another. "You know?"

"Exactly," the first woman says, her voice lowering even further. She glances at me, and I have to keep my eyes steadily focused on the shelf in front of me so she doesn't notice me creeping. And then she says, "Did you hear they're trying to protest it? Typical. These kinds of people are always mad about something."

A cringe so unholy runs through my body, and I have to take a deep breath to stabilize myself. I guess I exhale too loudly, because suddenly these two women are looking at me, shocked and almost offended that I dared eavesdrop. And I am looking at them because they're fucking trash.

"These kinds of people"? What? You can't come into *my* neighborhood—into my *house*—and talk this kind of bullshit. My jaw is getting tighter under this clench that I can't shake, and I feel as if I might throw up or say something that I really shouldn't. So I just look at them. I don't know what else to do. I cock my head to the side and wait like *Oh, all of a sudden you don't have anything else to say?* And they're backing away like *Wow, we really should've just bought salt and dipped.*

The second woman nudges the first, and they both spin on their heels, and scramble out of the aisle without giving me another look.

The aisle feels so empty now, and all I can do is stare at the shelves lined with jars and canisters. I can hear that lady's words in my head, the way her tone changed, the sound of her whisper. When I think about it, I shiver and shudder and roll my shoulders and shrink into myself. That voice is so ugly. It's so ugly, I feel I'll never be able to forget it.

Rafa comes over with another flyer. He walks up behind me and slowly pushes the red and white ad into my line of vision. I jump and smack him in the arm because I'm nervous—he startled me on purpose—and also because I want to cry. I can't cry in front of Rafa again, but the more I listen to my own breathing and the emptier the air is around me, the more the heaviness in my chest grows. I'm not stupid. I know there are millions of people like that lady in the world, tons of people who look down on you because you're not like them, but she has no right to say those things here. No right, not in *my* neighborhood.

Rafa wrinkles his nose, confused. He eyes me slowly, his brown eyes drawing over every line of my face, and suddenly I'm aware that I must be frowning really hard, because he looks concerned. "What's wrong?" he asks. "Is this about the Rexdale thing?"

"No," I say. No, just no.

I can't form any more words, and he doesn't push it. He looks at me again, and I look away because why is he looking at me like that, like he's trying to read me? His eyes are so intense. He must know something's off, because the next thing I know, he's stashing the flyer on the shelf and sighing loudly. "Cool. Can we go now? What are we even doing in here anyway?"

"Yeah, right." I shrug and say with more conviction, "Yeah, fuck this place. Trying to sell me curry for four dollars a pound. So waste."

I follow Rafa back outside, past the overeager greeter at the entrance, and back into the Ginger East air. Rafa won't stop looking at me. He's pacing a bit, taking uneven steps up and down the curb, stopping every now and then to glance at me. I don't want to look at him, so I bring out my phone to see if Kate texted me. She didn't, and I knew she wouldn't, but I needed a distraction. A distraction from this store, from everything.

Rafa creeps up beside me. His clothes are tinged with the smell of a thousand spices. "Did Kate text you?" he asks.

I shake my head and spin my phone around to show him, even though I know he's looking over my shoulder anyway. "Nothing."

He gives me a look like *Oh, okay. Cool,* but I bet he's thinking something like *If you're best friends, then why isn't she talking to you?* Even if he's not thinking that, it's now what *I'm* thinking, and I'm so frustrated, I want to die. I sigh loudly and put my phone away. "Let's go find food," I say. "I need to eat my feelings."

Rafa chuckles and finally stops pacing. He comes up to me, and I'm reminded again how much taller he's gotten. How much he seems to have grown. "What feelings?" he asks.

"*My* feelings."

"About?"

Those stupid-ass women talking shit about the kinds of people who live here. Spice of Life selling organic sea salt like all sea salt didn't just organically come from the ocean. Maree

189

being annoying and pretending she knows anything about this place when she doesn't. Not enough people caring about the protest. Kate acting as though she doesn't know me anymore. Ginger Store being gone. This place looking different than I remember. "Life."

He cocks his head to the side. "Oh. I thought you were going to say 'about you.'"

This time, I smack him in the arm as hard as I can, and he jumps back, laughing. "You're so annoying!" I yell, but I'm laughing too. I'm thrown out of my sour mood, almost forgetting all about that stupid lady and her stupid friend, because all I can think of is Rafa. "See? This is why I can't go anywhere with you—"

"Well, where are you trying to go with me, huh?" he asks, stepping up to me again. "Like on a date, or?"

"Oh my God, shut up." I feel light-headed as the word "date" repeats over and over in my head. A *date*? Damn, why would he even say that? Oh my God, why would he *think* that? I'm groaning as I back away, rubbing my temples to calm down. It's not working. He's still laughing, because obviously this is so funny to him. I wish I could be literally anywhere else but here—anywhere but here, and not with Rafa, because now he thinks I want to date him. Or maybe with Rafa, but somewhere cool and neutral like a park or the movies. The movies are neutral. It's also a date spot.

Wait. Do I want to date Rafa?

"Okay, but I am hungry, though," he calls to me, bringing me back to reality. "Where should we go? What else is good around here? I don't even know anymore."

I stop backing away and am finally able to face him now that a safe distance of pretty much one million feet is between us. I try to shrug casually, but my shoulders are still shaking with laughter, nerves, all of the above. "Man, I don't know. I . . ."

He raises an eyebrow when I stop talking. Out of the corner of my eye, I see Bo—Bo?— rush out of a convenience store a building away. I know that's Bo—I might have only seen him once since he moved away, but there's no mistaking those loafers and tight khakis. Damn, he really hipstered it up.

Rafa follows my gaze across the street as Bo scampers to the nearest crosswalk. Rafa is not subtle at all because he calls in a snarky voice, "Is that Beethoven Junior?" and Bo stops dead in his tracks as if someone threw a shoe at him. He whips around, trying to find the source of the voice— trying to figure out who here knows his full name. He really shouldn't have told it to us when we were young. No way we'd forget a name like that. He played himself.

When Bo finally spots Rafa, it takes him a minute to register who he is. He takes a few steps away from the crosswalk and toward us, squinting through his thick glasses. Maybe it's the shock of seeing me and Rafa together, or maybe it's the realization that he's been caught in Ginger East again on a school day, but he doubles back to the crosswalk and pretends he never saw us in the first place.

"Weird kid," Rafa says like it's the plainest fact ever, which it really is. The two of us exchange a look.

I manage to make it to the crosswalk before Bo bolts down the street, and tug softly on his ridiculously lush sweater. It feels seven layers thick. "Wow, how much did this cost?" I spit out, running my fingers over the fabric.

He shrugs my hand off. It's so slight that I barely feel his shoulder move under his sweater.

I frown. "Bo, actually?"

He glances my way, giving a hint of what I think is an apologetic smile. "Sorry. I'm kind of in a hurry."

"A hurry?"

He nods and then returns his full attention to the crosswalk light. He's focusing so hard that it feels as if he's silently willing it to change. Man, the second there's a crosswalk, no one wants to jaywalk anymore.

He's hiding something under his arm and has been holding it there since he ran out of that convenience store. I grab for it, but he turns and I catch his arm before I'm able to get it. "What's that, what's that?" I ask, tiptoeing around him to get a better look. He avoids me at all angles.

"It's nothing," he finally says. "It's just a book—it's mine."

"Well, obviously it's yours," I snort. "What book? Let me see."

"No."

"Why?"

"Because."

"Where're you going?"

"N-nowhere."

"Bro, you traveled all the way here to go nowhere?"

"I mean, it's none of your business," he retorts, a slight quiver in his voice. As soon as the light changes, he heads across the street, taking long strides without bothering to look back over his shoulder. He's so certain I won't follow him, even though I should. Even though I kind of want to.

He crosses the next street and beelines straight for Ginger Way. He's going to visit Kate.

CHAPTER TWENTY-ONE

Neither Kate nor Bo mentions anything in the chat about why the two of them are being really shady, hanging out together in secret. They're doing the most right now, and if I think about it any longer, I'll start feeling as though I'm some unwanted stepchild. They're acting like they're dating, but that's not possible. If they were, Kate would've told me.

Rafa gets a text from Marcus saying some of the soccer guys are playing for fun at a park near his house. We are standing side by side in front of the Eats as I watch the messages from Marcus come in one at a time. Rafa doesn't bother moving his phone this time.

Marcus: yo r u comin?? we hv 2 n 1 n need 1 mor
Marcus: wrr r u btw?? yo if u wr gunna skip thn u shuldve told me

I'm getting a headache. "In what world is *w-r-r* an abbreviation for 'where'?" I sigh. "Is this boy okay?"

"He's just very dedicated to his shorthand, that's all."

"Why are you friends with him?"

"What do you mean? He's not that bad," he says. I look in his eyes; he's completely serious. He really thinks Marcus isn't a crusty-ass gremlin. When I don't respond right away, he goes on, "Sometimes he's pretty cool. Like . . . uh, sometimes."

I chuckle. "That's not even convincing. You can't even name one time!"

"Why do I have to name one time?" he says, and laughs. "I said sometimes he can be cool, as in there are several times I thought he was semi-decent—"

"Semi-decent? That's enoughhh!" I can't stop laughing. He juts out his lip at me, and it makes me want to slap him, but I'm too busy gasping through chuckles. "If Marcus misses you so much, you can go. I don't mind."

"I don't wanna leave you, though," he says with a tilt of his head.

My throat dries with a last, strained laugh. "What are you talking about?" I gulp, a flurry of nerves attacking me slowly. They eat away at my good sense.

"Because you're by yourself . . . ? Right?" he tells me. Of course he just means he doesn't want to leave abruptly, but it's the way he says it. Why does he say things like that? "Unless you're gonna pull up on Bo or something."

"Tch, no," I scoff. "It's fine. I have tons of stuff to do, so it's cool if you have to go."

"Man, you know you don't have anything—"

"I have *tons* of stuff," I reiterate, pressing into every syllable and trying so hard not to smile. "Please leave."

He laughs and then reaches out for a fist bump. "See you at school," he says. I return it, my lips pursed tight. Only when his rideshare shows up and leaves do I let the wave of giddiness wash over me fully.

Rafa is right, though: I have nothing to do. I wait around the park until the school day ends, and go see Mr. Brown. Focusing on the protest will be better for me, anyway. Much more productive than trying to force my way back into my best friend's life.

By the time I leave Mr. Brown's house, I'm clutching twelve pamphlets and a clipboard to my chest, ready to ask residents if they want to learn more about the protest. Mr. Brown only printed fifty pamphlets because he didn't think many people would take any, so he split them unevenly among everyone and told us to get to work. "Get people to commit," he told us. "Tell them to come."

Paco grabs his stack and waits for me outside Mr. Brown's house. He offers a sheepish smile as I join him at the sidewalk, and he nods down the road, away from the intersection and deeper into the neighborhood. I had really wanted to spend the time alone, talking to people one-on-one, especially since I'm on Channel 9 today, but I've been feeling like I owe Paco an apology. The way he looks at me makes me feel like I do too, so I say, "Sorry about before," to appease him.

His face scrunches up. "For what?"

"For . . . before," I repeat, suddenly unsure what I'm talking about. "I think I may have cut you off or said something to you at—at Ginger Store that morning."

"I don't think so. You've been through a lot, so maybe you can't remember well," he says after a moment. I get it now: that look wasn't about me owing him an apology; it was about him feeling sorry for me.

I glance away. "It's whatever."

"I know I said some stuff . . . ," he goes on. "Listen, I didn't mean any disrespect when I said this place was unsafe. It's my home too. I grew up in these streets. But I *know* you remember the arcade. It wasn't that long ago. When that happened, we thought it'd be the end, but this, Ginger Store, is a different kind of hurt. It's someone's *house.* You know?" He even pauses a bit to gauge my reaction, search my face for some sort of acknowledgment.

But all I can say is, "Of course I remember the arcade," before my chest stings with weighted memories. My mouth is bitter with recollections of caution tape and police and screaming. People surrounding the doors, surrounding the windows, not letting us look inside. The crying went on forever, and then one day, it was done. The arcade closed. My friends left.

"Let's just hand these out," I tell him, waving my pile of pamphlets. "Let's split so we can cover more ground. I'll take this side and you take that side. Deal?"

He forces a stiff smile, and I know it's because he wants to talk more about the store and how everything is changing. He's so selfish. Why does he think I want to talk about how almost everything I'm used to is flipping around and turning into something I don't recognize? "I don't know," he tells me. "Let's go together instead. People might react better to a friendly face."

"What about my face isn't friendly?" I say, and he chuckles, shaking his head.

"I didn't mean it that way," he goes on. "I've talked to a lot of these people when we were trying to get participants out for that park cleanup. They'll recognize me. For the right reasons, anyway."

He chuckles again, and I get the faint inkling he thinks he's funny. I twist my lips into a frown on purpose. "Sounds like you're a hater."

"Come on," he says, and cuts across the road.

I follow as he approaches the first house. Inside, fast footsteps scuttle to the door when I knock, and I brace myself for who might be on the other side. Paco puffs out his chest, trying to appear bigger, more solid, than he is. He's no longer as clumsy and boyish as I remember him. He's much more like a man now, so mature with his own thoughts and everything. We used to be kids. I wonder for a second if he looks at me and still sees me the same. I wonder how easy it is for someone's feelings to change like that.

The door opens and a man who looks a lot younger in the face than he probably is blinks into the daylight. I force a smile, but it's Paco who speaks up. "Hey, good afternoon. I'm Paco and this is Nelo. We live around the corner there."

"Also on my social feed."

"Sorry?"

He sighs impatiently, eyes honing in on me. "I see your face maybe twice a day. It's ridiculous."

First my face isn't friendly, and now it's ridiculous? I try not to show how annoyed I am, but hearing it from someone who's essentially your neighbor hits differently. "So, um," I stutter as I pull out a pamphlet to give to him. He takes it reluctantly. "We're having a silent protest soon as a community initiative against the changes in the neighborhood."

He doesn't even blink. "What changes?"

Is he serious? Paco jumps in. "Uh. Well, for one, Ginger Store has been out of commission. Also, Spice of Life is infringing on local businesses. Sure, things have always been rough around here, but I think it's important that—"

"It's a free market," he cuts in, cocking his head to the side. "There's nothing much people can do about that, and I doubt a protest will actually help. Plus, no offense, shit like this always happens around here. You can't be protesting every five seconds."

This sour-ass man—is this Clyde-Craig?

I frown. "Uh, no offense to you either, but I don't really

think you should say that. . . ." He looks fully offended. "People out there say that kind of stuff all the time. How can you say the same things? You live here. You know what it's like. *They* don't. You should know better."

He breathes out heavily through his nostrils and takes a step back. "Right. Thanks for the info," he says, before he slams the door right in our faces. I almost want to kick his door back in. Is he kidding? What does he mean, he doesn't think a protest will help? Hasn't he ever heard of community?

"Okay," Paco says as we slump off the porch. "New plan: maybe let me handle the confrontational stuff."

I frown, glancing away. "I never said anything that wasn't true. How could he think that? Doesn't he see what's been happening?"

"Yeah, but . . ." He sighs, resigned. For a second, I'm grateful. I imagine Paco wanting to explain nuance to me, how people navigate disagreements, all of that, and I'm happy he doesn't lecture me. But on the other hand, I can tell he thinks I'm too young to understand, and I hate that even more. He continues down the road. "It's cool. Come on," he says.

The next house looks more pleasant, and when an older woman pulls open the door and smiles at us, I know this will be way easier than the other guy. Immediately I smile back and hand her a pamphlet. "Hi. I'm Nelo, this is Paco, and we—"

"I know who you are," she says, still smiling. "You"—she

points to Paco—"did that thing at the park with the kids, and you"—she turns to me—"I've seen you on the news more than once now."

I chuckle nervously. "Wh-what? More than once?"

"Well, you were giving an interview," she explains, gesturing back into her house, "and then I think you were in another video around here. Maybe at the intersection."

Ugh, the rant video. Can they even play that on TV? I suppress a groan and hand her a pamphlet—but quickly retract it when I realize I already gave her one. She smiles at my clumsiness. "Cool. Well, we're just here to tell you about the protest," I say.

"Mr. Brown from down the street is organizing it," Paco jumps in, nodding. "We're trying to get as many people to come out as possible. It's to help bring together the community and highlight some of the issues that residents are facing, like rent increases, safety issues, spikes in crime . . ."

Paco rambles on so easily, as if he's just been waiting to talk about what makes the neighborhood so scary. It's annoying.

"You know, this is a very good thing you people are doing. Very good," she says. In one swift movement, she reaches forward to touch my forearm. "And you, my dear, you're so— you're exactly what this place needs. Things have been falling apart, so it's nice to see young people who care enough to put it back together. It's our home, after all."

A genuine smile spreads across my lips. Wow, she *gets* it.

She knows why this sort of thing is important. "So you're coming?" I ask her. She starts nodding before I even finish talking. "All the details are in the pamphlet," I say. "And if you need anything, you know where to find me—er—us."

"I know. On TV." She laughs at that. "I'm only joking. I know you already—you're Janet's daughter."

When she shuts the door, Paco tries to high-five me, but I avoid him because that's too embarrassing right now. He grins. "That went pretty well," he says, following me to the next house. "Lucky she's a fan of your Hive Man clip."

I groan. "It's so weird that even old people are watching it."

"Awareness is everything," he goes on. "It doesn't matter who gets your message as long as they're getting it. The next step is action. It's a pretty simple model."

"There should be more action," I grumble. "Too much awareness feels, I don't know, counterproductive. If I know, and you know, and they know, then what's anyone doing about it? You know?"

He snorts. "You sound like this guy in my sociology class. He's way too idealistic."

I narrow my eyes at him. "Okay, but what's wrong with that?"

"It's naive."

Naive, again. I'm too this, too that, too childish, too naive, always.

"Sure," I grunt, and beeline for the next house without

waiting for him. If he only wanted to go door-to-door with me to make fun of me, I really wish he would've said so up front.

I head toward the third house and knock once before Paco joins me on the step. I'm ready to hand the pamphlet to whoever opens the door, but I'm not really prepared for the look of disgust and distaste I'm getting from this lady. She's younger-looking, and a small child is clinging to her leg. The kid is trying to push the door open wider, but the woman refuses to budge. "Hi," I utter, and hold out a pamphlet. She doesn't take it. "We're—"

"I know who you are," she says sharply.

Paco clears his throat as he glances at me. "Uh. Well, we're here to tell you a bit about a silent protest we're having in front of Spice of Life. It's a community-run effort trying to highlight the recent changes going on in the neighborhood."

"So is this another way you've decided to exploit us?" the woman asks.

Now it's my turn to look disgusted. "What?"

"You heard me," she goes on with a roll of her eyes. "You got tired of being on TV and you decided exploiting from within works best."

"Wh-what?" I'm so taken aback, I can hardly think. "Exploiting what? I—I mean, I was only on TV once and very recently—and only to talk about how horrible things have been—"

"Yes," she cuts in. "Just like everyone else talks about how horrible it is here. And so?"

"No, not like everyone else," I say, annoyed. "It's different."

"Because you live here?" She lets out a crass laugh that forces a shiver down my spine. It's so evil. "It didn't sound like you had much respect for this place in that—that video you posted—"

"I never posted that—"

"So you never posted it, but you seem to be doing well from it," she goes on. "In that Channel 9 interview this afternoon, talking as though we're better than accepting money that people are donating to us from the goodness of their hearts. You make us all sound like we're ungrateful—poor, ungrateful, all of us beggars."

"I didn't mean it like that," I tell her, trying to temper my voice. She rolls her eyes a million times over as if I'm lying. What's this lady's problem?

"Ma'am," Paco interrupts. "In all fairness, who's to even say the neighborhood will see any of that money? This sort of thing has happened before."

"Has it now?" she groans, snark dripping off her words. Quickly she snatches the pamphlet from the child and shoves it back into my hands. "I'm not going to this protest. It's a scam. If you people have nothing to do with your time, I hear that new spice store is hiring." And she shuts the door quietly with one resounding click.

CHAPTER TWENTY-TWO

Kate KK Tran has added **Bo Williams** to the chat.

Chinelo Sondra: wow of course

Bo Williams: of course what?

Chinelo Sondra: nothing

Bo Williams: you guys have a secret chat? since when?

Raf Morales: what about this seems like a secret to you???

Bo Williams: Rafa, that you in your pic? are you pro now?

Chinelo Sondra: oh my god don't say that, he's not even that good

Raf Morales: @Bo Williams not yet but give it half a year, trust

Raf Morales: @Chinelo Sondra you keep talkin that shit, i'm not giving you free tickets to any of my games in life ever

Chinelo Sondra: lol no one wants to see you fake injuries all up and down europe BYE

Raf Morales: wooooow so it's like that??

Bo Williams: uuuhhh do you guys need some privacy or?

Chinelo Sondra: ?? no??

Raf Morales: where's kate?

Bo Williams: i don't know

Chinelo Sondra: i dont know

Raf Morales: both of you dont know??

Chinelo Sondra: i've been doing street team stuff for the protest, so bo would have a better idea

Raf Morales: y'all live on the same street lol

Chinelo Sondra: i literally said i've been busy, rafael!!

Raf Morales: you're really out here like this after one interview lol

Chinelo Sondra: shut up lol!! this girl hasn't texted me since that day bo was here, so.

Bo Williams: sorry for blowing you off last time

Bo Williams: i promised i'd grab a book for mrs. tran since i saw it at the shop earlier

Chinelo Sondra: oh

Bo Williams: yeah

Bo Williams: but it wasn't that deep

Chinelo Sondra: seemed deep enough you bused all the way here for a book when amazon dot com exists

Bo Williams: well i was coming by anyway

Bo Williams: since kate called

Chinelo Sondra: called?

Bo Williams: yeah i was thinking you would come by too since you live so close

Chinelo Sondra: lol oh? is that why you ran from me at the crosswalk?

Raf Morales: bo it's like you're never at school

Bo Williams: you guys were skipping too

Raf Morales: true

Bo Williams: rafa, you don't live in g-east anymore do you?

Raf Morales: excuse????

Raf Morales: where the fuck is g-east?

Chinelo Sondra: LOL see! it's weird

Bo Williams: y'all are dumb

Bo Williams: that's what people call it around here. it's kinda cool

Raf Morales: it's dumb

Bo Williams: well maree calls it g-east

Raf Morales: whoa whoa wait who cares about this???

Chinelo Sondra: you watch her videos now @Bo Williams?

Bo Williams: no

Bo Williams: i mean i watched maybe tree

Bo Williams: three*

Bo Williams: saw her on tv the other day

Raf Morales: again?

Chinelo Sondra: about what?

Bo Williams: another interview for the fundrace and the neighborhood stuff. she keeps extending the goal because people are donating like mad

Raf Morales: has she talked to kate at all though?

Chinelo Sondra: doubtful

Bo Williams: kate hasn't mentioned it to me

Chinelo Sondra: wow okay

Chinelo Sondra: anyways

Bo Williams: nelo, are you doing any other interviews?

Chinelo Sondra: no way lol my mom almost booked it. she was like "why are you on TV?" and i had to convince her it was just clips from that rant that went viral so she wouldn't snap

Raf Morales: "we'd be a neighborhood that has a fundrace" is the best fuck you i've ever heard

Chinelo Sondra: LOL i didn't mean to say that! he was so bold, thinking we actually care about anything maree does

Bo Williams: i know eh? man, maree changed so much

Bo Williams: sometimes she puts on this accent and i'm like why are you talking like that?

Raf Morales: true

Chinelo Sondra: same!

Bo Williams: honestly she changed the most

Bo Williams: you're all pretty much the same as i remember you

Bo Williams: still rude as hell

Bo Williams: only maree is almost unrecognizable

Bo Williams: the way she talks, the way she looks

Kate KK Tran: www.youtube.com/E2Lw9YWLVts

Bo Williams: ???

Raf Morales: whats this?

Kate KK Tran: just watch it

I skip Maree's theme song, poking the progress bar impatiently until I see a still image of her newly highlighted hair. Actually, the more I look at it, the more it seems as if she got some ombré thing done. Either that or the lighting is playing tricks on me.

Maree looks to be in better spirits now. She smiles widely, bobbing her head back and forth to invisible music, and she can't help but giggle. "Hi, guys, hi!" she says with a wave. "I haven't made a real video in a minute, huh? Like, lately it's all been so depressing and about robbery and stuff. Give me some time, though. I have something *really cool* planned for you guys."

The video cuts to a close-up of her face where all she says is "really cool" in a low tone before it returns to a full shot of her and her lush hair, now modeled over her left shoulder. "So first of all, me and my friends want to say thank you for all your donations to the Ginger East FundRace to fight incidents of gang violence and just violence in general. It means so much to know I have some of the best, most thoughtful viewers out there, so a big thank-you to everyone who donated! Now on to the news . . ."

She takes a deep breath and breaks into a wide grin. "This video's called 'Surprise!' for a reason, y'all. There's been so much hype about the G-East situation, and people have been listening. Like, *legit* people. I've been talking to them and they want to partner with me to host a benefit concert to help raise awareness and more money for the cause. This is so dope for two reasons: one, because it's such an important cause that hasn't only affected my friend but others in the area, and two, because the only way we can get things to change is by reaching out to people in power who are willing to use their privilege for good. I'm so, so excited to announce more details for all my local fans. My fam." She laughs. "And if you're down to come, I think I might do a giveaway. Like, who doesn't live local and wants to win a pair of tickets and the opportunity to chill with me during the set? I'm *tel-ling* you, there's gonna be the best performers. Trust. Oh God, I'm so excited. I don't want to spill anything. I'll tell you guys later. Later. New video soon. Tell your friends. Bye-bye!" She waves and waves until the video cuts.

CHAPTER TWENTY-THREE

Mom comes into my room just as I'm about to leave for the bus on Monday. I'm pulling a sweater over my spaghetti strap tank top, and I hear her say, "I hope you're not going to take that sweater off at school," before I see her.

"No," I reply, wrestling the fabric over my head. "It's way too cold for that." It's too cold, but I know the only reason she's saying that is because it's a really fitted tank top, I apparently need a bigger bra, and there are boys at my school. Ugh. I don't want to think about boys like Marcus staring at my chest—I don't want to think about my growing chest, but now I am and I hate it.

"Uh-huh," she says, and then steps into my room. "You're already dressed, but when you come back, try this on." She tosses a bag from a lingerie store onto my bed. Oh my God, does she want me to die? "This is probably a better-size bra than what you're wearing."

"Moooom," I whine, nudging the bag to the end of my bed. "I don't need it."

She actually glances at my chest before she says, "Uh, yes, you do."

"I'm not wearing it. There's nothing wrong with the one I have right now. Plus, what if the new one isn't the right size? Then there's no point." I cross my arms.

Mom raises an eyebrow. "So do you want to go for a fitting?"

"N-no way."

"Try it on, then," she says, nodding to the bag. "I can return it tomorrow before work if it doesn't fit."

I glare at the bag.

"Go to the loans place for me before school?" She changes the subject easily, crossing her arms as she leans against the doorframe. "Tell Mr. Brown I'll see him before nightfall about, uh, a check."

I've been seeing too much of Mr. Brown lately. We're both probably a little sick of each other. He gives me pamphlets, I hand them out, people either say yes they'll come or no they won't—but each and every time, someone else recognizes me from some video. Most of the time, it's okay, but other times, I'm an exploiter, a famewhore, no better than Maree. Do people really look at her and look at me and think we're the same? Can't they see that I'm actually from here?

Not to mention, it's almost been a week since I saw Calvin, and I can't get that eerie description of this man jogging in the night out of my head. A part of me feels like this is inevitable—did I really think I'd be able to figure out who trashed the store? Did I really think it'd be impossible that it was someone from around here? And would Mr. Tran even care—would it make him want to stay? Kate called me naive, and I thought she was being annoying. Maybe she was being practical. Maybe she was just protecting herself.

"Chi-chi?" Mom says again. "Did you hear me?"

"Yeah, sure," I say with a grunt. "Mr. Brown, before nightfall."

She nods, satisfied with my answer, and then pushes a flyer into my hands. "It was on the door. Thought it might be something you'd be interested in."

It's an advertisement for Spice of Life. Damn, now they're going door-to-door? This flyer is specifically about a job fair for teenagers. Wow, they're trying it. They really want to employ all the youth in the area to work at their demonic spice cavern.

I frown. "You want me to get a job here?"

"Well, the bills aren't going to pay themselves," she says, but the immediate flash of regret in her eyes tells me she didn't mean to utter those words. I stare back at the paper and pretend to be studying the ugly Spice of Life logo extra hard, because I don't want to see that look on her face. Mom tries her hardest to keep up the facade that we have more than enough, but from time to time, it cracks. When the car breaks down and we have to get it towed to the house instead of a garage, the facade cracks. When the pantry empties bit by bit, it cracks. When we get more and more rent letters in the mail, it cracks.

"I mean," she continues hurriedly, "it'll teach you responsibility. And it'll also give you the opportunity to learn money management skills, like Kate has, because she's been working in her parents' store since she was young."

Just hearing about Ginger Store is enough to form a lump in my throat. It hasn't been open since the incident, I've barely even seen the Trans since then, and every day I'm trying to get people to come to a protest in support of what their family is dealing with. It's ironic. I don't know what's going on with the insurance claim, I don't know what's going on with my best friend, I don't know what's going on, period.

I cringe and fold the flyer to put into my bag. "I don't know. I can get a job somewhere else, if you want me to."

If she wants me to. She is frowning, and I think it's because she doesn't know how to tell me, yes, she needs my help. I don't know if I'm any better, because I don't know how to offer.

"What's wrong with this place?" Mom asks, nodding to the flyer. "It's huge. There's a better opportunity to get hired here than at other places."

"Yeah, but they're so, I don't know, capitalist."

Her frown deepens. "You've been listening to your dad too much."

"But you both used to say that."

"Our society is capitalist, Chi-chi. It's just the way it is."

"Yeah, but that doesn't mean I have to like it," I grumble, and grab my bag off the bed.

Mom literally won't stop frowning. "What's wrong with you today?"

"Nothing."

"How is Kate doing?" she asks.

"Kate?" I repeat. "She's—I don't know. She's cool."

Mom doesn't buy it. She's no longer apprehensive about the money thing. Now it's like all her teenage-daughter senses are tingling at once, and she's trying to figure out what the real, deeper issue is. She scans me up and down a few more times before she steps out of my way. "Okay. Tell her parents I said hello if you see them."

"I will."

"And I better not see your face on TV again."

"Mom, I swear those were all edited clips."

"Do I look like I was born yesterday?" she grunts, waving a hand from her head to her toes as if she's daring me to look. "Do you know how many people have been telling me they've seen you on the news?" And she starts rambling off people's names I don't know, like "Jerry that engineer" or "Marianne who's always baking those cakes." Uh, who? Damn. I bet each and every one of those people refers to me as "Janet's daughter."

Then she says, "TV is dangerous. I'm serious. When you're in a public forum, your words don't belong to you anymore. You can say whatever you want, but people will take only what they need."

I know that all too well now. "No more TV," I mumble. "I got it."

"Get to Mr. Brown's. Also tell me what you think," she says, "about the flyer."

"I will. Bye, Mom," I say as I duck past her.

What I didn't say was that I'm heading to the bus stop early after I hit up the loans place. What I didn't say was that I haven't spoken to Kate since last week and I don't really know how to break the silence.

When I walked by her house after watching the new Maree video, I saw some police officer roll up to the Trans' place. This tall, kinda rough-looking guy knocked on the door five times, even though they have a doorbell, while he was flipping through a notepad. The door opened and some-one let him in, though I couldn't see who. I have no idea if he had a list of suspects, or if he had new developments, or if he wanted to do a new interview with them or what. I thought Kate would've called or texted to tell me what was up, but she didn't, and I didn't ask.

I haven't been seeing Kate on the bus recently either. Whenever I text her to say hey, she doesn't get back to me as if she wants to talk to me. She'll reply mad late and say *Oh, I just saw this now.* I can take a hint. The only problem is, she's my best friend and it's not like I can ignore her or get a new best friend. I don't get how she's okay with ignoring me.

On top of that, she barely talks in the group chat, and

when she does, it's usually with Bo. I think they have inside jokes now. She said something and he replied with something really basic, and all she said was *LOL*. And I'm thinking, like, *Excuse me, that wasn't even that funny!* They've definitely become closer. I think they might be dating, but apparently that's just me being jealous. That's what Rafa says, anyway— that I'm *jealous.*

Rafa and I have been talking a lot too. We don't hang out often at school, because he still has his friends and I still hate them, but he texts me almost every day—in the morning, in the night, whenever. It feels as though we're secret friends, because no one at school knows we grew up together or that we talk as often as we do, but I'm okay with it. It's nice to have *someone*, especially after your best, closest friend in the whole world ditches you. And he gets me. I like that he always has.

People at school are deep in speculation about Maree's latest video. I must have missed the notification in our online school group, because there's a new post there about who the performers might be. There are ongoing polls, and the number one guess so far is Sol Cousins. I would actually die. Sure, no one really listens to him anymore, but I don't think we'd be mad if he rolled through for free. All of a sudden, we'd be bumping "I Ain't Never" like nothing had changed.

Some twelfth-grade girl did a whole chart on why she thinks Sol is headlining, and people are beginning to buy into it. Suddenly that impromptu pop-up shop downtown is making sense, because obviously he came here to talk to Maree's people about show dates. And yeah, it does make sense that he was spotted in Yorkville, because that's where Maree's publicist apparently lives, and maybe they were getting lunch. And damn, *of course* he isn't touring next month because he's actually going to be here, in Ginger East, performing for the less fortunate.

I want to believe this megastar is literally going to be across the street from Ginger Store, performing in that huge field, but there's no way this bitch knows Sol. No way.

CHAPTER TWENTY-FOUR

I rush to the main street and push the door open to Mr. Brown's loan shop. It's a lot heavier than it looks, so I have to lean into it and drag my feet a little as I go. He's at the counter behind the bulletproof glass, staring wide-eyed at me from behind his thick glasses. He doesn't budge. That bullet-proof glass is just for show; I know Mr. Brown isn't afraid of anyone.

"Hi, Mr. Brown," I say, approaching the counter.

He wrinkles his nose at me and lets his eyes fall back to his work. "I've been seeing too much of you, Chinelo," he drawls. "In real life, on the news . . ."

"Man, that's what I've been saying," I murmur. "They're replaying the interview?"

"Yes," he says. "All the time now on prime time."

"That explains why Mom won't stop snapping at me."

"Well, she cares," he says simply.

I don't know what to say to that, so my eyes scan the desk behind the glass instead. He's counting lines on some paper, lines filled with a bunch of different numbers that I can't make out from here. For a moment, his eyes flick up to meet mine. I bet he's wondering what I'm still doing here. To be honest, so am I.

"Oh yeah! So my mom said—"

"Hold on," he cuts in as he gets to his feet. He pushes back from the desk and moves to stand up, but the ceiling is a bit low for his tall frame. "Ack!" He massages his head as he slumps toward the back room. And I'm here thinking.

Just thinking.

Calvin's voice breaks into my thoughts. The entire conversation rolls over and over in my mind—"you definitely know him . . . got an accent . . . owns a shop on the road"—and my heart beats faster and faster once the realization hits me.

Mr. Brown.

Mr. Brown was the guy who was jogging late at night for some ridiculous reason, because who even goes out at nighttime around here—and it makes sense! He's so fit for his old age!

Mr. Brown comes back with a small envelope and settles into his chair. My eyes are wide, and my gaze is boring into his face, but it still takes him a second to notice.

"It's you," I whisper.

He is unimpressed. "What you want, girl?"

"You're . . . You went jogging that night when the store was bricked," I say as calmly as I can. "Is it true? W-were you . . . Did you see anything?"

He sighs again and pulls his glasses from his face, sets them down on the counter. The way he's looking so worn has me thinking I'm right, that Calvin was right. Excitement revs up in the pit of my stomach again. Excitement, and dread. For the past week, I was distracted by the protest, but now it looks as though I may be getting somewhere trying to figure out who did this to Ginger Store. Now if Mr. Brown saw who it was, if Mr. Brown says it's someone he didn't recognize, then that means there's no way it could've been someone from around here. Kate wouldn't have to move, and everyone could start getting their life back on track. If this could all happen before the protest? Even better. I rock back and forth on my heels, barely able to contain the energy that's zipping up my spine.

Mr. Brown leans toward the glass and says, "What makes you think I saw anything?"

"Uh, network. Networking," I tell him, thinking of Calvin's shady way of saying it.

"Who do you have to network with around here? I hope you're not talking to them boys at the liquor store."

I shake my head. "It's not them. It's just . . . a friend. A friend told me you know who bricked Ginger Store."

His mouth forms into a frown right away. "And which one of your friends said that?" he asks, his deep voice booming. I really thought he was going to give me a second to gather my thoughts, but the way he's launching into it tells me he's been asked before. "Listen, people keep asking me about it because I was out for a jog, but I'll tell you like I've been telling everyone: I didn't see *nothing.*"

"You had to have, though," I press on. "The kid behind the dumpster—or was it the back door—"

"No—"

"I mean, everyone pretty much already thinks it's those Avery boys—you know the ones. They both look so much like different young Justin Biebers, it's crazy—"

"I—what? No, child, no," he cuts in, waving his hands in front of me to get me to stop talking. "And who said anything about a boy?"

I frown. "Everyone? Apparently you?"

"I never said anything about a boy," he tells me. "I said it was a *kid* I saw duck past into the building. I never said anything about a boy."

CHAPTER TWENTY-FIVE

I'm still pretty early for history class despite Mom and the bra, and the detour at Mr. Brown's. The room is filled with the kinds of kids who always show up before the bell and don't care if it's uncool to be here before the teacher. They give me a once-over while I head to my seat and drop my bag onto the desk. I'm buzzing. I don't even care. Mr. Brown didn't say he didn't know the person who threw the brick, but he didn't say he knew who it was either. That means he probably doesn't. He probably didn't recognize the person because they're not from Ginger East. I've been avoiding telling Kate what I know, but this feels heavy enough. It feels real.

I take out my phone and scroll through my social while I wait. Crossing my legs under the desk, I lean into the phone screen like there's something really cool on it. Really, there's nothing. Almost all the apps are dead in the mornings because no one posts anything. It only gets really interesting after first period because some kids in my grade have second-period lunch. I don't know how they got so lucky.

Rafa changed his profile picture to one where he's wearing glasses—he doesn't need glasses—and lying on his bed.

His dark hair is disheveled but in the way that it looks like he did it on purpose, and he's biting his lip like he wants something. I swear, every picture this boy takes is a thirst trap. It's so weird to even think that.

I'm staring longer at his picture than I want to admit. My eyes hone in on the screen, fixating on his—face. Suddenly everything around me is blocked out but my phone and the hollow sound of my breathing as I lean closer and closer to the device in my hands.

Kate would honestly slap me if she saw me like this.

I should slap me.

But I don't know. He's good to look at. He has really matured. I can see it now. Even admitting that to myself is making my stomach twist a little, making my palms sweaty. My eyes roll over the ripples on his shirt, and my mind is saying, *Get it together.* My face is hot, my heartbeat is thudding loud in my chest, and my mind is like, *Didn't I just tell you to quit it?* My finger pokes the screen, enlarging the picture, and for one brave second, I dare myself to zoom in just a bit closer— meanwhile, my mind is all, *BITC*—

—but my concentration is broken when I hear a chair scrape across the floor. I'm thrown back into the classroom, emotionally exposed, and feeling like my mom told my teacher I went up a bra size. I quickly hit the like button on his picture and nearly break my thumb scrolling away. That didn't happen. None of that happened. Oh my God.

Vicky Sanchez uploaded a new profile picture too. She's hanging off one of her friends, I think some girl named Aliyah, and they're laughing. It's a cute picture, so I hit like and keep scrolling.

"Yo, yo!"

I'm nudged back to reality before I can really grasp what's going on. When I look up, blinking away the impression of Rafa's lips burned into my eyes from my screen, Kate is sitting beside me, dropping her bag onto the desk, and grinning while she untangles her earphones. The whole scene feels as though it came from some TV movie. Nothing feels real. Me? Sweating like I got caught on a blocked site at school. Kate? Laughing like normal, struggling with her earphones like normal, and about to show me something on her phone like normal.

"Did you see Rafa's picture?" she asks, pulling her chair closer to my desk so I can see her phone. She lowers her voice, to barely a whisper, and says, "It's kinda hot, but don't tell him I said anything."

My heart pounds in my chest double-time. I act like I'm not going to say anything, and then I utter, "Only *kinda*?"

She gasps and slams her hand down on the table. It has me jumping because it's so loud. "I knew it!" she says with a chuckle. "You like him, you like him—"

"What, no, shut up, shut up!" I say, flustered. I try to cover her mouth with my hands. She keeps dodging me, but I guess she's had practice with that these past few weeks. "I didn't mean it like that! I meant, like, yeah, he's a bit *more* than *kinda* hot, but that doesn't mean I think he's *actually* hot."

"You two would make a good couple," she muses.

I'm so flustered, I could die. "Based on what evidence—"

"And he's pretty much always talking to you in the chat, so."

"Excuse?" I gasp. "Says who?"

She snickers. "Are you dumb? You really haven't noticed?"

"I mean, I'm just saying," I tell her with a shrug. "I didn't even know you read the chat, so."

She rolls her eyes a million times and groans forever. "Woooow," she sighs, and then there's nothing more. She can be annoyed with me if she wants, but I didn't lie. When's the last time she said a word to me on there? And now she's showing up and pretending that we just talked last night or the night before or the night before that? No way. Kate's pretty much my sister, but she's not thinking straight if she thinks it's going to be like this.

"Forget that," Kate says with a wave of her hand. "Tell me about the brick stuff. How far have you gotten with that?" She's teasing me, snickering and poking me in the side, but she's about to be shocked by what I tell her. For a second, nervousness palms me in my chest, but then I remember that I don't have to hide it anymore. Mr. Brown pretty much confirmed that it was someone he didn't know who threw the brick. That's all I need to know, and I'm sure it'll be enough for the Trans to stay.

So I grin and say, "I figured it out," while I dance around in my seat. Kate gasps and does not join me in celebrating. "Legit, legit, I got it. I talked to Mr. Brown, and he said it was a kid he didn't recognize who must have thrown the brick."

"Wh-what? Wait . . ." Kate chuckles nervously. She shifts in her seat until she's facing me directly, and brushes her hair off her shoulders. It makes her neck look longer, makes her look as if she's sitting up super straight too. But the look on her face, the small tick above her eyebrows, shows she doesn't really believe me. "For real? How could he not have . . . Mr. Brown knows everyone."

"Exactly," I say, still cheesing. "Because it wasn't someone from around here! I told you! No one from Ginger East would be dumb enough to do something like this. I knew it, I knew it!"

Kate scoffs, "Right," and shifts back so she's facing the front of the room. Not quite the reaction I was hoping for. She should be celebrating with me. Forget the police for a second; forget everything else. This means that her family won't have to leave. Mr. Tran will know that we're still okay. He'll know that we're good people.

Kate is eerily silent, and I don't know what to do. The Kate I know wouldn't react like this, and I only know how to talk to the Kate I know. This new Kate puts up walls wherever she wants. She won't talk to me for days, ignores me in the group chat, and then decides she wants to show me something on her phone like it's all good. It's like whiplash. I can't keep up.

I rest my head on my hand, my elbow propping it up on the desk, and turn to her. "My turn to ask a question," I say as she glances at me.

She looks at me like I'm about to cuss her, and says, "Is this about your TV debut? Because I've already seen it."

I wince. With the way she said it, she might as well have slapped me. "Uh, no?"

"Okay, good."

Okay, good? What's her problem? "It's about you," I say, pressing into each word. That gets a sigh out of her. One sigh! I can't believe this. "What's been going on with you these days? I haven't seen you, haven't talked to you . . ."

"What do you mean?" She grimaces.

"This," I say, gesturing to the space between us, the remnants of her question in the air, the distance. "*This* is what I mean."

Kate's sigh transforms into sadness and a vulnerability that I can't understand. I wasn't expecting it, and I'm hit so bad when I see it. All of a sudden, all the bitterness at being ignored vanishes because I remember that her family is going through a lot, and I couldn't possibly understand. I couldn't *possibly*. But I do, and I want to understand more. Maybe she forgot, but her family is like my family too.

We glance at each other, and I'm lost in my own head, trying to make sense of what's going on in hers. Silence to my face is at least better than silence from a screen, but if this were back when we were younger, if this were *really* us, she'd spill first and add follow-up questions later. She would've helped me find out who bricked the store too. We'd sneak out of the house and hang in someone's backyard if the park wasn't safe, and we'd go over conspiracy theories and neighborhood gossip and stupid stuff. If we had any plan at all, she'd proof it, because that's how she is, always careful and fake reckless. Now it's like she's done being reckless completely. I can't tell if this is growing up or just growing, but I want out.

When I don't say anything, she pouts at me like a lost puppy. Well, I hate dogs, and if she was actually my friend, she'd remember that. I turn away and sit back in my seat. Man, I'm trying so hard not to be mad, but I am and it sucks.

Suddenly Kate stops pouting and sits bolt upright, folding her hands atop the desk as if someone smacked her into shape. I still don't look at her, but then she starts talking with this heavy voice: "Maree's doing a whole publicity thing for this— for her—just *everything*."

I don't say more than a "Yeah, unfortunately," because I don't know where she's going with this.

"Can I tell you something?" she asks as she leans in closer and speaks quieter. The fact that she thinks she even has to ask hurts in a weird way. She's never had to ask me that before because it was always assumed that yes, she can tell me anything, and yes, I'm always here. "The insurance is taking forever. Like, way longer than I thought was legal. At first, they said they weren't sure if they could approve it. Just because Dad was like, 'It's probably someone in the neighborhood,' they think he knows them, and they want to say it's an inside job or something. And I'm like, what? Why? Just *why?*" She grunts and rubs at her left eye.

"So what did the police say?"

She pauses. "What?"

"The police," I say again. "They were at your place over the weekend, right? I saw some guy come through."

"Oh, yeah." She takes her time answering, scrunching up her lips while she thinks. What's there to think about? Either they were there or they weren't, and they clearly were there. "They wanted to update us."

"Okay, so?" I prod. "What kinds of leads do they have? Are they searching outside Ginger East for this kid?"

"I don't know. I guess?" she replies. "They were talking to Dad and Jake or someone else. I don't know anything about that. It's not like the police can help us. Not really, anyway. It's the insurance money we need, you know?" She touches the ends of her hair while she speaks, her eyes downcast. "It's dumb. We have a cousin, a lawyer, who's kind of looking over everything for us in terms of the insurance claim. I said we should hire a real one, but I don't—I shouldn't have said that. You know?"

I nod at once. I do know. Kate's family is like mine: okay until. Until rent, until surprise bills, until someone loses their job. I know what she means without her having to say it.

Kate shrugs. She looks so tired. Her eyes aren't as bright as they normally are, and the color has been drained from her lips. "So the insurance is taking forever, but Mom said we can't wait around for them anymore. She snapped the other night, eh? Dad hasn't been doing so well and she just yelled at him. They got into a *big* fight. It was so awkward because I don't think Bo has ever seen my parents argue like that before."

My eyebrows rise immediately. "Bo?"

Her cheeks turn pink and she stutters like she knows she said something wrong. "Oh, um, yes. Yeah. We were hanging out . . ."

Hearing her say that stings. Whether she was avoiding me on purpose or not, the fact still stands that somehow Bo— Bo?!—is in the running to replace me. They better be secretly together or something, because the thought of Bo (Bo?!) taking my best-friend privileges is legit the worst.

"Anyway," she continues. "The point is: the insurance is stalled and everyone is mad. Dad is miserable, Mom is miserable, Jake is always at school, and I'm always at home. That's it—that's all you've missed." She throws up her hands like *Here, take it,* and then slouches back in her seat.

"You never told me, so I didn't know," I say. It's stating the obvious, but I'm in my feelings and I don't care. I want her to feel a little bit bad that she left her best friend out of her life for what felt like a million weeks.

"You've been busy with your protest thing."

"Not true. And we practically live next door to each other. You literally have to walk by my house to get anywhere."

"Okay, but I'm telling you now, so it's whatever."

That's a useless thing to say, but I'm not going to fight with her so early in the morning. It's not even worth it.

Instead I ask, "What about Maree, though?" Even saying her name is enough to get on Kate's bad side. She changes so fast. Her fatigue turns to anger in the blink of an eye. Her eyes narrow and she purses her lips extra, extra hard. Honestly, it's a big mood. "She's been collecting money all over the place, right?" I ask. "Don't tell me she hasn't even tried to talk to you."

Kate groans and laughs at the same time. It sounds demonic. "The joke is that you're actually surprised. That bitch didn't care from day one. And now she's hosting a benefit concert? For *whose benefit?* All she cares about is her image and her YouTube views."

"That's wrong," I say. "She has over thirty thousand in a FundRace somewhere, and she hasn't reached out to you once? That's fucked all the way up. That's stealing."

Kate nods, sitting back in her chair. "Yeah. Stealing.

You know what thirty thousand would mean to me? To my family?"

I know what it would mean to me: it would mean my best friend wouldn't have to leave.

I sit back in my chair too, and we're both just quiet. It's so different because I always know what to say. Now I'm stringing words together in my head and trying to test the mood. Nothing fits the way it used to.

One of the usual early-to-class kids bursts into the room and beelines straight for his friends. "Hey, guys!" He glances around nervously at all the new faces— namely mine and Kate's—and is soon so overtaken by his story that he doesn't care who's listening. "Maree's setting up for her interview in the caf. It's national news this time!"

Kate doesn't budge an inch. Not a hair on her head or an eyelash moves at the sound of the announcement. The boy who rushed in and his friends quickly scramble to their feet and make their way out of the classroom, followed by the people behind us, and the people behind them. The classroom is empty, with the echoes of chairs scraping floors and feet scampering to the doorway.

I look at Kate, and she's doing the most trying not to look at me. Her lips are pursed so tight and her eyes are bulging. I can't lie—I'm a little bit curious, so I get up and sling my bag over my shoulder.

"National news?" Kate mumbles. "Reporters have stopped

trying to get a hold of my parents, especially now that Maree announced the concert. It's their store, but all people want to know is what other people are telling them." I don't have to ask to know that I'm one of those "other people."

I frown. "You gotta talk to Maree."

Kate grunts and slouches in her seat.

"You have to," I say again. "You can't let her think this is okay. She's doing the most off what some kids did to *your* family. No, she can't play it like that."

A few more kids dash by the classroom door, rushing frantically in the direction of the cafeteria. I nudge Kate's leg with my foot and say, "Come on, let's go."

She makes a show of standing up and grabbing her bag, rolling her eyes and sighing loudly like I'm dragging her there, when she knows in her heart she wants to go too.

There's already a huge crowd gathering around the open caf doors. No one is being let inside. Kate and I wiggle our way into a snug spot between some tall twelfth graders and a group of first-year girls who smell like every body-spray sample at the mall. At first, it's a struggle to slip into the crowd, but it gets easier the further in we get—and the more people seem to recognize me.

"You were on TV, right?" one of the twelfth graders asks me, and I nod right away. He chuckles. "Yo, that's dope. I saw your other video too."

"Same," a girl with braids down to her knees pipes up.

Her eyebrows are perfectly shaped, and she makes a point to wiggle them at me as she says, "You're like Maree, but for *us*. You should be the one up there."

Kate groans at that, and I pretend I don't care so we can slip closer to the front. I don't want to be anything like Maree, but the girl's words are laced with an underlying acceptance that I'm not used to hearing. Not back at Ginger East, where some people think I'm wasting my time or exploiting them. This girl gets it.

Maree is sitting on one of the caf benches getting her makeup done. I recognize the makeup artist from a few of Maree's online pictures, but I don't say anything to Kate because then she'd know I've been on Maree's social pages, and at this point, that's as good as treason.

Maree waves every now and then to the crowd, and the bigger joke is that people are actually waving back. What? This girl isn't untouchable. She sits somewhere behind me in science class, and I pass her every day in the halls. We all do. All of a sudden, we're fawning over her like she's some other-worldly being. Like she's a real celebrity and not just some girl who got lucky on YouTube—some girl who threw her home and her old friends under the bus to get famous.

The reporter and camera people are setting up across from her. The reporter, a man I've never seen before, shakes her hand before showing her his notes. She nods along while her makeup artist friend applies lip gloss to her lower lip.

But then it happens. She sees us, me and Kate, nestled in with the others. At first it's subtle and I'm not sure she realizes it's us, but then she stops, slowly nudging her makeup artist friend away to get a closer look. To concentrate better.

The crowd gets antsy and a few people begin to look around to figure out who she's looking at. I hear someone whisper, "It's the Feds girl, that one from the news," and more and more eyes fall on me. Maree keeps her gaze trained on us. What's she thinking? She's just staring like she's got something to say, but she doesn't speak. Doesn't move. Kate is fuming beside me. I swear I can feel the warmth she's emitting. She's clenching her fists and trembling.

Then—"Ready to go?" the reporter asks Maree. Her gaze is broken and she smiles warmly at him, nodding. He gives her a microphone pack, and her friend helps mic her up.

Kate immediately spins on her heel and pushes her way out of the growing crowd. "Wait, wait!" I call after her. The group around us is eager to fill the space we left, and within seconds, it's like there was never an opening to begin with.

My eyes search the hall for Kate, and I catch a glimpse of her black-and-white high-tops heading toward the main doors. I chase after her and manage to grab on to her sweater before she makes it out. "Let go of me!" she snaps.

"No. What the hell?" I snap back. "You can't just *leave* school—"

"Why? Because I'm not a fake celebrity, I don't get to do whatever I want?"

"What? That's not fair—"

"Besides, you ditched school the other day to hang out with Rafa, and I didn't say anything."

"I didn't ditch to hang out with *him*, genius—I ditched to hang out with *you*," I tell her. She shuts up right away.

Kate crosses her arms and purses her lips hard for a few minutes. "I can't stay here. I don't want to listen to all her *bullshit*—I can't listen to other people talk about it either. She's ruining *everything*," she says. "I'm not staying." She tells me like it's a challenge and I'm going to try to stop her.

Instead I shrug. "Well, where are you going to go?"

"Home."

"Tch, okay," I say with a scoff. "Home, where you can watch the interview live on your TV?"

She frowns so hard, she starts looking more like her mom. It's scary. "Fine," she says, and brings out her phone. I bet she's texting Bo. She's probably asking him to come get her. He can't even drive! He's probably taking the bus here from Santa Ana, willing to skip class at the drop of a hat just because Kate says so. Oh my God, she's really trying to tell me that I have a thing for Rafa when she's been obsessed with Bo since she found out he's stylish and washes his face now?

I'm pouting, chewing the inside of my cheek as I watch her fingers move swiftly over her screen. "Who's that?" I ask.

"Jake."

"Jake?" I repeat, and she nods without looking at me. "What?"

"He said he'll sign me out from school. So it's technically

not skipping," she tells me, and makes a face like *You really thought, huh?*

I can't even say anything, so I just follow her to the office, where we sit on chairs outside the main doors, waiting for Jake to roll up. He gets to the school in about ten minutes, which really makes me wonder where he was when she messaged him. Jake looks slightly more put together than he did the last time I saw him. He's wearing another hoodie that Kate stole from him and he evidently stole back.

He walks up to the counter and talks to the receptionist. Kate jumps to her feet to join him at the desk, waving me over.

Our receptionist is a mean lady with mad thick bifocals. She's always squinting through them, even though I swear the point of glasses is to be able to see without doing that. "And you're signing out *whom?*" she asks sharply.

"Uh, my sister," Jake tells her as he finishes signing the attendance form. I creep up beside him, and he jumps a bit like he didn't see me there before. "What are you doing here?" he asks in a low tone.

I shrug. "I go to this school."

"That's not what I meant."

The receptionist almost pulls the form back to her side before Jake grabs it, gives a hint of an apologetic smile, and starts to scribble my name below Kate's. He writes a reason, "family stuff," and hands the form back to her.

"Hmmm . . ." The receptionist hums while she looks at the form. Her eyes do leaps between the page and my face, and the page and Jake's face. "Um—I don't think you can sign *her* out," she says finally, jutting her pen toward me. "Are—um— you see, school policy outlines that only a *relation* can sign out a student—"

"She is a relation," Jake tells her. "She's my sister too."

CHAPTER TWENTY-SIX

Being in the back of Jake's car is legit. Once Kate hooks up her phone to the sound system, the awkwardness from school disappears and we're rapping through all the samples in her soon-to-be-finished mixtape. A Midtown Project mix rattles the car, and Jake turns it down a little. "This is embarrassing," he grunts, even though I know for a fact that he likes exactly three Midtown songs. What's embarrassing is that he prefers the extremely emo "Cascade" to the clearly superior power pop "Breakout Summer." I bet he liked Sol's latest album too, him and his flop taste.

I lean toward the driver's seat, and Jake gives me a mean side-eye while he turns the corner. I say, "You got here so quick. Were you at school or something?"

"Kind of," he answers, and that's it.

I snort. "What does 'kind of at school' look like?" My phone buzzes in my hand, distracting me from Jake and the sharp turn around the corner he just took. It's a message from Rafa. My heart jumps because I'm nervous, or something like that. Memories of me practically drooling over his picture in the open flood my mind, and I shut my eyes to make them go away. I swipe on the message to see that he's sent me a screenshot of his social feed. His new profile picture is front and center, and underneath it, it's clearly visible that it's been liked by 291 people, one of whom is me. Because he's mad petty, he's underlined my name on the screenshot in red. Wow, I'm drying up. Whatever fleeting attraction I may have felt for him is gone because I remember boys are annoying and he isn't the exception; he's the rule.

I reply: *your point????*

His reply? Obnoxious kissy-face emojis. Ugh.

i liked vicky sanchez's latest pic too so you're not special bye, I text back.

He sends three more kissy-face emojis. I'm blocking this boy.

When I shove my phone away, Kate is turned around, staring at me from the passenger seat. "Who was that?" she asks plainly.

I shrug. "Rafa."

She raises an eyebrow, inquisitive and annoying, and purses her lips so hard, the color starts to seep out of them. I should've lied and said it was my mom or someone.

"He's just texting me stupid stuff," I go on, as if me saying this will actually help. It doesn't. Kate's lips relax, but her raised eyebrow is threatening to stay there forever. "Like, I liked his latest picture, and because he's obsessed with himself, he sent me a screenshot of it, like it means anything. It costs nothing to double tap on a picture, and it's not even that deep. He's just being a guy."

Kate juts out her lips while she thinks. She leans closer to Jake, nudging him in the arm twice, and says, "You think that's innocent behavior?"

He shakes his head. "No. Isn't Rafa that kid who used to like you?" he asks, locking eyes with me in the rearview mirror.

I cringe and groan and fall back on the seat and die, all in that order. "Why would you even say that?"

"Because it's true, right?" Jake replies, casting a sideways glance at Kate. "Isn't that what you said?"

Kate nods immediately. "Yes. Yes. Points were made."

"I don't want to hear any points," I say.

"Well, you're gonna, so just shut up," she teases with a snicker. "Listen. This boy used to visit you every single day, first thing in the morning, and ask you to come outside or go to the park with him. On his tenth birthday, he literally only invited you to the arcade until Maree complained and Rafa's mom told him he had to invite everyone else too. And didn't he kiss you once? Didn't you tell me he kissed you?"

My mouth is open—no sound, no air, no nothing. I'm in so much shock that I can barely form a proper thought. I shake my head, hoping that will be enough of a response until I can gather myself. When I'm finally able to speak, I say, "Uh—no? Wh-when did he ever? When did *I* ever?"

Kate turns to Jake. "I swear you said she told me this," she says.

"Why would he even remember that?" I cut in. "Rafa doesn't like me, and I never kissed him. Can we stop talking about this? What have I done to deserve being roasted this early in the morning, huh?" I quickly lean forward and flick her in the back of the head.

"Ow!" She yelps and moves away, laughing. "Okay. I didn't lie about anything. I'll ask him next time I see him."

"Don't you dare."

"I do what I want."

"Wow, so maybe I should ask Bo the same thing?"

She shuts up so fast that it has me laughing in the back. Even Jake notices and he does a quick double take at Kate as she bites her tongue. "S-shut up," she finally says, pushing out her words with a giggle. "Bo and I are just friends, obviously. It's not weird for me to have a close friend who's a boy. I know you don't know anything about that life, though."

I'm cackling. "Bit—"

"I'm dropping you guys off at the mall," Jake cuts in unceremoniously. That look he's giving me in the rearview mirror tells me he's interrupting on purpose too.

Kate says, "Fine," right away. I just shrug. The two of us haven't hung out together in what feels like forever, but I'm excited because it almost feels like we're real friends again.

Jake nods once. "Cool. I gotta head back to school, but tell Dad I'll be home later to update him on the insurance stuff."

My ears perk up. I even sit up a bit straighter too. "What's happening with the insurance?"

In a second, I know I wasn't meant to ask or know what was going on. Kate and Jake share the most obvious look of regret I've ever seen in my life. Even from where I'm sitting, I can see the way Jake's eyes crinkle and how Kate's lips purse tightly with unease. Wow, really? So much for being family. "I mean, it's all good. Don't tell me," I say, leaning back into my seat. Don't tell me. It's not really any of my business. I'm just waiting to hear good news about Ginger Store like everyone else in the neighborhood is.

"It's been approved," Kate blurts out. She says it quickly but still doesn't bother hiding her grimace. What a snake!

Still, I'm too happy to be annoyed at her. "What? Really?" I gasp. Warmth fills my cheeks and I can't help but smile, even if they're both the definition of suspect right now. I asked her literally an hour ago, and she told me it was stalled, but now it's approved? I don't have it in me to be mad; I'm just happy things can get back to normal. "Actually? That's so good! So—so when is the window being fixed, then? The insurance money will cover the window, right? I mean, it should. It better. Wait, does it?"

Jake clears his throat but says nothing. We drive in stuffy silence for a few more paces. Then Kate turns around to face me a bit better. She's smiling now too. "Yo, they're giving us a *lot* more than we thought we'd get," she tells me.

I grin. "Are you guys going to be rich?"

"It's all relative."

"Wow, okay, there," I say, and snicker. "When is Ginger Store reopening? Do you guys know yet?" She hesitates, opening and closing her mouth, stumbling over words she isn't going to say. I feel bad for even asking, so before she has a chance to answer, I cut in, "You know what, it's all good. It doesn't matter right now. I'm just happy it's reopening, period."

Kate eases into a smile, but I catch a look she and Jake share, and it reminds me that I'm left out. I don't know any more or any less than they want to tell me, and right now, it feels like they don't want to tell me anything.

Jake clears his throat again. He should really get some lozenges or something, like damn. "If we tell you any more about the insurance, how do we know it won't end up in some interview or whatever?" he says with a chuckle.

I slouch into the backseat. "Man, I'm done giving interviews."

Kate nudges Jake in the arm as she says, "You should see. At school, people are like, 'You're the Feds girl!' She's way too busy to talk to me." She turns and makes an ugly face at me. Is she serious right now? I force a chuckle, but she knows she's the one who's been ignoring me and spending all her free time with Bo.

Jake glances at me. "Are you gonna be at the protest?"

"Yeah," I say. "I'm helping organize. You're coming, right?"

"I got school."

"You always have school."

"Okay, and?" he snorts. "You'd always have school too, if you two delinquents actually went."

Kate laughs, and I'm sitting in the back like that wasn't even *that* funny. But I don't say anything because things have been so serious lately. Her laughing is a good sign.

CHAPTER TWENTY-SEVEN

Jake buys us food at the Eaton Center downtown before he goes back to school. Kate plans our return back to Ginger East strategically for three-thirty. Otherwise nosy people might wonder what we're doing rolling into the neighborhood so early.

Kate is ecstatic. She keeps humming and tapping her toes and twirling into walls. It has me laughing, and for a few moments, I feel as if things are on their way back to normal. The insurance came through and Ginger Store will reopen. After the protest, we'll be able to confront who bricked the window, Mr. Tran will chill, Kate won't be moving, and everything will go back to the way it should be.

"I gotta text Bo," she says suddenly while she whips out her phone. She's struggling a little because she only has one free hand. The other one is holding a strawberry banana smoothie.

Bo again? I catch myself before I roll my eyes, and instead just smile and shrug as pleasantly as I can manage. If Kate sees through it, she doesn't show it at all. She's too obsessed with her phone and her long message to Bo. Kate starts to giggle at whatever she's reading, whatever Bo is saying. I crane my neck a little, sipping on my own smoothie, while I try to read her screen. She giggles "Oh my God" and shifts away so I can't see. Now I roll my eyes. What are they talking about that she can't talk about with me? Is it couple stuff? Oh my God, are they a couple?

Three-thirty rolls around, and we're on a bus into Ginger East. The closest transit bus stops at the end of the main road, at the top of the hill. It's ten minutes walking before you even see Ginger Way. Kate steps off the bus before me and starts the long trek down the cracked sidewalk. She takes measured steps while she hums.

"The Eats?" she calls over her shoulder.

I nod. "The Eats."

When we walk into Jimmy's place, I start to wonder where the after-school-rush customers will sit because almost every table is taken up by protest volunteers. I recognize them mostly from Mr. Brown's house, and a few of them wave at me as we walk in.

Paco smiles immediately when he sees me. "Nelo," he says with a small nod. Kate gives a tight smile, but goes back to her phone. Paco doesn't seem fazed at all. He's always smiling these days because the protest is getting closer and closer. I think he thrives on this stuff, community organizing and things like that. "You wouldn't believe the numbers we're getting for the protest. Mr. Brown thinks more than two hundred people might show up. Crazy, right? He's thinking people may even come in from other neighborhoods, and all because of that interview you did."

I pretend not to notice how Kate flinches beside me as she scrolls through her phone. "I doubt it's the interview alone," I tell him. "People around here are just dedicated, that's all."

"Call it whatever you want."

"So what are we protesting, exactly?" Kate's voice hits like a knife to the chest. Paco and I look over in slow motion— everything is in slow motion now. She takes a hearty sip of her second strawberry smoothie before staring at us both, blank and uninspired. What the hell does this girl mean, what are we protesting? Is she trying to embarrass me? She's my best friend and she doesn't even know?

Paco gives a nervous chuckle, glancing at me like *Is she serious?* "Changes in the neighborhood, mostly," he explains. "Newer businesses come in that are failing to treat existing residents with respect. Property management companies are hiking up prices, knowing full well that the average income in Ginger East isn't that high and statistically won't reach astronomical levels over the next five years. Outside pressure from police to 'clean out' the area." He air-quotes "clean out," a regretful look on his face.

"Also people coming in, doing shitty things, and causing our crime rates to go up," I say, thinking of the store, and the arcade too.

"Ooooh," Kate sighs. She's giving me so much stress right now. "Cool."

"Cool," Paco echoes. "You'll be there, right?"

"Yeah, of course she will," I cut in, before Kate continues to embarrass me. She gives me a look, but I ignore her.

Paco smiles, relieved. "That's good to hear. It'd be cool if more young people can come out, so tell everyone," he says to her.

"Will Nelo be giving a speech?" Kate asks, looking me square in the eyes. Does she really think I won't fight her in front of Paco?

"No, I'm not giving a speech," I say pointedly. "The protest isn't about me."

Kate nods, seemingly content with my lack of continued exposure. Without another word, she reaches out for a flyer from Paco, which he graciously gives, and then she settles in at the only empty table in the place, by the far, far wall. I follow, giving Paco a regretful smile as I pass.

I stop by the counter to order fries. Jimmy scoops me a fresh plate full and hands it to me before I weave my way through the tables to find Kate. The lights aren't as bright in the back of the diner, but Kate's face is well lit from her phone. "So what did Bo say?" I ask as I sit down.

Kate glances at me. "About what?"

"About whatever you told him when we got off the bus."

"And what did I tell him?" she teases.

After a moment, I say, "Never mind." It's hard to keep the bitterness out of my voice.

I shove some fries into my mouth and fall into myself, being fake and pretending I'm unbothered, but it's hard not to see the hint of sadness in her eyes as she glances up at me again. "I—" She pauses when her phone starts to ring, and her eyebrows twist in confusion as she stares at the caller ID. "What?"

"Who is it?" I ask, which I know is a waste of time the moment I say it because I know she won't tell me.

Instead she holds up a finger, signaling for me to wait, and brings the phone to her ear. "Hello, hello? Hi. Dad?"

I busy myself with absolutely nothing. It's rough pretending.

Suddenly Kate's tone changes. The Eats is buzzing a few steps away from us with talk of protests and change, but tangible silence fills the space around us. She speaks lower and lower, almost whispering and murmuring responses into her phone. I shoot her a look like *What's going on?* and she fully turns around so she won't have to look at me. Rude.

She says bye a million times and hangs up. "What happened?" I ask immediately. If I don't ask, she'll probably find a way to avoid the subject forever. "Is your dad okay?"

"Yeah, he's good," she says, turning back to face me.

"Okay? Are you sure?"

"I'm sure, I'm sure." She smiles, almost timid, and busies

herself with the fries. She steals one and chews fast like a rodent. It's distracting. I'm two seconds away from giving up when she says, "Hey . . . you're my best friend, right?" Her voice is barely a murmur, the words creaking out with anxiousness.

I nod quickly, even though the impulse to clap back with *I thought you forgot* is really strong. "Of course, obviously," I tell her. My voice sounds desperate when I hear it come out of my mouth, and I kind of hate it, that desperation. "What's up?"

She toys with her fingers on the table. It's making me mad nervous. "Things at the house are okay," she says. "Dad's okay. He's fine. Actually, he's been talking to that Horst guy from that real estate company. Remember him? With the car and the—the name. I'm so used to Mom calling him 'vulture' that I almost forgot about it. Anyway, they have a meeting soon, apparently. . . ."

My jaw hangs slack in disbelief. Of all the things I imagined her saying in this very moment, this was officially the last. It's easier to picture her saying that she was giving up on her mixtape or she actually liked that trash album Sol Cousins put out, than it would have been to picture her saying this. We spent the whole afternoon together, and she said nothing. But now—now that she happened to have answered the phone in front of me, she wants to tell me Mr. Tran is taking another meeting with that Horst guy? How could he? How could she not tell me they were still talking?

Kate finally exhales. She looks relieved, like a huge weight has fallen off her chest and onto the diner floor. But me? I'm frantic. "What the hell?" I nearly snap, and she jumps in place. "Why's he meeting with him again? Like, what could he possibly have to say?"

"Man, I don't . . ." She sighs. "He's sell—He's more than likely going to sell the store. . . ."

"*More than likely?* What the fuck?"

She frowns—glares—and whatever relief she felt a second ago is clearly gone. "Yeah. *More than likely,*" she replies, sharp. "Why're you so mad at me?"

"I'm not mad at *you.* I just can't believe he's selling out, that's all."

"*Selling out?* Okay, fuck you," she snaps back. "This is why I didn't want to tell you! I *knew* I shouldn't have told you. You don't—you don't get it."

I roll my eyes. "I'm gonna go talk to Mr. Tran since all you've been doing lately is lying."

She grimaces. "Excuse me? Lying about what?"

I don't answer, just stuff another fry into my mouth and rush out of the Eats as fast as I can. Kate follows, talking rapid-fire behind me while I head to her house. "Why're you so mad about this? You have no right, you know that? It's not your family's store that had a brick thrown through it."

"You're right. So then *you* should be more mad than me. But instead you don't care who threw it or the fact that they're getting away with it right now while your dad is pretty much selling out—"

"Stop saying that! I do care. You really think I don't?"

"You're always brushing me off," I counter. "You don't want to talk about who bricked the store. Just admit it. You don't care that it was probably a kid from outside Ginger East. You don't care about who bricked the store because you don't actually care—"

"Don't you dare say I don't care about the store!" she nearly shrieks. "Or my family. Damn, why can't you leave it alone?"

I frown. "Why should I? You say you care, but then you say shit like that. Kate, this is snake behavior—it's Aries behavior!"

"I'm a Sagittarius, damn!"

"Look at me—does it look like I don't know that?"

"Listen, this is—I'm—it's complicated."

"How?" I say. "How is it complicated? Either you care or you don't. Either your dad is keeping the store or he's not. Ginger Store is part of the neighborhood, and you're just— he's just gonna—he just wants to sell it? To some guy who dares to go out in public with a name like 'Horst'?"

She frowns. "Man, that's just his name."

"I don't care!"

She groans and turns away from me. I get to her front step and knock, but she nudges me aside and opens the door with her key, mumbling something under her breath about me being impatient and dumb. I don't even care right now. As far as I'm concerned, I'm the only one around here making any kind of sense.

I kick off my shoes and rush into the living room. "Mr. Tran? Mr. Tran?" I call, making my way past the—boxes? There are boxes all over the place, piled one on top of the other. There are items poking out, items from the store, and rent notices about the house littered on every other box. All these damn notices. You'd think one would be enough.

I shuffle past a few boxes and call out again, "Mr. Tran?" before he emerges from the adjacent kitchen holding the house phone.

"Nelo," he says with a warm smile. He's trying to be welcoming, but I can't shake this frown, this quivering lip, this disappointment on my face. His smile slowly fades once he gets a better look at me. He's uneasy too, crossing the room to sit on the sofa.

Kate steps out from behind me and circles to the kitchen. Mr. Tran watches her go, thinking she has something to say to him, but she doesn't. He straightens the hemline of his shirt and avoids my eyes.

"Mr. Tran, did that guy call you just now?" I ask, and gesture to the phone lying on the table.

He has to look at the phone before he looks at me. "Yes," he answers plainly.

"The Horst guy?"

"*Mr.* Horst."

"I don't even care," I mumble, and cross my arms. He frowns at me, disappointed. I hate it when adults get all smug about being right and wrong and looking at me as if they're the only ones allowed to say anything. *I* should be the one who's disappointed, not him. "So that's it? You're selling? It's done?"

Mr. Tran turns on Kate as she reenters the room. He's talking to her with his eyes, trying to spell out some secret code. All she can do is shrug, look at me, and look at him.

Suddenly Mr. Tran sighs and sits up straighter. I want to believe he's tired of dancing around the issue, but he might be tired of dancing around me. "Nothing is 'done,'" he says in that plain, pacifying tone that I hate. "I've been talking to him and we're coming to an—an agreement."

"An agreement? So you're selling?" I repeat, bluntly. "How could you, though? Like, just like that?"

"The police are taking too long to investigate, as usual," he goes on, ignoring me. He's actually ignoring me! I'm *fuming*. "They come for statements and call for new evidence, but they have nothing. It's nothing." He clears his throat and smooths his knuckles down to his knees. "They will never find who did this, and you know how this neighborhood is."

I falter, my words stuttering past my lips. "Th-there's nothing wrong with the neighborhood."

He stares at me, that sickeningly sweet pacifying look, and if I could, I swear I'd just burst into tears right now. Mr. Tran never had any complaints about this place, and suddenly one thing happens to him, and he's over it? One thing happens to him from someone who doesn't even go here, and he's over it? No way. He doesn't think this can happen somewhere else? That Ginger East is special and bad people *only* do bad things here and bad shit *only* happens here? No fucking way.

"Nelo," he begins, and suddenly we're staring at each other—him trying to appear calm, and me trying not to cry. I can't believe this is happening.

"You're seriously thinking of leaving . . . ," I utter.

He doesn't move. I suck in my lips, bite down hard, and breathe deep to push the tears away. Fuck, fuck, fuck.

"Nothing is 'done,' like I said," he tells me. "I'm going to talk to Mr. Horst and see. That's all." He is so stern when he speaks, his voice so strict and crisp. I've never heard him speak this way about anything to anyone. He's so different from the Papa Tran I know. Where is the soft smile and the gentle laugh?

I inhale deeply, and feel my shoulders shake and my breath hitch in my throat. I'm trembling so hard now, and all I want to do is hide.

"And me, I've been at that store for many, many years. . . ." He nods slowly, sagely, as if the years are washing over him.

"I've thought for a long time that it was all I had, but maybe that's not true anymore. Maybe this is an opportunity."

"B-but you could reopen the store," I say, waving away his words. "With the insurance money. And fix the window. Right? Even with rent going up on your house, you don't have to sell the store. . . ."

He rolls his knuckles against his knees again and sighs so deeply. I am trembling again. "Many, many years," he repeats, and we lock eyes over the coffee table. "I don't want to go backward, Nelo. That is not where goodness exists. Sometimes things have to change to get better," he says carefully. He's being so delicate, like I'm about to scream or something. But I'm not going to scream—I'm not even going to yell. Hearing his words settle into my ears makes me want to cry even more. Loudly, angrily, sadly. Just cry. I shake my head, and he nods twice as fast, trying to pacify me again. "Yes, yes, they do," he goes on. "Change isn't always a bad thing, you know."

"I didn't—" My voice hitches in my throat again, and I gulp down the urge to cry. "I don't think that it is. It's just . . ."

Mr. Tran shakes his head and says again, slower, more practiced, "Sometimes things have to change to get better."

But better for who? The neighborhood was fine before. How could it have been bad if I grew up here with so many good people? That doesn't make sense. What's wrong with going backward?

I want to tell him that so badly, but the lump in my throat is growing bigger and my eyes are beginning to sting. Before I can blink, I turn away, back to the entrance, and wrestle my shoes on. I don't even bother to turn around when Kate calls my name.

CHAPTER TWENTY-EIGHT

I don't talk to Kate the next day. She's finally texting me, a million times too, and messaging me online. Lots of *talk to me* and *are you okay?* and even one *it's not even your store!* And I'm always two seconds away from blocking her because I never want to speak to her again. I know it's not my store, but if she doesn't understand why I'm sad about this whole selling thing, then she'll never get it. Mr. Tran sells, and then what? She has to move, someone else will move into her house, and I'll lose my best friend like I lost all my other best friends. For a while, it'll be okay and I'll get used to her not being here. But then I'll walk by the Ginger Store building or hear some dumb song on the radio, and I'll remember that one time we listened to the latest Midtown Project album for five hours in the store's back room. Then what am I supposed to do? Call her? Wait for her to forget who I am? It's the same cycle all over again and all of this just gets me feeling some type of way.

By Friday, Rafa notices that I've been dead in the group chat, so he messages me separately.

Raf Morales: whats wrong with you???

Raf Morales: you ok??*

Chinelo Sondra: ya

Raf Morales: ok but why are you lying tho??

Chinelo Sondra: i'm not lying, i'm good

Raf Morales: kate's worried

Chinelo Sondra: she told you that?

Raf Morales: she wrote it in the other chat

Raf Morales: the one you're ignoring

Chinelo Sondra: i'm not ignoring anything

Raf Morales: ok but why lie lol??

Raf Morales: don't think i don't know you

Raf Morales: watching unread messages pile up like you have something better to do

Chinelo Sondra: LOL shut up!

Raf Morales: because you're petty as hell

Chinelo Sondra: whoa whoa whoa

Chinelo Sondra: i swear i'm about to block you

Raf Morales: there's my girl

Chinelo Sondra: stoppppp

Another message comes through on the group chat. I see the notification from Bo drop down from the top of my screen first before I hear it, but I'm extra careful not to accidentally tap it, or the group chat will open and they'll see I read all the messages.

Wow, Rafa's right. I am petty.

Raf Morales: what're you up to these days?

Raf Morales: like after school

Raf Morales: i know you saw that notif just now from bo btw

Chinelo Sondra: lol damn can i live????

Chinelo Sondra: it's only bo so i don't care

Raf Morales: what you have against him anyway?

Chinelo Sondra: nothing

Chinelo Sondra: honestly nothing. i'm not that cool with him anymore. kate told me to add him.

Raf Morales: lol ohhhhhh

Chinelo Sondra: ???

Raf Morales: nothing

Raf Morales: you didnt answer my question

Chinelo Sondra: what question?

Raf Morales: you wanna hang out after school or nah?

Chinelo Sondra: where?

Raf Morales: i dont know, wherever

Chinelo Sondra: doing what?

Raf Morales: uh woooow

Raf Morales: illegal stuff obviously

Chinelo Sondra: if this is some excuse to get me to talk to kate, then no

Raf Morales: nooo she wont be there

Chinelo Sondra: why not?

Raf Morales: you wanna hang out with kate?

Raf Morales: over me?

Chinelo Sondra: lol i meannn

Chinelo Sondra: so who else is coming?

Raf Morales: no one

Chinelo Sondra: no one else? just us?

Raf Morales: thats what i said

It sounds like he's setting me up, and the second I agree, Kate and Bo are going to ambush me and make me talk to them. Make me talk about selling the store or Spice of Life bringing the ugly to Ginger East. I can think of literally nothing worse right now. Another notification from the group chat pops up, and I wait for it to fully disappear before I engage again.

Chinelo Sondra: I gotta be back in time for the protest though, so it can't be anything too illegal, just like 87% illegal

Raf Morales: no lines, got it

Chinelo Sondra: pleeeeeease

Raf Morales: next time we're on the bus, just get off at my stop

Chinelo Sondra: ummm

Chinelo Sondra: this entire thing sounds suspect

Raf Morales: suspect and petty

Raf Morales: the dream team

Chinelo Sondra: oh my GOD

I make a huge deal about it, but I'm actually thankful that Rafa asked to hang out. I need to get my mind off everything and chill out before the protest. Kate's been shooting me worried looks all week since I stormed out of her house, and I've been refusing to make eye contact or talk to her ever since. I don't hang out with her at lunch, instead opting to take a long, lonely walk around the block and pretend I'm not hungry as all hell when I get back to school. I even make sure I'm at the bus the second the bell rings so I don't have to run into her.

Today our usual seat is empty but I skip by it and—take a deep breath—cross into soccer player territory. I'm sitting a bit closer to the back, somewhere Rafa would usually sit, and I slide down as much as I can. My knees are pressed into the seat in front of me, and I bring out my phone, trying to look as busy and invisible as possible. Suddenly I am very aware of the fact that I'm not wearing the new bra Mom got me.

I get a jolt of panic whenever I hear someone else get on the bus. I'm thinking this is a bad idea and I should've sat in my usual seat, or maybe a seat down so I'd be saddled in with that weird eleventh-grade girl who always brings her tuba home to practice. I can hide beside a tuba. I feel so out in the open now.

A group of boys gets on the bus and they're loud as hell, so I know it's either a bunch of overexcited freshmen or the soccer team. I start concentrating extra hard on my phone so I don't have to make eye contact with anyone.

Kate texts me: *where are you???* I delete the notification without a thought. She can stop pretending to care about my feelings, especially now that she has Bo. I bet she already told him everything.

"Whoa, whoa, what's this? Feds girl?"

I cringe so hard at the sound of Marcus's voice. It's so intrusive too. His tongue wraps around his words, and when he speaks, it's as if he's licking your ears. He leans over into my seat, and for a second, I'm afraid he's going to sit beside me, but he doesn't. He leans, licks his lips, stares at me. Being under his gaze is so itchy. He says, "You're really close to where I sit. Why don't you hop back one?"

It takes too long to prepare the perfect clapback, so I just shrug, keep my eyes low, and say, "No thanks." If he was decent, he'd leave, but since he's not, he stays and I can still feel him breathing his hot, nasty-ass breath in my peripheral.

One of his friends squishes by him to a seat way behind me, but Marcus stays because he is scum. "Where's your friend?" he asks, and looks over his shoulder to the front of the bus. "The hot one. Asian."

"Obviously not here."

"You two break up or something?" he asks, chuckling as if he's the funniest guy ever. As if he's the first boy alive to ever assume two close female friends are more than friends.

I don't say anything to him, and he finally takes a hint. He slides into the seat behind me. I hate that he's so close, but it's way better that he's out of my face. It sucks that I can still hear him breathing behind me.

I busy myself with more mindless phone swiping, opening

app after app and closing them, and then pretending to text someone and then closing that, all so I don't look like a loner. Rafa eventually shows up, greets his friends, and exchanges some obnoxious words with them, before dropping into the seat beside me. This doesn't go unnoticed by Marcus, who then props up and leans over the back of the seat to talk to Rafa. "Yooo . . . ," he croons. My neck is tingling with how close he is. "You should've just said you broke up with your girl because of Raf. I heard he's got that effect on girls."

"Because he has that effect on you?" I sneer.

Rafa chokes back a chuckle, and Marcus's smug demeanor immediately shifts. He's no longer smirking; now he's just annoyed with me. "Yo, chill," he says sharply, and directs his attention to Rafa, who's doing a horrible job trying not to laugh. *"Fam."*

Rafa is grinning. "I mean, what'd she lie about?"

"Faaaaam."

"You said you joined the team last year because of me, though!"

Marcus frowns. "I never said that any *day*, fam!"

"Yeah, you did say that!" one of his friend's pipes up from behind us, and Marcus's brown skin is tinged with a hint of red. This is really all I want: Marcus, thoroughly roasted and set aside.

He kisses his teeth in defiance and crashes back down into his seat. Rafa is still chuckling when he glances at me, and

I look away, back at my phone for no real reason. I've typed out half a text to a sometimes-friend that I don't even want to send, so I hit the back button a million times before I stuff my phone away.

"Hi," Rafa says to me once he has kind of composed himself.

"Hi," I reply. It's strange that suddenly I can't think of any other words.

CHAPTER TWENTY-NINE

Rafa lives in the Cooksville area now, just west of Ginger East. I've only been there once or twice. I know it has sustainable-coffee shops, the kinds that are now popping up in Ginger East. I know it has corner shops and community centers that aren't littered with graffiti or cash advance advertisements. It's really sterile compared to Ginger East. Sometimes people smile at you when you walk by, and it makes you feel as if you have money. I can't explain how, but it just does.

Rafa puts in serious work getting rid of his friends when we get off the bus. They're being suspect and hanging around too long, or eyeing me like they want to talk to me but can't. Like he told them not to say anything to me, or something like that. I'm cool with it, though. I don't know them all by name, and I'm not really looking for any new friends, so I turn the other way and fake scroll through my messages. The group chat notifications are piling up. Two hundred and one, and counting.

"Are you gonna read them or no?" Rafa asks. He creeps up behind me, staring clear over my shoulder.

Hiding my phone, I spin around to face him. "No way. It's too late now, anyway."

"What d'you mean it's too late?" He snickers. "They're not going to kick you out. Just read them."

"Damn, don't you know how to mind your own business at all?" I say, and he bursts out laughing. His laugh is more charming than he is, and it puts me at ease, though I didn't know I was nervous before. What's there to be nervous about? I know Rafa. We're real friends now, just like old times. "Where are we going? What am I doing out here in Cooksville?"

"Hanging out with me, obviously." He says it as though I've been given the best gift ever. Normally I'd hate that, but it really has me grinning hard this time. I won't ever say it to Rafa, but in a way, this kind of is a gift. I spend all my time in Ginger East because it's where I'm from. It's the only way I know how to be. Rafa and I grew up in the same place, but he left just when we were becoming real people—teenagers with thoughts and feelings and real problems. He's so different now, and it's strange to think that it's because of this place, that another place could have shaped him like how Ginger East shaped me.

"Can I see your house?" I ask.

He's suspicious, narrowing his eyes at me. "Why you wanna see my house?"

"To make sure you're not homeless? I don't know."

He laughs. "I think my mom might be home."

Mama Morales is the cool mom. Growing up, we all thought that, mainly because she let Rafa grow his hair out as long as he wanted. His house also always had the best snacks. My house and Kate's house always had rice because our parents hate us, Bo's house always had cashews and other stuff nobody likes, and Maree's house was the worst because all she had was ham and cheese. Rafa's house had Pop-Tarts and cinnamon rolls and empanadas and ice cream. So much ice cream! It was heaven.

Mrs. Morales used to work in HR or something like that, but now that they live in Cooksville, she's a stay-at-home mom, which I think is weird because Rafa is her only kid and he's always at school or at practice, so she could definitely go do something else now if she wanted to. I wonder if Mr. Morales still works at that bank like he used to. He used to always come back mad late and leave for work super early. He got a promotion a while back. That's probably why they could afford to move, and why Mrs. Morales still looks like she's pushing thirty when she's really not.

Rafa lives in a two-story house, which is such a contrast to the bungalow he used to live in at Ginger East. He pushes open the door, and I'm immediately hit with the smell of seasoned beef, and that's how I *know* I'm not going home for dinner.

"Ma?" Rafa calls down the hallway.

Mrs. Morales pokes her head out of the kitchen and gasps loudly when she sees me. I don't think she knows it's me, because her eyebrows are twisting in that way when you're confused and trying to make sense of something. She's dusting her hands on a cloth as she approaches. "Who's this? A friend from school?" she asks, eyeing me up and down.

"Yeah," he says, and kicks off his shoes before trudging past her into the kitchen. "You remember Nelo, right?"

Hearing my name has her gasping again, but this time she grins and laughs and presses her hand to her mouth. "*Nelo?* From the neighborhood? The cute one from TV with the face?" she says, and chortles, and then quickly calls over her shoulder, saying something in Spanish.

Rafa calls back, "Ma, you can't *say* that!" He sounds more than a little touchy.

Mrs. Morales chuckles. "I can say whatever I want, babe. And it's true— it's true, you know," she says to me with a wink. I smile back politely even though I don't know what's true and what's not. "Come in, come in. Oh my goodness, you were on the news recently, and look at you . . ."

I take my time taking off my shoes and heading down the hallway while Mrs. Morales admires me from up close. It's uncomfortable because she's smiling so much and I'm just trying to get a good look at the inside of this house. This is definitely the nicest house I've ever been in. The hardwood floor doesn't creak, and the cream-colored walls are scuff-free. My

head even deeper. "That place is no good for children. It's not a good place to grow up."

"Wh-what?" I choke out with a nervous laugh. Is she kidding? Mrs. Morales is nodding like, *Yes, it's so tragic,* and all I can think of is how untrue that is. My mind can't move fast enough to spell out all the ways she's wrong. "N-no, uh, wait," I stutter. "Ginger East isn't that bad. I mean, growing up there was pretty cool. It's still cool. I don't have any complaints."

Mrs. Morales is still frowning, still feeling sorry for me. "You kids couldn't go out at night. It was dangerous to even go onto the main road sometimes in the day. And there was that old man, the one on the drugs, hmm. He would always approach the children, and it scared me so much—"

"It's not like that anymore, though," I interrupt. "He's dead now, anyway, so it's, like, ten times safer."

"And then the arcade."

I swallow, tense. "That was a long time ago."

Her smile is strained, sad, and she nods slowly. "I know, *mija,* how much you like that place," she tells me. Her words are a soothing back rub, a gesture that wants to tell me that everything will be fine. She's trying to pacify me. Why are adults always doing this to me? "But it's changed, hasn't it? It's changed a lot."

I shake my head right away. So sick of talking about change.

Suddenly I hear a familiar voice come from the living

room. I jump a little because it's maybe too familiar and I'm stuck wondering how this voice, how this person, got all the way out here. All the way out of Ginger East.

"Is that Mr. Brown?" I ask after a moment of silence. Mrs. Morales strains to hear, and I follow the voice to Rafa's massive living room and the TV blaring the local news. I'm immediately distracted by the pristine look and extreme cleanliness of the room. Some of the chairs are still covered in plastic, so I know they're just for decoration. I stand in front of the TV as Mr. Brown speaks too closely into a microphone that an off-camera interviewer sticks into his face. There's a huge brown building behind him. It's Spice of Life.

Rafa pops his head into the living room as Mr. Brown takes hold of the microphone. "Oh, Mr. Brown from the neighborhood," he says, coming to join me by the TV. "What's he doing on TV?"

"He's organizing the protest, remember?" I tell him.

"The one you're also organizing?"

"You made that joke already."

"Damn."

"We're thinking we might get over two hundred people or something," I tell him. "Are you coming, though?"

He shrugs. "Maybe. Depends."

I have no idea what he means by that, but I'm too enamored of Mr. Brown on TV to care. We always used to make fun of the low-budget local area news, but seeing Mr. Brown on it and seeing Ginger East not looking as though it's a poverty porn tourist spot lightens my spirits a bit. Just a bit, though. It's nice that the neighborhood's community efforts are being highlighted, but knowing why the protest is happening brings my mind back to Ginger Store and the Trans. And Kate.

". . . and the protest is tonight, correct?" the interviewer asks.

"Yes," Mr. Brown says cordially. "We're expecting a lot of young people. I'm sure you know of Chinelo Agu, who was on Channel 9 a while back. . . ."

"You're famous," Rafa gasps, and I have to laugh.

"Once again, we just want it to be peaceful," Mr. Brown continues. "It's really about the community coming together in the face of ugliness."

When he says "ugliness," the camera immediately pans to Spice of Life for a hot second before jolting back to Mr. Brown. This cameraman feels no ways about his job, does he?

Rafa disappears momentarily and returns with a bunch of snacks. I'm reminded why his house was always the best. He presses a cold water bottle into my hand, and it brings me back to the present, here in this model-home-looking living room with the brightest pot lights I've ever seen. "Come on, let's go outside for a bit," he says. "We can't sit in here. It's for decoration."

"I knew it."

He leads me to the backyard, which I'm happy to see isn't much bigger than mine. The grass is greener and there's a soccer net at the opposite end, snuggled away behind a six-seater patio set. There are two chairs and a table off to the side—and out of view of the sliding door—where he sets down the chips and cookies. I instantly grab the box and rip it open, drop into one of the chairs, and cram a cookie into my face.

Rafa opens his bottle of water and takes a gulp, swishes it around in his mouth a bit before swallowing. We lock eyes, and I reach for another cookie and take a huge bite, before I say, "So . . . your mom speaks Spanish now?"

He groans right away. "She practically learned yesterday and she's actually doing the most."

"And you speak Spanish now too?"

"I always have," he corrects me like he's actually right. This boy doesn't know any Spanish, and he knows it. If his mom just learned yesterday, then he learned this morning.

"Okay, so what'd your mom say?"

"What'd what?"

"What'd your mom say just now?" I ask again while he takes another gulp of his water. "What'd she say before you told her she shouldn't say that? Was she cussing me? Is that it?"

He smirks, the slightest tinge of red brushing his cheeks, and shakes his head. "No way, no. She wasn't."

"I bet she was," I tease, poking him in the arm. In his toned arm. "That's probably why you won't tell me. You think I'm too sensitive."

"Uh, obviously you're too sensitive. It's a byproduct of being so petty," he says, and snickers.

"I'm gonna need you to not call me petty—"

"I bet Kate thinks you're petty but she won't say it because you're too sensitive."

I'm laughing even though I don't want to. "Shut up, shut up," I chuckle, and swipe another cookie to occupy myself. Rafa is giving me sly looks like he knows he's right—he's always looking at me like that! Well, he's not right. No one can be that right all the time. "I'm not sensitive," I reiterate as clearly as I can with cookie stuck to the roof of my mouth.

"Sure," he says. I finish off the rest of his water, partially because it's the only bottle open and partially because I want to annoy him.

"Is that why you're not talking to her?" he asks.

"Honestly?" I sigh. "Haven't you ever tried minding your business?"

"I'm serious, though. Even Bo's kind of worried."

"About Kate?"

"About you."

I grimace. Bo, worried about me? Rafa has to know how stupid that sounds. "Why would he be?" I say. "If I'm not talking to Kate, why's it his problem? And it's not that I'm *not* talking to her, anyway. I don't have anything to say to her, so. It's not his business."

Rafa shrugs, but I know he doesn't buy anything I'm saying. He's quiet, contemplating, and I can suddenly feel all my frustrations bubble to the surface. My chest is pounding. My voice is echoing in my ears. "It's all just stupid," I spit out. "Everything is so brand-new now. Ever since the stuff happened with Ginger Store, Kate's been all weird and won't talk to me. Not really, anyway. She's making it seem as if it's all because I was in that video and on TV, but I know that can't be true.

"We're like this . . ." I hold up both my hands, flat and level to one another with my fingertips touching, and then I shift one hand a bit higher and one hand a bit lower. Rafa moves my hands, the higher one higher and the lower one lower, as if I'm some sort of puppet. His hands are warm and familiar against mine, and he doesn't let go right away. When I try to look at him, he stares at my fingers like he's concentrating on something so important. Normally I would think it wasn't that deep, but now I think it's cute.

He eventually lets go, and I have to steady myself without the weight of his hands under mine. When I don't continue, he stares at me, expectantly. He even has the nerve to ask: "So then what?"

"Uh." I clear my throat. "Then—uh—she's down here and I'm up here, right?" I wiggle each hand.

"How are you sure she's not the higher one?"

"Because it's my story," I say, and he laughs. "Focus, Rafael."

He says, "Focusing," and leans in closer. I might be imagining it, but either I can feel warmth emanating off him or my temperature is rising.

I purse my lips to keep from smiling. "I'm so serious right now. I'm up here, and she's down here, but we used to be like this." I bring both my hands back to the same level and touch my fingertips again. "We used to be the same, you know? When everything happened with the store . . . man, even when the protest came up, I thought she'd join with me. I thought we'd be in this together, like we always have, but it's as if she doesn't care at all. Can you believe that?"

"No," he says, his voice soft and tempered.

I scowl. "Well, it's true. Things aren't the way they used to be," I tell him, feeling my edge come back. "She's changed. The neighborhood has changed. Kate's always talking to Bo—and Mr. Tran, who used to be the coolest Tran, is probably selling the store to those bitch-ass real estate people! Honestly? Can you imagine Ginger East with a new high-rise? It's wack. Nothing in there is new—or maybe everything is new and that's the problem. I don't recognize anything anymore. That store, that place that sells shit with kale as if anyone can tell the difference between that and actual grass. And that spice store. All these new places coming in and changing the neighborhood . . ." My voice trails off once I lose steam. I'm caught in this confusion where my mind is done running, but I have no idea what I've said.

Rafa opens the other water bottle. He doesn't say anything to me while he's wrestling with the cap or sliding the bottle over to me. I'm too full of anger to drink any water, but I chug it anyway. It makes me feel heavier.

"I'm gonna tell you something," Rafa says. "You're probably not gonna like it, though."

"Don't say I'm overreacting."

"Yeah, no, not that," he tells me. He nudges the water closer to me, and I take another gulp to appease him. And then he says: "Mr. Tran has a right to sell his own store."

His words feel like a direct attack. My defenses are up immediately. "I never said he didn't, though."

"That's basically what you said."

"No, it's not."

"It is," he says effortlessly. "He doesn't owe you anything. His store got trashed and you're mad because he wants to take a payout from some real estate guys? To pay for his store that got trashed? Are you listening to yourself? Ginger Store isn't the *entire* neighborhood. And if things are different from how they used to be, if Kate thinks Bo is cool now, then you're not gonna die. Change can be good."

I frown and roll my eyes so hard, it feels like they're about to pop out of my head. But he's right about maybe one thing, and I'm mad that he is. I know Ginger Store isn't the whole neighborhood, but it's a big part of it. And it's *my* neighborhood. I've spent my entire life there, grew up there, and I still live there.

I am quiet for long enough that he probably feels like he won, which puts me deeper in my feelings because he definitely did *not* win that conversation. I'm just spent. My mind is tired and I don't know what I want.

Suddenly Rafa nudges the bag of chips closer to me, and I crack the smallest of smiles. I'm so bad at faking it because I take another look at the chips and start laughing like I wasn't just heavy in thought a second ago. "I hate you," I say.

He smirks and leans in closer beside me. "Why?"

"Because you always make me think about stuff," I tell him, and he laughs.

"Stuff?"

"Yes, stuff," I mumble, grazing my fingers over the chip bag. I glance at Rafa and we lock eyes briefly. I can't place the look in his eyes, but all of a sudden I'm hyper-aware of him staring at me, his closeness. "Sometimes you're just not ready for things to be different," I say slowly. "You know what I mean?"

He shakes his head.

And then he leans over and kisses me.

On the *lips*.

I shudder at the warmth of his mouth on mine, how comfortable but foreign it feels. And when I kiss him back, the shock is enough to crush me. It's deeper than anything I've ever experienced. It feels like home.

I break away, letting my tongue glide along the inside of my lip, and immediately feel the full force of my nervousness kick in. Me? And *Rafa*?

"Oh m-my God," I stutter. My voice sounds distant, like someone else's in my ears. He is looking at me like *Is this girl going to be all right?* and I'm imagining what it would be like to kiss him again, or maybe—I don't know—push my hands under his shirt or something so I can properly evaluate the ab situation, but I can't think straight—and I don't know why I'm even thinking about him like this! I don't want this. Do I?

"Are you okay?" he asks quietly.

I want to say no, but I'm just as fake as Kate. "Yes. Yeah," I utter. And that's it.

He frowns, unconvinced. "Are you sure? Because you can tell me if you're not. . . ."

"N-no, I'm good. I just, uh—" *Can't stop thinking about what your lips feel like.* Can't stop thinking, can't stop thinking, can't stop thinking. Has he thought about kissing me before? Is that the only reason he asked me to come over? Is that the only reason he's being so nice to me?

"I n-need to go home," I stutter out finally. "The protest is tonight, so I should, uh, go." My eyes dart immediately to the ground, where I swipe for my bag, and then I back away from the table.

"Nelo—"

"It's cool. I'll see you at school," I tell him, before slinging my backpack over my shoulder and beelining straight for the doors into the house.

Mrs. Morales is hovering by the sliding doors. I'm panicking, thinking she saw and she's about to lecture me, but it takes me a second to see that her shock is because I'm leaving and *not* because I've been kissing her son. "You're not staying for dinner?" she asks, taking a step toward me.

"No," I tell her, forcing a smile. She follows me to the doorway, where I crouch and begin wrestling my feet into my shoes. "No, I gotta get home. And then there's the protest. My mom called, so."

"Oh, yeah?" She smiles too, nodding. "How is she these days?"

"She's good. She's cool."

"Wow, you know, you're starting to look so much like her. So grown-up."

While I rise, her eyes are taking in every angle of my face, of my body, and I'm stuck under her gaze for ten long seconds. "I really have to go, Mrs. Morales," I mutter.

The trance is broken and she nods, a hint of disappointment in her smile. "Of course, of course. Tell her I said 'Hey.' "

"I will."

I spin around and pull open the front door. I don't want to look like I'm running away, but I am. I'm jogging out the door and down the driveway. I'm running to the sidewalk. I can't stop running.

Now that I'm alone, all of my caged feelings break free. My heart is thumping in my chest and I'm so nervous, I could die. What just happened? Things aren't supposed to be like this. I can't *like* him. Not like that, anyway.

My feet slow to a stop once I reach the intersection where the school bus dropped us off. It's so empty on the street.

I cross the road while I dig my phone out of my pocket. Honestly, I wonder if Rafa will call me—or if he won't call me because he doesn't know what to say, just like how I don't know what to say to him. I fumble my phone, almost dropping it a million times, while I think. While I play the kiss over and over again in my head. How good it felt. How familiar.

"You like him," I murmur to myself. "Or he likes you . . ."

We were *best* friends at a point, and I haven't spoken to him in ages, so when did he start thinking he liked me? Maybe because we've been spending so much time together, he feels like we have a different kind of bond now, because we're older and guys and girls apparently can't be just friends anymore.

Or, maybe he's always liked me. That's what Kate and Jake said, and why would they lie?

CHAPTER THIRTY

My fingers stumble over Jake's number. Jake is the only one
I know who has a car and might agree to come get me, aside
from my mom, who also has a car but might be more concerned with me being in Cooksville than anything. Luckily,
he picks up on the second ring. "Nelo?" he asks. "Why are you
calling me?"

"Uh . . . ," I mumble, staring around at the street. Cars fly
by, each kicking up more wind than the last, and I turn my
back on them so I can hear him better. "I don't know," I tell
him. "Are you at home?"

"Yeah," he answers. "What's up?"

"Can you come get me?"

There's a beat of silence before he says, "What?"

"I'm in Cooksville."

"Wait, why are you in Cooksville?"

"Long story. Can you just come get me?"

He snorts. "Were you kidnapped?"

"Maybe I was," I shoot back, my voice shaking through my
defensiveness. "Can you come get me, *please*? I don't wanna

call my mom. She can't leave work early, and I don't want to bother her."

He sighs and groans as though I'm forcing him to do something awful, like he'd sooner leave me here to die than drive the twenty extra minutes down the highway to find me. I really shouldn't be surprised that new Jake would rather let me die in Cooksville, since new Kate is keeping secrets with her new best friend, Bo. This entire family is on something. "Fine," he says eventually. "Don't move, okay? Where are you?"

"On some street corner, I don't know. There's some espresso bar here."

"Wow, okay," he chuckles. I don't like hearing him laugh on the phone so casually while I'm anything but casual. It really doesn't help that every time I'm not talking, I'm thinking about Rafa. And kissing him. "I'm coming. Go wait at the espresso place."

He hangs up first, and I instantly bolt across the street to hide out in the café. It's way warmer in here and smells like roasted coffee beans and cinnamon. The second I step in, the barista at the counter turns to me and grins. It stops me in my tracks. "Welcome," she calls.

I glance over my shoulder to make sure she's not talking to the person behind me. The barista seems to find this funny, and she giggles while she polishes the counter. "Can I get you anything?" she asks me.

There are at least four other people in the room, either typing away on tablets or reading books. It's so quiet and she's talking like we're the only two people in here. I make a point to walk closer to the counter and whisper, "No, I'm okay, thanks," so she doesn't have to yell across the room anymore.

"Okay, cool," she replies at the exact same volume as before. "Just so you know, we have white chocolate vanilla lattes on special this week. Our large size comes with an automatic donation to any of the charities we're affiliated with. You can take a look at those on our community board."

I nod quickly, hoping that will get her to stop talking so loud. "Yeah, cool. Thanks."

Another customer walks in, and the barista directs her attention to him. I take the opportunity to duck into the nearest empty booth and slouch down. I wait, and when my phone finally buzzes, it's Jake telling me he's outside—and not Rafa telling me he likes me or anything, thankfully.

I'm shocked to see Kate in the passenger seat, even though I really shouldn't be. Jake is her brother and I'm sure he asked her if she wanted to tag along. He probably doesn't know how difficult it's going to be for me to sit in a car with a girl who clearly doesn't see me as her best friend anymore.

Kate glances at me through the window, then avoids my eyes as I slink around to the backseat. The guilt hits me immediately, followed by anger, followed by fatigue. I'm always in such a rush to tell her everything, but this time, I keep my mouth firmly shut. "Thanks, Jake," I mutter, shifting my backpack onto the seat beside me.

"Yeah, it's cool," he says simply as he backs out of the café's parking spot. He glances at Kate before he looks at me in the rearview mirror. He can tell something's up because I didn't bother saying anything to Kate, but he stays quiet and pulls onto the road.

Kate turns around in her seat, and she's got this apologetic pout on like she didn't just snap at me a few days ago. I'm not about this, so I shrug, like *What do you want?* She flinches a little, looking more and more the victim. Does she really think I'm going to fight her right now? No way.

I sink farther down into my seat and reach for my phone—but quickly drop it when I realize I don't actually want to check it.

"So . . . ," Kate begins. "What are you doing all the way out here? I thought you were going to the protest. Did you miss the bus or something?"

I shrug. "No." I'm prepared to leave it at that, but her eyes are waiting, egging me on to continue. "Hanging out with Rafa."

"Whaaaat?" she gasps, and pulls out her phone, immediately swiping through to our group chat. "How did I miss this invite?"

There's no nice way to say "You weren't invited," so I sink further into my seat and focus on the moving pavement outside instead. The sooner we can get to Ginger East, the better, but it feels like Jake is driving slower and slower. At first I think he's doing it on purpose because he can sense the awkwardness and he enjoys watching me suffer or something, but traffic really is backing up. I crane my neck a little to see what's going on, if there's an accident, but a grocery truck blocks my view. Irony is a bitch.

Kate eventually stops scrolling once she realizes I'm not going to answer. She pockets her phone again and faces me as best she can, chewing on her lower lip, trying to figure out what to say. Finally she settles on, "How come you called Jake instead of me?"

"You don't drive, so."

She frowns. Wait, so now she's getting mad at me because I told her some facts?

"What's your issue?" she says.

"I mean, you *can't* drive, though."

"No, no," she groans. "I meant about today. Like, you knew you were going to hang out with Rafa and you didn't tell me? I was worried because you didn't text me—and besides, he's my friend too, you know."

"Well, it's not like we spent a lot of time talking, anyway."

Why did I say that? Her mouth zips shut and her face scrunches up, confused, while she tries to figure out if I'm talking about what she thinks I'm talking about. But then, before she can call me out, Jake cuts in and says, "That sounds like you and Bo." And he snickers. *Snickers.*

Shocked, Kate whips around to face Jake. "Shut uuuuup," she hisses.

He keeps snickering. "I'm just saying. Maybe you don't want to be there for those hangouts, just like how I don't want to be in the room next to yours when you and Bo are *hanging out*—"

"Jake!" she snaps.

The car goes quiet with nothing but Jake's stifled chuckles, the engine whirring in the background, and cars honking impatiently in front of us. Kate is avoiding my eyes again. She's doing such a good job of pretending I'm not staring right at her, mouth hung open, a million thoughts going through my head. "What the *hell*? Are . . . are you and Bo—"

"No," she interrupts, shaking her head. "We're not."

"Aren't you, though?" Jake pipes up, and Kate's nostrils flare in anger.

But it doesn't matter. My chest already hurts with this hollow feeling I've never felt before. It's betrayal, or something like it. It's being left behind or taken for granted or whatever. It's ugly, heavy, and empty at the same time, and I can't stand it. It hurts to think my best friend—one of my best friends ever—can't even tell me that she and Bo are . . . that they're . . .

"You guys are actually dating, aren't you," I say quietly. It's not even a question—it's a fact. It's true. The car goes quiet and Kate looks at me, but says nothing. Absolutely nothing. We tell each other everything. When did we stop being that person for each other?

She pouts again like I've said something to her so mean and so vile that she can't stand to answer. That's all I need to see before I reach for my bag beside me. I can't be in here anymore. Traffic has slowed to a full stop as Jake turns left at the top of the hill on our descent into Ginger East. Instinctively I grab the door handle and try to pull it open, but the car is still inching forward and the door is locked. "Open the—stop the car," I say, my jaw tense.

"We can't stop the car," Kate mumbles. "We're, like, not even home yet. Chill."

"Don't tell me to chill," I hiss, and she winces like I cut her. "Stop the car, *please*," I tell Jake.

Kate sighs. "We're literally approaching Ginger Way." She's right; we've inched forward enough that Ginger Store is in view, but the traffic seems to be getting worse and worse on the main road. Jake stops the car and waits. We're stuck for another three, four, five seconds before I pull for the door handle again. Jake locks the doors before I get to it. "Come on, don't be like this," Kate says.

"Be like what?" I snap. "You act like telling me anything is gonna kill you. Meanwhile, we're supposed to be 'friends.' Jake, open the door—"

"Why are you always so dramatic?" Kate groans, though her voice is small. "I mean, I was going to tell you—I haven't told anyone. Not even my other friends know."

"Bitch, what other friends?" I practically shriek.

Jake locks eyes with me in the rearview mirror and starts yelling at me—"What's your problem?"—but I unlock the door and bolt while he's distracted, and wrestle my backpack on before taking off down the road.

"Nelo!" I hear Kate call, but I keep running. The traffic gets denser as I make my way down the hill and past Ginger Store. It's backed up all the way down the road, and that's when I remember—the protest. The protest was supposed to start in the evening, so why's the road blocked this early?

I keep running, forgetting about Kate and instead focusing on what's going on. I jog past the abandoned duplex and past Mr. Brown's loans shop, which is closed. I jog past the good coffee place and the good, good coffee place, and that kale-sandwich-selling place. Jimmy from the Eats is standing in the doorway, arms crossed, and he gives me a grim look as I pass him. "Be careful, huh," he says to me.

"Of what?" I say.

He nods to the crowd ahead, and I slow my pace a little when I finally see it. The reason for the traffic. Police cars line the road in front of Spice of Life, and officers are standing at attention, circling, patrolling. My footsteps become lighter as I approach, as I scan the growing crowd. Residents are keeping their distance from police. Several protesters wearing all black huddle by the Spice of Life entranceway with their eyes closed, praying. *Praying.* Others are carrying signs in the air, engaging with shop owners, talking. Everything feels still but scary. Tense.

I slip through the crowds. They grow tighter and tighter around me until I emerge on the other side, facing Spice of Life. A barricade of officers is guarding the store, daring anyone to get close. When I take a step forward, their chests puff out and their anger grows. *Chill,* I want to say. *Chill, I live here.* But they don't look like they came for a conversation.

I sidestep a group of protesters with signs, and a small section of police immediately tracks me with their eyes like I'm some kind of criminal. They recognize me for sure, whether it's from the news or the video of me saying they probably vandalized the store. They mobilize, break away, and stand guard all around the store. "You're protecting the building?" I say, my eyes flying up to the straight-edged roof. My voice falls into the hum of the street. There's a buzz bouncing off every building, off every resident. "You're protecting the building when there are people who live here?" None of them even bats an eyelash at me. It's like they don't hear me at all.

Spice of Life looks ten times uglier under their watch. Its brick looks moldy and gray and shaky, just like the one officer who won't stop looking at me like I'm about to jump him. His arms fall to his sides the second he thinks I'm not watching, but when I turn back, he crosses them again, stern and strict.

Then one of the officers speaks up, all self-righteous. Like he went to school and I didn't, so there's no way I could know what he's about to tell me. "Listen, we're going to need you to step back. This building is private property," he says.

I want to laugh out of nervousness and rage, but I can't do anything besides frown. "This entire *street* is private property, bro."

His sneer grows deeper, more fierce. "It's *officer*—"

Mr. Brown's voice cuts through the chatter. I don't know how I didn't notice his tall figure beside the officers before. His face is set in that stubborn scowl while he gestures wildly, explaining something or other to this cop. The guy doesn't even look interested. "You can't obstruct traffic, sir," the officer says. "And you can't block people from entering another person's business." His eyes break away from Mr. Brown and scan the street again, making eye contact with each of the other cops. It's like they have a code.

Mr. Brown waves to the Spice of Life entranceway behind him. "We're not obstructing nothing," he says bluntly. "If people want to go and shop, they can go and shop. We're not blocking any doors. We're not the ones who come with barricades to intimidate people . . ." Mr. Brown trails off when he notices me standing a few paces away. A look of fear crosses his face, and he walks over, fast and harried, nearly knocking the officer down. "What are you doing here?"

"What do you mean? I'm on your committee," I tell him. "You even said I should go on the news, remember?"

Mr. Brown has a frantic look in his eyes. His anxiety is

mouth is slack with shock by the time I get to the kitchen. No cracked tiles, no uneven floor, nothing. It's like a model home.

Rafa notices me gawking and taps his chin, trying to get me to fix my face. I make a show of pressing my jaw back up where it belongs, and he laughs. Mrs. Morales zeroes in on us like a heat-seeking missile. She's still wiping her hands on that cloth, still smiling at me like I'm her prize puppy. "So are you two *studying*?" she asks, eyeing us both. The way she's saying it has me feeling cornered, and is making my face mad warm.

Rafa shakes his head. Wow, what a snake. He can't even lie?

"I know, I know," Mrs. Morales says, turning to me. "Nelo's so smart. You never had to study."

I can only smile. "I guess so," I say. "We're just hanging out."

"Oh?" she croons, sweeping over to the kitchen table. "So just *hanging out*, then?"

"Ma, honestly?" Rafa says. "Nelo's never left Ginger East and she has approximately one and a half friends, so that's why we're hanging out here instead."

I gasp. "Oh, so it's like that?"

He chuckles, smug and assured, and says, "Yeah, obviously."

But Mrs. Morales is frowning through it all as she shakes her head, looking at me with pity. I've gone from prize puppy to pathetic puppy in two seconds. "You still live there, huh?" she asks quietly. I nod like *Yeah, of course*, and she shakes her palpable, and it spreads to me the longer it takes for him to answer. The sounds around us are distracting. Voices rising and softening put me on edge. The electric buzz in the air grows louder and louder. And Mr. Brown's frantic look morphs into a grimace. He says, "You shouldn't be here."

"Why not? And why are there so many cops? It's . . ." I look around and notice that the officer Mr. Brown was talking to is giving me the nastiest look. It makes my stomach turn. He's distracted once another protestor steps to him, this short man I recognize from seeing him every now and then in the neighborhood. It looks like they're arguing about something. "Why are there so many cops?" I ask again.

"You really want to be asking me that question?" Mr. Brown huffs, annoyed. "If your mom doesn't know you're here, then you shouldn't be—"

"Nelo!"

I cringe at the sound of Kate's voice. It's the first time I've ever had that kind of reaction to her. My feet are itching to start running again, but the area is getting more and more crowded. I can't see a way out, and every time my eyes glance over to the police line, the police are glaring at me. What did I ever do to them? Something about their presence is haunting, like standing in the shadow of a tall, tall building. They shouldn't be here, they really shouldn't.

Someone calls Mr. Brown's name, and after giving me one last stern look, he hobbles through the restless crowd.

I hear Kate saying, "Sorry, sorry, excuse me," before I feel her hand on my arm, spinning me around to face her. She's glowering at me and I'm glowering back, and in this moment I'm sure we both hate each other more than anything else in the entire world.

Voices rise in the distance. Some protesters are done praying under the police's watchful eye and are beginning to get agitated. I can see it in how they move, turning their backs to oncoming officers and clenching their fists when they talk. Mr. Brown goes from group to group, telling them one thing or another, and they nod, stiff, with one eye always on the police.

Kate watches the circling officers, and I can feel her unease growing. She looks at me again, and the fear in her eyes dissipates at once. She's still mad.

One of the officers calls out to us. "Hey," he says, "you girls can't play here. You should leave."

I grimace. "Um, excuse me—?"

"We're going," Kate calls back over me. She grabs my arm and leads me away from the crowd to a quiet space at the corner of Ginger Way, where no one can see us. I look over my shoulder at a small group of officers advancing on protesters, but my view is cut off by the growing crowd.

The second Kate and I have some breathing room, I yank my arm away from her and take a step back. She doesn't even look hurt, and that's when I know she's actually here for a fight.

"You're being stupid," she says, drawing out every word. "I can't even believe you're mad about this. You really think I wasn't going to tell you about Bo? You're my *best* friend—"

I hold up a hand to silence her. "Shut," I say, pressing my index finger and thumb together.

She's fuming. "Excuse me?"

"I'm really not going to stand here and listen to you lie to me. Why not just tell me from the beginning, then?" I ask, crossing my arms defensively. "Mind yourself. You *know* you weren't going to tell me anything. You wanna know how I know? Because you haven't said a thing to me for an entire month. Ever since what happened at Ginger Store—"

"This has nothing to do with the store!"

Her voice cracks when she yells. Cars are honking, still backed up along the main road. Angry voices rise in the distance, chanting carries through the air.

"Yes, it does," I press again. "You know it as well as I do. You never cared about finding out who smashed the window because you knew your dad would sell anyway. You didn't care that selling meant we weren't gonna hang out anymore, and you're spending all your time with Bo, keeping secrets from me—"

"It's—no—listen. It's different; it's not what you think," she cuts in.

I grimace. "Not what I think? How do you know what I'm thinking?"

"He—he just *gets* me, okay?" She throws her arms into the air, exasperated. A strand of hair falls out of place, into her eyes, and she brushes it away in one harsh swipe. All I can do is shrug. She's suddenly anxious, and it's strange to think I made her that way. I didn't think asking her to be real with me would be this difficult. Maybe I don't understand after all.

The chatter rises around us, and I echo loud enough for her to hear, "He *gets* you?" and she nods right away. "I thought I got you."

"You do, ob-obviously," she stutters, still anxious. She's fidgeting, shifting her weight from one leg to the other. "But it's different with Bo. He's not from here anymore, you know? And you, you're in love with this place. He isn't, so sometimes he's just easier to talk to. He left, and now he knows what it's like to want other things. To want more in life."

I recoil from the harshness of her words. "Wow, so I don't? Is that what you really think of me? That I settle for every-thing?"

"I never said that," she groans. "God, you're always being so—"

"So what? Dramatic? Naive? I'm literally just repeating what you told me."

"Don't even," she warns. "You're always saying what-ever you want, like no one else's feelings matter, but it's not like you know how difficult things have been for my family this entire time. You think my parents wanted to stay here this long?"

I shake my head. "They wouldn't—"

"I'm serious. I'm *so* serious," she goes on, boastful and proud. I've never seen her this cocky, this enraged. It's even worse with the yelling in the distance. It's gotten louder, angrier. "You think they didn't want to move into a nicer house, or a nicer neighborhood, especially after what happened with the arcade? You think they were cool with rent going up? You really—you *really* think I wasn't tired of hearing them complain, month after month, year after year? How do you think I felt, not being able to do anything about it? And then—*and then*, when I thought things were finally going good, your video blows up and Maree decides to go online and tell the entire fucking world about the store, and now people are throwing money at her and reporters are everywhere talking to both of you and blowing everything out of proportion!"

"What . . . ? What's being blown out of proportion—"

"The insurance would've been fine on its own. We didn't need all this extra media attention," she goes on, her voice as rough as I've ever heard it. "It wasn't supposed to get this deep. No one was supposed to pay attention—no one ever pays attention to Ginger East. If I knew it was going to go down like this, I would've never thrown that stupid brick!"

Her words hit like a cold, hard slap in the face, and I stumble back to steady myself. There are sirens blaring around the corner, and I think of the police and the protest and this neighborhood changing. And then I hear it: the smash. The sound of glass shattering in the open air. People yelling, sirens, everything. I remember seeing glass pepper the sidewalk the morning Ginger Store was trashed. I remember seeing the brick. But now I can see Kate, my best friend, standing under the cover of night, breathing heavily while she throws it.

CHAPTER THIRTY-ONE

The sirens are getting louder and louder in the background, and soon we see people running away from the main road, away from Spice of Life. Kate and I are still rooted in place. Shock doubles over in my chest.

"What?" I ask. Kate is still fuming, still crossing her arms and rocking back and forth on her heels to try to calm herself. She's a ball of energy, and if I touch her, she may explode for real. "What?" I say again.

She ignores me, glancing my way once or twice but not long enough for me to really see her expression. She's so distant and I'm so, so confused. What did she say? "*You* threw it?" I mutter. "Everything . . . What? Why?"

All she does is shrug, defiant and cold, and I hate that she thinks that's a good enough answer. Can't she see that I'm mad too? I don't care if she doesn't think I have a right to be. "You're the worst," I sneer at her, and she rolls her eyes. "This entire time you *knew*, and you hid it from me."

"It's just . . . it's just a lot," she mutters, eyes downcast.

"It was a lot, but you didn't want to tell me. So you told Bo instead—because he *gets* you?"

She shrugs again, but the fight in her is disappearing. She's angry but her sagging shoulders and deep sigh prove she doesn't have it in her to be confrontational anymore.

I can't find words to say to her. This is the worst betrayal. I'm thinking about Ginger Store and the Trans—and how they've always treated me like family, and how my entire childhood, all my memories, revolve around them. I'm praying so hard not to blink, because I can feel the tears coming.

Has she ever really thought of me as family? She wanted out so much, but never told me. She never mentioned she didn't like living in Ginger East. Not once.

"Holy fuck, is it really that bad here?" I say, my voice barely a whisper.

She bites her lip and chokes back a whimper because she's about to cry too. The sirens echo, ringing in my ears, and shaking my chest. We've run out of words, and have nothing left to do but stand here and feel everything. We haven't been like this since we were young. Sometimes we'd yell at each other about nothing, stupid stuff, kid stuff. And then we'd sit outside at the curb after everyone else had gone home, letting the wind tickle our ankles as we hummed and sniffled and stared at the road. Actually, when I think about it, it's been a long time since I've seen Kitkat cry.

A loud pop sounds through the air, causing us both to flinch. I've never heard anything so loud—and I've never seen the sky so red, so cloudy. Pillars of red and white smoke erupt over the tops of the buildings. I know they're coming from the main road where the protest is. It's engulfing rooftops and low-rises in the distance, like some creepy smoke machine that's malfunctioning and threatening to eat everything in its path.

I think I hear Kate say something, but her voice is muffled and drowned out amid the screaming. People are yelling, loud police voices and loud civilian voices, all clashing a street away. My feet begin to move on their own, first sliding backward, then taking off toward the intersection. The protesters—Mr. Brown and Paco and everyone—I need to make sure they're okay.

Kate calls, "Where the hell do you think you're going?" but I am already too far gone to respond. I push forward, elbowing through growing crowds running in the opposite direction.

I cough as the smoke gets thicker. People rush out of the fog from out of nowhere, sidestepping me, brushing past as they split from the main road. My heartbeat is doing double time in my chest. The closer I get to the intersection, the more people I elbow through, the worse and worse I feel. I've never seen smoke like this. My bones rattle with nervousness as I step closer and closer to the main road. When my eyes finally glimpse the scene, it takes every fiber of my being to keep me rooted in place.

I've never been this *scared.*

That immense need to cry hits me tenfold. For a moment, I've forgotten about Kate and what she did to the store; now my eyes can only see the chaos of the street and what's happening to the neighborhood. Protesters and police at odds with each other, aggressive, yelling, violent. Passersby running, locking doors, pulling down their shades, hiding. Sirens are going mad in the background. The red smoke clears, only to have another cop shoot something—A flare? A bomb?—sky-high. A woman shrieks. I think I know her. I think she sold me a shawarma once.

I can feel people push past me as they run for cover, but I can't move. Everywhere I look, there's another corner of Ginger East that I can't un-see. It's ingrained in my mind like this now. The riot superimposes on my memories, brushing away the good with the ugliness of the street and the police, and I hate that I let it. I hate that I'm seeing any of this.

Someone body-checks me into the wall, and my back hits the window of the Eats. Hurried feet rush by, and I inch as close to the wall as I can to avoid the crowd.

The door to the Eats pops open, and I feel a hand struggle to pull me inside. Jimmy locks the door behind me and pushes an overturned table close to the window. I watch, shaken, as he puts down the shades and the metal barrier before guiding me farther into the store. "Stay away from the windows," he says. He sounds so calm, so assured. He's done this kind of thing before.

An older girl huddles by the corner, hugging a small boy as their eyes follow me in. I can't even speak. My voice is locked so deep in my chest, my mouth is so, so dry, and the steady stream of tears down my face won't let up.

"We have to figure out how to get you home," Jimmy muses. He's closed down the kitchen. The smell of grease and burgers lingers in the air, clinging to the walls, his clothes, the tables, everything. "You know Amelia?" he says to me. I can only nod. Her soft brown eyes scan me with familiarity. Amelia lives on my street, but I haven't seen her a lot in the past few years because she's in nursing at the community college. "We've been trying to get in touch with Enzo's parents," he says, nodding to the boy, "but they're not picking up. I'll have to take him myself. He has a key."

"I can go by myself," the boy mumbles into the thick of Amelia's sweater.

She's quick to chastise him. "No you can't. You see how bad it is out there?"

I open my mouth to say something, anything, but I can't. It's like I don't know any words. Instead an icy, jarring, "F-fuck," spills out from my lips as I press my hands into my eyes.

Jimmy gives me a patronizing look as he circles around Amelia to grab his jacket and keys. "We can go through the back. There shouldn't be too much commotion—"

The sound of the front window shattering breaks our

fabricated safety. Enzo yelps and I duck, letting my knees hit the floor. Jimmy is yelling—"Are you okay? Is everyone okay?"—and Enzo is crying. Amelia shushes him, shakes him, and she's crying too. My forehead touches the cold tile, and for a moment I feel like running headfirst into the protest was a mistake. Maybe this was all a mistake. Kate doesn't care, the police don't care, even some of the residents don't care. Why did I think this was worth it?

My voice creaks out, "I have to go, I have to go," and I crawl, frantic, across the floor. My palms touch the glass shards, accidentally press into them, and I wince and hiss my way to the door. Tears cloud my eyes as I stumble to my feet. Blood—*blood* trickles down my fingers and I absently, angrily, rub them across my knees. The glass burrows deeper but I don't care; can't feel much. Just need to get out. Need to get home.

Jimmy calls, "Nelo?" but I don't turn back.

"Hey! Hey!" a woman's voice cries in the restaurant, and I hear her fast footsteps before I feel her hoisting me up. Jimmy is hanging by the back door, but all I can see is the frightened look in this woman's eyes. She is the shawarma lady from earlier, and she's shaking more than I am. "Where do you think you're going?"

"H-home," I manage to say.

"Take her," Jimmy tells her. "Come through the back—"

"I can go alone," I say.

"Shush," the shawarma lady scolds me. Her scolding is laced with fear, and it's like the second she sees my hands and the crimson stain on my knees, her fears are justified. She holds me close and guides me to the back door. "I'll take you. You can't be outside alone."

"But—"

"Come, this way. The front street isn't safe," she says, rushing me toward the back door.

My shoulders are shaking and I try to push away from her, but she grabs hold of my arm and doesn't let go. I want to yell at her, tell her I can go alone, I'm fine, just leave me by myself, but the first word out of my mouth isn't a word at all; it's an ugly, throaty sob. My knees buckle but shawarma lady is ready and catches me, pulls me to my feet. "Let's go, let's go," she says, guiding me back down the street. She's coughing too. Her hand is pressed against her mouth and nose, but it's not helping at all.

I stand straighter after a few steps, sniffling and wiping my eyes. They're burning. Everything is burning in this smoke.

"Janet's daughter, right? You live down here?" she asks me, gesturing toward Ginger Way.

I nod. "Yeah," I say, my voice barely there. "Is—Where's Mr. Brown?"

She frowns into a cough as we walk, and presses her hand to her chest to keep it from rattling too much. "Don't worry about him. You think it's this easy to get rid of that man? Which house is yours?"

I don't say anything, but the shouting and panic around us is conversation enough. Protesters who fled Spice of Life crouch on front lawns chugging water bottles and washing out their eyes. I hear someone say "Milk!" and I immediately think of tear gas, how protesters would douse their faces in milk to alleviate the burn.

My mind is a swirl of yelling and smoke and blood and bad memories. And shattered glass, again. It's always shattered glass these days.

CHAPTER THIRTY-TWO

Jimmy says Enzo got home okay. So did the others. He comes late at night, looking weary and rattling with fatigue, and he speaks quickly before stepping off the porch and making his way down the darkened street. Mom stands behind me in the doorway, and the moment he leaves, she slams the door shut and bolts it. "Go to bed," she hisses, before stomping her way back to her room. I do as I'm told. I'm way too tired to think, to move, to cry, to do anything else but close my eyes. I tremble the entire night.

Social is buzzing the next morning. Everyone online is talking about the protest—or the "riot," as it's now been dubbed. It's infuriating how something that was supposed to be a silent demonstration is now being branded as a violent riot that injured fifteen people. I should stop scrolling through my phone, but I can't.

Mom comes into my room with a small jar of Mentholatum. She checks in on me every hour now that the daylight has exposed the scratches on my body. Scraped knees, scraped forearms, everything scraped. She doesn't even cuss me; she just swallows slow and frowns. When she gets close enough, I can see that it's fear buried deep in her brows and in the crevices of her mouth.

"Arms out," she orders. I do as she says, and she meticulously rubs the mentholated balm onto my cuts. They sting, but not as bad as they did the first time. When she's done, she says, "Come eat pepper soup."

"Right now?"

She stares.

"Can I eat it later?" I ask, eyes downcast. "I just need to check on something."

"Check fast," she says, and turns to leave.

I don't know why I bother going back to my phone. Looking at pictures and videos of what happened is making my blood boil, making me so much more tired than I already am—and I am exhausted. My eyes glaze over with each new image. I don't even cringe anymore when I see the video of the police officer getting out his baton and advancing on protestors. I don't blink when the sound of glass shattering shakes the crowd. I don't budge when I scroll past a GIF of me from my rant video, echoing with digital fervor: "Honestly, and don't tell anyone I said this, but this is *exactly* the kind of thing the Feds would do."

It's cold today. It's actually not so bad because cold weather is my favorite, so it distracts me a little. I have much nicer sweaters and hoodies and jackets than I do tank tops and stuff. Plus, my mom is next-level anxious these days whenever she sees me wear tanks with nothing else. She scans me to see if I'm wearing the new bra. I'm clearly not, but if she won't ask, then I won't say anything.

While I'm scrolling, I get a call from Kate, which I immediately decline. She knows she can come to my door, since we live four houses away from each other, but I can tell she doesn't know what to say to me. That's why she calls. She knows I won't answer.

Then Rafa texts me, and out of nowhere, I start thinking about kissing him again. All I see is the notification before I flip my phone over and stuff it into my sweater pocket. He's the one thing that manages to get me outside of my head and away from the problems of the neighborhood. I haven't talked to him since I ran out of his house, mainly because I'm not sure what I want to tell him, and partially because my mind, my body, is so rooted in Ginger East right now. In the community.

"Mom, I'm going outside," I call from my room. I grab a palmful of peppermint oil and run it through my pressed-out hair, catching all my edges and ends. I might like the colder weather, but that doesn't mean my hair does.

Mom is on the phone when she comes into the hallway. She's not done frowning as she waves me over and covers the phone with her hand. "Where? Where are you going?" Her voice is dry and tired.

"The park," I say. It feels like a lie. I don't really know if it is yet.

She narrows her eyes at me. "To do what?"

"I don't know. Relax?"

"And you can't relax in here?"

I sigh. "Mom, please?"

"It's not s-safe out there," she stutters, choking on the word.

"I'll be careful, I promise," I say, unsure if my reassurance even means anything. Yeah, I'll be careful, sure, but weren't the people at the protest careful too? They didn't deserve what happened to them.

Suddenly Mom hands the phone to me. "It's your dad," she says. My confusion is replaced with a relief that runs from my head to my toes and makes me feel safe.

"Hi, Dad," I say, taking the phone. "How are you?"

First, Dad chuckles like he always does. He has a really nice laugh, and I'm sad I didn't inherit it. Every time I hear it, it seems like nothing in the world can possibly be wrong. It's the exact thing I need to hear at this very second. "Chi-ne," he croons in his deep, throaty voice. "How are you? Your mom says you haven't been home a lot."

Chi-ne, Chi-ne. This is the nickname I'm used to. It sounds so good and so warm coming from my dad, and it makes me realize how much I've missed it. "I've been home," I say, turning away from Mom. She comes up behind me and starts to touch my hair, threading her fingers through it like she doesn't want me to leave. She starts talking—"Your hair is getting so long"—while I'm trying to have a conversation with Dad. They both always do this, speaking at the same time and expecting me to reply. I can't focus on two things at once! "I'm home now— Mom, it's the oil. I told you about the peppermint oil."

"But you're going out," Mom cuts in. She doesn't even bother hiding her unease.

"You're going out?" Dad asks. "Where are you going?"

"To the park," I tell him. "I wanted some fresh air. And to see what's . . . what became of everything."

"I've heard it's very dangerous there," he goes on like he didn't hear me. "I read online about the riot."

"It was a protest, Dad."

"But you see they're calling it a riot," he says. "You see how easy it is for them to call it whatever? Eh? So, just be careful. Maybe you should stay inside."

"I will be so careful, on God," I plead. "Please can I go?"

"Are you going with Kate?"

Hearing her name puts such a bitter taste in my mouth now. I have to gulp a million times to push it back down. "Uh, no. She's busy." Yeah, busy with her boyfriend and her insurance fraud.

"Oh?" His interest is piqued for some reason. "So you're going alone? I hope you're not going there to meet boys." I can't tell if he's trying to be funny so I just wait, big-eyed and stuck, unsure what to say next. And then he says, "Do you have a boyfriend now?" and I nearly drop the phone trying to squeeze it back into my mom's hands.

"N-no way," I call into the phone from a safe distance. "Bye, Dad! Bye, Mom. I'll be back soon. I'll be safe," I say to her, and rush as fast as I can down the hall.

This is the complete opposite of playing it cool, but I can't help it. Any mention of boys has me immediately thinking about Rafa. My mind is a wreck. He messaged me five times since this morning, but I won't read them. I know I should—I *really* should—but I don't even know what to say to him. I can guess what he wants to say to me. *Why'd you leave so fast?* or *You're doing the most about nothing.* Or I could be wrong, and he could be wondering if I'm okay, especially with what happened at the protest. Maybe he's worried since he hasn't heard from me. Maybe he's worried I won't want to be friends anymore.

The thought of staying friends makes me shudder as I step out my front door. What does that even look like now? Do friends who kiss each other still hang out normally? Does he still think about kissing me?

"Shut up, Nelo, damn," I hiss to myself, making my way down the steps to the sidewalk. Things were so much easier when I was younger. Why does it seem like the older you get, the more everything changes and the more miserable you are? And nothing stays the same. Not one thing.

I've said I'm going to the park so many times now that I

almost believe it, but when my feet get to the end of Ginger Way, I instead turn left toward Spice of Life.

So many businesses are closed today. A lot of them got damaged during the rioting, and the brokenness of the street is hard to miss. There's hardly anyone outside, hardly anyone in the few stores that are open. It's like a ghost town. Everyone's in mourning.

The closer I get to Spice of Life, the more the silence begins to make sense to me. The early morning crowd isn't in the stores because they're in the streets. People skip back and forth holding bags of recycling, while others sweep roads bathed in glass. Some are picking up debris and trash with gloved hands, while others organize piles and piles of bagged garbage. The site is like its own ecosystem. Everyone has their place.

"Nelo!" Paco calls. I look into the crowd and see him wave me over. I'm a bit nervous as I approach him, but I can't deny how happy I am to see he's okay. Even though I can still vividly see what the street looked like during the protest, how different and how angry, seeing Paco in good health makes me smile, if only a little.

As I walk over, I tiptoe around more than just the glass and rubble. Somehow, even though I convinced people to come out for the protest, I don't feel like I belong here.

"You're okay," I sigh, relieved. I want to hug him, but I am still trembling. "Have you heard from the others? Mr. Brown? Anyone?"

"They're good. He's fine. You know Mr. Brown's a tank."
Paco smiles shyly. "This place is a wreck. Definitely not in our
event plan."

"Uh-huh," I say, still looking around at the street.

"An-anyway." He clears his throat. "Reporters came by a
bit earlier. So weird, but one of the guys asked for you by
name. Dave? Said you'd probably have something to say."

I grunt. "I think I'm running out of things to say, honestly."

"I'm not so sure," he replies. "But everyone needs a break.
I get that. I can respect that." He reaches out for a fist bump,
and I oblige. We've become so much closer ever since Ginger Store got trashed. When we look onto the street, I know
we see the same thing, and that's comforting to me amid all
this.

Spice of Life stands, haggard, before us. I didn't take a
moment to really look at the building before, and from this
close, it's alarming. The front windows are smashed—more
than smashed. Some have huge gaping holes through them,
while others are completely gone. The pavement reflects in
the light, with all the glass that's littered on the ground. It
reminds me of Ginger Store the day it got bricked. People
roaming around, watching. Others are taking pictures. Some
are crying. And then there are people moving large chunks
of debris. So much debris. People hugging each other. And
glass, everywhere.

It's too much. It's too similar, it's too much, and it's always happening—why is this always happening?

I can't be here right now.

"I gotta go," I say, taking a quick step back.

Paco furrows his brows in shock. "Oh? I thought you maybe would help with the cleanup efforts—"

"I can't. I—I should, but I just need to go," I ramble off as I back away. If he says anything else to me, I can't hear it because I'm walking so fast in the opposite direction. For fuck's sake, why did I turn left? Didn't I know what I'd see here?

The park has always been a safe place, so I skip over my street and head to the winding path across from Ginger Store. The wind picks up a little, and I hunch my shoulders against it, walking quickly until I can get under the protection of the trees near the swings. They block out everything. I don't know how, but it's magic. I mean, I'm sure it's just the way the wind blows or how the rain falls or something, but to me, it's magic. My friends and I got stuck there in a storm once a few years back, but I barely felt any drops because the huge maple tree blocked them. Maree got soaked, though. When we were really young, she used to hate going on the swings and would stand at the edge of the sandpit, away from the trees, and watch everyone else with this snobby scowl on her face. She'd always catch a cold the next day and have to stay in while we all went out. Thinking back, there are so many memories I have where she is missing because she's sick. I can't imagine her getting ice cream in the winter with us or hanging upside down on the monkey bars at the park.

That's why it's strange to see her here, in real time and not in front of a screen where she's framed by views and likes. Her heels dig into the damp sand, and her back slouches while she sways slowly back and forth on the swing. Her arms are wrapped around the swing's chains, her eyes are downcast, and her lips are moving slowly like she's talking to herself, or praying. The entire scene is enough to throw me off. First the riot cleanup, and now this? Isn't there somewhere I can be sad in peace?

Before I can run, she senses me there and looks up, startled that someone else would dare appear at the park. But when she realizes it's me, she timidly smiles and waves. I force myself to wave back even though I don't really want to.

"Nelo, what's good?" she calls, still smiling. I join her at the swings, letting my feet dig into the sand too, and she grins, watching me. "What are the odds?"

"Of what?" I snort. "You being in my neighborhood, you actually talking to me, or me not running when I saw you just now?"

"Wow, okay," she laughs. Her laugh is so sharp and awkward, but hearing it ushers in this huge wave of nostalgia. Her mom used to laugh like that whenever we came to her house to ask for Maree. I could never read her mom, but hearing Maree sound like her puts me at ease. I take the swing next to her and let myself kick off from the ground, swinging gently back and forth.

"I guess all of them," she says. "Remember when you and Rafa were headed to the bus that one time? It seemed a bit like you didn't want to talk to me."

I sigh, unsure how to respond. "Yeah," I say, and leave it at that. The air is soothing against my face while I swing higher and higher above the ground.

"I didn't know, like, you guys still hang out," she says, and then looks at me. "You and Rafael, I mean."

My heart jumps when I hear his name, and I hate it. I hate that all my emotions are through the roof. "We don't hang out," I say, flatly. "We just take the same bus."

"It looked like you guys were still close," Maree goes on. "And you like all his pictures online."

"How do you even know that?"

"I can see your name in the list of people who liked them."

"Doesn't that just mean *you're* stalking him?"

She blushes so easily. Her pale skin lights up, even though she's deadpan, pretending like what I'm saying doesn't affect her. We're done talking for a second, and she takes a moment to kick off the ground, breaking into a weak, lazy swing. "Anyway," she presses on. "I was just saying. My friend used to date him, and she's like, 'He's a ho,' and I'm like, 'Well, *obviously* he is. He's a guy and he's hot. Therefore, ho.' But then she was like, 'Weren't you friends with him?' And I told her we don't talk anymore, even though we used to be, like, super close."

I nod lazily while Maree gives me a side glance to make sure I'm really listening. I mask my emotions with a frown so she doesn't think I'm interested. But maybe I'm frowning too hard, because she starts looking smug, like she's gotten through to me. What's her issue?

"But that's not the point," she finally continues, pushing her blond hair over her shoulder. "It's just, when I saw you guys together, I had thoughts."

I roll my eyes. "What kind of thoughts, Maree?"

"I thought you were *together* together."

"Why?" I chuckle nervously. I didn't know she's been watching me so hard. "Do we look like we're *together* together?"

"Well, I mean, either that or everyone around here hangs out without me," she says. "But then I realized he doesn't live in, um, G-East anymore. Actually, I think he lives closer to where I live. I should ask him."

Hearing her call it "G-East" makes me want to choke, but hearing her talk so much about Rafa puts me even deeper in my feelings than I want to be. I'm a wreck today. I'm *this* close to telling her about what happened at his house, which gives me a guilty, sick feeling in my stomach. I haven't really told anyone, not even Kate. Not like I would right now, anyway. She's more concerned with her Ginger East getaway plan.

And Bo. Does she even know there's a cleanup group? Does she even care?

I force a smile at Maree, but not because I hate her or anything. In fact, I do it because I don't hate her at all. "What are you doing all the way out here, then? In the hood," I add.

She snickers like we have an inside joke. "Came to check out the venue, check out my old neighborhood," she says. "The benefit concert is coming up soon, you know? Plus, I haven't been down here in a minute. To Ginger East." Then she sings, "G-East," like anyone asked for that.

"Girl, stop. That's your second strike. No one calls it that."

"What?"

"It's Ginger East."

"People call it 'G-East' sometimes," she says. "People where I'm from."

"I thought you were from here," I tease, and she rolls her eyes in a playful way.

"People where I live now, okay?" she says with a smirk. "Although, it's not that much different from here these days. All the suburbs are becoming the same."

"What do you mean 'not that much different'?"

"Nelo," she begins in a quiet voice, as if someone's lurking behind us. "Spice of Life moved in and people are pissed, right? That's why there was a riot yesterday. I saw it all on the news."

"Did the news also say it was supposed to be a peaceful

protest until the cops showed up?" I ask, doing absolutely nothing to hide the bitterness in my voice.

"You know they didn't," she says, with a roll of her eyes. "This place has changed, for real. I guess that's to be expected, but I just wasn't prepared. It's probably because I haven't been here in forever. You're probably like, 'Shut up, Maree. It's been like this since time,' and I get it. But it's different for me because I don't live here anymore."

Everything is putting a bad taste in my mouth and it won't go away, no matter how I try to swallow it down, no matter how much I try to pretend it isn't. The stuff with Ginger Store, then the stuff with Kate—then the stuff with Kate smashing the Ginger Store window—and then everything with the protest and Mr. Brown. And Rafa. Soon I am kicking off the ground and falling into a new lull, an easy swinging pace where I don't have to try. Eventually I say, "It's different for me too. And I've actually lived here forever."

There's a hint of sympathy in her smile that I didn't ask for and don't want. Or need. It's all I can do to ignore her and swing higher before the familiar buzz of my phone brings me back down. Groaning, I reach for it and flip it over in my hand to read the screen. It's a text message from Kate. Maree, being her regular, nosy self, leans over to look. "Is that Kate? You can text her back, if you want. I don't mind."

"Oh, you don't . . . mind?"

"I—sorry, I didn't mean it like that," she says. "I just

meant I don't want you to feel that I'm, like, preventing you from talking to Kate or something."

"Mmm."

"Hey," she gasps. "Is it—do you think she'll be cool if I, like, stop by her house or something? I know we don't talk at school, and I know the neighborhood is kinda in shambles right now, but I mean . . ."

I immediately shake my head, and Maree's bright smile begins to fade. It's like in that very moment, she realizes that walking into the house of the girl she essentially exploited and robbed for more YouTube clicks would not be okay.

I can see the shame in her eyes before she turns away from me. "You know, a lot of the money from the FundRace went to setting up the benefit concert," she says, measured and slow. "It's not that I wasn't going to actually donate it to Kate's family. I'm not a monster. It's just that my PR company—they control everything. They thought it'd be best to use it for a concert, so we could earn more and, you know—"

"Eventually donate it to actual victims?"

She winces at the sting in my words. "Yeah, exactly. Like, we have a full plan, but don't tell anyone. After the benefit concert, we want to bring in more youth workers at the community center, and maybe start youth business initiatives for kids who dropped out of school and stuff. It's legit, I swear."

I'm still skeptical. Everything Maree's saying is stuff that's been said before by richer companies and greedier people.

They try to come in and change things by saying everything residents want to hear, but at the end of it all, they don't know anything about places like this, and they don't actually care about people here either. They just like to talk.

I shrug. Kate made it clear that Ginger Store isn't my problem in the first place, so I can't say anything. "Yeah, whatever."

"It's true," she says. "You think I would really play you guys like that?"

"Tch, yes."

She frowns. "Y'all think so little of me."

"It's Kate you need to apologize to, not me," I say. "It's not *my* store that got vandalized." Vandalized. If we can even call it that anymore.

Maree is still frowning when she turns away, and for a second, she reminds me of those fake pouty models online. Everything about her is so picture-perfect and foreign, from the way she sighs to the way she looks over her shoulder at the massive field behind us, eyes traveling over every bump and hill. "Yeah." She's speaking so soft that her voice is almost lost in the wind. "I will. She's not talking to me, but I'll go see her. I owe her."

I nod and push my feet off the ground, and I'm swinging again.

"Hey . . ." Maree turns to me slowly, almost eerily. She bites her lip and hums while she thinks. "Hey, do you think she'll forgive me faster if I tell her who's coming to the benefit?"

"Uh, is it Sol Cousins?"

Maree is quiet for too long for me to really be comfortable. She's humming and smiling and being all shady. I gasp and immediately stick my feet into the sand, jerking forward and coming to a complete stop beside her. "It better not be. You know we've collectively moved on now. Don't tell me you liked that last album," I say.

Now it's her turn to kick her feet off the ground and start swinging.

CHAPTER THIRTY-THREE

MON 04/26 at 6:15 p.m.

Kate KK Tran: are you ok? call me

Kate KK Tran: did you see the other chat? it's really rough but tell me what you think

Kate KK Tran has sent a file: djkaytee_mtpxelastics.m4a

Kate KK Tran: i found that elastics beat for free, but it's fire, right?

Kate KK Tran: goes so good with midtown lol

FRI 04/30 at 4:57 p.m.

Kate KK Tran: sis hey

Kate KK Tran: ok fine I know I should've told you about bo

Kate KK Tran: and about the store

Kate KK Tran: i was scared you'd be mad

Kate KK Tran: nelo honestly?? are you ok? can you text me please??

Kate KK Tran: i was right when i said you were in love with this place and that's why i couldn't tell you

Kate KK Tran: you really think that if i said i wanted my family to move, you would've actually been like oh okay yeah true? no way. you honestly think ginger east is so great

Kate KK Tran: you think your feelings about this place are more important than mine

Kate KK Tran: it wasn't even your store, you get that??

Kate KK Tran: it's my family's store

Kate KK Tran: it's my store

Kate KK Tran: what the fuuuuuuck bro

Kate KK Tran: you're really not gonna text back??

Kate KK Tran: rafa said you won't talk to him. what happened?

Kate KK Tran: i'm sorry ok

Kate KK Tran: if that's what you want to hear

Kate KK Tran: i should've told you about the store and the brick and all that shit from the jump. you and i are so alike sometimes that it's hard

Kate KK Tran: it's just hard

Kate KK Tran: and bo's not like us anymore. you can't get mad at me for wanting his perspective too

Kate KK Tran: but maybe you're right. i should've told you first. about bo.

Kate KK Tran: since i like him and everything

Kate KK Tran: lowkey i thought you'd laugh at me because he was always such a nerd and i've had a crush on fine ass ray at school for A G E S and i know he's nothing like fine ass ray, but he's nice. and he's my friend

Kate KK Tran: he's our friend.

Kate KK Tran: don't be mad ok?? just text me

Kate KK Tran: please??

SAT 05/01 at 3:37 p.m.

Kate KK Tran: sis?

CHAPTER THIRTY-FOUR

Kate KK Tran: hey

Chinelo Sondra: hi

Kate KK Tran: omg!!

Kate KK Tran: i thought you were gonna leave me on read!!

Chinelo Sondra: can you come over?

Kate KK Tran: yes of course

Kate KK Tran: i'll be there in 2

I am nervous from the moment I put down my phone to the moment the front doorbell rings. It could also be because I'm groggy from sleeping most of the day yesterday, but that's not completely true. Kate has been to my house a million times before, but this time it feels as if a stranger is visiting. She might look and sound like Kate, but I don't understand the way she thinks. She said we were alike, but that really isn't true anymore.

Kate looks fidgety when I open the door. She's just as

anxious as I am. "Hey," she mumbles. She kicks off her shoes and follows me into the house.

Mom went to the store to get onions and tomato paste, so we have a bit of time to be real with each other. We sit in the living room on two adjacent sofas, clearing our throats and waiting for the other to speak first. She shies away from my gaze, and that's how I know she doesn't want to go first. Meanwhile, I am itching so bad to just fucking go *off.* For a second, I want to scream and say ugly things that will make her hate me forever, only because I want her to feel just as bad as I have these past few days. I want her to know what it feels like to really be alone. But I take a deep breath, and I realize that's just pettiness getting the better of me. I don't want to make Kate sad. I want to understand her.

I lean toward the side table beside the sofa and grab a stress ball the size of my hand. Mom got a bunch for her patients, and she keeps a few at home for times when she's stressed. Kate watches as I squash it between my hands. "If you're not holding the ball, then you can't speak. Deal?" I toss it over to her.

She catches it and swallows, hard. "Do you want to go first, then?"

I hold my hands open for her to toss the stress ball back. As soon as it's in my hands, I stare her dead in the face and ask, "Why'd you do it? Throw the brick, shut down the store, everything. Why?"

There's no shock or disappointment in her eyes, just

acceptance. She knew it was coming to this. I toss the ball to her and she catches it, squeezes it tightly in her hands. "Sometimes this place is so small. Just hear me out, okay? It's like being in a simulation or something. Everything's the same every day. I get that the neighborhood is becoming, like, foreign or whatever to you, but to me, it's always looked the same. It'll always be the same, and I don't know if that's a good thing anymore." She throws the ball back.

I catch it. "You didn't answer my question." She coughs out a smile and eases into the sofa a bit more when I say that. "You threw the brick because you wanted to leave? I don't understand. Was it really worth ruining your family's only source of income?"

She reaches out for the ball when I toss it. "Don't think of it like that," she scolds. "No offense, but if you don't know, then you just don't."

"So tell me," I blurt out—and then bite my tongue once I realize I'm not holding the ball.

"Dad wakes up mad early to get to the store, and Mom joins him around an hour later," she continues. "They work all day, almost every day, and for what? We might own the place, but we don't live there, so we also pay rent on our house— rent that just won't stop going up because of who knows why. Bigger chains or newer stores with money buying up prop- erty ten feet away from them, or whatever. So many For Sale signs taunting us. Real estate guys are swooping in every day, telling Dad how badly they want to build a condo over the store he built from the jump. And I could see in his face, in my mom's face, that they wanted to say yes. I don't know if they were staying because of me and Jake or what, but they wanted to get out." She swallows, hard, before she goes on. "They were tired too, you know? My parents. They wouldn't say it, but I knew they were. So I knew the brick was the only way out. After I did it, Dad started to actually think about life away from the store, like I knew he would. And with the brick, I figured if the insurance people could see it as an accident, then we'd be in the clear, and we'd have enough money and the opportunity to finally, finally leave."

"What if they didn't okay the insurance? What if you had gone to jail?"

She's deadpan when she waves the ball in my face, and I groan, like *Fine, keep going, then.*

"Ginger East may be sketch," she says, "but police know there's nothing illegal going down at the store. I knew when they saw the damage, they'd see it as a byproduct of living out here. They wouldn't think there was a real motive. Just petty crime in the area like always, you know?"

She's so convinced she's right, and I find it hard to disagree. We don't have the best track record. If something isn't gang affiliated, any cops who roll through always think crime is just part of the package living here. Unfortunately. They never care to look deeper, and I know Kate figured she'd get lucky that way. If the protest is anything to go by, the police think we have nothing better to do than destroy our own stores, our own property. Our own community. I can't blame her for thinking that the insurance people wouldn't suspect anything either.

I reach out for the ball, and she throws it to me a bit harder than she did before. "Do your parents know it was you? Did you tell them? What did they say?" And I toss it back.

Kate fumbles but eventually catches the ball before it hits the ground. "I told them. I had to," she mumbles, pushing her hair behind her ear. "Once the insurance got approved, Dad started talking to the police more. He really wanted to find out who did this, so he kept calling and calling them, and I felt so bad. Man, when I said it was me, he was *pissed*." She lets out a sad, uneasy chuckle, and I shrug, like, *Yeah, obviously. You played yourself.* "I was really . . . mad at myself too, actually. Because I made such a big deal about everything being for my family, but to see Dad like that made me think, like, 'Damn, what am I doing? Did I really think this was for real going to work?'"

She's looking at me like I have something to say to that. I open my hands for her to throw me the ball, but she holds on to it for another second. "I got lucky. I was naive. I was stupid as fuck too," she says, and then tosses it toward me.

I catch it. "Yeah, you were," I tell her, and she laughs a little, that same sad chuckle. "But I can't hate because that's bold. I think even if your dad was mad, he understands. Right?" She exaggerates a shrug, throws her arms up, and wiggles her shoulders on their way down. It has us both chuckling.

"What did your mom say?" I ask. "And Jake? Did they want to kill you?"

"Straight up murder," she says as I toss her the ball. "Jake thinks it's selfish of me. He's too cool, and all he does is dissociate. But when I tell you Mom and Dad cussed me for *hours*—" And she bursts out laughing. I laugh too because the mental image of Mr. and Mrs. Tran—the nicest, sweetest people—swearing so openly and harshly at their daughter is genuinely mad funny.

"I'm surprised you didn't hear from, like, down the street," she continues. "I couldn't even say nothing too. I just sat there and was like, 'Okay, true.'" I press my hand to my mouth to stop myself from laughing harder. She grins. "They said they don't want to see me anywhere near music until I'm done with college. Dad says I owe him for life, and I get that . . . but I don't think he gets me. To be honest, I think Mom is trying her hardest to understand too. More than anything, she thinks she's failed as a mother because she couldn't see how badly I wanted to leave."

I'm still chuckling when I say, "Why are moms always doing the most?"

She giggles too. "I don't know, man. But my parents are . . . it gets better every day."

I open my hands for the ball, and she throws it to me. I have to take a second to wipe my eyes because I laughed so hard, I literally cried. "So are you guys moving? Will your dad actually sell?" I ask eventually.

Kate bites her bottom lip and hesitates before she catches the ball. "I don't know."

"Do you want to move?"

"Ball," she says, and throws it back.

"Do you want to move?" I ask again, and toss the ball back as soon as it touches my fingers.

She waits a moment before saying, "I think so, yeah. The way Bo describes where he lives and what Santa Ana Academy is like . . . it just sounds so different." I can tell she wants to smile, but she pushes her lips together to stop herself. Does she think I'll get mad if she's happy about leaving? We've been laughing, like things are almost back to normal, yet she can't be completely real with me.

"It sounds like another dimension," she says, and then snorts because she definitely knows how cheesy that was. "You get it, though. We're all about this place, so we can't really know. But I feel like I *want* to know. Does this make sense?"

"I think so," I say. She throws me the ball, but I set it down on the table instead of squeezing it like I was. I'm trying to understand, but it's so hard to piece everything together. "So you want to leave," I repeat. She nods timidly and quickly, like she's afraid of her own answer. "And you didn't think you could tell me."

"You know I wanted to, but I wasn't sure how you'd take it."

"I don't know either," I mumble. "I was so worried that

selling the store meant I'd be losing my friend—my best friend. I couldn't see around it. Still can't."

Kate pouts apologetically. "You'd never lose me. Even if I moved away, we have real history." She reaches out for our secret handshake, the fist bump, and I bite back a bittersweet smile as I return it. "I should have said something to you. Bo kept saying I should. . . ."

Bo kept saying she should. In my head, I've painted him like some chicly dressed demon who swoops in and steals my best friend at the last second, but I need to be real with myself too. Bo isn't like that. He was never like that. He was always a bit shy and reserved. Now he dresses way better and pretends to be with it, but deep down inside, what if he's still that same awkward kid?

I'm quiet for long enough that Kate thinks something is wrong. She opens her mouth to speak but stops before she dives into her words. "You must really like him, huh?" I pipe up. She nods, and then blushes so hard, it makes *me* blush for even asking. "Why?" I ask.

"Why?" she repeats with a nervous chuckle. "I don't know. He's cool. He's good to talk to and we get along, but in a different way. He makes me laugh too," she adds. I doubt Bo is funny now, but I'll let her have this one.

"And he gets you?"

"He gets me, man," she says. Seeing her like this, calmer and lighter, makes me happier. Suddenly she points in the direction of the stress ball and makes grabby hands like I'm going to throw it to her. "What, are we not doing the ball anymore?" she asks.

"No."

"Can I ask *you* something, then?"

I pause for a moment before I stutter out, "Y-yeah, of course."

A sly smile creeps onto her face. I've just been grilling her for who knows how long, and she hasn't asked me anything. I mean, it's not like I have anything to add to the wider discussion of why she broke into Ginger Store, but still, watching her watch me, I feel vulnerable.

She asks, "Why's it so weird that it was Bo?"

Just like that, a spotlight is shining directly in my face. I'm fidgeting under her gaze. "It's not," I lie.

"You make it seem like it is. You hate him, don't you?"

"No, I don't."

"What if I was dating Rafa?"

My chest tightens at the sound of his name. "But you're not."

"But what if I was?" she presses again. "Would you have been cool with it? We all used to be friends, but you act like Bo's the worst person in the world or something. Like you can't believe it has to be him."

"That's not true."

"So, then, what is it?"

"It's . . ." I sigh loudly. "It's just . . . it's Bo." She's staring at me because she knows that isn't a good enough answer. *I know it isn't good enough either.* "He's not really anything special, right? He's just Bo. I thought if I was going to be replaced . . ." I can't even finish the thought. Being "replaced" sounds so childish but it's really how I felt. "If I was going to be replaced, I thought it'd be with someone cooler," I eventually say. "Someone else. It made me think Bo was suddenly this brand-new guy everyone liked more than me."

"Brand-new?" she snickers.

"You get what I mean."

"I do, I do," she says. "Well, he *is* cooler now, although maybe not as cool as you. He's different."

"Different?" I scoff.

"Yes, different. You don't think people can change? You think he's still the same kid who cleans his glasses with the front of his shirt because he cares more about actual dirt touching them than sweat?"

I burst out laughing at that. "I remember that!"

"Same," she says. "But he's not like that anymore, I promise."

"Yeah?"

"Yeah. He has, like, this cool, lint-free cloth now."

CHAPTER THIRTY-FIVE

Kate and I catch up like we haven't spoken in forever. Like we're old friends who happened to run into each other at the store after ten years in other cities.

We can't stop talking about Bo. I ask her what it's like to be dating him—to be dating a boy—and all she says is "It's *aight*" in a voice that has me rolling so hard that I nearly fall off the sofa. "It's cool, it's cool," she adds. "We click, so it's all good. I thought it would be too hard to get used to, but I'm adjusting."

"Adjusting," I repeat. My head rolls against the sofa seat and my chest is warm because I'm so in my feelings, but in a good way. I haven't felt this good in a while. Not since before the whole Rafa incident. Or maybe not *since* the Rafa incident.

In one swift motion, I push myself up and swing my feet to the ground. Kate glances at me, and she starts getting all serious when she sees my face. I think I'm finally ready to tell her about Rafa. You know, while I'm in a sharing mood. While I'm still delirious. While I'm still hiding.

"What's up?" she says, and I'm so shocked that she knows

I have something important to say. She knows me so well, it's scary.

I wait for her to sit upright too before I start speaking. "So . . . I saw Maree yesterday at the swings."

"Ugh, Maree?" Kate grimaces. "What was she doing all the way out here? Was she lost?"

"No, she was . . ." She was checking out the park before the concert, but a part of me wonders if she was drawn back here after everything that's been going on. Can a place really ever leave you? If Kate leaves, will she still remember what it's like to be here?

"She was what?" Kate asks. "Stealing from babies?"

I chuckle. "No, she was—she—I don't know. She didn't say," I lie. "We talked for a bit, and it was weird because she was normal for a hot second. But then I found myself wanting to tell her stuff, and I got all anxious because she's not really the person I tell stuff to. That was always you."

Kate moves closer and closer as I speak, her eyes wide like she's bracing herself for a shock. "So, what happened?"

"With what?"

"Like, what did you want to tell her?" she asks. She's leaning so close, it looks like she's about to fall off the sofa.

I take a deep, deep, deep breath and say, "Um, I kissed Rafa."

Her gasp morphs into the widest grin. "I *knew*—"

"Or, like, he kissed me first."

She's shrieking now. "BITCH—"

The front door rattles and we both jump to our feet. I can hear my mom come in and push the door shut behind her, humming some song she must've heard on the radio. Kate and I look at each other and simultaneously say, "Park! The park!" Soon we're grabbing our stuff and rushing past my mom in the hallway.

"Where—Kate?—Chi-chi, where are you going?" Mom asks while we wrestle on our shoes.

"Park, park," I tell her. "Bye, Mom!"

"Bye, Mom," Kate repeats, and we both giggle our way out the door.

Kate and I link arms as we walk the familiar path. The streets are still quiet, although every now and then, I hear the distinct ruffle of garbage bags and people shuffling around. When we get to the intersection, I take purposeful steps to the right, not bothering to turn back toward Spice of Life in case I see something I don't want to, something I'm not ready to see yet. It's selfish of me, but I don't know what else to do.

"Tell me how it all went down," Kate says, and I launch into the story of how I went from drooling over Rafa's picture in class to licking his face, with his mom just inside the house. We walk and stop a few times because Kate has to gather her thoughts and let out a, "Oh my God?" every now and then. I am an odd mixture of relief and nerves. One second, it's relief that finally, *finally* I'm able to tell someone about the whole Rafa thing. The other second, it's nervousness that I shouldn't have said anything to begin with. I still don't really know what I feel about Rafa. I'm still in between.

We're at the park, sitting side by side on the swings like we always do. Being here with Kate feels more like home. The wind is warmer, the swing seat doesn't cut into my thighs too hard, and the sand isn't getting into my canvas shoes, even though I'm digging my feet pretty far in. I have my best friend back. Things are beginning to feel normal again. A new normal.

"So let me get this straight," Kate says while she stares up at the sky. I'm about to kick off from the ground, but she grabs a hold of my swing's chain before I can move. "Rafa invites you to his house, he kisses you, you kiss him back, and then you just run?"

"Damn, you reduced that all the way down."

"Didn't I say he liked you?" she continues. "Right? I called it, remember?"

My cheeks are getting warmer and warmer, and she's watching me so hard, it makes me want to die. I start laughing instead and turn away so she can't see my face. "Stop talking to me," I whine.

"I knew it! You like him!"

"Shut uuuup, I don't," I tell her. "I can't. We're friends. It's so weird."

"It's not weird. And he's so hot now!" she says, and cackles.

"Please stop calling him hot—"

"What did he say after?" she asks, tapping her toes excitedly. "Like, yesterday?"

I turn back around to face her, my feet still dug into the ground. "I legit haven't spoken to him since," I whisper.

Kate's mouth falls open. "Uh, sorry?"

"I legit haven't spoken to him since," I repeat, and then whip back around.

Kate grabs my swing's chain and pulls it so I'm facing her again. "Are you being serious? You, who's been up and down TV with way too much to say about the Feds? You gotta text him back, fam."

"What do I say? I haven't even *looked* at any of the messages he sent me." I groan and push my face into my hands. Kate has to do the most as she tries to pull them off my face. "What if he hates me?"

"Nclo, no," she scoffs. "Give me your phone. We're gonna get you a boyfriend."

"Uglhhh."

"Let me see." Kate stretches her hand out for my phone. When I hand it over, she swipes in, inputting my password with ease, and immediately goes straight to Messenger. Her brows furrow as she reads the messages. Every now and then, she hmms and huhs, and her eyes get really big. I'm losing my mind waiting for her to say something, but it's like she knows how impatient I am and she just takes longer and longer to read through everything. She scrolls up and down, she pauses, and she gasps. Then she backtracks and reads again.

"What is it?" I finally spit out. "What did he say?"

Kate purses her lips and mm-hmms at me while she returns my phone. "You know Rafa. He's always been, like, too cool, even during that time when he didn't wash his hair for a month."

I nod frantically. "Yeah, and?"

"He likes you."

I gasp and groan, running my hands down my face. I even lose balance a bit, almost falling backward off the swing, before Kate reaches out to steady me. "Is that what he said?" I ask, my voice small. I'm nervous.

She wrinkles her nose while she thinks. "Hmm, no. But he didn't have to outright say it," she tells me. "Read the messages and see for yourself."

I shake my head immediately. "No, no way."

"What? Why?"

"If I read them, then that's it," I say. "I can't ever go back, and things will be—they'll be *different*, no matter what."

She's already rolling her eyes at me before I finish speaking. "This is coming from someone whose face has been all over the news leading up to the protest. You're so dramatic," she says. "Some things don't change at all."

"But some things do!"

"Well, I know one person who doesn't. She's been doing

the most since she was born," she says, snickering, and gives me a friendly push. It brings my head back down from whatever cloud it was threatening to float off to. "Give me your phone. I'll read them for you."

Kate puts on this weird, deep voice that I guess is supposed to sound like Rafa, but sounds more like she's someone's overly aggressive dad. I'll allow it this time.

"One," she begins, reading from my phone screen. "'Hey, you get home okay? I called you and you didn't answer. Let me know if you're okay.' Two. 'Hey, dot-dot-dot, woooow so I guess you actually don't want to talk to me? That's kinda fucked up, but whatever. You don't think you're overreacting?' Three. 'I know you're mad and stuff but at some point you're going to have to read these.' Four. 'I would've felt better if you left me on read.'

"Five. 'Listen—I'm *really* sorry. If I knew you were gonna react like that, I wouldn't have tried anything. It's, dot-dot-dot, I-D-K. I-D-K. I kinda saw that going differently.' Missed call at four-thirty-five p.m. Missed call at four-thirty-six p.m."

"That's back-to-back," I whisper.

"Yeah, and I bet you watched them both ring out, you snake," Kate says, and snorts. She continues. "Missed call at four-forty-eight p.m. Missed call at eight-fifty-five p.m. Six. Missed call at seven-fifteen a.m. Seven. Missed call at three-oh-four p.m.

"Eight. 'Wow you're really not gonna talk to me or

nothing? I get that you're still mad at me, and that's cool because fine, but I was kinda hoping you would at least pick up. I'm worried about you that's all. We're still good right?' Nine. 'I wanted to ask you something but I'm not gonna type it out. So call me back.' Ten. Missed call at twelve-oh-one p.m. Eleven. Missed call at one-forty-four p.m. Twelve. 'You're actually reading these? Call me, okay?' "

She hands the phone back to me. And I accidentally drop it.

Kate snickers. "You're wrecked, fam."

CHAPTER THIRTY-SIX

On Monday morning, I find a crumpled twenty-dollar bill in the space between my mattress and the wall. This is a good sign.

The second I step out of my room, Mom rushes to me, a thin sweater pulled over her work clothes. Her eyes glance over my face before she reaches for my arm, pulls up my sleeve a little, and checks on the scars from the protest. I'm surprised she doesn't show up with something else to rub onto my hands.

"Come on," she says quickly. "You're going to miss your bus."

"I know. I'm leaving right now," I tell her, but I stay rooted in place.

She takes a step away and beckons me to follow.

"Are we . . . driving?"

"No," she says. "I'm leaving now too, so we might as well go together. I can walk you—"

I groan and press my hands down my face. "Noooo, Mom, what? Why?"

"Don't ask me why—"

"It's perfectly safe outside," I plead. "The bus stop isn't

even that far. No one is going to—to . . ." I can't say it. The words "no one is going to kill me" are light on my tongue like a bad joke, but I know how heavy they would sound in my mom's ears. My scars from the protest on Friday have faded a little, along with Mom's apprehension. But it isn't completely gone. I guess that's to be expected.

I fumble through a non-response, groaning, "Well, just . . . I don't want you to be late for work because of me, so . . ."

"Of course," she says. "So grab your things and let's go."

There is literally nothing worse than this.

Kate meets me at the bus stop and acts really cool about my mom being there, but I can see in her eyes that she's dying to roast me. Every time my mom looks into the distance to see if the bus is coming, Kate looks at me like she's gathering intel. I hate it. I want it to be tomorrow already—tomorrow, when I will definitely respond to Rafa, I swear!

The bus comes and Mom watches it screech to a stop in front of us. She scoops me into a quick hug before the doors pull open. Mom isn't a huge hugger, so the importance isn't lost on me, but it's still awkward and I low-key wish it wasn't happening. She is more anxious than before and it's because of the protest. It's because of me.

"Bye, Mom," Kate says first as we board the bus.

"Bye," Mom says, and waves. She waits two seconds until she sees us drop safely into our seats, before she takes off back down the road.

The bus drives off. Kate stares out the window as the

pavement rolls past us. She is probably waiting until we get a safe distance away before she starts making fun of me. "Okay, shut up," I say preemptively. "I know what you're gonna say." I don't.

She chuckles, shocked. "What? I wasn't gonna say anything."

"Yeah, you were."

She slouches down in her seat. I do the same. "So what are you gonna do, by the way?" she asks. "If you see Rafa, are you gonna talk to him?"

I glance away, trying to pretend like the idea isn't freaking me out. The truth is, I haven't thought about what to say to him because I'm secretly hoping we never speak again. Which is a lie! Because I do want him to talk to me. Just maybe not today.

"I don't know," I mumble, doing a bad job of keeping it cool. Suddenly I look at the bus doors, imagining what it will be like once he gets on. Will he say hi to me first? Should I say hi to him? What if he doesn't say anything? If I see him at school, that's one thing. It'll be easier to ignore him. But on the bus, it's close quarters. Everyone, including all his stupid soccer friends, will be able to hear if he says anything to me, and I don't see that going in my favor. Plus, when it all comes down to it, I don't know what to say to him.

"Okay, let's talk about something else since you're clearly in your feelings," Kate pipes up, bringing out her phone. "Bo told me Santa Ana is planning an end-of-year trip to

Barcelona for his class. And they're not even graduating! Can you believe it?"

I scoff. "Yeah, kinda. It's Santa Ana."

"Look," Kate says, and we both lean in to scroll through her messages. It's weird as hell seeing them as a couple, but I'm getting used to it. I'm adjusting.

The bus turns into Cooksville, and my knees, my back, everything seizes up. Stress and nervousness I was ignoring suddenly pulsate through my chest. Kate still scrolls, and I focus as hard as humanly possible on the screen as the bus comes to a full stop. *Don't look up, don't look up.*

Kate looks because she hates me. I'm ready for her to start snickering or nudge me so hard in the arm that I fall into the aisle, but she doesn't. After a moment, she returns to her phone, scrolls until she gets to a meme about sausages. It's not funny, but I laugh anyway.

Suddenly the bus pulls away and I finally look around me. My anxiety quells. I spot Marcus in his usual seat. He is telling a story, loud and brash, to the soccer bros hanging off seats adjacent. I turn before he catches me looking.

"Rafa's not here," Kate says.

"Yeah, I know. . . ." My feelings are warped. I didn't really want to run into him, but that doesn't mean I didn't want to see him.

CHAPTER THIRTY-SEVEN

Avoiding Rafa is a bittersweet success, based solely on the fact that he didn't show up today. I feel empty. Don't want to eat anything, don't want to talk to anyone, don't want to be at school, really. Don't care that Tyrell's still mad about the outcome of some basketball game and almost got into the scrap of the century with Adam and his boys over it. Don't care that Miss Santana offered to pay Mr. Patel's class entrance fee for that web development competition—even though we all know it's because she's obsessed with him and no one wants to address it. Don't care that Jemma took a selfie with her new makeup palette and finally mastered the art of contour, although I do take the time to sift through all her picture likes to see if Rafa is one of them. He isn't, and I'm in my feelings about that too because Jemma actually looks so pretty in this picture and it deserves more likes.

Jake texts both Kate and me at 2:55. It's suspicious because he pretty much copy-pasted the same message. He says Horst is coming to the house and he's swinging by to grab Kate so he may as well get me too. He tells us to be outside the front doors at 3:01 or else he's leaving us here. He makes it seem like he's going to drive by and we have to jump in before he shuts the door. The image would normally make me laugh, but I don't even crack a smile when I see him coming down the road.

Kate nudges me, giving me a small pinch in my side. "You okay?"

I shrug and nod and hum. "I don't know."

"Did you text Rafa?" When I shake my head, she frowns. "Yo, you're being dumb. Just talk to him. Is it such a bad thing if you like him so much?"

I cringe. It takes me a second to realize I'm cringing so hard, overreacting, because I—I don't . . . "What?" I breathe out. "Says who?"

Kate snorts. "Are you kidding? That's obviously why you're so up your ass about this."

"N-no, it's not."

"It is," she says. "It's been a whole weekend. Why don't you call him or something?"

"Call?"

"Text him!"

"Text who?" Jake calls from the car. He honks twice, which is so embarrassing because he's literally right in front of us—and the whole school. People around us freeze as if this has anything to do with them. "Get in. We need to get home before rush hour. Otherwise you both owe me money."

"Why do we owe you money?" I say while Kate rushes into the passenger seat like someone is chasing her. "What's your issue?"

"Allowance— cut. Secret stash—mysteriously gone," she recounts while glaring at Jake. "I don't have anything else to give this fool. Plus, it's a free ride."

The school bus is technically also free, but I get what she means. I jump into the backseat and Jake speeds away, maneuvering around the first of the buses rolling in. He pulls onto the road, mumbling under his breath at the traffic around the school, and I lean forward, nearly resting my head on the shoulder of the driver's seat. "Thanks, Jake," I say.

We lock eyes in the rearview mirror. "Sure," he says.

I tilt my head. "Yo, if I give you a twenty, can you stop off and get me food before we get back home?"

He scoffs. "You don't have a twenty." Then I pull out the bill I found in my room this morning and wave it beside his head.

Kate gasps, sitting up straighter. "Can we get—okay, wait, can we grab bubble tea? Nelo," she says, turning to face me. "You know there's no good bubble tea place near Ginger East. You *know* that."

I laugh because she's being so serious. There really isn't, though. "Yeah, I'm down."

"Okay, down for what?" Jake cuts in. "I'm not driving you fools anywhere but home. You think I would've come pick you up if Mom and Dad didn't tell me to? As if you can't just take the bus."

"What if we give you a hundred dollars?" I ask.

"Like you have a hundred dollars," he says, snickering.

"You're right," I concede, which makes him snicker even more. "When I get a hundred dollars, I'll hire you to drive me around. That's probably the only work you'll get with your degree, anyway."

"That's *if* he gets his degree," Kate adds, and she reaches over her shoulder for a fist bump from me.

Jake slams on the brakes as revenge, and I almost go flying. He steps on the accelerator, and suddenly I'm thrown backward into my seat, disheveled and confused, which has him laughing in the front. It's only a matter of time before I'm splayed out across the backseat, laughing, just like I used to when we would all go for a ride in Mr. Tran's car. Or when we'd go to the park before sundown and end up burrowed in the tall grass during the summer, and Jake and his friends would come find us before our parents got worried. Jake would always let me sit on the handlebars of his bike. That was when we used to be really close.

"Jake, d'you remember that bike you used to have?" I ask suddenly. He eyes me in the rearview mirror while I sit up, brushing my hair out of my face. "And how sometimes you let me sit on the handlebars and—"

"You always almost died," Kate cuts in, giggling.

"Remember? You'd, like, always be screaming like you're about to fall off."

"I was about to fall off!"

"I remember," Jake says with the tiniest, most fleeting smile ever. Something about him saying he remembers something that means so much to me just has me feeling like—I don't know—things were *good*. And that my memories mean something to someone else too. My memories of the neighborhood and how we were all okay.

I'm gushing like an idiot in the backseat, sighing and smiling and content while I lean against the window. All it takes is for Jake to say, "Okay, this is your house. Get out," for me to break out of my nostalgia trap and feel the cool sting of spring air against my face. He presses the unlock button rapidly, over and over again, and eyes me carefully.

"Bye," I say, and push open the back door. "Kate, text later? If there's nothing but rice at my place, let's grab fries at the Eats if they're open." So many businesses are still doing half days here and there while the street gets back up and running. Or so I've heard, anyway. When I think about the main road, I shiver. People are saying the cleanup is almost complete by Spice of Life, but I don't know. I haven't seen it myself. Not yet.

Kate turns quickly in her seat, and pushes her two hands together in mock prayer. "Sorry, sis. I have plans later," she says, frowning. "I'll make it up to you. Promise."

She's never offered to make anything up to me, so I know her plans must include Bo in some capacity. I smile and try hard to look like I'm not mad, and that's because I'm not. I'm okay now. She doesn't owe me anything. "They're just fries, fam. It's not that deep," I tease. "See you later."

I climb out and wave them off as they make the two-second drive to their house down the road. I swing my backpack around so I can search for my house keys a bit easier. My hand scrapes the bottom of my bag, and the familiar cold metal is nowhere to be found. "Umm . . ." I rip open my bag and all but stick my head in, trying to get a better look around. Oh God, if I left my key inside my actual house, I'm going to die. Mom isn't home for another two hours.

Kate and Jake have already disappeared inside their house by the time I get it into my head to hang at their place for a while. Jake's car is parked lazily in the driveway, and dangerously close to a familiar silver sedan. It's pulled off to the side, immaculate and clean like it always is. It's Mr. Horst's car.

The Trans' front door pops open, and for a split second, I feel I should run. My feet are rooted in place while Mr. Horst steps onto the porch. Mr. Tran follows, and the two men shake hands. I know what that handshake must mean; I know why Mr. Tran is smiling the way he is. I know why he bows his head a little as Mr. Horst walks off the front step, heading briskly toward his car. I know why Mr. Tran waves at him and says, "Have a safe trip." It must be over. Ginger Store must really be gone.

Mr. Horst's silver car drives past, and I look away and pretend to be searching through my bag again. I shake it and hear the keys jangling—those bastards are in here, I know it!

When I look up again, Mr. Tran is still standing on his porch. I thought he would've gone inside right away, but he's smiling and waving at me from the doorway. It's been a long time since I've seen him look so—so normal. I wave back, unsure if a smile would look like I was trying too hard. Mr. Tran chuckles a bit and then calls, "You lost your key?"

"No, I found them," I call back, feeling my fingers finally hit the smooth metal in my bag.

Mr. Tran shakes his head. "It doesn't matter, come over. There's rice. I know how much it's your favorite food."

"Definitely not," I say, pursing my lips to keep from laughing. It's been ages since he's joked with me, and I know one reason why is because I was the literal worst to him the last time we saw each other. I owe him an apology, even if he is getting rid of Ginger Store. My home.

I think of Kate talking about all the things I don't know, how Mr. Tran worked tirelessly for us—for the community. That raging voice in my head that always wants to be right tries to yell as loud as it can, but the second a laugh breaches my lips, that voice is gone. All I can think of is how happy Mr. Tran looks and how I haven't seen him this happy in a while. And how this can be normal too.

CHAPTER THIRTY-EIGHT

In the evening, the sun is disappearing over the rooftops, and Mom is watching news while she texts my dad. She's so funny because, even though she's a really fast typer on the computer, she still texts with her index finger, poking the keys rapidly as if that makes up for the fact that she's only using one finger. I usually tease her for it, but I'm not trying to be heard with this extra huge piece of vanilla cake and tall glass of orange juice on the way to my room. I found it in the fridge and it was half-eaten, which means one of Mom's coworkers probably gave it to her. I'm not supposed to eat in my room, but Mom's stuck in her messages and she won't be out of there for a while.

I clasp the fork in my teeth with an iron grip and race to my room. The second I make it inside, an inch away from my bed, I drop the fork onto the covers and quickly put the juice and cake on my desk. My floor creaks when I tiptoe over to close the door a little. I don't hear any ruffling from Mom. I won.

I hope the cake and the juice will calm me while I go

through all my messages from Rafa. What's the last one he sent me? Something about how I should call him? He only wrote that because he saw I'd read the messages—or that Kate had read them out loud to me, anyway. She says I like him and that's why I'm so nervous, but how can she be so sure?

I think back to when we were kids and Rafa was one of my best friends. Like, we just clicked. We understood each other. Even after he moved away and became really popular, a small part of me always believed we were still cool with each other. And now this? This is something else.

It would have been so much easier if I didn't kiss him back. But I did, and I know deep down that means something.

I grab my fork and stuff a huge helping of cake into my mouth while I scroll through my phone. There's a new message since I checked last. I can hear everything in his voice, and it makes me smile while I read.

Raf Morales: hey
Raf Morales: sorry about everything. probably shouldn't have said you're overreacting . . .
Raf Morales: but anyway
Raf Morales: we can still be friends, right? and like actual real friends this time. not just online and shit, but at school too. like how things used to be
Raf Morales: when we were younger

Raf Morales: i don't like that you're not talking to me. i didn't think it would bother me so much but it kinda does, sooo

Raf Morales: and if you're wondering, i did really like you

Raf Morales: i mean i do really like you

Raf Morales: i mean i did for a long time and i do still currently sooo

Raf Morales: that's what's up

Raf Morales: but it's cool if you don't like me that way

Raf Morales: lol I mean i guess it's cool

Raf Morales: in theory

Raf Morales: anyway. even if you're being fake, i miss hanging out with you and i promise i won't be weird so call me or something

Raf Morales: we should chill tomorrow

I'm gushing hard—so hard that I reread every message a thousand times over. My heart pounds in my chest when I read that he likes me. My eyes roll over and over again when he implies theoretically that there's no way I wouldn't be attracted to him. It's such a Rafa thing to say, and I hate it and love it at the same time. I hate that I love it too.

I stretch out my legs and I lie on my back against the cold, wooden floor. All my anxiety and nervousness is replaced with relief. Or, what I guess relief feels like—this freeing calmness.

I like Rafa. I've known him almost half my life. We only

started speaking to each other because of everything that went down with Ginger Store and Kate—because of how things were changing with Ginger East. So, why is it so weird for our relationship to change too? Why am I so quick to say no to everything all the time?

I dial his number as I crawl into bed. The phone rings once, twice, before he answers, "Hello?" He sounds tired, but there's a gravelly quality to his voice that I like.

"Hey," I say. Meanwhile, my voice doesn't even sound like it's mine. It's so small and nervous. It's never been this small and nervous before.

And I don't know what else to say!

Fuck!

Suddenly he chuckles. "Why're you calling me?"

His voice, low and taunting, throws me out of my fantasy world, and I sit upright immediately. "Uh, didn't you say to call you?"

"When?"

"You sent me a long-ass message and said to call you."

"You left me on read for a million years. I didn't even know your phone was still working—"

"You're truly so dramatic, like it wasn't close to a million—and! You didn't even show up at school today, so what's with that?"

He sighs. "Well . . . yeah." An uneasy silence buzzes between us. My eyes dart to the wall as if it'll help me escape this awkwardness, and the realization that maybe he didn't show because of me. "Um, so . . . ," he continues. "Why're you calling me again?"

I groan for a long, long time. "Why're you trying to act like you didn't just pour out your soul to me on Messenger?"

That makes him laugh. I know it's partially because he's fake as hell and partially because I'm making him nervous. *I'm* making *him* nervous. That's so strange to even think about. He doesn't say anything else either. Just laughs.

"That's mad brave," I say quietly. Thinking about the messages makes me smile, and I can't help grinning. "Especially since you know I can screenshot it—"

"Don't even—"

"I won't, I won't," I say, and snicker. "I wouldn't do that. You know I'm not a snake."

"Do I know that?"

"You know that, yeah," I tell him.

We're quiet now. It's hard to know exactly what I want to say when there are so many thoughts swirling around in my head and only some of them make sense. I'm waiting for him to speak first. I want him to ask me a question I can say yes or no to. But then it hits me: if anyone has to say anything, it's me. If anyone's against something new and different, it's me. It hurts to even think that, but it's true.

The realization has me curling into a ball, snuggling my way back under my covers, and pressing the phone tight against my ear. "Um . . . ," I begin softly. "N-not yet."

"What do you mean?" he asks.

"Just not—not *now*, I guess," I say. "It's just a lot."

It's silent for a moment, and then he says, "What's a lot? Does this have to do with the store?"

"No. I meant, like, you and me."

"Oh . . . ," he sighs. And then he's quiet again.

My heart is thumping in my chest. I feel like I've disappointed him and he'll never want to talk to me again. I don't know why I'm thinking that. He never gave me a reason to think something like that before. I start stuttering through every explanation I can think of. "It's not that I don't *like* you, because o-obviously, uh, I do. I mean, I guess so. Kind of. I don't really know if I want things to be that way, and not so soon after we basically became friends again. Right?"

"I guess so."

I wait a second or two before I ask, "You're not mad, are you?"

"No," he says. "Why would I be mad?"

"Because . . . I don't know."

"I mean, we're still cool. That's whatever," he tells me. "You're always saying you want things to be the same, but that's not always going to happen, you know?" I'm waiting for the edge in his voice, but there is none. He's not angry with me. He's just telling me, like a teacher would tell a kid. To my ears, it sounds a bit like *Things change. You have to get over it*, and a part of that resonates with me.

I so badly want to ask if he's only saying this because he

wants me to date him, but I don't think I can joke with him like that right now. Still, I can hear his voice in my head and how he would reply. Probably with something like *Nelo, what the fuck?* and then I'd have to laugh because he's not intimidating. Not to me, anyway—not anymore.

Instead I say, "I know. I'm still adjusting," and it doesn't feel like a lie.

CHAPTER THIRTY-NINE

A new video about the benefit concert from Maree has been posted in T.L. Chats, but Kate won't let me watch it. Rafa sends it to me, which is weird at first, and becomes doubly weird when I don't see him on the bus. When I get to school, I see him by the field with some soccer people and immediately walk the opposite way. I want to talk to him, or text him and ask why he's here so early, but I don't because I don't know how. I am running away from everything these days—the neighborhood, Rafa, everything—and I hate it because it's not me. I don't know what my problem is.

Kate and I hang by the hall early in the morning before history class, and suddenly her phone starts ringing. "Is it Bo?" I tease her, pinching at her ribs and arms while she swats me off.

"Shut up, shut up!" she hisses, trying her best not to giggle. She darts away from me and tucks her hair behind her ear before she answers the phone. That's how I know it's him.

Now that Kate is distracted, I click on Maree's video. She forgoes her theme song again, which is how I know this is serious. Maree looks somber when the video loads up, but she smiles and waves anyway. "Hi, guys, and welcome to my channel," she says. So humble, like we don't already know who she is.

She's wearing less makeup, and her usually flouncy hair is tied into a tight ponytail behind her head. "So I wanted to first of all say a huuuuuge thanks to everyone who's donated to the FundRace and everyone who's bought tickets for this Saturday's show. It's gonna be amazing. I'm so ready to hang out with y'all." She forces a smile before her demeanor changes, and her eyes drop to the table. I haven't seen this side of her in a long time. She's so vulnerable that she almost doesn't look like the Maree from her videos. She looks like the Maree I remember.

"Yo, so . . ." And there it is—that accent, that distinct Ginger East, west end *thing*. Hearing it so candidly gives me such a rush, like she's speaking in a secret language only I understand. Like she's speaking to me. "I have to apologize to a good friend of mine. Well, she *was* a good friend, and we haven't really spoken in a while but, you know, in my heart, she's still my girl. I've been horrible lately, so I want to take this time now to apologize. I won't expose her name on here because some of y'all, man . . ." She laughs. "Some of y'all do the most. But I knew her when her name was Kitkat. Something really shitty happened to her and her family in the neighborhood where we grew up—this really awesome,

awesome place where I literally had the *best* time with my friends—and she didn't deserve that. No one does, obviously, but her especially. So, Kitkat, if you're watching—I'm sorry. And I hope I'll see you on Saturday. Take care, guys."

The video is thirty minutes old, but there are already so many comments. The top one says: *She'll probably forgive you. Honestly i'd love to have a best friend like you.*

"What's that?"

I hide my phone when I hear Kate approach. She eyes me suspiciously while I do my best to play it cool. "Are you talking to Rafa?" she asks.

"Uh, no," I tell her, and despite my deepest efforts, my face starts to get warm. Great. "It's — Maree posted a new video. Didn't you get the notification?"

"Please don't tell me you still watch that shit." She groans and pretends to be annoyed, but the next thing she says is: "What'd she say?"

I shrug. "Just stuff. You know the concert's on Saturday, right?"

She waves my words away like she never wants to hear about the concert again. "You know what else is on Saturday?" she says. "Mr. Horst's inspectors are visiting the store. Surveying, or something like that. He's coming by to sign the final papers after school today, though. It's a lot going on at once, but it's—it's *exciting.*"

She doesn't even have to say it because I can see in her

eyes how important this is for her. I remember how happy Mr. Tran looked when I saw Mr. Horst leaving his house, and it puts me right in my feelings. Happy feelings. "I get it; it's all good," I tell her.

"Yeah," she sighs. "Man, I have way more important things to worry about than Maree's stupid concert where Sol Cousins may or may not be showing up."

"Why can't she just confirm it?"

"Because she knows some people might not show up if it's true."

I laugh because, yeah, we collectively have really moved on. It's like a circuit: someone new will come up that we'd all die to see live. There's always someone.

There's a commotion down the hall, and I can hear girls talking loudly and footsteps approaching. I check my phone. It's not even time for first period. From around the corner comes Maree with her two latest friends, though, the closer they get, the more they start to look like two older friends. She's starting to keep them around longer.

When she sees us, she stops in her tracks. One of her friends whispers to the other, and the two of them flutter down the hall in the direction they came from, leaving Maree to make the long, awkward walk toward us. Kate nudges me and gives me a look like *What's going on?* I don't know either, so I keep quiet.

Maree twiddles her thumbs as she approaches, avoiding

our faces. Kate keeps looking at me like I know what's happening, so I have to flash her a look like *Stop looking at me, please.* Her eyes are vacant. She's dying to get away from Maree and this conversation.

"Hey, guys," Maree says quietly.

"Hi," Kate replies, short and sharp.

"So . . . I guess you saw the video?" She looks at Kate, hopeful.

But Kate shrugs and glances away. "I know everyone else probably has, but I've never watched one. Sorry."

Maree doesn't recoil or flinch from that one. She just nods slowly and says, "That's cool, that's fine. It's a bit presumptuous of me to think that, anyway, so I, um, I'm sorry."

Kate gives another shrug, although less defiant. She wasn't expecting that at all. "It's cool."

"Anyway," Maree continues. "I'm really sorry for how I just, like, used your story like that in the media and online. There's a lot that went on behind the scenes, but I know you don't care about any of that. It's not important. I, um, wanted to give you this. . . ." She reaches into her pocket and pulls out a card with a cheesy cartoon of a park on it, and hands it to Kate. When we both take a second longer to examine its grade-one Photoshop skills, she pipes up, "It's an invitation."

"Invitation?" I ask, peering closer at the card.

"Yeah," Maree says. "I made it on some photo app, so it's really shitty, but, anyway. It's for the concert. You can get in free and everything. I mean, obviously, like I wouldn't let you guys pay or anything. We can hang out like old times, you know?"

Kate is looking down at the card, so Maree directs her attention to me. Her eyes are pleading, and for a second, I clearly remember the cool Maree from when we were young and all so impressionable. But she hasn't been like that in a minute, and I don't think an apology video or specialized invitation or a possible sighting of Sol Cousins will change that.

Kate scoffs, folding the card in half and cramming it into her back pocket. Maree winces, bracing for the worst—like a smack to the face. It's tense as hell for a minute. Then Kate shakes her head, and says, "You can't just use people like that." It's as serious as I've ever heard her. Her tone has Maree locked up, not daring to move. "Just because you say a few nice words and post some clip on the internet, it's supposed to be all good? You forgot—you *forget* that we're people too."

Maree swallows hard. "Y-yeah, I know. I know."

"What you did isn't okay. Even if we don't live in your bougie-ass neighborhood and we're not super rich, it doesn't mean you can say whatever you want about us," she continues. "For weeks, you pretended like you could get away with it, like there weren't any consequences, like people weren't listening to what you were saying. But you *know* they were! That's how you got rich off this, isn't it? People listening to you?"

Maree winces under Kate's words and nods, even though she can't look Kate in the face anymore. "I never said—there was a lot of red tape, and a lot of people to answer to—"

"You should've thought of *me* first," Kate says, "not them. We're the ones who're supposed to be friends, remember? Isn't that what you told everyone on the news? That this happened to your 'friend'?"

I nudge Kate in the arm, but she shakes me off. Maree is ten seconds away from crying. I can see all the cues in her face: how she buttons up, how her cheeks grow red, how her eyes get droopy, how her bottom lip quivers. I can remember them all from when we were kids. "Chill. That's enough," I tell Kate.

"I'm done, I'm done," Kate says, crossing her arms. She doesn't bother looking at Maree anymore.

Maree sniffs and touches her eyelids softly. There's no way she's going to cry in front of us. Instead she inhales deeply and straightens up, brushing her hair off her shoulder. "Well, I'm sorry. I mean it, even if you don't believe me. And you don't have to accept my apology—that's whatever. But I want you to come on Saturday. I really do."

"I'll be there. I live there," Kate tells her. "You can wave at me from across the street."

Maree exhales in a huff but doesn't say anything else. She pretty much can't and she knows it. Her apologetic smile only extends to me as she turns and walks away.

I nudge Kate in the arm again, bringing her back down from whatever power trip she was on. "You good?" I ask.

She nods.

"No offense . . ." I purse my lips to keep from chuckling because she already looks so offended. "But you're *so* annoying."

She glares. "Why?"

"You're really going to act all righteous like you didn't break your own store window," I say, and laugh. It gets funnier the more I think about it. Kate smacks me in the arm, but she's laughing too, maybe even more than I am. "Maree might be fake, but at least she's real about it."

"Honestly, though. She's a pure vulture, just doing what she does best," she says, and snickers. "Circling."

CHAPTER FORTY

After school, Kate gets on the bus first and skips to our usual seat. She makes me sit first, even though I usually sit on the outside. "So you won't get any ideas about ditching me," she explains. When she makes these loud, annoying-ass kissy sounds, I nearly slap her across the face. I know who she's referring to, even though she's dead wrong.

"Wanna listen to something?" she asks, grinning, while she reaches for her phone and her earphones. "I'm almost done with the final mix. My parents have me on strict curfew now, so I have to be real quiet working on stuff in my room. Tell me what you think."

"What songs?" I ask, taking an earbud from her. She tinkers with her phone, pulling up the music app. "Which song?" I ask again, even though I can see her screen clearly from where I'm sitting. It's Midtown Project. I groan. "Can you stop with the Midtown Project throwbacks? Please accept that the hiatus was actually a breakup."

"This mix has a good beat, though," she protests. "It's fire. Just listen."

I try to, but my concentration is thrown when I hear a familiar voice. My heart feels like it has stopped beating and I'm in limbo, everything and nothing echoing in my ears at the same time. I focus on Kate's phone screen so hard that it's starting to give me a headache. Marcus's voice is loud—he comes down the aisle laughing and yelling about something with his usual group of asshole friends. And Rafa.

I actually want to die.

"Nelo, oh my God." Kate nudges me. I'm halfway to full slouch mode and I happen to be taking her earphones with me. "Stop being weird. I know it's hard, but wow, at least try."

"What's wrong with her?" Rafa asks. I'm shaking—I don't even want to look at him. I run my hands through my hair and fluff it out over my shoulder like I'm too important to engage in a conversation. Meanwhile, I'm sweating. I'm sweating *so* much! He's in the aisle, leaning against the seat in front of us, and he nods at me. "What's wrong with you?"

"Nothing," I say quietly.

Kate jumps in. "She's freaking out because Dad's officially signing over the store today."

"For real?" Rafa smirks and dips into the seat in front of us. "Are you guys gonna be rich?"

"N-no. Maybe," Kate says, coyly. She's only being modest because she knows she's wrong for getting excited about this, but that doesn't stop her from bouncing up and down in her seat like a kid on sugar. "These guys have been trying to buy out my dad for ages, so you know they probably threw in a bit extra. I'm going to ask Dad if he can sponsor my first-ever gig."

"When you're off punishment and graduate college," I add.

Kate frowns. "When I'm off punishment and graduate college."

Rafa points to Kate's earphones. "What are you listening to? Originals?"

She pauses a moment before handing him the set. "Kind of. . . . You might not like it, though."

"Why won't I like it?"

"It's Midtown Project," I blurt out, and Rafa immediately rolls his eyes a million times. "I mean, they're good, though, so your attitude? Unnecessary."

"Just listen," Kate says. "Please? I need a second opinion. Nelo's heard too many already, *and* she was there for my whole Midtowner phase, unlike *some* people."

He laughs. "What? Who was your favorite?" He turns to me. "Who was *your* favorite?"

"I'm, uh, really not trying to talk to you about Midtown Project on the bus, so."

Rafa settles into the seat in front of us, his back against the window. Kate goes through song after song, explaining the transitions. Even after the bus starts moving, he doesn't go sit with Marcus and the rest of them. He doesn't seem bothered, but I think it's nice of him. I'll find a way to tell him that later.

When it's his stop, he gets up and says bye like it's any other day, and I feel stupid for feeling sad. I was the one who said we should be friends in the first place. So why was I expecting a longer goodbye, or maybe a hug? Or a kiss? Or *something*?

"Ready?" Kate asks the second we step foot off the bus. She can't hide how excited she is anymore, and seeing her so happy rubs off on me in a way I didn't even know could happen. She's racing past Ginger Store, not even bothering to take a second glance at its boarded-up window or its dusty door handles. I feel guilty passing it without a final look, but Kate is far ahead and I really want to keep up this time.

Mr. Horst's car isn't outside yet. Kate hesitates a little when she reaches her front door. She shifts so I can't see her face when she walks in, but her footsteps tell me all I need to know. It's so weird that I have to watch her demeanor to understand what's going on at home. The Trans' home is my home too, but for the first time in a long time, I'm on the outside looking in. I see how Kate greets her parents patiently. I see how Mr. Tran, standing by the doorway folding up an old letter, gives her a measured response—"Welcome back"— with stifled warmth. I see how broken their bond is. But I know it'll get better with time. It'll change.

Mr. Tran is arranging store goods and books in an open

box. He takes the folded letter and places it into a new box, along with other letters and some other items. When he sees me, he smiles, genuinely. He looks lighter already. "You've come to see me sign away the store, huh?" he teases.

I'm giddy seeing him so at ease with me again, and I chuckle shyly and say, "Yeah, I guess so."

His smile is warm when he comes to squeeze my shoulder. "Come eat something while you wait. We have your favorite."

"Please don't say 'rice.'"

"It's rice!"

He jokingly squeezes my shoulder harder and I break into a whine. He's doing this to me on purpose, but I love it because it makes me feel like I belong here.

Jake comes into the living room with a file folder of papers and a sleek, black pen. He doesn't bat an eyelash when he sees me. Instead he sits on the sofa and spreads the documents across the table. He is so careful and meticulous when he puts the papers down, making sure they're all in order. Mr. Tran waltzes over and sits beside him, listening to Jake's explanation of the documents one by one. Their resemblance is so strong, and for the first time ever—for the first time since we were kids—I think, *Wow, Jake isn't that bad.*

"Nelo?"

Mrs. Tran steps out through the doorway for a hug. She hugs me tighter than she ever has before. "It's been so long since we've seen you. You've been on TV a lot, though."

"She's a celebrity now. She's too busy to come see us," Mr. Tran calls out, and it takes all my willpower to not scream at the top of my lungs.

Mrs. Tran flashes me a sly grin while she strokes my shoulder. "I'm happy you're here," she says.

"I am too," I tell her. "And I'm sorry . . . you know, for last time." When she raises a confused eyebrow at me, I stumble over my words, trying to get them out in the right order. "When I was here, and you guys were talking about selling . . . remember?" I look to Mr. Tran, who stares back from the sofa. "I said all those things to you about—about selling out and, like . . . just other horrible stuff. I didn't mean it, o-obviously. I was . . ." Scared. I was so scared.

Mrs. Tran pulls me into a hug and pats my back, but it's the smile from Mr. Tran that traps me. He nods gently beside Jake and says a soft, "Okay." Okay.

"He's here, he's here," Kate interrupts. She's been perched by the window, staring outside, and leaps to her feet when a car pulls into the driveway. She smooths out her shirt and stands taller. "Didn't mean to interrupt. Let's all agree to be cool, okay?"

"You're the one who needs to be cool, loser," Jake grunts.

"Ah, shush, shush," Mr. Tran says, rising to his feet. I fall back to the armchair closest to the kitchen and watch Mr. Horst enter and politely remove his shoes, before shaking both Mr. Tran's and Mrs. Tran's hands. "You remember my children," Mr. Tran says, gesturing to Kate, Jake, and then me. I give a humble wave from the back. Mr. Horst, only a little flustered by my being there, returns my wave as politely as a man like him knows how. It's not stiff and unwelcoming like I expected. It's actually much more casual.

Mr. Tran leads Mr. Horst to the sofa by the table. All the papers have already been signed by Mr. Tran at the bottom. Mr. Horst goes through and signs beside each signature while Mr. Tran watches with bated breath. We're all quiet, actually. No one wants to say anything. And what would we say, anyway? *Take good care of it,* or something like that. *This place means more to me and my friends than you'll ever know. Don't screw this up. I'm trusting you.*

Kate gestures into the kitchen. "Come on," she whispers. We gravitate to the wall farthest from the living room so we can talk in peace. Kate sits on the old kitchen table while I pull out a chair to join her. "This is surreal," she says, her voice still in a hush.

I nod quickly. "I can't believe it. He's really selling it."

"Yeah." Kate smiles suddenly, leaning so she can get a better look through the doorway. Mr. Horst is still signing and checking over each of the documents. "But hey, you know what Bo said when I told him about Dad selling the store? He was like—it's so stupid, don't laugh—but he was like, 'Oh, it's like a new phase, kinda.' Isn't that cool?"

I snort. "That's stupid as hell."

"Shut up."

"It is!" I continue, still chortling. "He's always been corny."

"But it's true, though," she says. "I've lived my entire life in that store, and now it's gone. It's not going to be mine anymore. It's not going to be *ours.*"

I'm chuckling but now it's out of nervousness.

Ours.

I mean, it is—it was. I feel like I should be signing my name on that paper too. Maybe it's selfish of me to even think that way, but we all have to let it go the same way Mr. Tran does. It might have been his, but if we didn't visit, it would have been nobody's.

"What are you gonna do?" she says, and snickers, kicking me in the leg. "Now that you won't have a place to get free ice cream on Tuesdays."

"Wow, enough about me," I say. "What about you guys? And your dad? What's he gonna do now that he doesn't have the store?"

"Dad'll be fine."

"D'you think he'll buy another store? Be like those Caribbean restaurants around Weston and have a Ginger Store two and a Ginger Store three—"

She bursts out laughing. "No, shut up, I don't know. He was a trained surgeon in Vietnam, you know. Maybe he'll try to get certified here or something, but I don't know if it's that deep with him, still."

I gasp and crane my neck toward the doorway again. Mr. Tran is bundling all the papers to give back to Mr. Horst, and suddenly the way he's holding that pen is suspect. It's too precise for a normal person. "For real?" I croak.

"Yeah, man."

"You learn something new every day."

"I've known from time. That's on you."

CHAPTER FORTY-ONE

On Saturday, the street is buzzing with quiet. Like when you feel the electricity in the air right before a storm.

The benefit concert is happening today. Soon there will be a ton of newcomers in Ginger East, maybe people who never once thought they'd come to "the ghetto," especially not after what happened with the protest. I try not to care, but I do. This is my home, after all. Kate says she doesn't care—about the people, about the benefit—but she's still the first person to share the image of the concert schedule in our group chat.

Kate KK Tran has shared an image.

Kate KK Tran: lookatthisbullshit

Bo Williams: so sol cousins not coming?

Raf Morales: nope. by now she would've said so

Bo Williams: she knows that's the only reason people would show

Bo Williams: typical maree

Chinelo Sondra: in what way is this typical??

Bo Williams: snake behavior

Chinelo Sondra: LOL

Chinelo Sondra: true

Kate KK Tran: if you guys go to this benefit concert, you're dead to me

Raf Morales: lol awkward. maree texted me free tickets

Bo Williams: lol why's she texting you?

Bo Williams: you still talk to her often?

Raf Morales: ummmm no

Chinelo Sondra: you're really gonna take free tickets

Chinelo Sondra: to a benefit concert??? rafael.

Kate KK Tran: exactly!! this is supposed to benefit underprivileged youth!!

Kate KK Tran: me. i am underprivileged

Kate KK Tran: my poor papa was never able to practice medicine here, as you know, as you are all aware

Bo Williams: truly, it's harder for immigrants to practice their professions when they move to the west because of our strict ass regulations

Bo Williams: i saw it all the time with relatives from the bahamas

Raf Morales: why did you get so serious?

Raf Morales: i'm not even going to this concert, chill

Chinelo Sondra: Rafa knows nothing about that immigrant struggle life since he was born in rexdale

Raf Morales: w o w

Bo Williams: rafa you're from rexdale???

Raf Morales: i'm obviously not from rexdale if we grew up in the same neighborhood, fam

Kate KK Tran: i mean you moved here kinda late though

Raf Morales: wow you too??

Kate KK Tran: ok shut up everyone!!

Kate KK Tran: who's coming to the store while the surveyors are here??

Bo Williams: maybe around 3

Raf Morales: i don't know yet

Chinelo Sondra: also don't know yet

Kate KK Tran: @*Chinelo Sondra* bitch you have nowhere else to go lol!!

Chinelo Sondra: SHUT UPP

Chinelo Sondra: there's something i gotta do first

Kate KK Tran: there's also something i gotta do first

Kate KK Tran: and i gotta ask you something in person

Raf Morales: is it about midtown project?

Kate KK Tran: LOL NO

Chinelo Sondra: lol let it die my guy!!

Raf Morales: never

Kate KK Tran: guys.

Kate KK Tran: the land dev people should be here in a few hours, so just text me when you get here if you're still coming!!

Kate KK Tran: i wanna see all of you

I immediately swipe out of the group chat and go to my chat with Rafa.

Chinelo Sondra: yo are you coming today or nah?

I wait for him to read the message. Ten seconds, twenty seconds, thirty seconds go by. He's probably holding his phone in his hand, refusing to click on the chat room. I don't want to think he's ignoring me, but if he is, I can't hold it against him. He did say we're still cool, but I can't help but feel like that's not completely true. I'm not sure whether I'm okay with things just the way they are either.

He finally reads the message and it takes twenty seconds for him to write back. Truly, I deserve this.

Raf Morales: yeah
Raf Morales: why?
Chinelo Sondra: just wondering
Chinelo Sondra: if i'm gonna see you or not
Raf Morales: oooohhhhhhh
Chinelo Sondra: shut uppp
Raf Morales: ok in that case, i don't know
Raf Morales: we'll see
Chinelo Sondra: omg you're so annoying
Raf Morales: mmmmm

I take my time getting ready, oiling my hair and pulling my favorite sweater—black, knit, tiger—over my head, and over the new bra Mom bought for me. Actually, it's so much more comfortable than the old one I had. It fits better.

Looking at myself in the mirror, I wonder why I avoided it for so long.

"I'm going out," I tell Mom as I head down the hall to the front door.

She is in the living room, lying down on the sofa, texting with one finger. "Be careful," she calls over her shoulder. "They're doing that concert today."

"I will. Mom, use two hands."

"What?"

I mimic texting with both hands, and all she does is frown. Frown!

"Don't talk to strangers," she says. "You and Kate make sure to come home after. And I don't want to see your face come up on some live TV report," she tells me, and resumes her archaic activity.

"Fine," I say. "But—Mom, look." And I hold my arms out, spinning around so she can get a 360-degree view. She cranes her neck and watches me twirl, but says nothing. "I'm wearing it," I tell her. "The bra."

"Obviously," she chortles, her voice sharp and almost cynical. "You really thought you'd get away with wearing your old one forever? People change. When you're stubborn, it hurts more."

"Wow, thanks." I sigh, and make my way to the door.

My phone beeps before I make it two steps. "It's from your dad," Mom calls. "He's sending it to everyone."

I open the message:

Dad: WELCOME TO THE 21ST CENTURY!

Our Phones >> Wireless

Cars >> Keyless

Tools >> Cordless

Leaders >> Shameless

Relationships >> Meaningless

Babies >> Fatherless

Government >> Useless

Parliament >> CLUELESS

Everything is becoming LESS but still our hope in God is—

Endless. In fact I am Speechless Because Salvation remains

Priceless!!

I really am going to die.

Chinelo: thanks dad!

Dad: Yes. . . . uwc.

I squeeze my feet into my shoes and jog across the street to the intersection at Ginger Way. I wasn't lying when I said there was something I had to do first. At the intersection, I go left and head back toward Spice of Life, where the cleanup crews are still sweeping, still gathering debris, still coordinating trucks to come take it away.

And Mr. Brown is there too.

He is okay; he's not walking with a limp or hiding scars on his hands. He directs crews and volunteers with a stern point of his finger, barking short commands in a way that makes you feel like he owns the place. And he does, kinda. If not for him organizing everything, we wouldn't have had the protest. We wouldn't have known that there are still people in the community who care.

I grin and wave when I see him. He doesn't do either, and I'm fine with that. "Hey, Mr. B.," I say.

He grimaces immediately. "Mr. *Brown*. I'm not a—a rapper."

I laugh so loud, it startles the nearest volunteer. "What?" Mr. Brown could definitely get away with a fitted cap and some high-tops, though. He probably wouldn't hear it from me, but he should try it sometime.

"What do you want?" he asks bluntly.

I try my best to curb my laughter, but it's hard. Mr. Brown cracks the smallest of smiles—a twitch at the corner of his mouth. It makes me laugh harder. I manage to take a deep breath and say, "Do you guys need help?"

His eyebrows arch. "Help? With . . . ?"

"The final bit of the cleanup," I say. "I know there's not much left to do, but I live here too, you know."

He purses his lips and nods, slowly. That's the best smile I'm going to get out of him after I dared to call him by a nickname. "Yeah, yep," he says, and gestures for me to follow him. "I hope you'll be available past the cleanup too."

"Yeah, Mr. Brown. I just said I live here."

"Because I'm thinking of a, hmm, a . . ." He pauses a second. "I guess a gathering. I'm trying to find out what people need in the community and how to help them get it. You understand? I think you should join."

"Me?" I say. "Legit?"

"Yes, legitimately."

I itch with excitement at the thought of working with other people who care about Ginger East as much as I do. Other people who live here. Other people who love the fries at the Eats but know to stay away from the milkshakes. Other people who know that the garbage truck doesn't really roll around until after five p.m., so you can get away with putting things at the curb late. Other people who remember Ginger Store, Vita ice cream, that sweet but musty hot chocolate smell.

"Yeah, of course," I tell him, trying not to grin. "I'm available whenever. Just tell me when."

Mr. Brown is trying not to smile too. He grabs a broom from a stack leaning against the wall and hands it to me as we approach a group of volunteers. And Kate. Kate is here and she has a broom.

We both freeze when we see each other and point like we can't believe what we're seeing. She cracks first. "What are you— Wait, don't answer that," she chuckles, shaking her head. "I know what you're doing here. I know what you're about."

"Yeah, fam. What are *you* doing here?" I ask.

"Are you joking?" She snorts. "I'm on major punishment, bro. Anytime my parents see an opportunity to punish me, they take it. The other day, I had to clean Mr. Jenkins's dog. I mean, are they serious? How do you even clean a dog?" I laugh before I realize I don't really know either. In a bathtub? "Man, I'm barely allowed to breathe without my parents knowing. They heard about the final sweep-up happening today and told me to come down here and clean until I drop, so here I am. Sweeping. Dropping," she adds with a flick of the broom.

"Well, good," I tease, and knock her ankles with the broom. She does the same to me, and if not for a loud tut from Mr. Brown, we both would've gone full war with the handles.

We lose track of time sweeping residual glass and rubble from the Spice of Life storefront. It is the last of the buildings to be cleaned. Actually, I try really hard not to look at it because I keep thinking it'll make me mad. But when I lift my head and look into the store, it just looks sad to me. There's no one, no sign of activity, nothing. No soul. A huge building like this and nothing to show for it. I still want the store gone from the neighborhood, but for a second, I only feel pity for its empty rows and untouched dried spices.

Kate pulls a large garbage bag past me to the heaping pile at the side of the road. I turn back around when I feel a tap on my shoulder and hear a muffled, "Chinelo?" behind me. It's

Dave from Channel 9 and a cameraman. I must look super distrusting of him because he holds his hands up in surrender like I'm about to snap. "Remember me? Dave Perillo. We did the interview . . ."

Perillo, got it.

"Yeah, I remember," I say.

He takes a long look around at the buildings and the storefront. "Things must have been really rough here lately."

"I mean, yeah," I blurt out. I don't mean it to come off rude, but if he has something he wants to ask me, I wish he'd just ask.

"We're doing another segment on the riots," he tells me. "I'm wondering if you'd speak with us, with permission from your mom again, of course. This is such a great backdrop, with the workers and the store . . ." His tone is ugly as he looks around in awe at the destroyed storefront, his "great backdrop."

"My mom's cool with it." She most definitely isn't, and she'll kill me if she ends up seeing the video. He doesn't question me, just starts setting up the shot with his cameraman. He wants to catch as much of Spice of Life's damaged building in the shot as possible, so he makes me stand directly in front of it. Kate comes into view but takes a whole step back once she notices the camera. "Come here," I hiss at her, and she backs up again. "Seriously, come here."

"Oh my God," she huffs, before tiptoeing into frame.

Dave raises an eyebrow, confused. "Um, who—what's this?"

"This is Kate Tran," I tell him, and she waves quickly. "Her family is . . . one of the reasons for the, uh, the protest."

He purses his lips, thinking. I can see the wheels turning: two pitiful teenagers is better than one. I already know the kind of story he's trying to sell.

They start filming. "This is Dave Perillo in Ginger East this afternoon, a week after the riots that shook this already fragile community." It takes all my will not to roll my eyes right now. "I'm joined again by Chinelo Agu, who you'll remember from our segment on the Ginger Store vandalism and her viral video spawned from that tragedy, as well as Kate Tran, another local who has seen firsthand the horrific events that shaped this catastrophe last week. Chinelo," he begins, turning to me. "What initiatives have sprung up as a result of the riots?"

"As a result of the *protest*," I say pointedly. "A lot of people have decided to come out and help with the cleanup efforts. It's been really great to see. I think it puts out a different image of the community too. People here really care about each other."

"There were reports that growing anti-corporate sentiment led to the altercation," he goes on. "Would you say this incident had a direct relation to what happened at Ginger Store?"

I shake my head, but it's Kate who jumps in before I can

answer. "No way. Ginger Store was . . . It's not related," she says, glancing at me shyly. "When people get agitated, they become unpredictable. I think that's normal."

"Exactly," I continue. "Plus, we're more than a building. A community is made up of people, not things." Even as I say that, I can't help but think of Ginger Store and how that building shaped so much of who I am. How it still does in some way.

"One last question before we let you both go," Dave says, and he's chuckling, so I know he's about to ask something stupid. Here goes. He asks me, "We hear Maree Porter, who used to be a resident of this area, is holding a benefit concert a few blocks down. Is that where you and the volunteers will be heading after the cleanup here?"

"Definitely not."

The afternoon trudges on. Dave wraps up his segment with some more shots of the store and leaves as fast as he showed up. I really hope that's the last I ever see of him.

We gotta get out of here too. I give Mr. Brown my broom back and thank him.

"No, thank *you*," he says, and smiles for real this time.

Kate and I make our way back to the intersection by Ginger Way. She's buzzing about the interview, almost frantic with how the whole thing went down. "I'm gonna get in so much trouble," she chortles. "Dad's gonna watch the news and be like, 'Who asked you to be on television?' And then they're probably going to make me wash ten million dogs, mow all the grass at the park or something, and then erase me from the earth."

I snort. "Sucks."

"They better not, though. Can you imagine if all they have is Jake?"

"Better one disgrace than two," I say, and she starts cackling like mad.

The intersection is louder than it was before we joined the volunteers. The closer we get, the more chatter and music we hear. The wind catches it and tosses it over the neighborhood, filling the air with a different kind of life. It's not anything I'm used to, but I'll allow it just for today.

There's a huge barricade set up around the park, and several buff security guys are guarding the entranceway. They're checking wristbands and monitoring a closed area where concertgoers seem to be hanging around and enjoying sponsored energy drinks. In the back, crowds are gathering for opening and secondary acts while two large screens on either side of the main stage show off every performance. Wow, Maree wasn't kidding. She's really trying it.

And across the street from all the chaos is Ginger Store. It's where we head once we're done soaking in the hectic scene. For the first time since the day of the incident, the plywood is gone and the large, gaping hole is bare, open for everyone to see. There's no police or caution tape this time. My feet gravitate there themselves, sliding across the sidewalk.

Kate's footsteps slow once she realizes that that's where I'm headed. She crosses her arms and tilts her head to the side, a smug look on her face. "There's nothing to see in there anymore," she sings. "Let it go. You gotta. I know I—I have."

"Yeah . . ." My eyes still wander, staring at the dustiness of the shelves and countertop. It's so surreal. Never in a million years did I ever think a place once so vibrant would end up dead like this. The bookshelf is empty. The perishables are probably well past their expiration date. A stagnant smell wafts forward. This isn't the store I remember. It's more like a shadow now.

I snap out of my trance and make my way back to the sidewalk, where Kate is still watching. She glances over her shoulder at the benefit across the street. Her distaste is palpable. I join her, arms crossed, both of us staring like we're too scared to cross the road.

"Hey," she speaks up, eyes still trained on the concert. "Did I tell you I heard from Maree's people?"

"No."

"Well, I did," she goes on. She's trying so hard to be still, to focus on the scene before us, not blink. I know her well enough to know she's pretending to keep it together. "Remember when she came up to us at school and was like, 'I'm so sorry. I've been the worst'? Well, now her people are calling my parents saying, like, there's going to be a 'delay' with the FundRace stuff." She air-quotes "delay" with rigid, angry fingers. "And I'm thinking, like, why wouldn't she call me herself? What's the point of trying to step to me in school, acting like you're about that, when you know you're still hiding behind your PR people?"

I scoff. "Not surprised."

"Not even disappointed," she utters. A cascade of applause erupts from across the street as more eager attendees rush the line, excitedly gripping wristbands and wrestling them on before disappearing into the park. They're probably trampling over used condoms right now and don't even realize it. Maree can hire whoever she wants to put up a stage and some screens, but deep down in her heart, she knows what this park is about. Because it's the same park we all used to hang out at.

"She was our friend too," I say, stating the obvious. Kate nods right away, because yeah, she gets it. That uncomfortable, niggling feeling of getting played by someone you know. Someone who's supposed to understand you better than most. Someone who shouldn't have betrayed you. Plenty of trash people come into Ginger East under the guise of wanting to help. You never think it'd be one of your own.

"It's the same," I go on. "Like, none of these people who claim to care about places like this actually do, you know? Maybe it's stupid of us to think Maree would've been different."

"Because she was one of us," she cuts in.

"Yeah," I say, "she was."

We're quiet for a moment or two more before Kate reaches

forward and play-slaps me in the arm. She tries to smile, but I know she's really taking everything hard. The light in her eyes is still there, but it's dim and it needs tending.

So I play-slap her back and say, "Let's just chill today. No Maree, no Horst talk, no nothing. Just you and me."

She chuckles. "And Bo."

"Fine."

"And Rafa."

I open and shut my mouth, soundless and nervous and floundering for some kind of coherent thought. I could just say "Fine" again, but a second "fine" might sound too forced. And "true" would probably sound too casual. "Cool" would definitely sound too enthusiastic!

I'm too quiet, and it takes one whole second for her to burst out laughing at my more-than-obvious silence. She wiggles her eyebrows at me, and I want to die. I'm happy she's not in her feelings about Maree anymore, but damn, at what cost?

Thankfully, a car pulls up in front of the store, and I know it must be Jake with the surveyor. The old-new Jake would've been mad that he was being woken up to do anything on a Saturday. But this new-new Jake doesn't seem to mind. He gets out of the car and shows the surveyor, a tall, stiff man, toward the building. When the surveyor notices that we're staring, Jake stops to introduce us as, "My sister and my . . . sister."

The surveyor smiles. "Nice to meet you." He doesn't wait

for a reply before he and Jake shuttle themselves toward the store.

Across the street, there's an eruption of noise and a flurry of action on the two screens, and Kate cranes her neck to try to get a better look at the crowd. "Is it Sol?" she yells, and I laugh like it's the funniest thing. I have to grab her arm to steady myself, even though we're both swaying with laughter. One of the security guards across the street eyes us suspiciously, but we don't care because we're used to it.

"There's no way," I tell her before I drop down onto the curb. She joins me, pulling her knees in together. We strain to hear whichever performer is on, but it's no use. We don't know the song.

Bo is the first to show up, and he's wearing brogues, which I think is mad funny but also very chic. He sits next to Kate, and the two of them hold hands from time to time, but pretend they aren't. Bo also brings this kale sandwich from that bougie sandwich shop that opened down the street, and all I can think is *Of course Bo likes kale now.* He splits it into uneven pieces and hands one to me. I take a bite only because he's watching. Honestly, it's an ugly sandwich and it tastes horrible. I learn a lot about Bo from the sheer fact that he thinks I'd like this.

Then Rafa shows up with my favorite ice cream. I'm filled with a new kind of happiness I didn't even know I could feel. "Yo . . . ," I gasp, eyeing the decadent chocolate ice cream bar in my hands. "Where'd you find this?"

He pouts, confused. Why does he look so good confused? "Like, at the store?"

"Just any store?"

"You do know they sell Vita ice cream at pretty much every grocery store in the area, right?" he asks bluntly. I'm too busy unwrapping the bar to respond. I should say thank you, and it's on the tip of my tongue, but so is the ice cream bar, and I like it so much more.

Soon afterward, there's another eruption of noise and another act takes the stage, but we don't move an inch. Kate calls again, "Is it Sol?" and she and I laugh. The boys don't pay us and our inside jokes any attention because they know we've been together so long that we're two halves of one whole. After all this time, we're almost the same person.

Kate eventually brings out her phone. "D'you guys want to listen to something? Shut up. It's not Midtown Project," she adds hastily before Rafa even opens his mouth. "Get hype. The mixtape is done."

He gasps. "For real?"

"Yeah, for real."

"Good," Bo chuckles. "I'm tired of looping the same snippets online."

Kate giggles, her face pulsing red. "Don't even. It's taken me forever, but here." She switches on her phone and turns up the volume on her app. The music across the street is loud, but we can hear the first beat of her mixtape, the deep bass of Midtown Project's "Cheap Date," crystal clear like we're in our own vacuum, our own world. Bo gasps and nods his head as the song picks up. Kate can't stop grinning. When the next song starts, she locks eyes with me and we both laugh. I don't know why, but it doesn't matter.

We're tired because it feels like we've been here forever—with each other all day, like we used to. Sunrise to sundown. I'm near chewing on the ice cream bar stick when I shift slightly and rest my head on Rafa's shoulder. I'm nervous and thinking maybe I shouldn't have done that, but it's too late to move my head and pretend it was an accident. He stiffens under the weight, but I can see the smallest smile catch the corner of his lips. He wraps his arm around my shoulders and pulls me in closer. I feel so at ease like this. I smile wider than I ever have about anything, and for a second, I think, *Wow, we're the same too.*

The crowd across the street grows bigger as the sun sets, blocking whatever view we have of the stage. Man, from here, we really can't see shit, but from what we can hear, we're not missing anything.

ACKNOWLEDGMENTS

How surreal is this!

Firstly, thank you to my family: my parents and my siblings (farm animal squad), my aunts, my uncles, my cousins, my grandma. I am blessed to be going through this life with all of you.

Everyone says it only takes one yes, so thank you to Farrah Penn for being my very, very first through Author Mentor Match. It's so affirming when someone else sees the good in your work, and you really helped me prepare for the road ahead.

To my amazing agent, Claire Friedman, who is always on top of everything I'm not (usually because I'm crying somewhere under a chocolate sheet cake). I really appreciate your time and energy, and it's been such an honor to work with you. Here's to many more years and many more successes!

The amazing editorial, design, and publicity teams at HarperCollins Canada and Delacorte Press shaped this book in so many ways, and I am so thankful to have worked with them. To my editors, Suzanne Sutherland and Monica Jean, who have been the perfect advocates for me and this book, and to Alex Hightower, whose enthusiasm will always mean the world to me: thank you all so much for your patience, your expertise, and above all, your understanding.

To Bex Glendining, thank you so much for your beautiful illustrations. I was literally obsessed with your style before I was told you'd be our artist, so thank you for agreeing and thank you for producing such a beautiful cover truly indicative of this story's spirit.

Thanks to the Toronto Writer Crew, especially Liselle, Kess, June, Elora, Debbie, Sarena and Sasha, Ashley, Dan, and Kelly, for being inspiring, talented, and within arm's reach. Thank you also to Jane for being a sounding board and a good friend.

Much love to the AMM fam, with a special hello to all of R3, for being my very first writing community; my trash fam for continually making unsavory life choices with me (trash weekend! sleeping on the street! bronchitis!) and never letting me stay in the garbage can alone too long; and my friends at the Festival of Literary Diversity (FOLD) in Brampton, where I first shared my work with an audience and learned so much by being around such beautifully talented artists.

To Nhi, who I really should be addressing as Dr. Nhi because how cool is that, thank you so much! I didn't know how to write this without exposing how we first met each other (the socially acceptable answer is: ages ago on the internet), but thank you for reading over my work time and time again, and thank you for this latest round. I appreciate your authenticity and enthusiasm, always.

Also to all my online friends who I met through various fandoms and who have become real and true friends over the years: thank you and I'm always cheering for you, until whenever.

Thanks to me, honestly and truly, for sticking it out this long and believing with infallible certainty that this dream was worth pursuing. I've had a copy of *Little Women* by Louisa May Alcott on my shelf since I was maybe five, and even though I legit didn't read it for twenty-plus years, I have always found it inspiring that my first name was already on a book cover.

Also, boldly, to Chimamanda Ngozi Adichie, who doesn't know me at all personally but who I met twice (once in London, once in Toronto) and who, when I told her I was a writer, encouraged me to keep going. This ended up being the best and only advice necessary. Daalu, Ma.

And finally, to the corner of Mississauga, Ontario, I will always call home, where I met my first friends and then promptly ditched them after school to be on time for *Pokémon* (what to do when school ends the same time your favorite show comes on): you are where my heart has remained.

ABOUT THE AUTHOR

LOUISA ONOMÉ holds a BA in professional writing from York University and lives in Toronto. *Like Home* is her debut novel.

louisaonome.com

GET
Underlined

**A Community of YA Book Nerds
& Aspiring Writers!**

READ

Book recommendations, reading lists, YA news

LIFE

Quizzes, book trailers, author videos

PERKS

Giveaways, merch, sneak peeks

CREATE

Community stories, writing contests and advice

We want to hear YOUR story!
**Create an account to write original stories,
connect with fellow book nerds and authors, build
a personal bookshelf, and get access to content
based on your interests!**

GetUnderlined.com
@GetUnderlined

Want a chance to be featured? Use #GetUnderlined on social!